JANE
AUSTEN

THE
BEDSIDE
AUSTEN

CLASSICS FOR PLEASURE

CHANCELLOR
PRESS

Sense and Sensibility first published in Great Britain in 1811
Emma first published in Great Britain in 1816
Northanger Abbey first published in Great Britain in 1818
Pride and Prejudice first published in Great Britain in 1813
Mansfield Park first published in Great Britain in 1814
Persuasion first published in Great Britain in 1818

This volume first published in Great Britain in 1993 by
Chancellor Press
an imprint of
Reed Consumer Books Limited
Michelin House, 81 Fulham Road, London SW3 6RB
and Auckland, Melbourne, Singapore and Toronto

ISBN 1 85152 358 8
A CIP catalogue record for this book is available at the British Library

Printed in Great Britain by William Clowes Ltd.

CONTENTS

Sense and Sensibility

Elinor and Marianne Dashwood, together with their mother and younger sister are left homeless when their father dies, as the family estate, Norland Park in Sussex, passes to their half-brother, Mr John Dashwood. The new heir and his wife are cold and miserly. They ignore old Mr Dashwood's request to provide for his wife and daughters. Mrs Dashwood and her daughters take a cottage in Devon, on the estate of their cousin Sir John Middleton. Marianne, a passionate romantic, despairs of ever finding true love. There is a mutual attraction between Elinor and Edward Ferrars, the brother of her sister-in-law, Mrs John Dashwood. His sister does not approve, nor does his overbearing mother. Before leaving Norland Elinor notices a coolness in Edward's manner towards her.

Life in Devon is quiet but comfortable. The Dashwoods adjust to their reduced circumstances with good grace. Sir John is a friendly man, with an endless supply of guests at his home, Barton Park. His wife Lady Middleton is an insipid woman, solely interested in her young children. The Dashwoods are frequently pressed to join in the activities at Barton Park.

Mrs Jennings, Lady Middleton's mother, was a good-humoured, merry, fat, elderly woman, who talked a great deal, seemed very happy, and rather vulgar. She was full of jokes and laughter, and before dinner was over had said many witty things on the subject of lovers and husbands; hoped they had not left their hearts behind them in Sussex, and pretended to see them blush whether they did or not. Marianne was vexed at it for her sister's sake, and turned her eyes towards Elinor to see how she bore these attacks, with an earnestness which gave Elinor far more pain than could arise from such commonplace raillery as Mrs Jennings's.

Colonel Brandon, the friend of Sir John, seemed no more adapted by resemblance of manner to be his friend, than Lady Middleton was to be his wife, or Mrs Jennings to be Lady Middleton's mother. He was silent and grave. His appearance however was not unpleasing, in spite of his being in the opinion of Marianne and Margaret an absolute old bachelor, for he was on the wrong side of five and thirty; but though his face was not handsome his countenance was sensible, and his address was particularly gentlemanlike.

There was nothing in any of the party which could recommend them as companions to the Dashwoods; but the cold insipidity of Lady Middleton was so particularly repulsive, that in comparison of it the gravity of Colonel Brandon, and even the boisterous mirth of Sir John and his mother-in-law was interesting. Lady Middleton seemed to be roused to enjoyment only by the entrance of her four noisy children after dinner, who pulled her about, tore her clothes, and put an end to every kind of discourse except what related to themselves.

In the evening, as Marianne was discovered to be musical, she was invited to play. The instrument was unlocked, every body prepared to be charmed, and Marianne, who sang very well, at their request went through the chief of the songs which Lady Middleton had brought into the family on her marriage, and which perhaps had lain ever since in the same position on the piano-forté, for her ladyship had celebrated that event by giving up music, although by her mother's account she had played extremely well, and by her own was very fond of it.

Marianne's performance was highly applauded. Sir John was loud in his admiration at the end of every song, and as loud in his conversation with the others while every song lasted. Lady Middleton frequently called him to order, wondered how any one's attention could be diverted from music for a moment, and asked Marianne to sing a particular song which Marianne had just finished. Colonel Brandon alone, of all the party, heard her without being in raptures. He paid her only the compliment of attention; and she felt a respect for him on the occasion, which the others had reasonably forfeited by their shameless want of taste. His pleasure in music, though it amounted not to that extatic delight which alone could sympathize with her own, was estimable when contrasted against the horrible insensibility of the others; and she was reasonable enough to allow that a man of five and thirty might well have outlived all acuteness of feeling and every exquisite power of enjoyment. She was perfectly disposed to make every allowance for the colonel's advanced state of life which humanity required.

CHAPTER EIGHT

MRS JENNINGS WAS A widow, with an ample jointure. She had only two daughters, both of whom she had lived to see respectably married, and she had now therefore nothing to do but to marry all the rest of the world. In the promotion of this object she was zealously active, as far as her ability reached; and missed no opportunity of projecting weddings amongst all the young people of her acquaintance. She was remarkably quick in the discovery of attachments, and had enjoyed the advantage of raising the blushes and the vanity of many a young lady by insinuations of her power over such a young man; and this kind of discernment enabled her soon after her arrival at Barton decisively to pronounce that Colonel Brandon was very much in love with Marianne Dashwood. She rather suspected it to be so, on the very first evening of their being together, from his listening so attentively while she sang to them; and when the visit was returned by the Middletons' dining at the cottage, the fact was ascertained by his listening to her again. It must be so. She was perfectly convinced of it. It would be an excellent match, for *he* was rich and *she* was handsome. Mrs Jennings had been anxious to see Colonel Brandon well married, ever since her connection with Sir John first brought him to her knowledge; and she was always anxious to get a good husband for every pretty girl.

The immediate advantage to herself was by no means inconsiderable, for it supplied her with endless jokes against them both. At the park she laughed at the colonel, and in the cottage at Marianne. To the former her raillery was probably, as far as it regarded only himself, perfectly indifferent; but to the latter it was at first incomprehensible; and when its object was understood, she hardly knew whether most to laugh at its absurdity, or censure its impertinence, for she considered it as an unfeeling reflection on the colonel's advanced years, and on his forlorn condition as an old bachelor.

Mrs Dashwood, who could not think a man five years younger than herself, so exceedingly ancient as he appeared to the youthful fancy of her daughter, ventured to clear Mrs Jennings from the probability of wishing to throw ridicule on his age.

'But at least, mama, you cannot deny the absurdity of the accusation, though you may not think it intentionally illnatured. Colonel

Brandon is certainly younger than Mrs Jennings, but he is old enough to be *my* father; and if he were ever animated enough to be in love, must have long outlived every sensation of the kind. It is too ridiculous! When is a man to be safe from such wit, if age and infirmity will not protect him?'

'Infirmity!' said Elinor, 'do you call Colonel Brandon infirm? I can easily suppose that his age may appear much greater to you than to my mother; but you can hardly deceive yourself as to his having the use of his limbs!'

'Did not you hear him complain of the rheumatism? and is not that the commonest infirmity of declining life?'

'My dearest child,' said her mother laughing, 'at this rate you must be in continual terror of *my* decay; and it must seem to you a miracle that my life has been extended to the advanced age of forty.'

'Mama, you are not doing me justice. I know very well that Colonel Brandon is not old enough to make his friends yet apprehensive of losing him in the course of nature. He may live twenty years longer. But thirty-five has nothing to do with matrimony.'

'Perhaps,' said Elinor, 'thirty-five and seventeen had better not have any thing to do with matrimony together. But if there should by any chance happen to be a woman who is single at seven and twenty, I should not think Colonel Brandon's being thirty-five any objection to his marrying *her*.'

'A woman of seven and twenty,' said Marianne, after pausing a moment, 'can never hope to feel or inspire affection again, and if her home be uncomfortable, or her fortune small, I can suppose that she might bring herself to submit to the offices of a nurse, for the sake of the provision and security of a wife. In his marrying such a woman therefore there would be nothing unsuitable. It would be a compact of convenience, and the world would be satisfied. In my eyes it would be no marriage at all, but that would be nothing. To me it would seem only a commercial exchange, in which each wished to be benefited at the expence of the other.'

'It would be impossible, I know,' replied Elinor, 'to convince you that a woman of seven and twenty could feel for a man of thirty-five any thing near enough to love, to make him a desirable companion for her. But I must object to your dooming Colonel Brandon and his wife to the constant confinement of a sick chamber, merely because he chanced to complain yesterday (a very cold damp day) of a slight rheumatic feel in one of his shoulders.'

'But he talked of flannel waistcoats,' said Marianne, 'and with me a flannel waistcoat is invariably connected with aches, rheumatisms, and every species of ailment that can afflict the old and the feeble.'

'Had he been only in a violent fever, you would not have despised him half so much. Confess, Marianne, is not there something interesting to you in the flushed cheek, hollow eye, and quick pulse of a fever?'

Soon after this, upon Elinor's leaving the room, 'Mama,' said Marianne, 'I have an alarm on the subject of illness, which I cannot conceal from you. I am sure Edward Ferrars is not well. We have now been here almost a fortnight, and yet he does not come. Nothing but real indisposition could occasion this extraordinary delay. What else can detain him at Norland?'

'Had you any idea of his coming so soon?' said Mrs Dashwood. '*I* had none. On the contrary, if I have felt any anxiety at all on the subject, it has been in recollecting that he sometimes shewed a want of pleasure and readiness in accepting my invitation, when I talked of his coming to Barton. Does Elinor expect him already?'

'I have never mentioned it to her, but of course she must.'

'I rather think you are mistaken, for when I was talking to her yesterday of getting a new grate for the spare bedchamber, she observed that there was no immediate hurry for it, as it was not likely that the room would be wanted for some time.'

'How strange this is! what can be the meaning of it! But the whole of their behaviour to each other has been unaccountable! How cold, how composed were their last adieus! How languid their conversation the last evening of their being together! In Edward's farewell there was no distinction between Elinor and me: it was the good wishes of an affectionate brother to both. Twice did I leave them purposely together in the course of the last morning, and each time did he most unaccountably follow me out of the room. And Elinor, in quitting Norland and Edward, cried not as I did. Even now her self-command is invariable. When is she dejected or melancholy? When does she try to avoid society, or appear restless and dissatisfied in it?'

CHAPTER NINE

THE DASHWOODS WERE now settled at Barton with tolerable comfort to themselves. The house and the garden, with all the objects surrounding them, were now become familiar, and the ordinary pursuits which had given to Norland half its charms, were engaged in again with far greater enjoyment than Norland had been able to afford, since the loss of their father. Sir John Middleton, who called on them every day for the first fortnight, and who was not in the habit of seeing much occupation at home, could not conceal his amazement on finding them always employed.

Their visitors, except those from Barton Park, were not many; for, in spite of Sir John's urgent entreaties that they would mix more in the neighbourhood, and repeated assurances of his carriage being always at their service, the independence of Mrs Dashwood's spirit overcame the wish of society for her children; and she was resolute in declining to visit any family beyond the distance of a walk. There were but few who could be so classed; and it was not all of them that were attainable. About a mile and a half from the cottage, along the narrow winding valley of Allenham, which issued from that of Barton, as formerly described, the girls had, in one of their earliest walks, discovered an ancient respectable looking mansion which, by reminding them a little of Norland, interested their imagination and made them wish to be better acquainted with it. But they learnt, on inquiry, that its possessor, an elderly lady of very good character, was unfortunately too infirm to mix with the world, and never stirred from home.

The whole country about them abounded in beautiful walks. The high downs which invited them from almost every window of the cottage to seek the exquisite enjoyment of air on their summits, were an happy alternative when the dirt of the valleys beneath shut up their superior beauties; and towards one of these hills did Marianne and Margaret one memorable morning direct their steps, attracted by the partial sunshine of a showery sky, and unable longer to bear the confinement which the settled rain of the two preceding days had occasioned. The weather was not tempting enough to draw the two others from their pencil and their book, in spite of Marianne's declaration that the day would be lastingly fair, and that every threatening cloud would be drawn off from their hills; and the two girls set off together.

They gaily ascended the downs, rejoicing in their own penetration at every glimpse of blue sky; and when they caught in their faces the animating gales of an high south-westerly wind, they pitied the fears which had prevented their mother and Elinor from sharing such delightful sensations.

'Is there a felicity in the world,' said Marianne, 'superior to this? – Margaret, we will walk here at least two hours.'

Margaret agreed, and they pursued their way against the wind, resisting it with laughing delight for about twenty minutes longer, when suddenly the clouds united over their heads, and a driving rain set full in their face. – Chagrined and surprised, they were obliged, though unwillingly, to turn back, for no shelter was nearer than their own house. One consolation however remained for them, to which the exigence of the moment gave more than usual propriety; it was that of running with all possible speed down the steep side of the hill which led immediately to their garden gate.

They set off. Marianne had at first the advantage, but a false step brought her suddenly to the ground, and Margaret, unable to stop herself to assist her, was involuntarily hurried along, and reached the bottom in safety.

A gentleman carrying a gun, with two pointers playing round him, was passing up the hill and within a few yards of Marianne, when her accident happened. He put down his gun and ran to her assistance. She had raised herself from the ground, but her foot had been twisted in the fall, and she was scarcely able to stand. The gentleman offered his services, and perceiving that her modesty declined what her situation rendered necessary, took her up in his arms without farther delay, and carried her down the hill. Then passing through the garden, the gate of which had been left open by Margaret, he bore her directly into the house, whither Margaret was just arrived, and quitted not his hold till he had seated her in a chair in the parlour.

Elinor and her mother rose up in amazement at their entrance, and while the eyes of both were fixed on him with an evident wonder and a secret admiration which equally sprung from his appearance, he apologized for his intrusion by relating its cause, in a manner so frank and so graceful, that his person, which was uncommonly handsome, received additional charms from his voice and expression. Had he been even old, ugly, and vulgar, the grati-tude and kindness of Mrs Dashwood would have been secured by any act of attention to her child; but the influence of youth, beauty, and elegance, gave an interest to the action which came home to her feelings.

She thanked him again and again; and with a sweetness of address which always attended her, invited him to be seated. But this he declined, as he was dirty and wet. Mrs Dashwood then begged to know to whom she was obliged. His name, he replied, was Willoughby, and his present home was at Allenham, from whence he hoped she would allow him the honour of calling tomorrow to inquire after Miss Dashwood. The honour was readily granted, and he then departed, to make himself still more interesting, in the midst of an heavy rain.

His manly beauty and more than common gracefulness were

instantly the theme of general admiration, and the laugh which his gallantry raised against Marianne, received particular spirit from his exterior attractions – Marianne herself had seen less of his person than the rest, for the confusion which crimsoned over her face, on his lifting her up, had robbed her of the power of regarding him after their entering the house. But she had seen enough of him to join in all the admiration of the others, and with an energy which always adorned her praise. His person and air were equal to what her fancy had ever drawn for the hero of a favourite story; and in his carrying her into the house with so little previous formality, there was a rapidity of thought which particularly recommended the action to her. Every circumstance belonging to him was interesting. His name was good, his residence was in their favourite village, and she soon found out that of all manly dresses a shooting-jacket was the most becoming. Her imagination was busy, her reflections were pleasant, and the pain of a sprained ancle was disregarded.

Sir John called on them as soon as the next interval of fair weather that morning allowed him to get out of doors; and Marianne's accident being related to him, he was eagerly asked whether he knew any gentleman of the name of Willoughby at Allenham.

'Willoughby!' cried Sir John; 'what, is *he* in the country? That is good news however; I will ride over tomorrow, and ask him to dinner on Thursday.'

'You know him then,' said Mrs Dashwood.

'Know him! to be sure I do. Why, he is down here every year.'

'And what sort of a young man is he?'

'As good a kind of fellow as ever lived, I assure you. A very decent shot, and there is not a bolder rider in England.'

'And is *that* all you can say for him?' cried Marianne, indignantly. 'But what are his manners on more intimate acquaintance? What his pursuits, his talents and genius?'

Sir John was rather puzzled.

'Upon my soul,' said he, 'I do not know much about him as to all *that*. But he is a pleasant, good humoured fellow, and has got the nicest little black bitch of a pointer I ever saw. Was she out with him today?'

But Marianne could no more satisfy him as to the colour of Mr Willoughby's pointer, than he could describe to her the shades of his mind.

'But who is he?' said Elinor. 'Where does he come from? Has he a house at Allenham?'

On this point Sir John could give more certain intelligence; and he told them that Mr Willoughby had no property of his own in the country; that he resided there only while he was visiting the old lady at Allenham Court, to whom he was related, and whose possessions he was to inherit; adding, 'Yes, yes, he is very well worth catching, I can tell you, Miss Dashwood; he has a pretty little estate of his own in Somersetshire besides; and if I were you, I would not give him up to my younger sister in spite of all this tumbling down hills. Miss Marianne must not expect to have all the men to herself. Brandon will be jealous, if she does not take care.'

'I do not believe,' said Mrs Dashwood, with a good humoured smile, 'that Mr Willoughby will be incommoded by the attempts of either of *my* daughters towards what you call *catching* him. It is not an employment to which they have been brought up. Men are very safe with us, let them be ever so rich. I am glad to find, however, from what you say, that he is a respectable young man, and one whose acquaintance will not be ineligible.'

'He is as good a sort of fellow, I believe, as ever lived,' repeated Sir John. 'I remember last Christmas at a little hop at the park, he danced from eight o'clock till four, without once sitting down.'

'Did he indeed?' cried Marianne with sparkling eyes, 'and with elegance, with spirit?'

'Yes; and he was up again at eight to ride to covert.'

'That is what I like; that is what a young man ought to be. Whatever be his pursuits, his eagerness in them should know no moderation, and leave him no sense of fatigue.'

'Aye, aye, I see how it will be,' said Sir John, 'I see how it will be. You will be setting your cap at him now, and never think of poor Brandon.'

'That is an expression, Sir John,' said Marianne, warmly, 'which I particularly dislike. I abhor every common-place phrase by which wit is intended; and "setting one's cap at a man," or "making a conquest," are the most odious of all. Their tendency is gross and illiberal; and if their construction could ever be deemed clever, time has long ago destroyed all its ingenuity.'

Sir John did not much understand this reproof; but he laughed as heartily as if he did, and then replied,

'Aye, you will make conquests enough, I dare say, one way or other. Poor Brandon! he is quite smitten already, and he is very well worth setting your cap at, I can tell you, in spite of all this tumbling about and spraining of ancles.'

CHAPTER TEN

MARIANNE'S PRESERVER, AS Margaret, with more elegance than precision, stiled Willoughby, called at the cottage early the next morning to make his personal inquiries. He was received by Mrs Dashwood with more than politeness; with a kindness which Sir John's account of him and her own gratitude prompted; and every thing that passed during the visit, tended to assure him of the sense, elegance, mutual affection, and domestic comfort of the family to whom accident had now introduced him. Of their personal charms he had not required a second interview to be convinced.

Miss Dashwood had a delicate complexion, regular features and a remarkably pretty figure. Marianne was still handsomer. Her form, though not so correct as her sister's, in having the advantage of height, was more striking; and her face was so lovely, that when in the common cant of praise she was called a beautiful girl, truth was less violently outraged than usually happens. Her skin was very brown, but from its transparency, her complexion was uncommonly brilliant; her features were all good; her smile was sweet and attractive, and in her eyes, which were very dark, there was a life, a spirit, an eagerness which could hardly be seen without delight. From Willoughby their expression was at first held back, by the embarrassment which the remembrance of his assistance created. But when this passed away, when her spirits became collected, when she saw that to the perfect good-breeding of the gentleman, he united frankness and vivacity, and above all, when she heard him declare that of music and dancing he was passionately fond, she gave him such a look of approbation as secured the largest share of his discourse to herself for the rest of his stay.

It was only necessary to mention any favourite amusement to engage her to talk. She could not be silent when such points were introduced, and she had neither shyness nor reserve in their discussion. They speedily discovered that their enjoyment of dancing and music was mutual, and that it arose from a general conformity of judgment in all that related to either. Encouraged by this to a further examination of his opinions, she proceeded to question him on the subject of books; her favourite authors were brought forward and dwelt upon with so rapturous a delight, that any young man of five and twenty must have been insensible indeed, not to become an immediate convert to the excellence of such works, however disregarded before. Their taste was strikingly alike. The same books, the same passages were idolized by each – or if any difference appeared, any objection arose, it lasted no longer than till the force of her arguments and the brightness of her eyes could be displayed. He acquiesced in all her decisions, caught all her enthusiasm; and long before his visit concluded, they conversed with the familiarity of a long-established acquaintance.

'Well, Marianne,' said Elinor, as soon as he had left them, 'for *one* morning I think you have done pretty well. You have already ascertained Mr Willoughby's opinion in almost every matter of importance. You know what he thinks of Cowper and Scott; you are certain of his estimating their beauties as he ought, and you have received every assurance of his admiring Pope no more than is proper. But how is your acquaintance to be long supported, under such extraordinary dispatch of every subject for discourse? You will soon have exhausted each favourite topic. Another meeting will suffice to explain his sentiments on picturesque beauty, and second marriages, and then you can have nothing farther to ask.' –

'Elinor,' cried Marianne, 'is this fair? is this just? are my ideas so scanty? But I see what you mean. I have been too much at my ease, too happy, too frank. I have erred against every common-place notion of decorum; I have been open and sincere where I ought to have been reserved, spiritless, dull, and deceitful: – had I talked only of the weather and the roads, and had I spoken only once in ten minutes, this reproach would have been spared.'

'My love,' said her mother, 'you must not be offended with Elinor – she was only in jest. I should scold her myself, if she were capable of wishing to check the delight of your conversation with our new friend.' – Marianne was softened in a moment.

Willoughby, on his side, gave every proof of his pleasure in their acquaintance, which an evident wish of improving it could offer. He came to them every day. To inquire after Marianne was at first his excuse; but the encouragement of his reception, to which every day gave greater kindness, made such an excuse unnecessary before it had ceased to be possible, by Marianne's perfect recovery. She was confined for some days to the house; but never had any confinement been less irksome. Willoughby was a young man of good abilities, quick imagination, lively spirits, and open, affectionate manners. He was exactly formed to engage Marianne's heart, for with all this, he joined not only a captivating person, but a natural ardour of mind which was now roused and increased by the example of her own, and which recommended him to her affection beyond every thing else.

His society became gradually her most exquisite enjoyment. They read, they talked, they sang together; his musical talents were considerable; and he read with all the sensibility and spirit which Edward had unfortunately wanted.

In Mrs Dashwood's estimation, he was as faultless as in Marianne's; and Elinor saw nothing to censure in him but a propensity, in which he strongly resembled and peculiarly delighted her sister, of saying too much what he thought on every occasion, without attention to persons or circumstances. In hastily forming and giving

They sang together.

his opinion of other people, in sacrificing general politeness to the enjoyment of undivided attention where his heart was engaged, and in slighting too easily the forms of worldly propriety, he displayed a want of caution which Elinor could not approve, in spite of all that he and Marianne could say in its support.

Marianne began now to perceive that the desperation which had seized her at sixteen and a half, of ever seeing a man who could satisfy her ideas of perfection, had been rash and unjustifiable. Willoughby was all that her fancy had delineated in that unhappy hour and in every brighter period, as capable of attaching her; and his behaviour declared his wishes to be in that respect as earnest, as his abilities were strong.

Her mother too, in whose mind not one speculative thought of their marriage had been raised, by his prospect of riches, was led before the end of a week to hope and expect it; and secretly to congratulate herself on having gained two such sons-in-law as Edward and Willoughby.

Colonel Brandon's partiality for Marianne, which had so early been discovered by his friends, now first became perceptible to Elinor, when it ceased to be noticed by them. Their attention and wit were drawn off to his more fortunate rival; and the raillery which the other had incurred before any partiality arose, was removed when his feelings began really to call for the ridicule so justly annexed to sensibility. Elinor was obliged, though unwillingly, to believe that the sentiments which Mrs Jennings had assigned him for her own satisfaction, were now actually excited by her sister; and that however a general resemblance of disposition between the parties might forward the affection of Mr Willoughby, an equally striking opposition of character was no hindrance to the regard of Colonel Brandon. She saw it with concern; for what could a silent man of five and thirty hope, when opposed by a very lively one of five and twenty? and as she could not even wish him successful, she heartily wished him indifferent. She liked him – in spite of his gravity and reserve, she beheld in him an object of interest. His manners, though serious, were mild; and his reserve appeared rather the result of some oppression of spirits, than of any natural gloominess of temper. Sir John had dropt hints of past injuries and disappointments, which justified her belief of his being an unfortunate man, and she regarded him with respect and compassion.

Perhaps she pitied and esteemed him the more because he was slighted by Willoughby and Marianne, who, prejudiced against him for being neither lively nor young, seemed resolved to undervalue his merits.

'Brandon is just the kind of man,' said Willoughby one day, when they were talking of him together, 'whom every body speaks well of, and nobody cares about; whom all are delighted to see, and nobody remembers to talk to.'

'That is exactly what I think of him,' cried Marianne.

'Do not boast of it, however,' said Elinor, 'for it is injustice in both of you. He is highly esteemed by all the family at the park, and I never see him myself without taking pains to converse with him.'

'That he is patronized by *you*,' replied Willoughby, 'is certainly in his favour; but as for the esteem of the others, it is a reproach in itself. Who would submit to the indignity of being approved by such women as Lady Middleton and Mrs Jennings, that could command the indifference of any body else?'

'But perhaps the abuse of such people as yourself and Marianne, will make amends for the regard of Lady Middleton and her mother. If their praise is censure, your censure may be praise, for they are not more undiscerning, than you are prejudiced and unjust.'

'In defence of your protégé you can even be saucy.'

'My protégé, as you call him, is a sensible man; and sense will always have attractions for me. Yes, Marianne, even in a man between thirty and forty. He has seen a great deal of the world; has been abroad; has read, and has a thinking mind. I have found him capable of giving me much information on various subjects, and he has always answered my inquiries with the readiness of good-breeding and good nature.'

'That is to say,' cried Marianne contemptuously, 'he has told you that in the East Indies the climate is hot, and the mosquitoes are troublesome.'

'He *would* have told me so, I doubt not, had I made any such inquiries, but they happened to be points on which I had been previously informed.'

'Perhaps,' said Willoughby, 'his observations may have extended to the existence of nabobs, gold mohrs, and palanquins.'

'I may venture to say that *his* observations have stretched much farther than your candour. But why should you dislike him?'

'I do not dislike him. I consider him, on the contrary, as a very respectable man, who has every body's good word and nobody's notice; who has more money than he can spend, more time than he knows how to employ, and two new coats every year.'

'Add to which,' cried Marianne, 'that he has neither genius, taste, nor spirit. That his understanding has no brilliancy, his feelings no ardour, and his voice no expression.'

'You decide on his imperfections so much in the mass,' replied Elinor, 'and so much on the strength of your own imagination, that the commendation I am able to give of him is comparatively cold and insipid. I can only pronounce him to be a sensible man, well-bred, well-informed, of gentle address, and I believe possessing an amiable heart.'

'Miss Dashwood,' cried Willoughby, 'you are now using me unkindly. You are endeavouring to disarm me by reason, and to convince me against my will. But it will not do. You shall find me as stubborn as you can be artful. I have three unanswerable reasons for disliking Colonel Brandon: he has threatened me with rain when I wanted it to be fine; he has found fault with the hanging of my curricle, and I cannot persuade him to buy my brown mare. If it will be any satisfaction to you, however, to be told, that I believe his character to be in other respects irreproachable, I am ready to confess it. And in return for an acknowledgment, which must give me some pain, you cannot deny me the privilege of disliking him as much as ever.'

CHAPTER ELEVEN

LITTLE HAD MRS DASHWOOD or her daughters imagined when they first came into Devonshire, that so many engagements would arise to occupy their time as shortly presented themselves, or that they should have such frequent invitations and such constant visitors as to leave them little leisure for serious employment. Yet such was the case. When Marianne was recovered, the schemes of amusement at home and abroad, which Sir John has been previously forming, were put in execution. The private balls at the park then began; and parties on the water were made and accomplished as often as a showery October would allow. In every meeting of the kind Willoughby was included; and the ease and familiarity which naturally attended these parties were exactly calculated to give increasing intimacy to his acquaintance with the Dashwoods, to afford him opportunity of witnessing the excellencies of Marianne, of marking his animated admiration of her, and of receiving, in her behaviour to himself, the most pointed assurance of her affection.

Elinor could not be surprised at their attachment. She only wished that it were less openly shewn; and once or twice did venture to suggest the propriety of some self-command to Marianne. But

Marianne abhorred all concealment where no real disgrace could attend unreserve; and to aim at the restraint of sentiments which were not in themselves illaudable, appeared to her not merely an unnecessary effort, but a disgraceful subjection of reason to common-place and mistaken notions. Willoughby thought the same; and their behaviour, at all times, was an illustration of their opinions.

When he was present she had no eyes for any one else. Every thing he did, was right. Every thing he said, was clever. If their evenings at the park were concluded with cards, he cheated himself and all the rest of the party to get her a good hand. If dancing formed the amusement of the night, they were partners for half the time; and when obliged to separate for a couple of dances, were careful to stand together and scarcely spoke a word to any body else. Such conduct made them of course most exceedingly laughed at; but ridicule could not shame, and seemed hardly to provoke them.

Mrs Dashwood entered into all their feelings with a warmth which left her no inclination for checking this excessive display of them. To her it was but the natural consequence of a strong affection in a young and ardent mind.

This was the season of happiness to Marianne. Her heart was devoted to Willoughby, and the fond attachment to Norland, which she brought with her from Sussex, was more likely to be softened than she had thought it possible before, by the charms which his society bestowed on her present home.

Elinor's happiness was not so great. Her heart was not so much at ease, nor her satisfaction in their amusements so pure. They afforded her no companion that could make amends for what she had left behind, nor that could teach her to think of Norland with less regret than ever. Neither Lady Middleton nor Mrs Jennings could supply to her the conversation she missed; although the latter was an everlasting talker, and from the first had regarded her with a kindness which ensured her a large share of her discourse. She had already repeated her own history to Elinor three or four times; and had Elinor's memory been equal to her means of improvement, she might have known very early in their acquaintance all the particulars of Mr Jenning's last illness, and what he said to his wife a few minutes before he died. Lady Middleton was more agreeable than her mother, only in being more silent. Elinor needed little observation to perceive that her reserve was a mere calmness of manner with which sense had nothing to do. Towards her husband and mother she was the same as to them; and intimacy was therefore neither to be looked for nor desired. She had nothing to say one day that she had not said the day before. Her insipidity was invariable, for even her spirits were always the same; and though she did not oppose the parties arranged by her husband, provided every thing were conducted in style and her two eldest children attended her, she never appeared to receive more enjoyment from them, than she might have experienced in sitting at home; – and so little did her presence add to the pleasure of the others, by any share in their conversation, that they were sometimes only reminded of her being amongst them by her solicitude about her troublesome boys.

In Colonel Brandon alone, of all her new acquaintance, did Elinor find a person who could in any degree claim the respect of abilities, excite the interest of friendship, or give pleasure as a companion. Willoughby was out of the question. Her admiration and regard, even her sisterly regard, was all his own; but he was a lover; his attentions were wholly Marianne's, and a far less agreeable man might have been more generally pleasing. Colonel Brandon, unfortunately for himself, had no such encouragement to think only of Marianne, and in conversing with Elinor he found the greatest consolation for the total indifference of her sister.

Elinor's compassion for him increased, as she had reason to suspect that the misery of disappointed love had already been known by him. This suspicion was given by some words which accidentally dropt from him one evening at the park, when they were sitting down together by mutual consent, while the others were dancing. His eyes were fixed on Marianne, and, after a silence of some minutes, he said with a faint smile. 'Your sister, I understand, does not approve of second attachments.'

'No,' replied Elinor, 'her opinions are all romantic.'

'Or rather, as I believe, she considers them impossible to exist.'

'I believe she does. But how she contrives it without reflecting on the character of her own father, who had himself two wives, I know not. A few years however will settle her opinions on the reasonable basis of common sense and observation; and then they may be more easy to define and to justify than they now are, by any body but herself.'

'This will probably be the case,' he replied; 'and yet there is something so amiable in the prejudices of a young mind, that one is sorry to see them give way to the reception of more general opinions.'

'I cannot agree with you there,' said Elinor. 'There are inconveniences attending such feelings as Marianne's, which all the charms of enthusiasm and ignorance of the world cannot atone for. Her

systems have all the unfortunate tendency of setting propriety at
nought; and a better acquaintance with the world is what I look
forward to as her greatest possible advantage.'

After a short pause he resumed the conversation by saying –

'Does your sister make no distinction in her objections against a
second attachment? or is it equally criminal in every body? Are those
who have been disappointed in their first choice, whether from the
inconstancy of its object, or the perverseness of circumstances, to
be equally indifferent during the rest of their lives?'

'Upon my word, I am not acquainted with the minutia of her
principles. I only know that I never yet heard her admit any instance
of a second attachment's being pardonable.'

'This,' said he, 'cannot hold; but a change, a total change of
sentiments – No, no, do not desire it, – for when the romantic
refinements of a young mind are obliged to give way, how
frequently are they succeeded by such opinions as are but too
common, and too dangerous! I speak from experience. I once knew
a lady who in temper and mind greatly resembled your sister, who
thought and judged like her, but who from an inforced change –
from a series of unfortunate circumstances' – Here he stopt suddenly;
appeared to think that he had said too much, and by his countenance
gave rise to conjectures, which might not otherwise have entered
Elinor's head. The lady would probably have passed without
suspicion, had he not convinced Miss Dashwood that what
concerned her ought not to escape his lips. As it was, it required
but a slight effort of fancy to connect his emotion with the tender
recollection of past regard. Elinor attempted no more. But Marianne, in her place, would not have done so little. The whole story
would have been speedily formed under her active imagination; and
every thing established in the most melancholy order of disastrous
love.

CHAPTER TWELVE

As ELINOR AND MARIANNE were walking together the next morning
the latter communicated a piece of news to her sister, which in spite
of all that she knew before of Marianne's imprudence and want of
thought, surprised her by its extravagant testimony of both. Marianne told her, with the greatest delight, that Willoughby had given
her a horse, one that he had bred himself on his estate in Somerset-

shire, and which was exactly calculated to carry a woman. Without considering that it was not in her mother's plan to keep any horse, that if she were to alter her resolution in favour of this gift, she must buy another for the servant, and keep a servant to ride it, and after all, build a stable to receive them, she had accepted the present without hesitation, and told her sister of it in raptures.

'He intends to send his groom into Somersetshire immediately for it,' she added, 'and when it arrives, we will ride every day. You shall share its use with me. Imagine to yourself, my dear Elinor, the delight of a gallop on some of these downs.'

Most unwilling was she to awaken from such a dream of felicity, to comprehend all the unhappy truths which attended the affair; and for some time she refused to submit to them. As to an additional servant, the expence would be a trifle; mama she was sure would never object to it; and any horse would do for *him*; he might always get one at the park; as to a stable, the merest shed would be sufficient. Elinor then ventured to doubt the propriety of her receiving such a present from a man so little, or at least so lately known to her. This was too much.

'You are mistaken, Elinor,' said she warmly, 'in supposing I know very little of Willoughby. I have not known him long indeed, but I am much better acquainted with him, than with any other creature in the world, except yourself and mama. It is not time or opportunity that is to determine intimacy; – it is disposition alone. Seven years would be insufficient to make some people acquainted with each other, and seven days are more than enough for others. I should hold myself guilty of greater impropriety in accepting a horse from my brother, than from Willoughby. Of John I know very little, though we have lived together for years; but of Willoughby my judgment has long been formed.'

Elinor thought it wisest to touch that point no more. She knew her sister's temper. Opposition on so tender a subject would only attach her the more to her own opinion. But by an appeal to her affection for her mother, by representing the inconveniences which that indulgent mother must draw on herself, if (as would probably be the case) she consented to this increase of establishment, Marianne was shortly subdued; and she promised not to tempt her mother to such imprudent kindness by mentioning the offer, and to tell Willoughby when she saw him next, that it must be declined.

She was faithful to her word; and when Willoughby called at the cottage, the same day, Elinor heard her express her disappointment to him in a low voice, on being obliged to forego the acceptance of his present. The reasons for this alteration were at the same time related, and they were such as to make further entreaty on his side impossible. His concern however was very apparent; and after expressing it with earnestness, he added in the same low voice – 'But, Marianne, the horse is still yours, though you cannot use it now. I shall keep it only till you can claim it. When you leave Barton to form your own establishment in a more lasting home, Queen Mab shall receive you.'

This was all overheard by Miss Dashwood; and in the whole of the sentence, in his manner of pronouncing it, and in his addressing her sister by her christian name alone, she instantly saw an intimacy so decided, a meaning so direct, as marked a perfect agreement between them. From that moment she doubted not of their being engaged to each other; and the belief of it created no other surprise, than that she, or any of their friends, should be left by tempers so frank, to discover it by accident.

Margaret related something to her the next day, which placed this matter in a still clearer light. Willoughby had spent the preceding evening with them, and Margaret, by being left some time in the parlour with only him and Marianne, had had opportunity for observations, which, with a most important face, she communicated to her eldest sister, when they were next by themselves.

'Oh! Elinor,' she cried, 'I have such a secret to tell you about Marianne. I am sure she will be married to Mr Willoughby very soon.'

'You have said so,' replied Elinor, 'almost every day since they first met on Highchurch Down; and they had not known each other a week, I believe, before you were certain that Marianne wore his picture round her neck; but it turned out to be only the miniature of our great uncle.'

'But indeed this is quite another thing. I am sure they will be married very soon, for he has got a lock of her hair.'

'Take care, Margaret. It may be only the hair of some great uncle of *his*.'

'But indeed, Elinor, it is Marianne's. I am almost sure it is, for I saw him cut it off. Last night after tea, when you and mama went out of the room, they were whispering and talking together as fast as could be, and he seemed to be begging something of her, and presently he took up her scissors and cut off a long lock of her hair, for it was all tumbled down her back; and he kissed it, and folded it up in a piece of white paper, and put it into his pocket-book.'

From such particulars, stated on such authority, Elinor could not withhold her credit: nor was she disposed to it, for the circumstance was in perfect unison with what she had heard and seen herself.

He cut off a long lock of her hair.

Margaret's sagacity was not always displayed in a way so satisfactory to her sister. When Mrs Jennings attacked her one evening at the park, to give the name of the young man who was Elinor's particular favourite, which had been long a matter of great curiosity to her, Margaret answered by looking at her sister, and saying, 'I must not tell, may I, Elinor?'

This of course made every body laugh; and Elinor tried to laugh too. But the effort was painful. She was convinced that Margaret had fixed on a person, whose name she could not bear with composure to become a standing joke with Mrs Jennings.

Marianne felt for her most sincerely; but she did more harm than good to the cause, by turning very red, and saying in an angry manner to Margaret,

'Remember that whatever your conjectures may be, you have no right to repeat them.'

'I never had any conjectures about it,' replied Margaret; 'it was you who told me of it yourself.'

This increased the mirth of the company, and Margaret was eagerly pressed to say something more.

'Oh! pray, Miss Margaret, let us know all about it,' said Mrs Jennings. 'What is the gentleman's name?'

'I must not tell, ma'am. But I know very well what it is; and I know where he is too.'

'Yes, yes, we can guess where he is; at his own house at Norland to be sure. He is the curate of the parish I dare say.'

'No, *that* he is not. He is of no profession at all.'

'Margaret,' said Marianne with great warmth, 'you know that all this is an invention of your own, and that there is no such person in existence.'

'Well then he is lately dead, Marianne, for I am sure there was such a man once, and his name begins with an F.'

Most grateful did Elinor feel to Lady Middleton for observing at this moment, 'that it rained very hard,' though she believed the interruption to proceed less from any attention to her than from her ladyship's great dislike of all such inelegant subjects of raillery as delighted her husband and mother. The idea however started by her, was immediately pursued by Colonel Brandon, who was on every occasion mindful of the feelings of others; and much was said on the subject of rain by both of them. Willoughby opened the piano-forte, and asked Marianne to sit down to it; and thus amidst the various endeavours of different people to quit the topic, it fell to the ground. But not so easily did Elinor recover from the alarm into which it had thrown her.

A party was formed this evening for going on the following day to see a very fine place about twelve miles from Barton, belonging to a brother-in-law of Colonel Brandon, without whose interest it could not be seen, as the proprietor, who was then abroad, had left strict orders on that head. The grounds were declared to be highly beautiful, and Sir John, who was particularly warm in their praise, might be allowed to be a tolerable judge, for he had formed parties to visit them, at least, twice every summer for the last ten years. They contained a noble piece of water; a sail on which was to form a great part of the morning's amusement; cold provisions were to be taken, open carriages only to be employed, and every thing conducted in the usual style of a complete party of pleasure.

To some few of the company, it appeared rather a bold under-taking, considering the time of year, and that it had rained every day for the last fortnight; – and Mrs Dashwood, who had already a cold, was persuaded by Elinor to stay at home.

CHAPTER THIRTEEN

THEIR INTENDED EXCURSION to Whitwell turned out very different from what Elinor had expected. She was prepared to be wet through, fatigued, and frightened; but the event was still more unfortunate, for they did not go at all.

By ten o'clock the whole party were assembled at the park, where they were to breakfast. The morning was rather favourable, though it had rained all night, as the clouds were then dispersing across the sky, and the sun frequently appeared. They were all in high spirits and good humour, eager to be happy, and determined to submit to the greatest inconveniences and hardships rather than be otherwise.

While they were at breakfast the letters were brought in. Among the rest there was one for Colonel Brandon; – he took it, looked at the direction, changed colour, and immediately left the room.

'What is the matter with Brandon?' said Sir John.

Nobody could tell.

'I hope he has had no bad news,' said Lady Middleton. 'It must be something extraordinary that could make Colonel Brandon leave my breakfast table so suddenly.'

In about five minutes he returned.

'No bad news, Colonel, I hope;' said Mrs Jennings, as soon as he entered the room.

'None at all, ma'am, I thank you.'

'Was it from Avignon? I hope it is not to say that your sister is worse.'

'No, ma'am. It came from town, and is merely a letter of business.'

'But how came the hand to discompose you so much, if it was only a letter of business? Come, come, this won't do, Colonel; so let us hear the truth of it.'

'My dear Madam,' said Lady Middleton, 'recollect what you are saying.'

'Perhaps it is to tell you that your cousin Fanny is married?' said Mrs Jennings, without attending to her daughter's reproof.

'No, indeed, it is not.'

'Well, then, I know who it is from, Colonel. and I hope she is well.'

'Whom do you mean, ma'am?' said he, colouring a little.

'Oh! you know who I mean.'

'I am particularly sorry, ma'am,' said he, addressing Lady Middleton, 'that I should receive this letter today, for it is on business which requires my immediate attendance in town.'

'In town!' cried Mrs Jennings. 'What can you have to do in town at this time of year?'

'My own loss is great,' he continued, 'in being obliged to leave so agreeable a party; but I am the more concerned, as I fear my presence is necessary to gain your admittance at Whitwell.'

What a blow upon them all was this!

'But if you write a note to the housekeeper, Mr Brandon,' said Marianne eagerly, 'will it not be sufficient?'

He shook his head.

'We must go,' said Sir John. – 'It shall not be put off when we are so near it. You cannot go to town till tomorrow, Brandon, that is all.'

'I wish it could be so easily settled. But it is not in my power to delay my journey for one day!'

'If you would but let us know what your business is,' said Mrs Jennings, 'we might see whether it could be put off or not.'

'You would not be six hours later,' said Willoughby, 'if you were to defer your journey till our return.'

'I cannot afford to lose *one* hour.' –

Elinor then heard Willoughby say in a low voice to Marianne, 'There are some people who cannot bear a party of pleasure. Brandon is one of them. He was afraid of catching cold I dare say, and invented this trick for getting out of it. I would lay fifty guineas the letter was of his own writing.'

'I have no doubt of it.' replied Marianne.

'There is no persuading you to change your mind, Brandon, I know of old,' said Sir John, 'when once you are determined on any thing. But, however, I hope you will think better of it. Consider, here are the two Miss Careys come over from Newton, the three Miss Dashwoods walked up from the cottage, and Mr Willoughby got up two hours before his usual time, on purpose to go to Whitwell.'

Colonel Brandon again repeated his sorrow at being the cause of disappointing the party; but at the same time declared it to be unavoidable.

'Well then, when will you come back again?'

'I hope we shall see you at Barton,' added her ladyship, 'as soon as you can conveniently leave town; and we must put off the party to Whitwell till you return.'

'You are very obliging. But it is so uncertain, when I may have it in my power to return, that I dare not engage for it at all.'

'Oh! he must and shall come back,' cried Sir John. 'If he is not here by the end of the week, I shall go after him.'

'Aye, so do, Sir John,' cried Mrs Jennings, 'and then perhaps you may find out what his business is.'

'I do not want to pry into other men's concerns. I suppose it is something he is ashamed of.'

Colonel Brandon's horses were announced.

'You do not go to town on horseback, do you?' added Sir John.

'No. Only to Honiton. I shall then go post.'

'Well, as you are resolved to go, I wish you a good journey. But you had better change your mind.'

'I assure you it is not in my power.'

He then took leave of the whole party.

'Is there no chance of my seeing you and your sisters in town this winter, Miss Dashwood?'

'I am afraid, none at all.'

'Then I must bid you farewell for a longer time than I should wish to do.'

To Marianne, he merely bowed and said nothing.

'Come, Colonel,' said Mrs Jennings, 'before you go, do let us know what you are going about.'

He wished her a good morning, and attended by Sir John, left the room.

The complaints and lamentations which politeness had hitherto restrained, now burst forth universally; and they all agreed again and again how provoking it was to be so disappointed.

'I can guess what his business is, however,' said Mrs Jennings exultingly.

'Can you ma'am?' said almost every body.

'Yes; it is about Miss Williams, I am sure.'

'And who is Miss Williams?' asked Marianne.

'What! do not you know who Miss Williams is? I am sure you must have heard of her before. She is a relation of the Colonel's, my dear; a very near relation. We will not say how near, for fear

of shocking the young ladies.' Then lowering her voice a little, she
said to Elinor. 'She is his natural daughter.'

'Indeed!'

'Oh! yes; and as like him as she can stare. I dare say the Colonel
will leave her all his fortune.'

When Sir John returned, he joined most heartily in the general
regret on so unfortunate an event; concluding however by
observing, that as they were all got together, they must do something by way of being happy; and after some consultation it was
agreed, that although happiness could only be enjoyed at Whitwell,
they might procure a tolerable composure of mind by driving about
the country. The carriages were then ordered; Willoughby's was
first, and Marianne never looked happier than when she got into it.
He drove through the park very fast, and they were soon out of
sight; and nothing more of them was seen till their return, which
did not happen till after the return of all the rest. They both seemed
delighted with their drive, but said only in general terms that they
had kept in the lanes, while the others went on the downs.

It was settled that there should be a dance in the evening, and
that every body should be extremely merry all day long. Some more

'I have found you out in spite of all your tricks.'

of the Careys came to dinner, and they had the pleasure of sitting down nearly twenty to table, which Sir John observed with great contentment. Willoughby took his usual place between the two elder Miss Dashwoods. Mrs Jennings sat on Elinor's right hand; and they had not been long seated, before she leant behind her and Willoughby and said to Marianne, loud enough for them both to hear, 'I have found you out in spite of all your tricks. I know where you spent the morning.'

Marrianne coloured, and replied very hastily, 'Where, pray?' –

'Did not you know,' said Willoughby, 'that we had been out in my curricle?'

'Yes, yes, Mr Impudence, I know that very well, and I was determined to find out *where* you had been to. – I hope you like your house, Miss Marianne. It is a very large one I know, and when I come to see you, I hope you will have new-furnished it, for it wanted it very much, when I was there six years ago.'

Marianne turned away in great confusion. Mrs Jennings laughed heartily; and Elinor found that in her resolution to know where they had been, she had actually made her own woman enquire of Mr Willoughby's groom, and that she had by that method been informed that they had gone to Allenham, and spent a considerable time there in walking about the garden and going all over the house.

Elinor could hardly believe this to be true, as it seemed very unlikely that Willoughby should propose, or Marianne consent, to enter the house while Mrs Smith was in it, with whom Marianne had not the smallest acquaintance.

As soon as they left the dining-room, Elinor enquired of her about it; and great was her surprise when she found that every circumstance related by Mrs Jennings was perfectly true. Marianne was quite angry with her for doubting it.

'Why should you imagine, Elinor, that we did not go there, or that we did not see the house? Is not it what you have often wished to do yourself?'

'Yes, Marianne, but I would not go while Mrs Smith was there, and with no other companion than Mr Willoughby.'

'Mr Willoughby however is the only person who can have a right to shew that house; and as we went in an open carriage, it was impossible to have any other companion. I never spent a pleasanter morning in my life.'

'I am afraid,' replied Elinor, 'that the pleasantness of an employment does not always evince its propriety.'

'On the contrary, nothing can be stronger proof of it, Elinor; for if there had been any real impropriety in what I did, I should have been sensible of it at the time, for we always know when we are acting wrong, and with such a conviction I could have had no pleasure.'

'But, my dear Marianne, as it has already exposed you to some very impertinent remarks, do you not now begin to doubt the discretion of your own conduct?'

'If the impertinent remarks of Mrs Jennings are to be the proof of impropriety in conduct, we are all offending every moment of all our lives. I value not her censure any more than I should do her commendation. I am not sensible of having done any thing wrong in walking over Mrs Smith's grounds, or in seeing her house. They will one day be Mr Willoughby's, and . . .'

'If they were one day to be your own, Marianne, you would not be justified in what you have done.'

She blushed at this hint; but it was even visibly gratifying to her; and after a ten minutes' interval of earnest thought, she came to her sister again, and said with great good humour, 'Perhaps, Elinor, it *was* rather ill-judged in me to go to Allenham; but Mr Willoughby wanted particularly to shew me the place; and it is a charming house I assure you. – There is one remarkably pretty sitting room up stairs; of a nice comfortable size for constant use, and with modern furniture it would be delightful. It is a corner room, and has windows on two sides. On one side you look across the bowling-green, behind the house, to a beautiful hanging wood, and on the other you have a view of the church and village, and, beyond them, of those fine bold hills that we have so often admired. I did not see it to advantage, for nothing could be more forlorn than the furniture, – but if it were newly fitted up – a couple of hundred pounds. Willoughby says, would make it one of the pleasantest summer-rooms in England.'

Could Elinor have listened to her without interruption from the others, she would have described every room in the house with equal delight.

CHAPTER FOURTEEN

THE SUDDEN TERMINATION of Colonel Brandon's visit at the park, with his steadiness in concealing its cause, filled the mind and raised the wonder of Mrs Jennings for two or three days; she was a great wonderer, as every one must be who takes a very lively interest in all the comings and goings of all their acquaintance. She wondered with little intermission what could be the reason of it; was sure there must be some bad news, and thought over every kind of distress that could have befallen him, with a fixed determination that he should not escape them all.

'Something very melancholy must be the matter, I am sure,' she said. 'I could see it in his face. Poor man! I am afraid his circumstances may be bad. The estate at Delaford was never reckoned more than two thousand a year, and his brother left every thing sadly involved. I do think he must have been sent for about money matters, for what else can it be? I wonder whether it is so. I would give any thing to know the truth of it. Perhaps it is about Miss Williams and, by the bye, I dare say it is, because he looked so conscious when I mentioned her. May be she is ill in town; nothing in the world more likely, for I have a notion she is always rather sickly. I would lay any wager it is about Miss Williams. It is not so very likely he should be distressed in his circumstances *now*, for he is a very prudent man, and to be sure must have cleared the estate by this time. I wonder what it can be! May be his sister is worse at Avignon, and has sent for him over. His setting off in such a hurry seems very like it. Well, I wish him out of all his trouble with all my heart, and a good wife into the bargain.'

So wondered, so talked Mrs Jennings. Her opinion varying with every fresh conjecture, and all seeming equally probable as they arose. Elinor, though she felt really interested in the welfare of Colonel Brandon, could not bestow all the wonder of his going so suddenly away, which Mrs Jennings was desirous of her feeling; for besides that the circumstance did not in her opinion justify such lasting amazement or variety of speculation, her wonder was otherwise disposed of. It was engrossed by the extraordinary silence of her sister and Willoughby on the subject, which they must know to be peculiarly interesting to them all. As this silence continued, every day made it appear more strange and more incompatible with the disposition of both. Why they should not openly acknowledge to her mother and herself, what their constant behaviour to each other declared to have taken place, Elinor could not imagine.

She could easily conceive that marriage might not be immediately in their power; for though Willoughby was independent, there was no reason to believe him rich. His estate had been rated by Sir John at about six or seven hundred a year; but he lived at an expense to which that income could hardly be equal, and he had himself often complained of his poverty. But for this strange kind of secrecy maintained by them relative to their engagement, which in fact concealed nothing at all, she could not account; and it was so wholly contradictory to their general opinions and practice, that a doubt sometimes entered her mind of their being really engaged, and this doubt was enough to prevent her making any inquiry of Marianne.

Nothing could be more expressive of attachment to them all, than Willoughby's behaviour. To Marianne it had all the distinguishing tenderness which a lover's heart could give, and to the rest of the family it was the affectionate attention of a son and a brother. The cottage seemed to be considered and loved by him as his home; many more of his hours were spent there than at Allenham; and if no general engagement collected them at the park, the exercise which called him out in the morning was almost certain of ending there, where the rest of the day was spent by himself at the side of Marianne, and by his favourite pointer at her feet.

One evening in particular, about a week after Colonel Brandon had left the country, his heart seemed more than usually open to every feeling of attachment to the objects around him; and on Mrs Dashwood's happening to mention her design of improving the cottage in the spring, he warmly opposed every alteration of a place which affection had established as perfect with him.

'What!' he exclaimed – 'Improve this dear cottage! No. *That* I will never consent to. Not a stone must be added to its walls, not an inch to its size, if my feelings are regarded.'

'Do not be alarmed,' said Miss Dashwood, 'nothing of the kind will be done; for my mother will never have money enough to attempt it.'

'I am heartily glad of it,' he cried. 'May she always be poor, if she can employ her riches no better.'

'Thank you, Willoughby. But you may be assured that I would not sacrifice one sentiment of local attachment of yours, or of any one whom I loved, for all the improvements in the world. Depend upon it that whatever unemployed sum may remain, when I make up my accounts in the spring, I would even rather lay it uselessly by than dispose of it in a manner so painful to you. But are you really so attached to this place as to see no defect in it?'

'I am,' said he. 'To me it is faultless. Nay, more, I consider it as the only form of building in which happiness is attainable, and were I rich enough, I would instantly pull Combe down, and build it up again in the exact plan of this cottage.'

'With dark narrow stairs, and a kitchen that smokes, I suppose,' said Elinor.

'Yes,' cried he in the same eager tone, 'with all and every thing belonging to it; – in no one convenience or *in*convenience about it, should the least variation be perceptible. Then, and then only, under such a roof, I might perhaps be as happy at Combe as I have been at Barton.'

'I flatter myself,' replied Elinor, 'that even under the disadvantage of better rooms and a broader staircase, you will hereafter find your own house as faultless as you now do this.'

'There certainly are circumstances,' said Willoughby, 'which might greatly endear it to me; but this place will always have one claim on my affection, which no other can possibly share.'

Mrs Dashwood looked with pleasure at Marianne, whose fine eyes were fixed so expressively on Willoughby, as plainly denoted how well she understood him.

'How often did I wish,' added he, 'when I was at Allenham this time twelvemonth, that Barton cottage was inhabited! I never passed within view of it without admiring its situation, and grieving that no one should live in it. How little did I then think that the very first news I should hear from Mrs Smith, when I next came into the country, would be that Barton cottage was taken: and I felt an immediate satisfaction and interest in the event, which nothing but a kind of prescience of what happiness I should experience from it, can account for. Must it not have been so, Marianne?' speaking to her in a lowered voice. Then continuing his former tone, he said, 'And yet this house you would spoil, Mrs Dashwood? You would rob it of its simplicity by imaginary improvement! and this dear parlour, in which our acquaintance first began, and in which so many happy hours have been since spent by us together, you would degrade to the condition of a common entrance, and every body would be eager to pass through the room which has hitherto contained within itself, more real accommodation and comfort than any other apartment of the handsomest dimensions in the world could possibly afford.'

Mrs Dashwood again assured him that no alteration of the kind should be attempted.

'You are a good woman,' he warmly replied. 'Your promise makes me easy. Extend it a little farther, and it will make me happy. Tell me that not only your house will remain the same, but that I shall ever find you and yours as unchanged as your dwelling; and that you will always consider me with the kindness which has made every thing belonging to you so dear to me.'

The promise was readily given, and Willoughby's behaviour during the whole of the evening declared at once his affection and happiness.

'Shall we see you tomorrow to dinner?' said Mrs Dashwood when he was leaving them. 'I do not ask you to come in the morning, for we must walk to the park, to call on Lady Middleton.'

He engaged to be with them by four o'clock.

CHAPTER FIFTEEN

MRS DASHWOOD'S VISIT to Lady Middleton took place the next day, and two of her daughters went with her; but Marianne excused herself from being of the party under some trifling pretext of employment; and her mother, who concluded that a promise had been made by Willoughby the night before of calling on her while they were absent, was perfectly satisfied with her remaining at home.

On thier return from the park they found Willoughby's curricle and servant in waiting at the cottage, and Mrs Dashwood was convinced that her conjecture had been just. So far it was all as she had foreseen; but on entering the house she beheld what no foresight had taught her to expect. They were no sooner in the passage than Marianne came hastily out of the parlour apparently in violent affliction, with her handkerchief at her eyes; and without noticing them ran up stairs. Surprised and alarmed they proceeded directly into the room she had just quitted, where they found only Willoughby, who was leaning against the mantle-piece with his back towards them. He turned round on their coming in, and his countenance shewed that he strongly partook of the emotion which overpowered Marianne.

'Is any thing the matter with her?' cried Mrs Dashwood as she entered − 'is she ill?'

'I hope not,' he replied, trying to look cheerful; and with a forced smile presently added, 'It is I who may rather expect to be ill − for I am now suffering under a very heavy disappointment!'

'Disappointment!'

'Yes, for I am unable to keep my engagement with you. Mrs Smith has this morning exercised the privilege of riches upon a poor dependant cousin, by sending me on business to London. I have just received my dispatches, and taken my farewell of Allenham; and by way of exhilaration I am now come to take my farewell of you.'

'To London! − and are you going this morning?'

'Almost this moment.'

Apparently in violent affliction.

'This is very unfortunate. But Mrs Smith must be obliged; – and her business will not detain you from us long I hope.'

He coloured as he replied, 'You are very kind, but I have no idea of returning into Devonshire immediately. My visits to Mrs Smith are never repeated within the twelvemonth.'

'And is Mrs Smith your only friend? Is Allenham the only house in the neighbourhood to which you will be welcome? For shame, Willoughby. Can you wait for an invitation here?'

His colour increased; and with his eyes fixed on the ground he only replied, 'You are too good.'

Mrs Dashwood looked at Elinor with surprise. Elinor felt equal amazement. For a few moments every one was silent. Mrs Dashwood first spoke.

'I have only to add, my dear Willoughby, that at Barton cottage you will always be welcome; for I will not press you to return here immediately, because you only can judge how far *that* might be pleasing to Mrs Smith; and on this head I shall be no more disposed to question your judgment than to doubt your inclination.'

'My engagements at present,' replied Willoughby confusedly, 'are of such a nature – that – I dare not flatter myself – '

He stopt. Mrs Dashwood was too much astonished to speak, and another pause succeeded. This was broken by Willoughby, who said with a faint smile, 'It is folly to linger in this manner. I will not torment myself any longer by remaining among friends whose society it is impossible for me now to enjoy.'

He then hastily took leave of them all and left the room. They saw him step into his carriage, and in a minute it was out of sight.

Mrs Dashwood felt too much for speech, and instantly quitted the parlour to give way in solitude to the concern and alarm which this sudden departure occasioned.

Elinor's uneasiness was at least equal to her mother's. She thought of what had just passed with anxiety and distrust. Willoughby's behaviour in taking leave of them, his embarrassment, and affection of cheerfulness, and, above all, his unwillingness to accept her mother's invitation, a backwardness so unlike a lover, so unlike himself, greatly disturbed her. One moment she feared that no serious design had ever been formed on his side; and the next that some unfortunate quarrel had taken place between him and her sister; – the distress in which Marianne had quitted the room was such as a serious quarrel could most reasonably account for, though when she considered what Marianne's love for him was, a quarrel seemed almost impossible.

But whatever might be the particulars of their separation, her sister's affliction was indubitable; and she thought with the tenderest compassion of that violent sorrow which Marianne was in all probability not merely giving way to as a relief, but feeding and encouraging as a duty.

In about half an hour her mother returned, and though her eyes were red, her countenance was not uncheerful.

'Our dear Willoughby is now some miles from Barton, Elinor,' said she, as she sat down to work, 'and with how heavy a heart does he travel?'

'It is all very strange. So suddenly to be gone! It seems but the work of a moment. And last night he was with us so happy, so cheerful, so affectionate? And now after only ten minutes notice – Gone too without intending to return! – Something more than what he owned to us must have happened. He did not speak, he did not behave like himself. *You* must have seen the difference as well as I. What can it be? Can they have quarrelled? Why else should he have shewn such unwillingness to accept your invitation here?' –

'It was not inclination that he wanted, Elinor; I could plainly see *that*. He had not the power of accepting it. I have thought it all over I assure you, and I can perfectly account for every thing that at first seemed strange to me as well as to you.'

'Can you indeed?'

'Yes. I have explained it to myself in the most satisfactory way; – but you, Elinor, who love to doubt where you can – It will not satisfy *you*, I know; but you shall not talk *me* out of my trust in it. I am persuaded that Mrs Smith suspects his regard for Marianne, disapproves of it, (perhaps because she has other views for him,) and on that account is eager to get him away; – and that the business which she sends him off to transact, is invented as an excuse to dismiss him. This is what I believe to have happened. He is moreover aware that she *does* disapprove the connection, he dares not therefore at present confess to her his engagement with Marianne, and he feels himself obliged, from his dependent situation, to give into her schemes, and absent himself from Devonshire for a while. You will tell me, I know, that this may, or may *not* have happened; but I will listen to no cavil, unless you can point out any other method of understanding the affair as satisfactory as this. And now, Elinor, what have you to say?'

'Nothing, for you have anticipated my answer.'

'Then you would have told me, that it might or might not have happened. Oh! Elinor, how incomprehensible are your feelings! You had rather take evil upon credit than good. You had rather look out for misery for Marianne and guilt for poor Willoughby, than an apology for the latter. You are resolved to think him blameable, because he took leave of us with less affection than his usual behaviour has shewn. And is no allowance to be made for inadvertence, or for spirits depressed by recent disappointment? Are no probabilities to be accepted, merely because they are not certainties? Is nothing due to the man whom we have all so much reason to love, and no reason in the world to think ill of? To the possibility of motives unanswerable in themselves, though unavoidably secret for a while? And, after all, what is it you suspect him of?'

'I can hardly tell you myself. – But suspicion of something unpleasant is the inevitable consequence of such an alteration as we have just witnessed in him. There is great truth, however, in what you have now urged of the allowances which ought to be made for him, and it is my wish to be candid in my judgment of every body.

Willoughby may undoubtedly have very sufficient reasons for his conduct, and I will hope that he has. But it would have been more like Willoughby to acknowledge them at once. Secrecy may be advisable; but still I cannot help wondering at its being practised by him.'

'Do not blame him, however, for departing from his character, where the deviation is necessary. But you really do admit the justice of what I have said in his defence? – I am happy – and he is acquitted.'

'Not entirely. It may be proper to conceal their engagement (if they *are* engaged) from Mrs Smith – and if that is the case, it must be highly expedient for Willoughby to be but little in Devonshire at present. But this is no excuse for their concealing it from us.'

'Concealing it from us! my dear child, do you accuse Willoughby and Marianne of concealment? This is strange indeed, when your eyes have been reproaching them every day for incautiousness.'

'I want no proof of their affection,' said Elinor; 'but of their engagement I do.'

'I am perfectly satisfied of both.'

'Yet not a syllable has been said to you on the subject, by either of them.'

'I have not wanted syllables where actions have spoken so plainly. Has not his behaviour to Marianne and to all of us, for at least the last fortnight, declared that he loved and considered her as his future wife, and that he felt for us the attachment of the nearest relation? Have we not perfectly understood each other? Has not my consent been daily asked by his looks, his manner, his attentive and affectionate respect? My Elinor, is it possible to doubt their engagement? How could such a thought occur to you? How is it to be supposed that Willoughby, persuaded as he must be of your sister's love, should leave her, and leave her perhaps for months, without telling her of his affection; – that they should part without a mutual exchange of confidence?'

'I confess,' replied Elinor, 'that every circumstance except *one* is in favour of their engagement; but that *one* is the total silence of both on the subject, and with me it almost outweighs every other.'

'How strange this is! You must think wretchedly indeed of Willoughby, if after all that has openly passed between them, you can doubt the nature of the terms on which they are together. Has he been acting a part in his behaviour to your sister all this time? Do you suppose him really indifferent to her?'

'No, I cannot think that. He must and does love her I am sure.'

'But with a strange kind of tenderness, if he can leave her with such indifference, such carelessness of the future, as you attribute to him.'

'You must remember, my dear mother, that I have never considered this matter as certain. I have had my doubts, I confess; but they are fainter than they were, and they may soon be entirely done away. If we find they correspond, every fear of mine will be removed.'

'A mighty concession indeed! If you were to see them at the altar, you would suppose they were going to be married. Ungracious girl! But *I* require no such proof. Nothing in my opinion has ever passed to justify doubt; no secrecy has been attempted; all has been uniformly open and unreserved. You cannot doubt your sister's wishes. It must be Willoughby therefore who you suspect. But why? Is he not a man of honour and feeling? Has there been any inconsistency on his side to create alarm? can he be deceitful?'

'I hope not, I believe not,' cried Elinor. 'I love Willoughby, sincerely love him; and suspicion of his integrity cannot be more painful to yourself than to me. It has been involuntary, and I will not encourage it. I was startled, I confess, by the alteration in his manners this morning; – he did not speak like himself, and did not return your kindness with any cordiality. But all this may be explained by such a situation of his affairs as you have supposed. He had just parted from my sister, had seen her leave him in the greatest affliction; and if he felt obliged, from a fear of offending Mrs Smith, to resist the temptation of returning here soon, and yet aware that by declining your invitation, by saying that he was going away for some time, he should seem to act an ungenerous, a suspicious part by our family, he might well be embarrassed and disturbed. In such a case, a plain and open avowal of his difficulties would have been more to his honour I think, as well as more consistent with his general character; – but I will not raise objections against any one's conduct on so illiberal a foundation, as a difference in judgment from myself, or a deviation from what I may think right and consistent.'

'You speak very properly. Willoughby certainly does not deserve to be suspected. Though *we* have not known him long, he is no stranger in this part of the world; and who has ever spoken to his disadvantage? Had he been in a situation to act independently and marry immediately, it might have been odd that he should leave us without acknowledging every thing to me at once: but this is not the case. It is an engagement in some respects not prosperously begun, for their marriage must be at a very uncertain distance;

and even secrecy, as far as it can be observed, may now be very advisable.'

They were interrupted by the entrance of Margaret; and Elinor was then at liberty to think over the representations of her mother, to acknowledge the probability of many, and hope for the justice of all.

They saw nothing of Marianne till dinner time, when she entered the room and took her place at the table without saying a word. Her eyes were red and swollen; and it seemed as if her tears were even then restrained with difficulty. She avoided the looks of them all, could neither eat nor speak, and after some time, on her mother's silently pressing her hand with tender compassion, her small degree of fortitude was quite overcome, she burst into tears and left the room.

This violent oppression of spirits continued the whole evening. She was without any power, because she was without any desire of command over herself. The slightest mention of any thing relative to Willoughby overpowered her in an instant; and though her family were most anxiously attentive to her comfort, it was impossible for them, if they spoke at all, to keep clear of every subject which her feelings connected with him.

CHAPTER SIXTEEN

MARIANNE WOULD HAVE thought herself very inexcusable had she been able to sleep at all the first night after parting from Willoughby. She would have been ashamed to look her family in the face the next morning, had she not risen from her bed in more need of repose than when she lay down in it. But the feelings which made such composure a disgrace, left her in no danger of incurring it. She was awake the whole night, and she wept the greatest part of it. She got up with an headache, was unable to talk, and unwilling to take any nourishment; giving pain every moment to her mother and sisters, and forbidding all attempt at consolation from either. Her sensibility was potent enough!

When breakfast was over she walked out by herself, and wandered about the village of Allenham, indulging the recollection of past enjoyment and crying over the present reverse for the chief of the morning.

The evening passed off in the equal indulgence of feeling. She played over every favourite song that she had been used to play to Willoughby, every air in which their voices had been oftenest joined, and sat at the instrument gazing on every line of music that he had written out for her, till her heart was so heavy that no farther sadness could be gained; and this nourishment of grief was every day applied. She spent whole hours at the piano-forté alternately singing and crying; her voice often totally suspended by her tears. In books too, as well as in music, she courted the misery which a contrast between the past and present was certain of giving. She read nothing but what they had been used to read together.

Such violence of affliction indeed could not be supported for ever; it sunk within a few days into a calmer melancholy; but these employments, to which she daily recurred, her solitary walks and silent meditations, still produced occasional effusions of sorrow as lively as ever.

No letter from Willoughby came; and none seemed expected by Marianne. Her mother was surprised, and Elinor again became uneasy. But Mrs Dashwood could find explanations whenever she wanted them, which at least satisfied herself.

'Remember, Elinor,' said she, 'how very often Sir John fetches our letters himself from the post, and carries them to it. We have already agreed that secrecy may be necessary, and we must acknowledge that it could not be maintained if their correspondence were to pass through Sir John's hands.'

Elinor could not deny the truth of this, and she tried to find in it a motive sufficient for their silence. But there was one method so direct, so simple, and in her opinion so eligible of knowing the real state of the affair, and of instantly removing all mystery, that she could not help suggesting it to her mother.

'Why do you not ask Marianne at once,' said she, 'whether she is or is not engaged to Willoughby? From you, her mother, and so kind, so indulgent a mother, the question could not give offence. It would be the natural result of your affection for her. She used to be all unreserve, and to you more especially.'

'I would not ask such a question for the world. Supposing it possible that they are not engaged, what distress would not such an inquiry inflict! At any rate it would be most ungenerous. I should never deserve her confidence again, after forcing from her a confession of what is meant at present to be unacknowledged to any one. I know Marianne's heart: I know that she dearly loves me, and that I shall not be the last to whom the affair is made known, when circumstances make the revealment of it eligible. I would not attempt to force the confidence of any one; of a child much less;

because a sense of duty would prevent the denial which her wishes might direct.'

Elinor thought this generosity overstrained, considering her sister's youth, and urged the matter farther, but in vain; common sense, common care, common prudence, were all sunk in Mrs Dashwood's romantic delicacy.

It was several days before Willoughby's name was mentioned before Marianne by any of her family; Sir John and Mrs Jennings, indeed, were not so nice; their witticisms added pain to many a painful hour; – but one evening, Mrs Dashwood, accidentally taking up a volume of Shakespeare, exclaimed,

'We have never finished Hamlet, Marianne; our dear Willoughby went away before we could get through it. We will put it by, and when he comes again . . . But it may be months, perhaps, before *that* happens.'

'Months!' cried Marianne, with strong surprise. 'No – nor many weeks.'

Mrs Dashwood was sorry for what she had said; but it gave Elinor pleasure, as it produced a reply from Marianne so expressive of confidence in Willoughby and knowledge of his intentions.

One morning, about a week after his leaving the country, Marianne was prevailed on to join her sisters in their usual walk, instead of wandering away by herself. Hitherto she had carefully avoided every companion in her rambles. If her sisters intended to walk on the downs, she directly stole away towards the lanes; if they talked of the valley, she was as speedy in climbing the hills, and could never be found when the others set off. But at length she was secured by the exertions of Elinor, who greatly disapproved such continual seclusion. They walked along the road through the valley, and chiefly in silence, for Marianne's *mind* could not be controlled, and Elinor, satisfied with gaining one point, would not then attempt more. Beyond the entrance of the valley, where the country, though still rich, was less wild and more open, a long stretch of the road which they had travelled on first coming to Barton, lay before them; and on reaching that point, they stopped to look around them, and examine a prospect which formed the distance of their view from the cottage, from a spot which they had never happened to reach in any of their walks before.

Amongst the objects in the scene, they soon discovered an animated one; it was a man on horseback riding towards them. In a few minutes they could distinguish him to be a gentleman; and in a moment afterwards Marianne rapturously exclaimed,

'It is he; it is indeed; – I know it is!' – And was hastening to meet him, when Elinor cried out,

'Indeed, Marianne, I think you are mistaken. It is not Willoughby. The person is not tall enough for him, and has not his air.'

'He has, he has,' cried Marianne, 'I am sure he has. His air, his coat, his horse. I knew how soon he would come.'

She walked eagerly on as she spoke; and Elinor, to screen Marianne from particularity, as she felt almost certain of its not being Willoughby, quickened her pace and kept up with her. They were soon within thirty yards of the gentleman. Marianne looked again; her heart sunk within her; and abruptly turning round, she was hurrying back, when the voices of both her sisters were raised to detain her, a third, almost as well known as Willoughby's, joined them in begging her to stop, and she turned round with surprise to see and welcome Edward Ferrars.

He was the only person in the world who could at that moment

Begging her to stop.

be forgiven for not being Willoughby; the only one who could have gained a smile from her; but she dispersed her tears to smile on *him*, and in her sister's happiness forgot for a time her own disappointment.

He dismounted, and giving his horse to his servant, walked back with them to Barton, whither he was purposely coming to visit them.

He was welcomed by them all with great cordiality, but especially by Marianne, who shewed more warmth of regard in her reception of him than even Elinor herself. To Marianne, indeed, the meeting between Edward and her sister was but a continuation of that unaccountable coldness which she had often observed at Norland in their mutual behaviour. On Edward's side, more particularly, there was a deficiency of all that a lover ought to look and say on such an occasion. He was confused, seemed scarcely sensible of pleasure in seeing them, looked neither rapturous nor gay, said little but what was forced from him by questions, and distinguished Elinor by no mark of affection. Marianne saw and listened with increasing surprise. She began almost to feel a dislike of Edward; and it ended, as every feeling must end with her, by carrying back her thoughts to Willoughby, whose manners formed a contrast sufficiently striking to those of his brother elect.

After a short silence which succeeded the first surprise and inquiries of meeting, Marianne asked Edward if he came directly from London. No, he had been in Devonshire a fortnight.

'A fortnight!' she repeated, surprised at his being so long in the same county with Elinor without seeing her before.

He looked rather distressed as he added, that he had been staying with some friends near Plymouth.

'Have you been lately in Sussex?' said Elinor.

'I was at Norland about a month ago.'

'And how does dear, dear Norland look?' cried Marianne.

'Dear, dear Norland,' said Elinor, 'probably looks much as it always does at this time of year. The woods and walks thickly covered with dead leaves.'

'Oh!' cried Marianne, 'with what transporting sensations have I formerly seen them fall! How have I delighted, as I walked, to see them driven in showers about me by the wind! What feelings have they, the season, the air altogether inspired! Now there is no one to regard them. They are seen only as a nuisance, swept hastily off, and driven as much as possible from the sight.'

'It is not every one,' said Elinor, 'who has your passion for dead leaves.'

'No; my feelings are not often shared, not often understood. But *sometimes* they are.' – As she said this, she sunk into a reverie for a few moments; – but rousing herself again, 'Now, Edward,' said she, calling his attention to the prospect, 'here is Barton valley. Look up to it, and be tranquil if you can. Look at those hills! Did you ever see their equals? To the left is Barton park, amongst those woods and plantations. You may see one end of the house. And there, beneath that farthest hill, which rises with such grandeur, is our cottage.'

'It is a beautiful country,' he replied; 'but these bottoms must be dirty in winter.'

'How can you think of dirt, with such objects before you?'

'Because,' replied he, smiling, 'among the rest of the objects before me, I see a very dirty lane.'

'How strange!' said Marianne to herself as she walked on.

'Have you an agreeable neighbourhood here? Are the Middletons pleasant people?'

'No, not at all,' answered Marianne, 'we could not be more unfortunately situated.'

'Marianne,' cried her sister, 'how can you say so? How can you be so unjust? They are a very respectable family, Mr Ferrars; and towards us have behaved in the friendliest manner. Have you forgot, Marianne, how many pleasant days we have owed to them?'

'No,' said Marianne in a low voice, 'nor how many painful moments.'

Elinor took no notice of this, and directing her attention to their visitor, endeavoured to support something like discourse with him by talking of their present residence, its conveniences, &c. extorting from him occasional questions and remarks. His coldness and reserve mortified her severely; she was vexed and half angry; but resolving to regulate her behaviour to him by the past rather than the present, she avoided every appearance of resentment or displeasure, and treated him as she thought he ought to be treated from the family connection.

CHAPTER SEVENTEEN

MRS DASHWOOD WAS surprised only for a moment at seeing him; for his coming to Barton was, in her opinion, of all things the most natural. Her joy and expressions of regard long outlived her wonder. He received the kindest welcome from her; and shyness, coldness, reserve could not stand against such a reception. They had begun to fail him before he entered the house, and they were quite overcome by the captivating manners of Mrs Dashwood. Indeed a man could not very well be in love with either of her daughters, without extending the passion to her, and Elinor had the satisfaction of seeing him soon become more like himself. His affections seemed to reanimate towards them all, and his interest in their welfare again became perceptible. He was not in spirits however; he praised their house, admired its prospects, was attentive, and kind; but still he was not in spirits. The whole family perceived it, and Mrs Dashwood, attributing it to some want of liberality in his mother, sat down to table indignant against all selfish parents.

'What are Mrs Ferrars's views for you at present, Edward?' said she, when dinner was over and they had drawn round the fire; 'are you still to be a great orator in spite of yourself?'

'No. I hope my mother is now convinced that I have no more talents than inclination for a public life!'

'But how is your fame to be established? for famous you must be to satisfy all your family, and with no inclination for expence, no affection for strangers, no profession, and no assurance, you may find it a difficult matter.'

'I shall not attempt it. I have no wish to be distinguished; and I have every reason to hope I never shall. Thank Heaven! I cannot be forced into genius and eloquence.'

'You have no ambition, I well know. Your wishes are all moderate.'

'As moderate as those of the rest of the world, I believe. I wish as well as every body else to be perfectly happy; but like every body else it must be in my own way. Greatness will not make me so.'

'Strange if it would!' cried Marianne. 'What have wealth or grandeur to do with happiness?'

'Grandeur has but little,' said Elinor, 'but wealth has much to do with it.'

'Elinor, for shame!' said Marianne; 'money can only give happiness where there is nothing else to give it. Beyond a competence, it can afford no real satisfaction, as far as mere self is concerned.'

'Perhaps,' said Elinor, smiling, 'we may come to the same point. *Your* competence and *my* wealth are very much alike, I dare say, and without them, as the world goes now, we shall both agree that every kind of external comfort must be wanting. Your ideas are only more noble than mine. Come, what is your competence?'

'About eighteen hundred or two thousand a-year; not more than *that*.'

Elinor laughed. '*Two* thousand a-year! *One* is my wealth! I guessed how it would end.'

'And yet two thousand a-year is a very moderate income,' said Marianne. 'A family cannot well be maintained on a smaller. I am sure I am not extravagant in my demands. A proper establishment of servants, a carriage, perhaps two, and hunters, cannot be supported on less.'

Elinor smiled again, to hear her sister describing so accurately their future expences at Combe Magna.

'Hunters' repeated Edward – 'But why must you have hunters? Every body does not hunt.'

Marianne coloured as she replied, 'But most people do.'

'I wish,' said Margaret, striking out a novel thought, 'that somebody would give us all a large fortune apiece!'

'Oh that they would!' cried Marianne, her eyes sparkling with animation, and her cheeks glowing with the delight of such imaginary happiness.

'We are all unanimous in that wish, I suppose,' said Elinor, 'in spite of the insufficiency of wealth.'

'Oh dear!' cried Margaret, 'how happy I should be! I wonder what I should do with it!'

Marianne looked as if she had no doubt on that point.

'I should be puzzled to spend a large fortune myself,' said Mrs Dashwood, 'if my children were all to be rich without my help.'

'You must begin your improvements on this house,' observed Elinor, 'and your difficulties will soon vanish.'

'What magnificent orders would travel from this family to London,' said Edward, 'in such an event! What a happy day for booksellers, music-sellers, and print-shops! You, Mrs Dashwood, would give a general commission for every new print of merit to be sent you – and as for Marianne, I know her greatness of soul, there would not be music enough in London to content her. And books! – Thomson, Cowper, Scott – she would buy them all over and over again; she would buy up every copy, I believe, to prevent their falling into unworthy hands; and she would have every book that tells her how to admire an old twisted tree. Should not you, Marianne? Forgive me, if I am very saucy. But I was willing to shew you that I had not forgot our old disputes.'

'I love to be reminded of the past, Edward – whether it be melancholy or gay, I love to recall it – and you will never offend me by talking of former times. You are very right in supposing how my money would be spent – some of it, at least – my loose cash would certainly be employed in improving my collection of music and books.'

'And the bulk of your fortune would be laid out in annuities on the authors or their heirs.'

'No, Edward, I should have something else to do with it.'

'Perhaps then you would bestow it as a reward on that person who wrote the ablest defence of your favourite maxim, that no one can ever be in love more than once in their life – for your opinion on that point is unchanged, I presume?'

'Undoubtedly. At my time of life opinions are tolerably fixed. It is not likely that I should now see or hear anything to change them.'

'Marianne is as steadfast as ever, you see,' said Elinor, 'she is not at all altered.'

'She is only grown a little more grave than she was.'

'Nay, Edward,' said Marianne, '*you* need not reproach me. You are not very gay yourself.'

'Why should you think so!' replied he, with a sigh. 'But gaiety never was a part of *my* character.'

'Nor do I think it a part of Marianne's,' said Elinor, 'I should hardly call her a lively girl – she is very earnest, very eager in all she does – sometimes talks a great deal and always with animation – but she is not often really merry.'

'I believe you are right,' he replied, 'and yet I have always set her down as a lively girl.'

'I have frequently detected myself in such kind of mistakes,' said Elinor, 'in a total misapprehension of character in some point or other: fancying people so much more gay or grave, or ingenious or stupid than they really are, and I can hardly tell why or in what the deception originated. Sometimes one is guided by what they say of themselves, and very frequently by what other people say of them, without giving oneself time to deliberate and judge.'

'But I thought it was right, Elinor,' said Marianne, 'to be guided wholly by the opinion of other people. I thought our judgments were given us merely to be subservient to those of our neighbours. This has always been your doctrine, I am sure.'

'No, Marianne, never. My doctrine has never aimed at the subjection of the understanding. All I have ever attempted to influence has been the behaviour. You must not confound my meaning. I am guilty, I confess, of having often wished you to treat our acquaintance in general with greater attention; but when have I advised you to adopt their sentiments or conform to their judgment in serious matters?'

'You have not been able to bring your sister over to your plan of general civility,' said Edward to Elinor. 'Do you gain no ground?'

'Quite the contrary,' replied Elinor, looking expressively at Marianne.

'My judgment,' he returned, 'is all on your side of the question; but I am afraid my practice is much more on your sister's. I never wish to offend, but I am so foolishly shy, that I often seem negligent, when I am only kept back by my natural awkwardness. I have frequently thought that I must have been intended by nature to be fond of low company, I am so little at my ease among strangers of gentility!'

'Marianne has not shyness to excuse any inattention of hers,' said Elinor.

'She knows her own worth too well for false shame,' replied Edward. 'Shyness is only the effect of a sense of inferiority in some way or other. If I could persuade myself that my manners were perfectly easy and graceful, I should not be shy.'

'But you would still be reserved,' said Marianne, 'and that is worse.'

Edward stared – 'Reserved! Am I reserved, Marianne?'

'Yes, very.'

'I do not understand you,' replied he, colouring. 'Reserved! – how, in what manner? What am I to tell you? What can you suppose?'

Elinor looked surprised at his emotion, but trying to laugh off the subject, she said to him, 'Do not you know my sister well enough to understand what she means? Do not you know she calls every one reserved who does not talk fast, and admire what she admires as rapturously as herself?'

Edward made no answer. His gravity and thoughtfulness returned on him in their fullest extent – and he sat for some time silent and dull.

CHAPTER EIGHTEEN

ELINOR SAW, WITH great uneasiness, the low spirits of her friend. His visit afforded her but a very partial satisfaction, while his own enjoyment in it appeared so imperfect. If was evident that he was unhappy; she wished it were equally evident that he still distinguished her by the same affection which once she had felt no doubt of inspiring; but hitherto the continuance of his preference seemed very uncertain; and the reservedness of his manner towards her contradicted one moment what a more animated look had intimated the preceding one.

He joined her and Marianne in the breakfast-room the next morning before the others were down; and Marianne, who was always eager to promote their happiness as far as she could, soon left them to themselves. But before she was half way upstairs she heard the parlour door open, and, turning round, was astonished to see Edward himself come out.

'I am going into the village to see my horses,' said he, 'as you are not ready for breakfast; I shall be back again presently.'

Edward returned to them with fresh admiration of the surrounding country; in his walk to the village, he had seen many parts of the valley to advantage; and the village itself, in a much higher situation than the cottage, afforded a general view of the whole, which had exceedingly pleased him. This was a subject which ensured Marianne's attention, and she was beginning to describe her own admiration of these scenes, and to question him more minutely on the objects that had particularly struck him, when Edward interrupted her by saying, 'You must not inquire too far, Marianne – remember I have no knowledge in the picturesque, and I shall offend you by my ignorance and want of taste if we come to particulars. I shall call hills steep, which ought to be bold; surfaces strange and uncouth, which ought to be irregular and rugged; and distant objects out of sight, which ought only to be indistinct through the soft medium of a hazy atmosphere. You must be satisfied with such admiration as I can honestly give. I call it a very fine country – the hills are steep, the woods seem full of fine timber, and the valley looks comfortable and snug – with rich meadows and several neat farm houses scattered here and there. It exactly answers my idea of a fine country, because it unites beauty with utility – and I dare say it is a picturesque one too, because you admire it; I can easily believe it to be full of rocks and promontories, grey moss and brush wood, but these are all lost on me. I know nothing of the picturesque.'

'I am afraid it is but too true,' said Marianne; 'but why should you boast of it?'

'I suspect,' said Elinor, 'that to avoid one kind of affectation, Edward here falls into another. Because he believes many people pretend to more admiration of the beauties of nature than they really feel, and is disgusted with such pretensions, he affects greater indifference and less discrimination in viewing them himself than he possesses. He is fastidious and will have an affectation of his own.'

'It is very true,' said Marianne, 'that admiration of landscape scenery is become a mere jargon. Every body pretends to feel and tries to describe with the taste and elegance of him who first defined what picturesque beauty was. I detest jargon of every kind, and sometimes I have kept my feelings to myself, because I could find no language to describe them in but what was worn and hackneyed out of all sense and meaning.'

'I am convinced,' said Edward, 'that you really feel all the delight in a fine prospect which you profess to feel. But, in return, your sister must allow me to feel no more than I profess. I like a fine prospect, but not on picturesque principles. I do not like crooked, twisted, blasted trees. I admire them much more if they are tall, straight and flourishing. I do not like ruined, tattered cottages. I am not fond of nettles, or thistles, or heath blossoms. I have more pleasure in a snug farm-house than a watch-tower – and a troop of tidy, happy villagers please me better than the finest banditti in the world.'

Marianne looked with amazement at Edward, with compassion at her sister. Elinor only laughed.

The subject was continued no farther; and Marianne remained thoughtfully silent, till a new object suddenly engaged her attention. She was sitting by Edward, and in taking his tea from Mrs Dashwood, his hand passed so directly before her, as to make a ring, with a plait of hair in the centre, very conspicuous on one of his fingers.

'I never saw you wear a ring before, Edward,' she cried. 'Is that Fanny's hair? I remember her promising to give you some. But I should have thought her hair had been darker.'

Marianne spoke inconsiderately what she really felt – but when she saw how much she had pained Edward, her own vexation at

Came to take a survey of the guest.

her want of thought could not be surpassed by his. He coloured very deeply, and giving a momentary glance at Elinor, replied, 'Yes; it is my sister's hair. The setting always casts a different shade on it you know.'

Elinor had met his eye, and looked conscious likewise. That the hair was her own, she instantaneously felt as well satisfied as Marianne; the only difference in their conclusions was, that what Marianne considered as a free gift from her sister, Elinor was conscious must have been procured by some theft or contrivance unknown to herself. She was not in a humour, however, to regard it as an affront, and affecting to take no notice of what passed, by instantly talking of something else, she internally resolved henceforward to catch every opportunity of eyeing the hair and of satisfying herself, beyond all doubt, that it was exactly the shade of her own.

Edward's embarrassment lasted some time, and it ended in an absence of mind still more settled. He was particularly grave the whole morning. Marianne severely censured herself for what she had said; but her own forgiveness might have been more speedy, had she known how little offence it had given her sister.

Before the middle of the day, they were visited by Sir John and Mrs Jennings, who, having heard of the arrival of a gentleman at the cottage, came to take a survey of the guest. With the assistance of his mother-in-law, Sir John was not long in discovering that the name of Ferrars began with an F. and this prepared a future mine of raillery against the devoted Elinor, which nothing but the newness of their acquaintance with Edward could have prevented from being immediately sprung. But, as it was, she only learned from some very significant looks, how far their penetration, founded on Margaret's instructions, extended.

Sir John never came to the Dashwoods without either inviting them to dine at the park the next day, or to drink tea with them that evening. On the present occasion, for the better entertainment of their visitor, towards whose amusement he felt himself bound to contribute, he wished to engage them for both.

'You *must* drink tea with us tonight,' said he, 'for we shall be quite alone – and tomorrow you must absolutely dine with us, for we shall be a large party.'

Mrs Jennings enforced the necessity. 'And who knows but you may raise a dance,' said she. 'And that will tempt *you*, Miss Marianne.'

'A dance!' cried Marianne. 'Impossible! Who is to dance?'

'Who! why yourselves, and the Careys, and the Whitakers to be sure – What! you thought nobody could dance because a certain person that shall be nameless is gone!'

'I wish with all my soul,' cried Sir John, 'that Willoughby were among us again.'

This, and Marianne's blushing, gave new suspicions to Edward. 'And who is Willoughby?' said he, in a low voice, to Miss Dashwood, by whom he was sitting.

She gave him a brief reply. Marianne's countenance was more communicative. Edward saw enough to comprehend, not only the meaning of others, but such of Marianne's expressions as had puzzled him before; and when their visitors left them, he went immediately round to her and said, in a whisper, 'I have been guessing. Shall I tell you my guess?'

'What do you mean?'

'Shall I tell you?'

'Certainly.'

'Well then; I guess that Mr Willoughby hunts.'

Marianne was surprised and confused, yet she could not help smiling at the quiet archness of his manner, and, after a moment's silence, said,

'Oh! Edward! How can you? – But the time will come I hope . . . I am sure you will like him.'

'I do not doubt it,' replied he, rather astonished at her earnestness and warmth; for had he not imagined it to be a joke for the good of her acquaintance in general, founded only on a something or a nothing between Mr Willoughby and herself, he would not have ventured to mention it.

CHAPTER NINETEEN

EDWARD REMAINED A week at the cottage; he was earnestly pressed by Mrs Dashwood to stay longer; but as if he were bent only on self-mortification, he seemed resolved to be gone when his enjoyment among his friends was at the height. His spirits, during the last two or three days, though still very unequal, were greatly improved – he grew more and more partial to the house and environs – never spoke of going away without a sigh – declared his time to be wholly disengaged – even doubted to what place he should go when he left them – but still, go he must. Never had any week passed so quickly – he could hardly believe it to be gone. He said so repeatedly; other things he said too, which marked the turn of his feelings and gave the lie to his actions. He had no pleasure at Norland; he detested being in town; but either to Norland or London, he must go. He valued their kindness beyond any thing, and his greatest happiness was in being with them. Yet he must leave them at the end of a week, in spite of their wishes and his own, and without any restraint on his time.

Elinor placed all that was astonishing in this way of acting to his mother's account; and it was happy for her that he had a mother whose character was so imperfectly known to her, as to be the general excuse for every thing strange on the part of her son. Disappointed, however, and vexed as she was, and sometimes displeased with his uncertain behaviour to herself, she was very well disposed on the whole to regard his actions with all the candid allowances and generous qualifications, which had been rather more painfully extorted from her, for Willoughby's service, by her mother. His want of spirits, of openness, and of consistency, were most usually attributed to his want of independence, and his better knowledge of Mrs Ferrars's disposition and designs. The shortness of his visit, the steadiness of his purpose in leaving them, originated in the same fettered inclination, the same inevitable necessity of temporizing with his mother. The old, well-established grievance of duty against will, parent against child, was the cause of all. She would have been glad to know when these difficulties were to cease, this opposition was to yield, – when Mrs Ferrars would be reformed, and her son be at liberty to be happy. But from such vain wishes, she was forced to turn for comfort to the renewal of her confidence in Edward's affection, to the remembrance of every mark of regard in look or word which fell from him while at Barton, and above all to that flattering proof of it which he constantly wore round his finger.

'I think, Edward,' said Mrs Dashwood, as they were at breakfast the last morning, 'you would be a happier man if you had any profession to engage your time and give an interest to your plans and actions. Some inconvenience to your friends, indeed, might result from it – you would not be able to give them so much of your time. But (with a smile) you would be materially benefited in one particular at least – you would know where to go when you left them.'

'I do assure you,' he replied, 'that I have long thought on this point, as you think now. It has been, and is, and probably will always be a heavy misfortune to me, that I have had no necessary business to engage me, no profession to give me employment, or afford me any thing like independence. But unfortunately my own nicety, and the nicety of my friends, have made me what I am, an idle, helpless being. We never could agree in our choice of a profession. I always preferred the church, as I still do. But that was not smart enough for my family. They recommended the army. That was a great deal too smart for me. The law was allowed to be genteel enough; many young men, who had chambers in the Temple, made a very good appearance in the first circles, and drove about town in very knowing gigs. But I had no inclination for the law, even in this less abstruse study of it, which my family approved. As for the navy, it had fashion on its side, but I was too old when the subject was first started to enter it – and, at length, as there was no necessity for my having any profession at all, as I might be as dashing and expensive without a red coat on my back as with one, idleness was pronounced on the whole to be the most advantageous and honourable, and a young man of eighteen is not in general so earnestly bent on being busy as to resist the solicitations of his friends to do nothing I was therefore entered at Oxford and have been properly idle ever since.'

'The consequence of which, I suppose, will be,' said Mrs Dashwood, 'since leisure has not promoted your own happiness, that your sons will be brought up to as many pursuits, employments, professions, and trades as Columella's.'

'They will be brought up,' said he, in a serious accent, 'to be as unlike myself as is possible. In feeling, in action, in condition, in every thing.'

'Come, come; this is all an effusion of immediate want of spirits, Edward. You are in a melancholy humour, and fancy that any one unlike yourself must be happy. But remember that the pain of parting from friends will be felt by every body at times, whatever be their education or state. Know your own happiness. You want nothing but patience – or give it a more fascinating name, call it hope. Your mother will secure to you, in time, that independence you are so anxious for; it is her duty, and it will, it must ere long become her happiness to prevent your whole youth from being wasted in discontent. How much may not a few months do?'

'I think,' replied Edward, 'that I may defy many months to produce any good to me.'

This desponding turn of mind, though it could not be communicated to Mrs Dashwood, gave additional pain to them all in the parting, which shortly took place, and left an uncomfortable impression on Elinor's feelings especially, which required some trouble and time to subdue. But as it was her determination to subdue it, and to prevent herself from appearing to suffer more than what all her family suffered on his going away, she did not adopt the method so judiciously employed by Marianne, on a similar occasion, to augment and fix her sorrow, by seeking silence, solitude and idleness. Their means were as different as their objects, and equally suited to the advancement of each.

Elinor sat down to her drawing-table as soon as he was out of the house, busily employed herself the whole day, neither sought nor avoided the mention of his name, appeared to interest herself almost as much as ever in the general concerns of the family, and if, by this conduct, she did not lessen her own grief, it was at least prevented from unnecessary increase, and her mother and sisters were spared much solicitude on her account.

Such behaviour as this, so exactly the reverse of her own, appeared no more meritorious to Marianne, than her own had seemed faulty to her. The business of self-command she settled very easily – with strong affections it was impossible, with calm ones it could have no merit. That her sister's affections *were* calm, she dared not deny, though she blushed to acknowledge it; and of the strength of her own, she gave a very striking proof, by still loving and respecting that sister, in spite of this mortifying conviction.

Without shutting herself up from her family, or leaving the house in determined solitude to avoid them, or laying awake the whole night to indulge meditation, Elinor found every day afforded her leisure enough to think of Edward, and of Edward's behaviour, in every possible variety which the different state of her spirits at different times could produce, – with tenderness, pity, approbation, censure and doubt. There were moments in abundance, when, if not by the absence of her mother and sisters, at least by the nature of their employments, conversation was forbidden among them, and every effect of solitude was produced. Her mind was inevitably at liberty; her thoughts could not be chained elsewhere; and the past and the future, on a subject so interesting, must be before her, must force her attention, and engross her memory, her reflection, and her fancy.

From a reverie of this kind, as she sat at her drawing-table, she was roused one morning, soon after Edward's leaving them, by the arrival of company. She happened to be quite alone. The closing of the little gate, at the entrance of the green court in front of the house, drew her eyes to the window, and she saw a large party walking up to the door. Amongst them were Sir John and Lady Middleton and Mrs Jennings, but there were two others, a gentleman and lady, who were quite unknown to her. She was sitting near the window, and as soon as Sir John perceived her, he left the rest of the party to the ceremony of knocking at the door, and stepping across the turf, obliged her to open the casement to speak to him, though the space was so short between the door and the window, as to make it hardly possible to speak at one without being heard at the other.

'Well,' said he, 'we have brought you some strangers. How do you like them?'

'Hush! they will hear you.'

'Never mind if they do. It is only the Palmers. Charlotte is very pretty, I can tell you. You may see her if you look this way.'

As Elinor was certain of seeing her in a couple of minutes, without taking that liberty, she begged to be excused.

'Where is Marianne? Has she run away because we are come? I see her instrument is open.'

'She is walking, I believe.'

They were now joined by Mrs Jennings, who had not patience enough to wait till the door was opened before she told *her* story. She came hallooing to the window, 'How do you do, my dear? How does Mrs Dashwood do? And where are your sisters? What! all alone! you will be glad of a little company to sit with you. I have brought my other son and daughter to see you. Only think of their coming so suddenly! I thought I heard a carriage last night, while we were drinking our tea, but it never entered my head that it could be them. I thought of nothing but whether it might not be Colonel Brandon come back again; so I said to Sir John, I do think I hear a carriage; perhaps it is Colonel Brandon come back again – '

Elinor was obliged to turn from her, in the middle of her story, to receive the rest of the party; Lady Middleton introduced the two strangers; Mrs Dashwood and Margaret came down stairs at the same time, and they all sat down to look at one another, while Mrs Jennings continued her story as she walked through the passage into the parlour, attended by Sir John.

Mrs Palmer was several years younger than Lady Middleton, and totally unlike her in every respect. She was short and plump, had a very pretty face, and the finest expression of good humour in it that could possibly be. Her manners were by no means so elegant as her sister's, but they were much more prepossessing. She came in with a smile, smiled all the time of her visit, except when she laughed, and smiled when she went away. Her husband was a grave looking young man of five or six and twenty, with an air of more fashion and sense than his wife, but of less willingness to please or be pleased. He entered the room with a look of self-consequence, slightly bowed to the ladies, without speaking a word, and, after briefly surveying them and their apartments, took up a newspaper from the table and continued to read it as long as he stayed.

Mrs Palmer, on the contrary, who was strongly endowed by nature with a turn for being uniformly civil and happy, was hardly seated before her admiration of the parlour and every thing in it burst forth.

'Well! what a delightful room this is! I never saw anything so charming! Only think, mama, how it is improved since I was here last! I always thought it such a sweet place, ma'am! (turning to Mrs Dashwood,) but you have made it so charming! Only look, sister, how delightful every thing is! How I should like such a house for myself! Should not you, Mr Palmer?'

Mr Palmer made her no answer, and did not even raise his eyes from the newspaper.

'Mr Palmer does not hear me,' said she, laughing, 'he never does sometimes. It is so ridiculous!'

This was quite a new idea to Mrs Dashwood, she had never been used to find wit in the inattention of any one, and could not help looking with surprise at them both.

Mrs Jennings in the mean time, talked on as loud as she could, and continued her account of their surprise the evening before, on seeing their friends, without ceasing till every thing was told. Mrs Palmer laughed heartily at the recollection of their astonishment, and every body agreed, two or three times over, that it had been quite an agreeable surprise.

'You may believe how glad we all were to see them,' added Mrs Jennings, leaning forwards towards Elinor, and speaking in a low voice as if she meant to be heard by no one else, though they were seated on different sides of the room; 'but, however, I can't help

'I declare they are quite charming.'

wishing they had not travelled quite so fast, nor made such a long journey of it, for they came all round by London upon account of some business, for you know (nodding significantly and pointing to her daughter) it was wrong in her situation. I wanted her to stay at home and rest this morning, but she would come with us; she longed so much to see you all!'

Mrs Palmer laughed, and said it would not do her any harm.

'She expects to be confined in February,' continued Mrs Jennings.

Lady Middleton could no longer endure such a conversation, and therefore exerted herself to ask Mr Palmer if there was any news in the paper.

'No, none at all,' he replied, and read on.

'Here comes Marianne,' cried Sir John. 'Now, Palmer, you shall see a monstrous pretty girl.'

He immediately went into the passage, opened the front door, and ushered her in himself. Mrs Jennings asked her, as soon as she appeared, if she had not been to Allenham; and Mrs Palmer laughed so heartily at the question, as to shew she understood it. Mr Palmer looked up on her entering the room, stared at her some minutes, and then returned to his newspaper. Mrs Palmer's eye was now caught by the drawings which hung round the room. She got up to examine them.

'Oh! dear, how beautiful these are! Well! how delightful! Do but look, mama, how sweet! I declare they are quite charming; I could look at them for ever.' And then sitting down again, she very soon forgot that there were any such things in the room.

When Lady Middleton rose to go away, Mr Palmer rose also, laid down the newspaper, stretched himself, and looked at them all round.

'My love, have you been asleep?' said his wife, laughing.

He made her no answer; and only observed, after again examining the room, that it was very low pitched, and that the ceiling was crooked. He then made his bow and departed with the rest.

Sir John had been very urgent with them all to spend the next day at the park. Mrs Dashwood, who did not chuse to dine with them oftener than they dined at the cottage, absolutely refused on her own account; her daughters might do as they pleased. But they had no curiosity to see how Mr and Mrs Palmer ate their dinner, and no expectation of pleasure from them in any other way. They attempted, therefore, likewise to excuse themselves; the weather was uncertain and not likely to be good. But Sir John would not be satisfied – the carriage should be sent for them and they must come. Lady Middleton too, though she did not press their mother, pressed them. Mrs Jennings and Mrs Palmer joined their entreaties, all seemed equally anxious to avoid a family party; and the young ladies were obliged to yield.

'Why should they ask us?' said Marianne, as soon as they were gone. 'The rent of this cottage is said to be low, but we have it on very hard terms, if we are to dine at the park whenever any one is staying either with them, or with us.'

'They mean no less to be civil and kind to us now,' said Elinor, 'by these frequent invitations than by those which we received from them a few weeks ago. The alteration is not in them, if their parties are grown tedious and dull. We must look for the change elsewhere.'

CHAPTER TWENTY

As THE MISS DASHWOODS entered the drawing-room of the park the next day, at one door, Mrs Palmer came running in at the other, looking as good humoured and merry as before. She took them all most affectionately by the hand, and expressed great delight in seeing them again.

'I am so glad to see you!' said she, seating herself between Elinor and Marianne, 'for it is so bad a day I was afraid you might not come, which would be a shocking thing, as we go away again tomorrow. We must go, for the Westons come to us next week you know. It was quite a sudden thing our coming at all, and I knew nothing of it till the carriage was coming to the door, and then Mr Palmer asked me if I would go with him to Barton. He is so droll! He never tells me any thing! I am so sorry we cannot stay longer; however we shall meet again in town very soon, I hope.'

They were obliged to put an end to such an expectation.

'Not go to town!' cried Mrs Palmer, with a laugh, 'I shall be quite disappointed if you do not. I could get the nicest house in the world for you, next door to our's, in Hanover-square. You must come, indeed. I am sure I shall be very happy to chaperon you at any time till I am confined, if Mrs Dashwood should not like to go into public.'

They thanked her; but were obliged to resist all her entreaties.

'Oh! my love,' cried Mrs Palmer to her husband, who just then entered the room – 'You must help me persuade the Miss Dash-woods to go to town this winter.'

Her love made no answer; and after slightly bowing to the ladies, began complaining of the weather.

'How horrid all this is!' said he. 'Such weather makes every thing and every body disgusting. Dulness is as much produced within doors as without, by rain. It makes one detest all one's acquaintance. What the devil does Sir John mean by not having a billiards room in his house? How few people know what comfort is! Sir John is as stupid as the weather.'

The rest of the company soon dropt in.

'I am afraid, Miss Marianne,' said Sir John, 'you have not been able to take your usual walk to Allenham today.'

Marianne looked very grave and said nothing.

'Oh! don't be so sly before us,' said Mrs Palmer; 'for we know all about it, I assure you; and I admire your taste very much, for I think he is extremely handsome. We do not live a great way from him in the country, you know. Not above ten miles, I dare say.'

'Much nearer thirty,' said her husband.

'Ah! well! there is not much difference. I never was at his house; but they say it is a sweet pretty place.'

'As vile a spot as I ever saw in my life,' said Mr Palmer.

Marianne remained perfectly silent, though her countenance betrayed her interest in what was said.

'Is it very ugly?' continued Mrs Palmer – 'then it must be some other place that is so pretty I suppose.'

When they were seated in the dining room, Sir John observed with regret that they were only eight altogether.

'My dear,' said he to his lady, 'it is very provoking that we should be so few. Why did you not ask the Gilberts to come to us today?'

'Did not I tell you, Sir John, when you spoke to me about it before, that it could not be done? They dined with us last.'

'You and I, Sir John,' said Mrs Jennings, 'should not stand upon such ceremony.'

'Then you would be very ill-bred,' cried Mr Palmer.

'My love, you contradict every body,' – said his wife with her usual laugh. 'Do you know that you are quite rude?'

'I did not know I contradicted any body in calling your mother ill-bred.'

'Aye, you may abuse me as you please,' said the good-natured old lady, 'you have taken Charlotte off my hands, and cannot give her back again. So there I have the whip hand of you.'

Charlotte laughed heartily to think that her husband could not get rid of her; and exultingly said, she did not care how cross he was to her, as they must live together. It was impossible for any one to be more thoroughly good-natured, or more determined to be happy than Mrs Palmer. The studied indifference, insolence, and discontent of her husband gave her no pain: and when he scolded or abused her, she was highly diverted.

'Mr Palmer is so droll!' said she, in a whisper, to Elinor. 'He is always out of humour.'

Elinor was not inclined, after a little observation, to give him credit for being so genuinely and unaffectedly ill-natured or ill-bred as he wished to appear. His temper might perhaps be a little soured by finding, like many others of his sex, that through some unaccountable bias in favour of beauty, he was the husband of a very silly woman, – but she knew that this kind of blunder was too common for any sensible man to be lastingly hurt by it. – It was rather a wish of distinction she believed, which produced his contemptuous treatment of every body, and his general abuse of every thing before him. It was the desire of appearing superior to other people. The motive was too common to be wondered at; but the means, however they might succeed by establishing his superiority in ill-breeding, were not likely to attach any one to him except his wife.

'Oh! my dear Miss Dashwood,' said Mrs Palmer soon afterwards, 'I have got such a favour to ask of you and your sister. Will you come and spend some time at Cleveland this Christmas? Now, pray do, – and come while the Westons are with us. You cannot think how happy I shall be! It will be quite delightful! – My love,' applying to her husband, 'don't you long to have the Miss Dashwoods come to Cleveland?'

'Certainly,' – he replied with a sneer – 'I came into Devonshire with no other view.'

'There now' – said his lady, 'you see Mr Palmer expects you; so you cannot refuse to come.'

They both eagerly and resolutely declined her invitation.

'But indeed you must and shall come. I am sure you will like it of all things. The Westons will be with us, and it will be quite delightful. You cannot think what a sweet place Cleveland is; and we are so gay now, for Mr Palmer is always going about the country canvassing against the election; and so many people come to dine with us that I never saw before, it is quite charming! But, poor fellow! it is very fatiguing to him! for he is forced to make every body like him.'

Elinor could hardly keep her countenance as she assented to the hardship of such an obligation.

'How charming it will be,' said Charlotte, 'when he is in Parliament! – won't it? How I shall laugh! It will be so ridiculous to see all his letters directed to him with an M.P. – But do you know, he says, he will never frank for me? He declares he won't. Don't you, Mr Palmer?'

Mr Palmer took no notice of her.

'He cannot bear writing, you know,' she continued – 'he says it is quite shocking.'

'No;' said he, 'I never said any thing so irrational. Don't palm all your abuses of language upon me.'

'There now; you see how droll he is. This is always the way with him! Sometimes he won't speak to me for half a day together, and then he comes out with something so droll – all about any thing in the world.'

She surprised Elinor very much as they returned into the drawing-room by asking her whether she did not like Mr Palmer excessively.

'Certainly;' said Elinor, 'he seems very agreeable.'

'Well – I am so glad you do. I thought you would, he is so pleasant; and Mr Palmer is excessively pleased with you and your sisters I can tell you, and you can't think how disappointed he will be if you don't come to Cleveland – I can't imagine why you should object to it.'

Elinor was again obliged to decline her invitation; and by changing the subject, put a stop to her entreaties. She thought it probable that as they lived in the same county, Mrs Palmer might be able to give some more particular account of Willoughby's general character, than could be gathered from the Middletons' partial acquaintance with him; and she was eager to gain from any one, such a confirmation of his merits as might remove the possibility of fear for Marianne. She began by inquiring if they saw much of Mr Willoughby at Cleveland, and whether they were intimately acquainted with him.

'Oh! dear, yes; I know him extremely well,' replied Mrs Palmer – 'Not that I ever spoke to him indeed; but I have seen him for ever in town. Somehow or other I never happened to be staying at Barton while he was at Allenham. Mama saw him here once before; – but I was with my uncle at Weymouth. However, I dare say we should have seen a great deal of him in Somersetshire, if it had not happened very unluckily that we should never have been in the country together. He is very little at Combe, I believe; but if he were ever so much there, I do not think Mr Palmer would visit him, for he is in the opposition you know, and besides it is such a way off. I know why you inquire about him, very well; your sister is to marry him. I am monstrous glad of it, for then I shall have her for a neighbour you know.'

'Upon my word,' replied Elinor, 'you know much more of the matter than I do, if you have any reason to expect such a match.'

'Don't pretend to deny it, because you know it is what every body talks of. I assure you I heard of it in my way through town.'

'My dear Mrs Palmer!'

'Upon my honour I did – I met Colonel Brandon Monday morning in Bond-street, just before we left town, and he told me of it directly.'

'You surprise me very much. Colonel Brandon tell you of it! Surely you must be mistaken. To give such intelligence to a person who could not be interested in it, even if it were true, is not what I should expect Colonel Brandon to do.'

'But I do assure you it was so, for all that, and I will tell you how it happened. When we met him, he turned back and walked with us; and so we began talking of my brother and sister, and one thing and another, and I said to him, "So, Colonel, there is a new family come to Barton cottage, I hear, and mama sends me word they are very pretty, and that one of them is going to be married to Mr Willoughby of Combe Magna. Is it true, pray? for of course you must know, as you have been in Devonshire so lately.'

'And what did the Colonel say?'

'Oh! – he did not say much; but he looked as if he knew it to be true, so from that moment I set it down as certain. It will be quite delightful, I declare! When is it to take place?'

'Mr Brandon was very well I hope.'

'Oh! yes, quite well; and so full of your praises, he did nothing but say fine things of you.'

'I am flattered by his commendation. He seems an excellent man; and I think him uncommonly pleasing.'

'So do I. – He is such a charming man, that it is quite a pity he should be so grave and so dull. Mama says *he* was in love with your sister too. – I assure you it was a great compliment if he was, for he hardly ever falls in love with any body.'

'Is Mr Willoughby much known in your part of Somersetshire?' said Elinor.

'Oh! yes, extremely well; that is, I do not believe many people are acquainted with him, because Combe Magna is so far off; but they all think him extremely agreeable I assure you. Nobody is more liked than Mr Willoughby wherever he goes, and so you may tell your sister. She is a monstrous lucky girl to get him, upon my honour; not but that he is much more lucky in getting her, because she is so very handsome and agreeable, that nothing can be good enough for her. However I don't think her hardly at all handsomer than you, I assure you; for I think you both excessively pretty, and so does Mr Palmer too I am sure, though we could not get him to own it last night.'

Mrs Palmer's information respecting Willoughby was not very material; but any testimony in his favour, however small, was pleasing to her.

'I am so glad we are got acquainted at last,' continued Charlotte. – 'And now I hope we shall always be great friends. You can't think how much I longed to see you! It is so delightful that you should live at the cottage! Nothing can be like it to be sure! And I am so glad your sister is going to be well married! I hope you will be a great deal at Combe Magna. It is a sweet place by all accounts.'

'You have been long acquainted with Colonel Brandon, have not you?'

'Yes, a great while; ever since my sister married. – He was a particular friend of Sir John's. I believe,' she added in a low voice, 'he would have been very glad to have had me, if he could. Sir John and Lady Middleton wished it very much. But mama did not think the match good enough for me, otherwise Sir John would have mentioned it to the Colonel, and we should have been married immediately.'

'Did not Colonel Brandon know of Sir John's proposal to your mother before it was made? Had he never owned his affection to yourself?'

'Oh! no; but if mama had not objected to it, I dare say he would have liked it of all things. He had not seen me then above twice, for it was before I left school. However I am much happier as I am. Mr Palmer is just the kind of man I like.'

CHAPTER TWENTY-ONE

THE PALMERS RETURNED to Cleveland the next day, and the two families at Barton were again left to entertain each other. But this did not last long; Elinor had hardly got their last visitors out of her head, had hardly done wondering at Charlotte's being so happy without a cause, at Mr Palmer's acting so simply, with good abilities, and at the strange unsuitableness which often existed between husband and wife, before Sir John's and Mrs Jennings's active zeal in the cause of society, procured her some other new acquaintance to see and observe.

In a morning's excursion to Exeter, they had met with two young ladies, whom Mrs Jennings had the satisfaction of discovering to be her relations, and this was enough for Sir John to invite them directly to the park, as soon as their present engagements at Exeter were over. Their engagements at Exeter instantly gave way before such an invitation, and Lady Middleton was thrown into no little alarm on the return of Sir John, by hearing that she was very soon to receive a visit from two girls whom she had never seen in her life, and of whose elegance, – whose tolerable gentility even, she could have no proof; for the assurances of her husband and mother on that subject went for nothing at all. Their being her relations too made it so much the worse; and Mrs Jennings's attempts at consolation were therefore unfortunately founded, when she advised her daughter not to care about their being so fashionable; because they were all cousins and must put up with one another. As it was impossible however now to prevent their coming, Lady Middleton resigned herself to the idea of it, with all the philosophy of a well-bred woman, contenting herself with merely giving her husband a gentle reprimand on the subject five or six times every day.

The young ladies arrived, their appearance was by no means ungenteel or unfashionable. Their dress was very smart, their manners very civil, they were delighted with the house, and in raptures with the furniture, and they happened to be so doatingly fond of children that Lady Middleton's good opinion was engaged in their favour before they had been an hour at the Park. She declared them to be very agreeable girls indeed, which for her ladyship was enthusiastic admiration. Sir John's confidence in his own judgment rose with this animated praise, and he set off directly for the cottage to tell the Miss Dashwoods of the Miss Steeles' arrival, and to assure them of their being the sweetest girls in the world. From such commendation as this, however, there was not much to be learned; Elinor well knew that the sweetest girls in the world were to be met with in every part of England, under every possible variation of form, face, temper and understanding. Sir John wanted the whole family to walk to the Park directly and look at his guests. Benevolent, philanthropic man! It was painful to him even to keep a third cousin to himself.

'Do come now,' said he – 'pray come – you must come – I declare you shall come – You can't think how you will like them. Lucy is monstrous pretty, and so good humoured and agreeable! The children are all hanging about her already, as if she was an old acquaint-

ance. And they both long to see you of all things, for they have
heard at Exeter that you are the most beautiful creatures in the
world; and I have told them it is all very true, and a great deal
more. You will be delighted with them I am sure. They have
brought the whole coach full of playthings for the children. How
can you be so cross as not to come? Why they are your cousins,
you know, after a fashion. *You* are my cousins, and they are my
wife's, so you must be related.'

But Sir John could not prevail. He could only obtain a promise
of their calling at the Park within a day or two, and then left them
in amazement at their indifference, to walk home and boast anew
of their attractions to the Miss Steeles, as he had been already
boasting of the Miss Steeles to them.

When their promised visit to the Park and consequent introduction
to these young ladies took place, they found in the appearance of
the eldest, who was nearly thirty, with a very plain and not a
sensible face, nothing to admire; but in the other, who was not
more than two or three and twenty, they acknowledged considerable
beauty; her features were pretty, and she had a sharp quick eye, and
a smartness of air, which though it did not give actual elegance or
grace, gave distinction to her person. – Their manners were particularly civil, and Elinor soon allowed them credit for some kind of
sense, when she saw with what constant and judicious attentions
they were making themselves agreeable to Lady Middleton. With
her children they were in continual raptures, extolling their beauty,
courting their notice, and humouring all their whims; and such of
their time as could be spared from the importunate demands which
this politeness made on it, was spent in admiration of whatever her
ladyship was doing, if she happened to be doing any thing, or in
taking patterns of some elegant new dress, in which her appearance
the day before had thrown them into unceasing delight. Fortunately
for those who pay their court through such foibles, a fond mother,
though, in pursuit of praise for her children, the most rapacious of
human beings, is likewise the most credulous; her demands are
exorbitant; but she will swallow any thing; and the excessive affection and endurance of the Miss Steeles towards her offspring, were
viewed therefore by Lady Middleton without the smallest surprise
or distrust. She saw with maternal complacency all the impertinent
incroachments and mischievous tricks to which her cousins
submitted. She saw their sashes untied, their hair pulled about their
ears, their work-bags searched, and their knives and scissors stolen
away, and felt no doubt of its being a reciprocal enjoyment. It

Mischievous tricks.

suggested no other surprise than that Elinor and Marianne should sit so composedly by, without claiming a share in what was passing.

'John is in such spirits today!' said she, on his taking Miss Steele's pocket handkerchief, and throwing it out of window – 'He is full of monkey tricks.'

And soon afterwards, on the second boy's violently pinching one of the same lady's fingers, she fondly observed, 'How playful William is!'

'And here is my sweet little Annamaria,' she added, tenderly caressing a little girl of three years old, who had not made a noise for the last two minutes; 'And she is always so gentle and quiet – Never was there such a quiet little thing!'

But unfortunately in bestowing these embraces, a pin in her lady-ship's head dress slightly scratching the child's neck, produced from this pattern of gentleness, such violent screams, as could hardly be outdone by any creature professedly noisy. The mother's consternation was excessive; but it could not surpass the alarm of the Miss Steeles, and every thing was done by all three, in so critical an emergency, which affection could suggest as likely to assuage the agonies of the little sufferer. She was seated in her mother's lap, covered with kisses, her wound bathed with lavender-water, by one of the Miss Steeles, who was on her knees to attend her, and her mouth stuffed with sugar plums by the other. With such a reward for her tears, the child was too wise to cease crying. She still screamed and sobbed lustily, kicked her two brothers for offering to touch her, and all their united soothings were ineffectual till Lady Middleton luckily remembering that in a sense of similar distress last week, some apricot marmalade had been successfully applied for a bruised temple, the same remedy was eagerly proposed for this unfortunate scratch, and a slight intermission of screams in the young lady on hearing it, gave them reason to hope that it would not be rejected. – She was carried out of the room therefore in her mother's arms, in quest of this medicine, and as the two boys chose to follow, though earnestly entreated by their mother to stay behind, the four young ladies were left in a quietness which the room had not known for many hours.

'Poor little creature!' said Miss Steele, as soon as they were gone. 'It might have been a very sad accident.'

'Yet I hardly know how,' cried Marianne, 'unless it had been under totally different circumstances. But this is the usual way of heightening alarm, where there is nothing to be alarmed at in reality.'

'What a sweet woman Lady Middleton is!' said Lucy Steele.

Marianne was silent; it was impossible for her to say what she did not feel, however trivial the occasion, and upon Elinor therefore the whole task of telling lies when politeness required it, always fell. She did her best when thus called on, by speaking of Lady Middleton with more warmth than she felt, though with far less than Miss Lucy.

'And Sir John too,' cried the elder sister, 'what a charming man he is!'

Here too, Miss Dashwood's commendation, being only simple and just, came in without any eclat. She merely observed that he was perfectly good humoured and friendly.

'And what a charming little family they have! I never saw such fine children in my life – I declare I quite doat upon them already, and indeed I am always distractedly fond of children.'

'I should guess so,' said Elinor with a smile, 'from what I have witnessed this morning.'

'I have a notion,' said Lucy, 'you think the little Middletons rather too much indulged; perhaps they may be the outside of enough; but it is so natural in Lady Middleton; and for my part, I love to see children full of life and spirits; I cannot bear them if they are tame and quiet.'

'I confess,' replied Elinor, 'that while I am at Barton Park, I never think of tame and quiet children with any abhorrence.'

A short pause succeeded this speech, which was first broken by Miss Steele, who seemed very much disposed for conversation, and who now said rather abruptly, 'And how do you like Devonshire, Miss Dashwood? I suppose you were very sorry to leave Sussex.'

In some surprise at the familiarity of this question, or at least of the manner in which it was spoken, Elinor replied that she was.

'Norland is a prodigious beautiful place, is not it?' added Miss Steele.

'We have heard Sir John admire it excessively,' said Lucy, who seemed to think some apology necessary for the freedom of her sister.

'I think every one *must* admire it,' replied Elinor, 'who ever saw the place; though it is not to be supposed that any one can estimate its beauties as we do.'

'And had you a great many smart beaux there? I suppose you have not so many in this part of the world; for my part, I think they are a vast addition always.'

'But why should you think,' said Lucy, looking ashamed of her sister, 'that there are not as many genteel young men in Devonshire as Sussex?'

'Nay, my dear, I'm sure I don't pretend to say that there an't. I'm sure there's a vast many smart beaux in Exeter; but you know, how could I tell what smart beaux there might be about Norland; and I was only afraid the Miss Dashwoods might find it dull at Barton, if they had not so many as they used to have. But perhaps you young ladies may not care about the beaux, and had as lief be without them as with them. For my part, I think they are vastly agreeable, provided they dress smart and behave civil. But I can't bear to see them dirty and nasty. Now there's Mr Rose at Exeter, a prodigious smart young man, quite a beau, clerk to Mr Simpson you know, and yet if you do but meet him of a morning, he is not fit to be seen. – I suppose your brother was quite a beau, Miss Dashwood, before he married, as he was so rich?'

'Upon my word,' replied Elinor, 'I cannot tell you, for I do not perfectly comprehend the meaning of the word. But this I can say, that if he ever was a beau before he married, he is one still, for there is not the smallest alteration in him.'

'Oh! dear! one never thinks of married mens' being beaux – they have something else to do.'

'Lord! Anne,' cried her sister, 'you can talk of nothing but beaux; – you will make Miss Dashwood believe you think of nothing else.' And then to turn the discourse, she began admiring the house and the furniture.

This specimen of the Miss Steeles was enough. The vulgar freedom and folly of the eldest left her no recommendation, and as Elinor was not blinded by the beauty, or the shrewd look of the youngest, to her want of real elegance and artlessness, she left the house without any wish of knowing them better.

Not so, the Miss Steeles. – They came from Exeter, well provided with admiration for the use of Sir John Middleton, his family, and all his relations, and no niggardly proportion was now dealt out to his fair cousins, whom they declared to be the most beautiful, elegant, accomplished, and agreeable girls they had ever beheld, and with whom they were particularly anxious to be better acquainted. – And to be better acquainted therefore, Elinor soon found was their inevitable lot, for as Sir John was entirely on the side of the Miss Steeles, their party would be too strong for opposition, and that kind of intimacy must be submitted to, which consists of sitting an hour or two together in the same room almost every day. Sir John could do no more; but he did not know that any more was required; to be together was, in his opinion, to be intimate, and while his continual schemes for their meeting were effectual, he had not a doubt of their being established friends.

To do him justice, he did every thing in his power to promote their unreserve, by making the Miss Steeles acquainted with whatever he knew or supposed of his cousins' situations in the most delicate particulars, – and Elinor had not seen them more than twice, before the eldest of them wished her joy on her sister's having been so lucky as to make a conquest of a very smart beau since she came to Barton.

' 'Twill be a fine thing to have her married so young to be sure,' said she, 'and I hear he is quite a beau, and prodigious handsome. And I hope you may have as good luck yourself soon, – but perhaps you may have a friend in the corner already.'

Elinor could not suppose that Sir John would be more nice in proclaiming his suspicions of her regard for Edward, than he had been with respect to Marianne; indeed it was rather his favourite joke of the two, as being somewhat newer and more conjectural; and since Edward's visit, they had never dined together, without his drinking to her best affections with so much significancy and so many nods and winks, as to excite general attention. The letter F— had been likewise invariably brought forward, and found productive of such countless jokes, that its character as the wittiest letter in the alphabet had been long established with Elinor.

The Miss Steeles, as she expected, had now all the benefit of these

Drinking to her best affections.

jokes, and in the eldest of them they raised a curiosity to know the name of the gentleman alluded to, which, though often impertinently expressed, was perfectly of a piece with her general inquisitiveness into the concerns of their family. But Sir John did not sport long with the curiosity which he delighted to raise, for he had at least as much pleasure in telling the name, as Miss Steele had in hearing it.

'His name is Ferrars,' said he, in a very audible whisper; 'but pray do not tell it, for it's a great secret.'

'Ferrars!' repeated Miss Steele; 'Mr Ferrars is the happy man, is he? What! your sister-in-law's brother, Miss Dashwood? a very agreeable young man to be sure; I know him very well.'

'How can you say so, Anne?' cried Lucy, who generally made an amendment to all her sister's assertions. 'Though we have seen him once or twice at my uncle's, it is rather too much to pretend to know him very well.'

Elinor heard all this with attention and surprise. 'And who was this uncle? Where did he live? How came they acquainted?' She wished very much to have the subject continued, though she did not chuse to join in it herself; but nothing more of it was said, and for the first time in her life, she thought Mrs Jennings deficient either in curiosity after petty information, or in a disposition to communicate it. The manner in which Miss Steele had spoken of Edward, increased her curiosity; for it struck her as being rather ill-natured and suggested the suspicion of that lady's knowing, or fancying herself to know something to his disadvantage. – But her curiosity was unavailing, for no farther notice was taken of Mr Ferrars's name by Miss Steele when alluded to, or even openly mentioned by Sir John.

CHAPTER TWENTY-TWO

MARIANNE, WHO HAD never much toleration for any thing like impertinence, vulgarity, inferiority of parts, or even difference of taste from herself, was at this time particularly ill-disposed, from the state of her spirits, to be pleased with the Miss Steeles, or to encourage their advances; and to the invariable coldness of her behaviour towards them, which checked every endeavour at intimacy on their side, Elinor principally attributed that preference of herself which soon became evident in the manners of both, but especially of Lucy, who missed no opportunity of engaging her in conversation, or of striving to improve their acquaintance by an easy and frank communication of her sentiments.

Lucy was naturally clever; her remarks were often just and amusing; and as a companion for half an hour Elinor frequently found her agreeable; but her powers had received no aid from education, she was ignorant and illiterate, and her deficiency of all mental improvement, her want of information in the most common particulars, could not be concealed from Miss Dashwood, in spite of her constant endeavour to appear to advantage. Elinor saw, and pitied her for, the neglect of abilities which education might have rendered so respectable; but she saw, with less tenderness of feeling, the thorough want of delicacy, of rectitude, and integrity of mind, which her attentions, her assiduities, her flatteries at the Park betrayed; and she could have no lasting satisfaction in the company of a person who joined insincerity with ignorance; whose want of instruction prevented their meeting in conversation on terms of equality, and whose conduct towards others, made every shew of attention and deference towards herself perfectly valueless.

'You will think my question an odd one, I dare say,' said Lucy to her one day as they were walking together from the park to the cottage – 'pray, are you personally acquainted with your sister-in-law's mother, Mrs Ferrars?'

Elinor *did* think the question a very odd one, and her countenance expressed it, as she answered that she had never seen Mrs Ferrars.

'Indeed!' replied Lucy; 'I wonder at that, for I thought you must have seen her at Norland sometimes. Then perhaps you cannot tell me what sort of a woman she is?'

'No;' returned Elinor, cautious of giving her real opinion of Edward's mother, and not very desirous of satisfying, what seemed impertinent curiosity – 'I know nothing of her.'

'I am sure you think me very strange, for inquiring about her in such a way;' said Lucy, eyeing Elinor attentively as she spoke; 'but perhaps there may be reasons – I wish I might venture; but however I hope you will do me the justice of believing that I do not mean to be impertinent.'

Elinor made her a civil reply, and they walked on for a few minutes in silence. It was broken by Lucy, who renewed the subject again by saying with some hesitation,

'I cannot bear to have you think me impertinently curious. I am sure I would rather do any thing in the world than be thought so by a person whose good opinion is so well worth having as yours. And I am sure I should not have the smallest fear of trusting *you*;

Amiably bashful.

indeed I should be very glad of your advice how to manage in such an uncomfortable situation as I am; but however there is no occasion to trouble *you*. I am sorry you do not happen to know Mrs Ferrars.'

'I am sorry I do *not*,' said Elinor, in great astonishment, 'if it could be of any use to *you* to know my opinion of her. But really, I never understood that you were at all connected with that family, and therefore I am a little surprised, I confess, at so serious an inquiry into her character.'

'I dare say you are, and I am sure I do not at all wonder at it. But if I dared tell you all, you would not be so much surprised. Mrs Ferrars is certainly nothing to me at present, – but the time *may* come – how soon it will come must depend upon herself – when we may be very intimately connected.'

She looked down as she said this, amiably bashful, with only one side glance at her companion to observe its effect on her.

'Good heavens!' cried Elinor, 'what do you mean? Are you acquainted with Mr Robert Ferrars? Can you be?' And she did not feel much delighted with the idea of such a sister-in-law.

'No;' replied Lucy, 'not to Mr *Robert* Ferrars – I never saw him in my life; but,' fixing her eyes upon Elinor, 'to his elder brother.'

What felt Elinor at that moment? Astonishment, that would have been as painful as it was strong, had not an immediate disbelief of the assertion attended it. She turned towards Lucy in silent amazement, unable to divine the reason or object of such a declaration, and though her complexion varied, she stood firm in incredulity and felt in no danger of an hysterical fit, or a swoon.

'You may well be surprised,' continued Lucy; 'for to be sure you could have had no idea of it before; for I dare say he never dropped the smallest hint of it to you or any of your family; because it was always meant to be a great secret, and I am sure has been faithfully kept so by me to this hour. Not a soul of all my relations know of it but Anne and I never should have mentioned it to you, if I had not felt the greatest dependance in the world upon your secrecy; and I really thought my behaviour in asking so many questions about Mrs Ferrars, must seem so odd, that it ought to be explained. And I do not think Mr Ferrars can be displeased, when he knows I have trusted you, because I know he had the highest opinion in the world of all your family, and looks upon yourself and the other Miss Dashwoods, quite as his own sisters.' – She paused.

Elinor for a few moments remained silent. Her astonishment at what she heard was at first too great for words; but at length forcing herself to speak, and to speak cautiously, she said with a calmness of manner, which tolerably well concealed her surprise and solicitude – 'May I ask if your engagement is of long standing?'

'We have been engaged these four years.'

'Four years!'

'Yes.'

Elinor, though greatly shocked, still felt unable to believe it.

'I did not know,' said she, 'that you were even acquainted till the other day.'

'Our acquaintance, however, is of many years date. He was under my uncle's care, you know, a considerable while.'

'Your uncle!'

'Yes; Mr Pratt. Did you never hear him talk of Mr Pratt?'

'I think I have,' replied Elinor, with an exertion of spirits, which increased with her increase of emotion.

'He was four years with my uncle, who lives at Longstaple, near Plymouth. It was there our acquaintance begun, for my sister and me was often staying with my uncle, and it was there our engagement was formed, though not till a year after he had quitted as a pupil; but he was almost always with us afterwards. I was very unwilling to enter into it, as you may imagine, without the knowledge and approbation of his mother; but I was too young and loved him too well to be so prudent as I ought to have been. – Though you do not know him so well as me, Miss Dashwood, you must have seen enough of him to be sensible he is very capable of making a woman sincerely attached to him.'

'Certainly,' answered Elinor, without knowing what she said; but after a moment's reflection, she added with revived security of Edward's honour and love, and her companion's falsehood – 'Engaged to Mr Edward Ferrars! – I confess myself so totally surprised at what you tell me, that really – I beg your pardon; but surely there must be some mistake of person or name. We cannot mean the same Mr Ferrars.'

'We can mean no other,' cried Lucy smiling. 'Mr Edward Ferrars, the eldest son of Mrs Ferrars of Park-street, and brother of your sister-in-law, Mrs John Dashwood, is the person I mean; you must allow that *I* am not likely to be deceived, as to the name of the man on who all my happiness depends.'

'It is strange,' replied Elinor in a most painful perplexity, 'that I should never have heard him even mention your name.'

'No; considering our situation, it was not strange. Our first care has been to keep the matter secret. – You knew nothing of me, or my family, and therefore there could be no *occasion* for ever mentioning my name to you, and as he was always particularly afraid of his sister's suspecting any thing, *that* was reason enough for his not mentioning it.'

She was silent. – Elinor's security sunk; but her self-command did not sink with it.

'Four years you have been engaged,' said she with a firm voice.

'Yes; and heaven knows how much longer we may have to wait. Poor Edward! It puts him quite out of heart.' Then taking a small miniature from her pocket, she added, 'To prevent the possibility of mistake, be so good as to look at this face. It does not do him justice to be sure, but yet I think you cannot be deceived as to the person it was drew for. – I have had it above these three years.'

She put it into her hands as she spoke, and when Elinor saw the painting, whatever other doubts her fear of a too hasty decision, or her wish of detecting falsehood might suffer to linger in her mind, she could have none of its being Edward's face. She returned it almost instantly, acknowledging the likeness.

'I have never been able,' continued Lucy, 'to give him my picture in return, which I am very much vexed at, for he has been always so anxious to get it! But I am determined to set for it the very first opportunity.'

'You are quite in the right;' replied Elinor calmly. They then proceeded a few paces in silence. Lucy spoke first.

'I am sure,' said she, 'I have no doubt in the world of your faithfully keeping this secret, because you must know of what importance it is to us, not to have it reach his mother; for she would never approve of it, I dare say. I shall have no fortune, and I fancy she is an exceeding proud woman.'

'I certainly did not seek your confidence,' said Elinor; 'but you do me nor more than justice in imagining that I may be depended on. Your secret is safe with me; but pardon me if I express some surprise at so unnecessary a communication. You must at least have felt that my being acquainted with it could not add to its safety.'

As she said this, she looked earnestly at Lucy, hoping to discover something in her countenance; perhaps the falsehood of the greatest part of what she had been saying; but Lucy's countenance suffered no change.

'I was afraid you would think I was taking a great liberty with you,' said she, 'in telling you all this. I have not known you long to be sure, personally at least, but I have known you and all your family by description a great while; and as soon as I saw you, I felt almost as if you was an old acquaintance. Besides in the present case, I really thought some explanation was due to you after my making such particular inquiries about Edward's mother; and I am so unfortunate, that I have not a creature whose advice I can ask. Anne is the only person that knows of it, and she has no judgment at all; indeed she does me a great deal more harm than good, for I am in constant fear of her betraying me. She does not know how to hold her tongue, as you must perceive, and I am sure I was in the greatest fright in the world t'other day, when Edward's name was mentioned by Sir John, lest she should out with it all. You can't think how much I go through in my mind from it altogether. I only wonder that I am alive after what I have suffered for Edward's sake these last four years. Every thing in such suspense and uncertainty; and seeing him so seldom — we can hardly meet above twice a-year. I am sure I wonder my heart is not quite broke.'

Here she took out her handkerchief; but Elinor did not feel very compassionate.

'Sometimes,' continued Lucy, after wiping her eyes, 'I think whether it would not be better for us both, to break off the matter entirely.' As she said this, she looked directly at her companion. 'But ·then at other times I have not resolution enough for it. – I cannot bear the thoughts of making him so miserable, as I know the very mention of such a thing would do. And on my own account too – so dear as he is to me – I don't think I could be equal to it. What would you advise me to do in such a case, Miss Dashwood? What would you do yourself?'

'Pardon me,' replied Elinor, startled by the question; 'but I can give you no advice under such circumstances. Your own judgment must direct you.'

'To be sure,' continued Lucy, after a few minutes silence on both sides, 'his mother must provide for him sometime or other; but poor Edward is *so* cast down about it! Did not you think him dreadful low-spirited when he was at Barton? He was so miserable when he left us at Longstaple, to go to you, that I was afraid you would think him quite ill.'

'Did he come from your uncle's then, when he visited us?'

'Oh! yes; he had been staying a fortnight with us. Did you think he came directly from town?'

'No,' replied Elinor, most feelingly sensible of every fresh circumstance in favour of Lucy's veracity; 'I remember he told us, that he had been staying a fortnight with some friends near Plymouth.' She remembered too, her own surprise at the time, at his mentioning nothing farther of those friends, at his total silence with respect even to their names.

'Did not you think him sadly out of spirits?' repeated Lucy.

'We did indeed, particularly so when he first arrived.'

'I begged him to exert himself for fear you should suspect what was the matter; but it made him so melancholy, not being able to stay more than a fortnight with us, and seeing me so much affected. – Poor fellow! – I am afraid it is just the same with him now; for he writes in wretched spirits. I heard from him just before I left Exeter;' taking a letter from her pocket and carelessly showing the direction to Elinor. 'You know his hand, I dare say, a charming one it is; but that is not written so well as usual. – He was tired, I dare say, for he had just filled the sheet to me as full as possible.'

Elinor saw that it *was* his hand, and she could doubt no longer. The picture, she had allowed herself to believe, might have been accidentally obtained; it might not have been Edward's gift; but a correspondence between them by letter, could subsist only under a positive engagement, could be authorized by nothing else; for a few moments, she was almost overcome – her heart sunk within her, and she could hardly stand; but exertion was indispensably necessary, and she struggled so resolutely against the oppression of her feelings, that her success was speedy, and for the time complete.

'Writing to each other,' said Lucy, returning the letter into her pocket, 'is the only comfort we have in such long separations. Yes, *I* have one other comfort in his picture; but poor Edward has not even *that*. If he had but my picture, he says he should be easy. I gave him a lock of my hair set in a ring when he was at Longstaple last, and that was some comfort to him, he said, but not equal to a picture. Perhaps you might notice the ring when you saw him?'

'I did,' said Elinor, with a composure of voice, under which was concealed an emotion and distress beyond any thing she had ever felt before. She was mortified, shocked, confounded.

Fortunately for her, they had now reached the cottage, and the conversation could be continued no farther. After sitting with them a few minutes, the Miss Steeles returned to the Park, and Elinor was then at liberty to think and be wretched.

Emma

Emma

EMMA WOODHOUSE, handsome, clever, and rich, with a comfortable home and happy disposition, seemed to unite some of the best blessings of existence; and had lived nearly twenty-one years in the world with very little to distress or vex her.

She was the youngest of the two daughters of a most affectionate, indulgent father, and had, in consequence of her sister's marriage, been mistress of his house from a very early period. Her mother had died too long ago for her to have more than an indistinct remembrance of her caresses, and her place had been supplied by an excellent woman as governess, who had fallen little short of a mother in affection.

Sixteen years had Miss Taylor been in Mr Woodhouse's family, less as a governess than a friend, very fond of both daughters, but particularly of Emma. Between *them* it was more the intimacy of sisters. Even before Miss Taylor had ceased to hold the nominal office of governess, the mildness of her temper had hardly allowed her to impose any restraint; and the shadow of authority being now long passed away, they had been living together as friend and friend very mutually attached, and Emma doing just what she liked; highly esteeming Miss Taylor's judgment, but directed chiefly by her own.

The real evils indeed of Emma's situation were the power of having rather too much of her own way, and a disposition to think a little too well of herself; these were the disadvantages which threatened alloy to her many enjoyments. The danger, however, was at present so unperceived, that they did not by any means rank as misfortunes with her.

Sorrow came – a gentle sorrow – but not all in the shape of any disagreeable consciousness. – Miss Taylor married. It was Miss Taylor's loss which first brought grief. It was on the wedding-day of this beloved friend that Emma first sat in mournful thought of any continuance. The wedding over and the bride-people gone, her father and herself were left to dine together, with no prospect of a third to cheer a long evening. Her father composed himself to sleep after dinner, as usual, and she had then only to sit and think of what she had lost.

The event had every promise of happiness for her friend. Mr Weston was a man of unexceptionable character, easy fortune, suitable age and pleasant manners; and there was some satisfaction in considering with what self-denying, generous friendship she had always wished and promoted the match; but it was a black morning's work for her. The want of Miss Taylor would be felt every hour of every day. She recalled her past kindness – the kindness, the affection of sixteen years – how she had taught and how she had played with her from five years old – how she had devoted all her powers to attach and amuse her in health – and how nursed her through the various illnesses of childhood. A large debt of gratitude was owing here; but the intercourse of the last seven years, the equal footing and perfect unreserve which had soon followed Isabella's marriage on their being left to each other, was yet a dearer, tenderer recollection. It had been a friend and companion such as few possessed, intelligent, well-informed, useful, gentle, knowing all the ways of the family, interested in all its concerns, and peculiarly interested in herself, in every pleasure, every scheme of her's; – one to whom she could speak every thought as it arose, and who had such an affection for her as could never find fault.

How was she to bear the change? – It was true that her friend was going only half a mile from them; but Emma was aware that great must be the difference between a Mrs Weston only half a mile from them, and a Miss Taylor in the house; and with all her advantages, natural and domestic, she was now in great danger of suffering from intellectual solitude. She dearly loved her father, but he was no companion for her. He could not meet her in conversation, rational or playful.

The evil of the actual disparity in their ages (and Mr Woodhouse had not married early) was much increased by his constitution and habits; for having been a valetudinarian all his life, without activity of mind or body, he was a much older man in ways than in years; and though everywhere beloved for the friendliness of his heart and his amiable temper, his talents could not have recommended him at any time.

Her sister, though comparatively but little removed by matrimony, being settled in London, only sixteen miles off, was much beyond her daily reach; and many a long October and November evening must be struggled through at Hartfield, before Christmas brought the next visit from Isabella and her husband and their little children to fill the house and give her pleasant society again.

Highbury, the large and populous village almost amounting to a town, to which Hartfield, in spite of its separate lawn and shrubberies and name, did really belong, afforded her no equals. The Woodhouses were first in consequence here. All looked up to them.

She had many acquaintance in the place, for her father was universally civil, but not one among them who could be accepted in lieu of Miss Taylor for even half a day. It was a melancholy change; and Emma could not but sigh over it and wish for impossible things, till her father awoke, and made it necessary to be cheerful. His spirits required support. He was a nervous man, easily depressed; fond of every body that he was used to, and hating to part with them; hating change of every kind. Matrimony, as the origin of change, was always disagreeable; and he was by no means yet reconciled to his own daughter's marrying, nor could ever speak of her but with compassion, though it had been entirely a match of affection, when he was now obliged to part with Miss Taylor too; and from his habits of gentle selfishness and of being never able to suppose that other people could feel differently from himself, he was very much disposed to think Miss Taylor had done as sad a thing for herself as for them, and would have been a great deal happier if she had spent all the rest of her life at Hartfield. Emma smiled and chatted as cheerfully as she could, to keep him from such thoughts; but when tea came, it was impossible for him not to say exactly as he had said at dinner.

'Poor Miss Taylor! – I wish she were here again. What a pity it is that Mr Weston ever thought of her!'

'I cannot agree with you, papa; you know I cannot. Mr Weston is such a good-humoured, pleasant, excellent man that he thoroughly deserves a good wife; – and you would not have had Miss Taylor live with us for ever and bear all my odd humours, when she might have a house of her own?'

'A house of her own! – but where is the advantage of a house of her own? This is three times as large. – And you have never any odd humours, my dear.'

'How often we shall be going to see them and they coming to see us! – We shall be always meeting! *We* must begin, we must go and pay our wedding-visit very soon.'

'My dear, how am I to get so far? Randalls is such a distance. I could not walk half so far.'

'No papa, nobody thought of your walking. We must go in the carriage to be sure.'

'The carriage! But James will not like to put the horses to for such a little way; – and where are the poor horses to be while we are paying our visit?'

'They are to be put into Mr Weston's stable, papa. You know we have settled all that already. We talked it all over with Mr Weston last night. And as for James, you may be very sure he will always like going to Randalls, because of his daughter's being housemaid there. I only doubt whether he will ever take us anywhere else. That was your doing, papa. You got Hannah that good place. Nobody thought of Hannah till you mentioned her – James is so obliged to you!'

'I am very glad I did think of her. It was very lucky, for I would not have had poor James think himself slighted upon any account; and I am sure she will make a very good servant; she is a civil, pretty-spoken girl; I have a great opinion of her. Whenever I see her, she always curtseys and asks me how I do, in a very pretty manner; and when you have had her here to do needlework, I observe she always turns the lock of the door the right way and never bangs it. I am sure she will be an excellent servant; and it will be a great comfort to poor Miss Taylor to have somebody about her that she is used to see. Whenever James goes over to see his daughter you know, she will be hearing of us. He will be able to tell her how we all are.'

Emma spared no exertions to maintain this happier flow of ideas, and hoped, by the help of backgammon, to get her father tolerably through the evening, and be attacked by no regrets but her own. The backgammon-table was placed; but a visitor immediately afterwards walked in and made it unnecessary.

Mr Knightley, a sensible man about seven or eight-and-thirty, was not only a very old and intimate friend of the family, but particularly connected with it as the elder brother of Isabella's husband. He lived about a mile from Highbury, was a frequent visitor and always welcome, and at this time more welcome than usual, as coming directly from their mutual connections in London. He had returned to a later dinner after some days absence, and now walked up to Hartfield to say that all were well in Brunswick-square. It was a happy circumstance and animated Mr Woodhouse for some time. Mr Knightley had a cheerful manner which always did him good; and his many inquiries after 'poor Isabella' and her children were answered most satisfactorily. When this was over, Mr Woodhouse gratefully observed,

'It is very kind of you, Mr Knightley, to come out at this late hour to call upon us. I am afraid you must have had a shocking walk.'

'Not at all, sir. It is a beautiful, moonlight night; and so mild that I must draw back from your great fire.'

'But you must have found it very damp and dirty. I wish you may not catch cold.'

'Dirty, sir! Look at my shoes. Not a speck on them.'

'Well! that is quite surprizing for we have had a vast deal of rain here. It rained dreadfully hard for half an hour, while we were at breakfast. I wanted them to put off the wedding.'

'By the bye – I have not wished you joy. Being pretty well aware of what sort of joy you must both be feeling, I have been in no hurry with my congratulations. But I hope it all went off tolerably well. How did you all behave? Who cried most?'

'Ah! poor Miss Taylor! 'tis a sad business.'

'Poor Mr and Miss Woodhouse, if you please; but I cannot possibly say "poor Miss Taylor." I have a great regard for you and Emma; but when it comes to the question of dependence or independence! – At any rate, it must be better to have only one to please, than two.'

'Especially when *one* of those two is such a fanciful, troublesome creature!' said Emma playfully. 'That, is what you have in your head, I know – and what you would certainly say if my father were not by.'

'I believe it is very true, my dear, indeed,' said Mr Woodhouse with a sigh. 'I am afraid I am sometimes very fanciful and troublesome.'

'My dearest papa! You do not think I could mean *you*, or suppose Mr Knightley to mean *you*. What a horrible idea! Oh, no! I meant only myself. Mr Knightley loves to find fault with me you know – in a joke – it is all a joke. We always say what we like to one another.'

Mr Knightley, in fact, was one of the few people who could see faults in Emma Woodhouse, and the only one who ever told her of them: and though this was not particularly agreeable to Emma herself, she knew it would be so much less so to her father, that she would not have him really suspect such a circumstance as her not being thought perfect by every body.

'Emma knows I never flatter her,' said Mr Knightley; 'but I meant no reflection on any body. Miss Taylor has been used to have two persons to please; she will now have but one. The chances are that she must be a gainer.'

'Well,' said Emma, willing to let it pass – 'you want to hear about the wedding, and I shall be happy to tell you, for we all behaved charmingly. Every body was punctual, every body in their best looks. Not a tear, and hardly a long face to be seen. Oh! no, we all felt that we were going to be only half a mile apart, and were sure of meeting every day.'

'Dear Emma bears every thing so well,' said her father. 'But, Mr Knightley, she is really very sorry to lose poor Miss Taylor, and I am sure she *will* miss her more than she thinks for.'

Emma turned away her head, divided between tears and smiles.

'It is impossible that Emma should not miss such a companion,' said Mr Knightley. 'We should not like her so well as we do, sir, if we could suppose it. But she knows how much the marriage is to Miss Taylor's advantage; she knows how very acceptable it must be at Miss Taylor's time of life to be settled in a home of her own, and how important to her to be secure of a comfortable provision, and therefore cannot allow herself to feel so much pain as pleasure. Every friend of Miss Taylor must be glad to have her so happily married.'

'And you have forgotten one matter of joy to me,' said Emma, 'and a very considerable one – that I made the match myself. I made the match, you know, four years ago; and to have it take place, and be proved in the right, when so many people said Mr Weston would never marry again, may comfort me for any thing.'

Mr Knightley shook his head at her. Her father fondly replied, 'Ah! my dear, I wish you would not make matches and foretell things, for whatever you say always comes to pass. Pray do not make any more matches.'

'I promise you to make none for myself, papa; but I must, indeed, for other people. It is the greatest amusement in the world! And after such success you know! – Every body said that Mr Weston would nevery marry again. Oh dear, no! Mr Weston, who had been a widower so long, and who seemed so perfectly comfortable without a wife, so constantly occupied either in his business in town or among his friends here, always acceptable wherever he went, always cheerful – Mr Weston need not spend a single evening in the year alone if he did not like it. Oh, no! Mr Weston certainly would never marry again. Some people even talked of a promise to his wife on her death-bed, and others of the son and the uncle not letting him. All manner of solemn nonsense was talked on the subject, but I believe none of it. Ever since the day (about four years ago) that Miss Taylor and I met with him in Broadway-lane, when, because it began to mizzle; he darted away with so much gallantry, and borrowed two umbrellas for us from Farmer Mitchell's, I made up my mind on the subject. I planned the match from that hour; and when such success has blessed me in this instance, dear papa, you cannot think that I shall leave off match-making.'

'I do not understand what you mean by "success;" ' said Mr Knightley. 'Success supposes endeavour. Your time has been properly and delicately spent, if you have been endeavouring for the last four years to bring about this marriage. A worthy employment for a young lady's mind! But if, which I rather imagine, your making

'Two umbrellas for us.'

the match, as you call it, means only your planning it, your saying to yourself one idle day, "I think it would be a very good thing for Miss Taylor if Mr Weston were to marry her," and saying it again to yourself every now and then afterwards, – why do you talk of success? where is your merit? – what are you proud of? – you made a lucky guess; and *that* is all that can be said.'

'And have you ever known the pleasure and triumph of a lucky guess? – I pity you. – I thought you cleverer – for depend upon it, a lucky guess is never merely luck. There is always some talent in it. And as to my poor word "success," which you quarrel with, I do not know that I am so entirely without any claim to it. You have drawn two pretty pictures – but I think there may be a third

– a something between the do-nothing and the do-all. If I had not promoted Mr Weston's visits here, and given many little encouragements, and smoothed many little matters, it might not have come to any thing after all. I think you must know Hartfield enough to comprehend that.'

'A straight-forward, open-hearted man, like Weston, and a rational unaffected woman, like Miss Taylor, may be safely left to manage their own concerns. You are more likely to have done harm to yourself, than good to them, by interference.'

'Emma never thinks of herself, if she can do good to others;' rejoined Mr Woodhouse, understanding but in part. 'But, my dear, pray do not make any more matches, they are silly things, and break up one's family circle grievously.'

'Only one more, papa; only for Mr Elton. Poor Mr Elton! You like Mr Elton, papa, – I must look about for a wife for him. There is nobody in Highbury who deserves him – and he has been here a whole year, and has fitted up his house so comfortably that it would be a shame to have him single any longer – and I thought when he was joining their hands to-day, he looked so very much as if he would like to have the same kind office done for him! I think very well of Mr Elton, and this is the only way I have of doing him a service.'

'Mr Elton is a very pretty young man to be sure, and a very good young man, and I have great regard for him. But if you want to shew him any attention, my dear, ask him to come and dine with us some day. That will be a much better thing. I dare say Mr Knightley wil be so kind as to meet him.

'With a great deal of pleasure, sir, at any time,' said Mr Knightley laughing; 'and I agree with you entirely that it will be a much better thing. Invite him to dinner, Emma, and help him to the best of the fish and chicken, but leave him to chuse his own wife. Depend upon it, a man of six or seven-and-twenty can take care of himself.'

CHAPTER TWO

MR WESTON WAS A NATIVE of Highbury, and born of a respectable family, which for the last two or three generations had been rising into gentility and property. He had recieved a good education, but on succeeding early in life to a small independence, had become indisposed for any of the more homely pursuits in which his brothers were engaged; and had satisfied an active cheerful mind and social temper by entering into the militia of his county, then embodied.

Captain Weston was a general favourite; and when the chances of his military life had introduced him to Miss Churchill, of a great Yorkshire family, and Miss Churchill fell in love with him, nobody was surprised except her brother and his wife, who had never seen him, and who were full of pride and importance, which the connection would offend.

Miss Churchill, however, being of age, and with the full command of her fortune – though her fortune bore no proportion to the family-estate – was not to be dissuaded from the marriage, and it took place to the infinite mortification of Mr & Mrs Churchill, who threw her off with due decorum. It was an unsuitable connection, and did not produce much happiness. Mrs Weston ought to have found more in it, for she had a husband whose warm heart and sweet temper made him think every thing due to her in return for the great goodness of being in love with him; but though she had one sort of spirit, she had not the best. She had resolution enough to pursue her own will in spite of her brother, but not enough to refrain from unreasonable regrets at that brother's unreasonable anger, nor from missing the luxuries of her former home. They lived beyond their income, but still it was nothing in comparison of Enscombe: she did not cease to love her husband, but she wanted at once to be the wife of Captain Weston, and Miss Churchill of Enscombe.

Captain Weston, who had been considered, especially by the Churchills, as making such an amazing match, was proved to have much the worst of the bargain; for when his wife died after a three years' marriage, he was rather a poorer man than at 'first, and with a child to maintain. From the expence of the child, however, he was soon relieved. The boy had, with the additional softening claim of a lingering illness of his mother's, been the means of a sort of reconciliation; and Mr and Mrs Churchill, having no children of their own, nor any other young creature of equal kindred to care for, offered to take the whole charge of little Frank soon after her decease. Some scruples and some reluctance the widower-father may be supposed to have felt; but as they were overcome by other considerations, the child was given up to the care and the wealth of the Churchills, and he had only his own comfort to seek and his own situation to improve as he could.

A complete change of life became desirable. He quitted the militia and engaged in trade, having brothers already established in a good way in London, which afforded him a favourable opening. It was a concern which brought just employment enough. He had still a small house in Highbury, where most of his leisure days were spent; and between useful occupation and the pleasures of society, the next eighteen or twenty years of his life passed cheerfully away. He had, by that time, realized an easy competence – enough to secure the purchase of a little estate adjoining Highbury, which he had always longed for – enough to marry a woman as portionless even as Miss Taylor, and to live according to the wishes of his own family and social disposition.

It was now some time since Miss Taylor had begun to influence his schemes; but as it was not the tyrannic influence of youth on youth, it had not shaken his determination of never settling till he could purchase Randalls, and the sale of Randalls was long looked forward to: but he had gone steadily on, with these objects in view, till they were accomplished. He had made his fortune, bought his house, and obtained his wife; and was beginning a new period of existence with every probability of greater happiness than in any yet passed through. He had never been an unhappy man; his own temper had secured him from that, even in his first marriage; but his second must shew him how delightful a well-judging and truly amiable woman could be, and must give him the pleasantest proof of its being a great deal better to chuse than to be chosen, to excite gratitude than to feel it.

He had only himself to please in his choice: his fortune was his own; for as to Frank, it was more than being tacitly brought up as his uncle's heir, it had become so avowed an adoption as to have him assume the name of Churchill on coming of age. It was most unlikely, therefore, that he should ever want his father's assistance. His father had no apprehension of it. The aunt was a capricious woman, and governed her husband entirely; but it was not in Mr Weston's nature to imagine that any caprice could be strong enough to affect one so dear, and, as he believed, so deservedly dear. He saw his son every year in London, and was proud of him; and his fond report of him as a very fine young man had made Highbury feel a sort of pride in him too. He was looked on as sufficiently belonging to the place to make his merit and prospects a kind of common concern.

Mr Frank Churchill was one of the boasts of Highbury, and a lively curiosity to see him prevailed, though the compliment was so little returned that he had never been there in his life. His coming to visit his father had been often talked of but never achieved.

Now, upon his father's marriage, it was very generally proposed, as a most proper attention, that the visit should take place. There

was not a dissentient voice on the subject, either when Mrs Perry
drank tea with Mrs and Miss Bates, or when Mrs and Miss Bates
returned the visit. Now was the time for Mr Frank Churchill to
come among them; and the hope strengthened when it was understood that he had written to his new mother on the occasion. For
a few days every morning visit in Highbury included some mention
of the handsome letter Mrs Weston had received. 'I suppose you
have heard of the handsome letter Mr Frank Churchill had written
to Mrs Weston? I understand it was a very handsome letter, indeed.
Mr Woodhouse told me of it. Mr Woodhouse saw the letter, and
he says he never saw such a handsome letter in his life.'

It was, indeed, a highly-prized letter. Mrs Weston had, of course,
formed a very favourable idea of the young man, and such a pleasing
attention was an irresistible proof of his great good sense, and a
most welcome addition to every source and every expression of
congratulation which her marriage had already secured. She felt
herself a most fortunate woman; and she had lived long enough to
know how fortunate she might well be thought, where the only
regret was for a partial separation from friends, whose friendship
for her had never cooled, and who could ill bear to part with her!

She knew that at times she must be missed; and could not think,
without pain, of Emma's losing a single pleasure, or suffering an
hour's ennui, from the want of her companionableness: but dear
Emma was of no feeble character; she was more equal to her situation than most girls would have been, and had sense and energy
and spirits that might be hoped would bear her well and happily
through its little difficulties and privations. And then there was such
comfort in the very easy distance of Randalls from Hartfield, so
convenient for even solitary female walking, and in Mr Weston's
disposition and circumstances, which would make the approaching
season no hindrance to their spending half the evenings in the week
together.

Her situation was altogether the subject of hours of gratitude to
Mrs Weston, and of moments only of regret; and her satisfaction –
her more than satisfaction – her cheerful enjoyment was just and so
apparent, that Emma, well as she knew her father, was sometimes
taken by surprise at his being still able to pity 'poor Miss Taylor,'
when they left her at Randalls in the centre of every domestic
comfort, or saw her go away in the evening attended by her pleasant
husband to a carriage of her own. But never did she go without Mr
Woodhouse's giving a gentle sigh, and saying:

'Ah! poor Miss Taylor. She would be very glad to stay.'

There was no recovering Miss Taylor – nor much likelihood of ceasing to pity her: but a few weeks brought some alleviation to Mr Woodhouse. The compliments of his neighbours were over; he was no longer teased by being wished joy of so sorrowful an event; and the wedding-cake, which had been a great distress to him, was all eat up. His own stomach could bear nothing rich, and he could never believe other people to be different from himself. What was unwholesome to him, he regarded as unfit for any body; and he had, therefore, earnestly tried to dissuade them from having any wedding-cake at all, and when that proved vain, as earnestly tried to prevent any body's eating it. He had been at the pains of

With a slice of Mrs Weston's wedding-cake.

consulting Mr Perry, the apothecary, on the subject. Mr Perry was an intelligent, gentlemanlike man, whose frequent visits were one of the comforts of Mr Woodhouse's life; and, upon being applied to, he could not but acknowledge, (though it seemed rather against the bias of inclination,) that wedding-cake might certainly disagree with many – perhaps with most people, unless taken moderately. With such an opinion, in confirmation of his own, Mr Woodhouse hoped to influence every visitor of the new-married pair; but still the cake was eaten; and there was no rest for his benevolent nerves till it was all gone.

There was a strange rumour in Highbury of all the little Perrys being seen with a slice of Mrs Weston's wedding-cake in their hands: but Mr Woodhouse would never believe it.

CHAPTER THREE

Mr Woodhouse was fond of society in his own way. He liked very much to have his friends come and see him; and from various united causes, from his long residence at Hartfield, and his good nature, from his fortune, his house, and his daughter, he could command the visits of his own little circle, in a great measure as he liked. He had not much intercourse with any families beyond that circle; his horror of late house and large dinner-parties made him unfit for any acquaintance, but such as would visit him on his own terms. Fortunately for him, Highbury, including Randalls in the same parish, and Donwell Abbey in the parish adjoining, the seat of Mr Knightley, comprehended many such. Not unfrequently, through Emma's persuasion, he had some of the chosen and the best to dine with him, but evening-parties were what he preferred, and, unless he fancied himself at any time unequal to company, there was scarcely an evening in the week in which Emma could not make up a card-table for him.

Real, long-standing regard brought the Westons and Mr Knightley; and by Mr Elton, a young man living alone without liking it, the privilege of exchanging any vacant evening of his own blank solitude for the elegancies and society of Mr Woodhouse's drawing-room and the smiles of his lovely daughter, was in no danger of being thrown away.

After these came a second set; among the most come-at-able of whom were Mrs and Miss Bates and Mrs Goddard, three ladies almost always at the service of an invitation from Hartfield, and who were fetched and carried home so often that Mr Woodhouse thought it no hardship for either James or the horses. Had it taken place only once a year, it would have been a grievance.

Mrs Bates, the widow of a former vicar of Highbury, was a very old lady, almost past every thing but tea and quadrille. She lived with her single daughter in a very small way, and was considered with all the regard and respect which a harmless old lady, under such untoward circumstances, can excite. Her daughter enjoyed a most uncommon degree of popularity for a woman neither young, handsome, rich, nor married. Miss Bates stood in the very worst predicament in the world for having much of the public favour; and she had no intellectual superiority to make atonement to herself, or frighten those who might hate her, into outward respect. She had never boasted either beauty or cleverness. Her youth had passed without distinction, and her middle of life was devoted to the care of a failing mother, and the endeavour to make a small income go as far as possible. And yet she was a happy woman, and a woman whom no one named without good-will. It was her own universal good-will and contented temper which worked such wonders. She loved every body, was interested in every body's happiness, quick-sighted to every body's merits; thought herself a most fortunate creature, and surrounded with blessings in such an excellent mother and so many good neighbours and friends, and a home that wanted for nothing. The simplicity and cheerfulness of her nature, her contented and grateful spirit, were a recommendation to every body and a mine of felicity to herself. She was a great talker upon little matters, which exactly suited Mr Woodhouse, full of trivial communications and harmless gossip.

Mrs Goddard was the mistress of a School – not of a seminary, or an establishment, or any thing which professed, in long sentences of refined nonsense, to combine liberal acquirements with elegant morality upon new principles and new systems – and where young ladies for enormous pay might be screwed out of health and into vanity – but a real, honest, old-fashioned Boarding-school, where a reasonable quantity of accomplishments were sold at a reasonable price, and where girls might be sent to be out of the way and scramble themselves into a little education, without any danger of coming back prodigies. Mrs Goddard's school was in high repute – and very deservedly; for Highbury was reckoned a particularly healthy spot; she had an ample house and garden, gave the children plenty of wholesome food, let them run about a great deal in the summer, and in winter dressed their chilblains with her own hands.

It was no wonder that a train of twenty young couple now walked after her to church. She was a plain, motherly kind of woman, who had worked hard in her youth, and now thought herself entitled to the occasional holiday of a tea-visit; and having formerly owed much to Mr Woodhouse's kindness, felt his particular claim on her to leave her neat parlour hung round with fancy-work whenever she could, and win or lose a few sixpences by his fireside.

These were the ladies whom Emma found herself very frequently able to collect; and happy was she, for her father's sake, in the power; though, as far as she was herself concerned, it was no remedy for the absence of Mrs Weston. She was delighted to see her father look comfortable, and very much pleased with herself for contriving things so well; but the quiet prosings of three such women made her feel that every evening so spent, was indeed one of the long evenings she had fearfully anticipated.

As she sat one morning, looking forward to exactly such a close of the present day, a note was brought from Mrs Goddard, requesting, in most respectful terms, to be allowed to bring Miss Smith with her; a most welcome request: for Miss Smith was a girl of seventeen whom Emma knew very well by sight and had long felt an interest in, on account of her beauty. A very gracious invitation was returned, and the evening no longer dreaded by the fair mistress of the mansion.

Harriet Smith was the natural daughter of somebody. Somebody had placed her, several years back, at Mrs Goddard's school, and somebody had lately raised her from the condition of scholar to that of parlour-boarder. This was all that was generally known of her history. She had no visible friends but what had been acquired at Highbury, and was now just returned from a long visit in the country to some young ladies who had been at school there with her.

She was a very pretty girl, and her beauty happened to be of a sort which Emma particularly admired. She was short, plump and fair, with a fine bloom, blue eyes, light hair, regular features, and a look of great sweetness; and before the end of the evening, Emma was as much pleased with her manners as her person, and quite determined to continue the acquaintance.

She was not struck by any thing remarkably clever in Miss Smith's conversation, but she found her altogether engaging – not inconveniently shy, not unwilling to talk – and yet so far from pushing, shewing so proper and becoming a deference, seeming so pleasantly grateful for being admitted to Hartfield, and so artlessly impressed by the appearance of every thing in so superior a style to what she had been used to, that she must have good sense and deserve encouragement. Encouragement should be given. Those soft blue eyes and all those natural graces should not be wasted on the inferior society of Highbury and its connections. The acquaintance she had already formed were unworthy of her. The friends from whom she had just parted, though very good sort of people, must be doing her harm. They were a family of the name of Martin, whom Emma well knew by character, as renting a large farm of Mr Knightley, and residing in the parish of Donwell – very creditably she believed – she knew Mr Knightley thought highly of them – but they must be coarse and unpolished, and very unfit to be the intimates of a girl who wanted only a little more knowledge and elegance to be quite perfect. *She* would notice her; she would improve her; she would detach her from her bad acquaintance, and introduce her into good society; she would inform her opinions and her manners. It would be an interesting, and certainly a very kind undertaking; highly becoming her own situation in life, her leisure, and powers.

She was so busy in admiring those soft blue eyes, in talking and listening, and forming all these schemes in the in-betweens, that the evening flew away at a very unusual rate; and the supper-table, which always closed such parties, and for which she had been used to sit and watch the due time, was all set out and ready, and moved forwards to the fire, before she was aware. With an alacrity beyond the common impulse of a spirit which yet was never indifferent to the credit of doing every thing well and attentively, with the real good-will of a mind delighted with its own ideas, did she then do all the honours of the meal, and help and recommend the minced chicken and scalloped oysters with an urgency which she knew would be acceptable to the early hours and civil scruples of their guests.

Upon such occasions poor Mr Woodhouse's feelings were in sad warfare. He loved to have the cloth laid, because it had been the fashion of his youth; but this conviction of suppers being very unwholesome made him rather sorry to see any thing put on it; and while his hospitality would have welcomed his visitors to every thing, his care for their health made him grieve that they would eat.

Such another small basin of thin gruel as his own, was all that he could, with thorough self-approbation, recommend, though he might constrain himself, while the ladies were comfortably clearing the nicer things, to say:

'Mrs Bates, let me propose your venturing on one of these eggs. An egg boiled very soft is not unwholesome. Serle understands boiling an egg better than anybody. I would not recommend an egg boiled by any body else – but you need not be afraid – they are very small, you see – one of our small eggs will not hurt you. Miss Bates, let Emma help you to a *little* bit of tart – a *very* little bit. Ours are all apple tarts. You need not be afraid of unwholesome preserves here. I do not advise the custard. Mrs Goddard, what say you to *half* a glass of wine? A *small* half glass – put into a tumbler of water? I do not think it could disagree with you.'

Emma allowed her father to talk – but supplied her visitors in a much more satisfactory style, and on the present evening had particular pleasure in sending them away happy. The happiness of Miss Smith was quite equal to her intentions. Miss Woodhouse was so great a personage in Highbury, that the prospect of the introduction had given as much panic as pleasure – but the humble, grateful, little girl went off with highly gratified feelings, delighted with the affability with which Miss Woodhouse had treated her all the evening, and actually shaken hands with her at last!

CHAPTER FOUR

HARRIET SMITH'S INTIMACY at Hartfield was soon a settled thing. Quick and decided in her ways, Emma lost no time in inviting, encouraging, and telling her to come very often; and as their acquaintance increased, so did their satisfaction in each other. As a walking companion, Emma had very early forseen how useful she might find her. In that respect Mrs Weston's loss had been important. Her father never went beyond the shrubbery, where two divisions of the grounds sufficed him for his long walk, or his short, as the year varied; and since Mrs Weston's marriage her exercise had been too much confined. She had ventured once alone to Randalls, but it was not pleasant; and a Harriet Smith, therefore, one whom she could summon at any time to a walk, would be a valuable addition to her privileges. But in every respect as she saw more of her, she approved her, and was confirmed in all her kind designs.

Harriet certainly was not clever, but she had a sweet, docile, grateful disposition; was totally free from conceit; and only desiring to be guided by any one she looked up to. Her early attachment to herself was very amiable; and her inclination for good company, and power of appreciating what was elegant and clever, shewed that there was no want of taste, though strength of understanding must not be expected. Altogether she was quite convinced of Harriet

Smith's being exactly the young friend she wanted – exactly the something which her home required. Such a friend as Mrs Weston was out of the question. Two such could never be granted. Two such she did not want. It was quite a different sort of thing – a sentiment distinct and independent. Mrs Weston was the object of a regard, which had its basis in gratitude and esteem. Harriet would be loved as one to whom she could be useful. For Mrs Weston there was nothing to be done; for Harriet every thing.

Her first attempts at usefulness were in an endeavour to find out who were the parents; but Harriet could not tell. She was ready to tell every thing in her power, but on this subject questions were vain. Emma was obliged to fancy what she liked – but she could never believe that in the same situation *she* should not have discovered the truth. Harriet had no penetration. She had been satisfied to hear and believe just what Mrs Goddard chose to tell her; and looked no farther.

Mrs Goddard, and the teachers, and the girls, and the affairs of the school in general, formed naturally a great part of her conversation – and but for her acquaintance with the Martins of Abbey-Mill-Farm, it must have been the whole. But the Martins occupied her thoughts a good deal; she had spent two very happy months with them, and now loved to talk of the pleasures of her visit, and describe the many comforts and wonders of the place. Emma encouraged her talkativeness – amused by such a picture of another set of beings, and enjoying the youthful simplicity which could speak with so much exultation of Mrs Martin's having '*two* parlours, two very good parlours indeed; one of them quite as large as Mrs Goddard's drawing-room; and of her having an upper maid who had lived five-and-twenty years with her; and of their having eight cows, two of them Alderneys, and one a little Welch cow, a very pretty little Welch cow, indeed; and of Mrs Martin's saying, as she was so fond of it, it should be called *her* cow; and of their having a very handsome summer-house in their garden, where some day next year they were all to drink tea: – a very handsome summer-house, large enough to hold a dozen people.'

For some time she was amused, without thinking beyond the immediate cause; but as she came to understand the family better, other feelings arose. She had taken up a wrong idea, fancying it was a mother and daughter, a son and son's wife, who all lived together; but when it appeared that the Mr Martin, who bore a part in the narrative, and was always mentioned with approbation for his great good-nature in doing something or other, was a single man; that there was no young Mrs Martin, no wife in the case; she did suspect danger to her poor little friend from all this hospitality and kindness – and that if she were not taken care of, she might be required to sink herself for ever.

With this inspiriting notion, her questions increased in number and meaning; and she particularly led Harriet to talk more of Mr Martin, – and there was evidently no dislike to. Harriet was very ready to speak of the share he had had in their moonlight walks and merry evening games; and dwelt a good deal upon his being so very good-humoured and obliging. 'He had gone three miles round one day, in order to bring her some walnuts, because she had said how fond she was of them – and in every thing else he was so very obliging! He had his shepherd's son into the parlour one night on purpose to sing to her. She was very fond of singing. He could sing a little himself. She believed he was very clever, and understood every thing. He had a very fine flock, and while she was with them, he had been bid more for his wool than any body in the country. She believed every body spoke well of him. His mother and sisters were very fond of him. Mrs Martin had told her one day, (and there was a blush as she said it,) that it was impossible for any body to be a better son; and therefore she was sure whenever he married he would make a good husband. Not that she *wanted* him to marry. She was in no hurry at all.'

'Well done, Mrs Martin!' thought Emma. 'You know what you are about.'

'And when she had come away, Mrs Martin was so very kind as to send Mrs Goddard a beautiful goose: the finest goose Mrs Goddard had ever seen. Mrs Goddard had dressed it on a Sunday, and asked all the three teachers, Miss Nash, and Miss Prince, and Miss Richardson, to sup with her.'

'Mr Martin, I suppose, is not a man of information beyond the line of his own business. He does not read?'

'Oh, yes! – that is, no – I do not know – but I believe he has read a good deal – but not what you would think any thing of. He reads the Agricultural Reports and some other books, that lay in one of the window seats – but he reads all *them* to himself. But sometimes of an evening, before we went to cards, he would read something aloud out of the Elegant Extracts – very entertaining. And I know he has read the Vicar of Wakefield. He never read the Romance of the Forest, nor the Children of the Abbey. He had never heard of such books before I mentioned them, but he is determined to get them now as soon as ever he can.'

The next question was:

'What sort of looking man is Mr Martin?'

'Oh! not handsome – not at all handsome. I thought him very plain at first, but I do not think him so plain now. One does not, you know, after a time. But, did you never see him? He is in Highbury every now and then, and he is sure to ride through every week in his way to Kingston. He has passed you very often.'

'That may be – and I may have seen him fifty times, but without having any idea of his name. A young farmer, whether on horseback or on foot, is the very last sort of person to raise my curiosity. The yeomanry are precisely the order of people with whom I feel I can have nothing to do. A degree or two lower, and a creditable appearance might interest me; I might hope to be useful to their families in some way or other. But a farmer can need none of my help, and is therefore in one sense as much above my notice as in every other he is below it.'

'To be sure. Oh! yes, it is not likely you should ever have observed him – but he knows you very well indeed – I mean by sight.'

'I have no doubt of his being a very respectable young man. I know indeed that he is so; and as such wish him well. What do you imagine his age to be?'

'He was four-and twenty the 8th of last June, and my birth-day is the 23rd – just a fortnight and a day's difference! which is very odd!'

'Only four-and-twenty. That is too young to settle. His mother is perfectly right not to be in a hurry. They seem very comfortable as they are, and if she were to take any pains to marry him, she would probably repent it. Six years hence, if he could meet with a good sort of young woman in the same rank as his own, with a little money, it might be very desirable.'

'Six years hence! dear Miss Woodhouse, he would be thirty years old!'

'Well, and that is as early as most men can afford to marry, who are not born to an independence. Mr Martin, I imagine, has his fortune entirely to make – cannot be at all beforehand with the world. Whatever money he might come into when his father died, whatever his share of the family property, it is, I dare say, all afloat, all employed in his stock, and so forth; and though, with diligence and good luck, he may be rich in time, it is next to impossible that he should have realised any thing yet.'

'To be sure, so it is. But they live very comfortably. They have no in-doors man – else they do not want for any thing; and Mrs Martin talks of taking a boy another year.'

'I wish you may not get into a scrape, Harriet, whenever he does marry; – I mean as to being acquainted with his wife – for though his sisters, from a superior education, are not to be altogether objected to, it does not follow that he might marry any body at all fit for you to notice. The misfortune of your birth ought to make you particularly careful as to your associates. There can be no doubt of your being a gentleman's daughter, and you must support your claim to that station by every thing within your own power, or there will be plenty of people who would take pleasure in degrading you.'

'Yes, to be sure – I suppose there are. But while I visit at Hartfield, and you are so kind to me, Miss Woodhouse, I am not afraid of what any body can do.'

'You understand the force of influence pretty well, Harriet; but I would have you so firmly established in good society, as to be independent even of Hartfield and Miss Woodhouse. I want to see you permanently well connected – and to that end it will be advisable to have as few odd acquaintance as may be; and, therefore, I say that if you should still be in this country when Mr Martin marries, I wish you may not be drawn in, by your intimacy with the sisters, to be acquainted with the wife, who will probably be some mere farmer's daughter, without education.'

'To be sure. Yes. Not that I think Mr Martin would ever marry any body but what had had some education – and been very well brought up. However, I do not mean to set up my opinion against your's – and I am sure I shall not wish for the acquaintance of his wife. I shall always have a great regard for the Miss Martins, especially Elizabeth, and should be very sorry to give them up, for they are quite as well educated as me. But if he married a very ignorant, vulgar woman, certainly I had better not visit her, if I can help it.'

Emma watched her through the fluctuations of this speech, and saw no alarming symptoms of love. The young man had been the first admirer, but she trusted there was no other hold, and that there would be no serious difficulty on Harriet's side to oppose any friendly arrangement of her own.

They met Mr Martin the very next day, as they were walking on the Donwell Road. He was on foot, and after looking very respectfully at her, looked with most unfeigned satisfaction at her companion. Emma was not sorry to have such an opportunity of survey; and walking a few yards forward, while they talked together, soon made her quick eye sufficiently acquainted with Mr Robert Martin. His appearance was very neat, and he looked like a sensible young man, but his person had no other advantage; and when he came to be contrasted with gentlemen, she thought he

Emma was not sorry to have such an opportunity of survey.

must lose all the ground he had gained in Harriet's inclination. Harriet was not insensible of manner; she had voluntarily noticed her father's gentleness with admiration as well as wonder. Mr Martin looked as if he did not know what manner was.

They remained but a few minutes together, as Miss Woodhouse must not be kept waiting; and Harriet then came running to her with a smiling face, and in a flutter of spirits, which Miss Wood-house hoped very soon to compose.

'Only think of our happening to meet him! – How very odd! It was quite a chance, he said, that he had not gone round by Randalls. He did not think we ever walked this road. He thought we walked towards Randalls most days. He has not been able to get the Romance of the Forest yet. He was so busy the last time he was at Kingston that he quite forgot it, but he goes again to-morrow. So very odd we should happen to meet! Well, Miss Woodhouse, is he like what you expected? What do you think of him? Do you think him so very plain?'

'He is very plain, undoubtedly – remarkably plain: – but that is nothing, compared with his entire want of gentility. I had no right to expect much, and I did not expect much; but I had no idea that he could be so very clownish, so totally without air. I had imagined him, I confess, a degree or two nearer gentility.'

'To be sure,' said Harriet, in a mortified voice, 'he is not so genteel as real gentlemen.'

'I think, Harriet, since your acquaintance with us, you have been repeatedly in the company of some, such very real gentlemen, that you must yourself be struck with the difference in Mr Martin. At Hartfield you have had very good specimens of well educated, well bred men. I should be surprized if, after seeing them, you could be in company with Mr Martin again without perceiving him to be a very inferior creature – and rather wondering at yourself for having ever thought him at all agreeable before. Do not you begin to feel that now? Were not you struck? I am sure you must have been struck by his awkward look and abrupt manner – and the uncouthness of voice, which I heard to be wholly unmodulated as I stood here.'

'Certainly, he is not like Mr Knightley. He has not such a fine air and way of walking as Mr Knightley. I see the difference plain enough. But Mr Knightley is so very fine a man!'

'Mr Knightley's air is so remarkably good, that it is not fair to compare Mr Martin with *him*. You might not see one in a hundred, with *gentleman* so plainly written as in Mr Knightley. But he is not the only gentleman you have been lately used to. What say you to Mr Weston and Mr Elton? Compare Mr Martin with either of *them*. Compare their manner of carrying themselves; of walking; speaking; of being silent. You must see the difference.'

'Oh, yes! – there is a great difference. But Mr Weston is almost an old man. Mr Weston must be between forty and fifty.'

'Which makes his good manners the more valuable. The older a person grows, Harriet, the more important it is that their manners should not be bad – the more glaring and disgusting any loudness, or coarseness, or awkwardness becomes. What is passable in youth, is detestable in later age. Mr Martin is now awkward and abrupt; what will he be at Mr Weston's time of life?'

'There is no saying, indeed!' replied Harriet, rather solemnly.

'But there may be pretty good guessing. He will be a completely gross, vulgar farmer – totally inattentive to appearances, and thinking of nothing but profit and loss.'

'Will he, indeed, that will be very bad.'

'How much his business engrosses him already, is very plain from the circumstances of his forgetting to enquire for the book you recommended. He was a great deal too full of the market to think of any thing else – which is just as it should be, for a thriving man. What has he to do with books? And I have no doubt that he *will* thrive and be a very rich man in time – and his being illiterate and coarse need not disturb *us*.'

'I wonder he did not remember the book' – was all Harriet's answer, and spoken with a degree of grave displeasure which Emma thought might be safely left to itself. She, therefore, said no more for some time. Her next beginning was,

'In one respect, perhaps, Mr Elton's manners are superior to Mr Knightley's or Mr Weston's. They have more gentleness. They might be more safely held up as a pattern. There is an openness, quickness, almost a bluntness in Mr Weston, which every body likes in *him* because there is so much good humour with it – but that would not do to be copied. Neither would Mr Knightley's down-right, decided, commanding sort of manner – though it suits *him* very well; his figure and look, and situation in life seem to allow it; but if any young man were to set about copying him, he would not be sufferable. On the contrary, I think a young man might be very safely recommended to take Mr Elton as a model. Mr Elton is good humoured, cheerful, obliging, and gentle. He seems to me, to be grown particularly gentle of late. I do not know whether he has any design of ingratiating himself with either of us, Harriet, by additional softness, but it strikes me that his manners are softer than they used to be. If he means anything, it must be to please you. Did not I tell you what he said of you the other day?'

She then repeated some warm personal praise which she had drawn from Mr Elton, and now did full justice to; and Harriet blushed and smiled, and said she had always thought Mr Elton very agreeable.

Mr Elton was the very person fixed on by Emma for driving the young farmer out of Harriet's head. She thought it would be an excellent match; and only too palpably desirable, natural, and prob-able, for her to have much merit in planning it. She feared it was what every body else must think of and predict. It was not likely, however, that any body should have equalled her in the date of the plan, as it had entered her brain during the very first evening of Harriet's coming to Hartfield. The longer she considered it, the greater was her sense of its expediency. Mr Elton's situation was most suitable, quite the gentleman himself, and without low connections; at the same time not of any family that could fairly object to the doubtful birth of Harriet. He had a comfortable home for her, and Emma imagined a very sufficient income; for though the vicarage of Highbury was not large, he was known to have some independent property; and she thought very highly of him as a good-humoured, well-meaning, respectable young man, without any deficiency of useful understanding or knowledge of the world.

She had already satisfied herself that he thought Harriet a beautiful girl, which she trusted, with such frequent meetings at Hartfield, was foundation enough on his side; and on Harriet's, there could be little doubt that the idea of being preferred by him would have all the usual weight and efficacy. And he was really a very pleasing young man, a young man whom any woman not fastidious might like. He was reckoned very handsome; his person much admired in general, though not by her, there being a want of elegance of feature which she could not dispense with: – but the girl who could be gratified by a Robert Martin's riding about the country to get walnuts for her, might very well be conquered by Mr Elton's admiration.

CHAPTER FIVE

'I DO NOT KNOW WHAT your opinion may be, Mrs Weston,' said Mr Knightley, 'of this great intimacy between Emma and Harriet Smith, but I think it a bad thing.'

'A bad thing! Do you really think it a bad thing? – why so?'

'I think they will neither of them do the other any good.'

'You surprize me! Emma must do Harriet good: and by supplying her with a new object of interest, Harriet may be said to do Emma good. I have been seeing their intimacy with the greatest pleasure. How very differently we feel! – Not think they will do each other any good! This will certainly be the beginning of one of our quarrels about Emma, Mr Knightley.'

'Perhaps you think I am come on purpose to quarrel with you, knowing Weston to be out, and that you must still fight your own battle.'

'Mr Weston would undoubtedly support me, if he were here, for he thinks exactly as I do on the subject. We were speaking of it only yesterday, and agreeing how fortunate it was for Emma, that there should be such a girl in Highbury for her to associate with. Mr Knightley, I shall not allow you to be a fair judge in this case. You are so much used to live alone, that you do not know the value of a companion; and perhaps no man can be a good judge of the comfort a woman feels in the society of one of her own sex, after being used to it all her life. I can imagine your objection to Harriet Smith. She is not the superior young woman which Emma's friend ought to be. But on the other hand, as Emma wants to see her better informed, it will be an inducement to her to read more herself. They will read together. She means it, I know.'

'Emma has been meaning to read more ever since she was twelve years old. I have seen a great many lists of her drawing up at various times of books that she meant to read regularly through – and very good lists they were – very well chosen, and very neatly arranged – sometimes alphabetically, and sometimes by some other rule. The list she drew up when only fourteen – I remember thinking it did her judgment so much credit, that I preserved it some time; and I dare say she may have made out a very good list now. But I have done with expecting any course of steady reading from Emma. She will never submit to any thing requiring industry and patience, and a subjection of the fancy to the understanding. Where Miss Taylor failed to stimulate, I may safely affirm that Harriet Smith will do nothing. – You could never persuade her to read half so much as you wished. – You know you could not.'

'I dare say,' replied Mrs Weston, smiling, 'that I thought so *then*; – but since we have parted, I can never remember Emma's omitting to do any thing I wished.'

'There is hardly any desiring to refresh such a memory as *that*' said Mr Knightley, feelingly; and for a moment or two he had done. 'But I,' he soon added, 'who have had no such charm thrown over my senses, must still see, hear, and remember. Emma is spoiled by being the cleverest of her family. At ten years old, she had the misfortune of being able to answer questions which puzzled her sister at seventeen. She was always quick and assured, Isabella slow and diffident. And ever since she was twelve, Emma has been mistress of the house and of you all. In her mother she lost the only person able to cope with her. She inherits her mother's talents, and must have been under subjection to her.'

'I should have been sorry, Mr Knightley, to be dependent on *your* recommendation, had I quitted Mr Woodhouse's family and wanted another situation; I do not think you would have spoken a good word for me to any body. I am sure you always thought me unfit for the office I held.'

'Yes,' he said, smiling. 'You are better placed *here*; very fit for a wife, but not at all for a governess. But you were preparing yourself to be an excellent wife all the time you were at Hartfield. You might not give Emma such a complete education as your powers would seem to promise; but you were receiving a very good education from *her*, on the very material matrimonial point of submitting your own will, and doing as you were bid; and if Weston had asked me to recommend him a wife, I should certainly have named Miss Taylor.'

'Thank you. There will be very little merit in making a good wife to such a man as Mr Weston.'

'Why, to own the truth, I am afraid you are rather thrown away, and that with every disposition to bear, there will be nothing to be borne. We will not despair, however. Weston may grow cross from the wantonness of comfort, or his son may plague him.'

'I hope not *that*. – It is not likely. No, Mr Knightley, do not foretell vexation from that quarter.'

'Not I, indeed. I only name possibilities. I do not pretend to Emma's genius for foretelling and guessing. I hope, with all my heart, the young man may be a Weston in merit, and a Churchill in fortune. – But Harriet Smith – I have not half done about Harriet Smith. I think her the very worst sort of companion that Emma could possibly have. She knows nothing herself, and looks upon Emma as knowing every thing. She is a flatterer in all her ways; and so much the worse, because undesigned. Her ignorance is hourly flattery. How can Emma imagine she has anything to learn herself, while Harriet is presenting such a delightful inferiority? And as for Harriet, I will venture to say that *she* cannot gain by the acquaintance. Hartfield will only put her out of conceit with all the other places she belongs to. She will grow just refined enough to be uncomfortable with those among whom birth and circumstances have placed her home. I am much mistaken if Emma's doctrines give any strength of mind, or tend at all to make a girl adapt herself rationally to the varieties of her situation in life. – They only give a little polish.'

'I either depend more upon Emma's good sense than you do, or am more anxious for her present comfort; for I cannot lament the acquaintance. How well she looked last night!'

'Oh! you would rather talk of her person than her mind, would you? Very well; I shall not attempt to deny Emma's being pretty.'

'Pretty! say beautiful rather. Can you imagine any thing nearer perfect beauty than Emma altogether – face and figure?'

'I do not know what I could imagine, but I confess that I have seldom seen a face or figure more pleasing to me than her's. But I am a partial old friend.'

'Such an eye! – the true hazle eye – and so brilliant! regular features, open countenance, with a complexion! oh! what a bloom of full health, and such a pretty height and size; such a firm and upright figure. There is health, not merely in her bloom, but in her air, her head, her glance. One hears sometimes of a child being 'the picture of health;' now Emma always gives me the idea of being the complete picture of grown-up health. She is loveliness itself. Mr Knightley, is not she?'

'I have not a fault to find with her person,' he replied. 'I think her all you describe. I love to look at her; and I will add this praise, that I do not think her personally vain. Considering how very handsome she is, she appears to be little occupied with it; her vanity lies another way. Mrs Weston, I am not to be talked out of my dislike of her intimacy with Harriet Smith, or my dread of its doing them both harm.'

'And I, Mr Knightley, am equally stout in my confidence of its not doing them any harm. With all dear Emma's little faults, she is an excellent creature. Where shall we see a better daughter, or a kinder sister, or a truer friend? No, no; she has qualities which may be trusted; she will never lead any one really wrong; she will make no lasting blunder; where Emma errs once, she is in the right a hundred times.'

'Very well; I will not plague you any more. Emma shall be an angel, and I will keep my spleen to myself till Christmas brings John and Isabella. John loves Emma with a reasonable and therefore not a blind affection, and Isabella always thinks as he does; except when he is not quite frightened enough about the children. I am sure of having their opinions with me.'

'I know that you all love her really too well to be unjust or unkind; but excuse me, Mr Knightley, if I take the liberty (I consider myself, you know, as having somewhat of the privilege of speech that Emma's mother might have had) the liberty of hinting that I do not think any possible good can arise from Harriet Smith's intimacy being made a matter of much discussion among you. Pray excuse me; but supposing any little inconvenience may be apprehended from the intimacy, it cannot be expected that Emma, accountable to nobody but her father, who perfectly approves the acquaintance, should put an end to it, so long as it is a source of pleasure to herself. It has been so many years my province to give advice, that you cannot be surprized, Mr Knightley, at this little remains of office.'

'Not at all,' cried he; 'I am much obliged to you for it. It is very good advice, and it shall have a better fate than your advice has often found; for it shall be attended to.'

'Mrs John Knightley is easily alarmed, and might be made unhappy about her sister.'

'Be satisfied,' said he, 'I will not raise any outcry. I will keep my ill-humour to myself. I have a very sincere interest in Emma. Isabella does not seem more my sister; has never excited a greater interest; perhaps hardly so great. There is an anxiety, a curiosity in what one feels for Emma. I wonder what will become of her!'

'So do I,' said Mrs Weston gently; 'very much.'

'She always declares she will never marry, which, of course, means just nothing at all. But I have no idea that she has yet ever seen a man she cared for. It would not be a bad thing for her to be very much in love with a proper object. I should like to see Emma in love, and in some doubt of a return; it would do her good. But there is nobody hereabouts to attach her; and she goes so seldom from home.'

'There does, indeed, seem as little to tempt her to break her resolution, at present,' said Mrs Weston, 'as can well be; and while she is so happy at Hartfield, I cannot wish her to be forming any attachment which would be creating such difficulties, on poor Mr Woodhouse's account. I do not recommend matrimony at present to Emma, though I mean no slight to the state I assure you.'

Part of her meaning was to conceal some favourite thoughts of her own and Mr Weston's on the subject, as much as possible. There were wishes at Randalls respecting Emma's destiny, but it was not desirable to have them suspected; and the quiet transition which Mr Knightley soon afterwards made to 'What does Weston think of the weather; shall we have rain?' convinced her that he had nothing more to say or surmise about Hartfield.

CHAPTER SIX

EMMA COULD NOT FEEL a doubt of having given Harriet's fancy a proper direction and raised the gratitude of her young vanity to a very good purpose, for she found her decidedly more sensible than before of Mr Elton's being a remarkably handsome young man, with most agreeable manners; and as she had no hesitation in following up the assurance of his admiration, by agreeable hints, she was soon pretty confident of creating as much liking on Harriet's side, as there could be any occasion for. She was quite convinced of Mr Elton's being in the fairest way of falling in love, if not in love already. She had no scruple with regard to him. He talked of Harriet, and praised her so warmly, that she could not suppose any thing wanting which a little time would not add. His perception of the striking improvement of Harriet's manner, since her introduction at Hartfield, was not one of the least agreeable proofs of his growing attachment.

'You have given Miss Smith all that she required,' said he; 'you have made her graceful and easy. She was a beautiful creature when she came to you, but, in my opinion, the attractions you have added are infinitely superior to what she received from nature.'

'I am glad you think I have been useful to her; but Harriet only wanted drawing out, and receiving a few, very few hints. She had all the natural grace of sweetness of temper and artlessness in herself. I have done very little.'

'If it were admissible to contradict a lady,' said the gallant Mr Elton –

'I have perhaps given her a little more decision of character, have taught her to think on points which had not fallen in her way before.'

'Exactly so; that is what principally strikes me. So much super-added decision of character! Skilful has been the hand.'

'Great has been the pleasure, I am sure. I never met with a disposition more truly amiable.'

'I have no doubt of it.' And it was spoken with a sort of sighing animation, which had a vast deal of the lover. She was not less pleased another day with the manner in which he seconded a sudden wish of her's, to have Harriet's picture.

'Did you ever have your likeness taken, Harriet?' said she: 'Did you ever sit for your picture?'

Harriet was on the point of leaving the room, and only stopt to say, with a very interesting naïveté,

'Oh! dear, no, never.'

No sooner was she out of sight, than Emma exclaimed,

'What an exquisite possession a good picture of her would be! I would give any money for it. I almost long to attempt her likeness myself. You do not know it I dare say, but two or three years ago I had a great passion for taking likenesses, and attempted several of my friends and was thought to have a tolerable eye in general. But from one cause or another, I gave it up in disgust. But really, I could almost venture, if Harriet would sit to me. It would be a delight to have her picture!'

'Let me entreat you,' cried Mr Elton; 'it would indeed be a delight! Let me entreat you, Miss Woodhouse, to exercise so charming a talent in favour of your friend. I know what your drawings are. How could you suppose me ignorant? Is not this room rich in specimens of your landscapes and flowers; and has not Mrs Weston some inimitable figure-pieces in her drawing-room, at Randalls?'

Yes, good man! – thought Emma – but what has all that to do with taking likenesses? You know nothing of drawing. Don't pretend to be in raptures about mine. Keep your raptures for Harriet's face. 'Well, if you give me such kind encouragement, Mr. Elton, I believe I shall try what I can do. Harriet's features are very delicate, which makes a likeness difficult; and yet there is a peculiarity in the shape of the eye and the lines about the mouth which one ought to catch.'

'Exactly so – The shape of the eye and the lines about the mouth – I have not a doubt of your success. Pray, pray attempt it. As you will do, it will indeed, to use your own words, be an exquisite possession.'

'But I am afraid, Mr Elton, Harriet will not like to sit. She thinks so little of her own beauty. Did not you observe her manner of answering me? How completely it meant, "why should my picture be drawn?" '

'Oh! yes, I observed it, I assure you. It was not lost on me. But still I cannot imagine she would not be persuaded.'

Harriet was soon back again, and the proposal almost immediately made; and she had no scruples which could stand many minutes against the earnest pressing of both the others. Emma wished to go to work directly, and therefore produced the portfolio containing her various attempts at portraits, for not one of them had ever been finished, that they might decide together on the best size for Harriet. Her many beginnings were displayed. Minatures, half-lengths, whole lengths, pencil, crayon, and water-colours had been all tried in turn. She had always wanted to do everything, and had made more progress both in drawing and music than many might have done with so little labour as she would ever submit to. She played and sang; – and drew in almost every style; but steadiness had always been wanting; and in nothing had she approached the degree of excellence which she would have been glad to command, and ought not to have failed of. She was not much deceived as to her own skill, either as an artist or a musician, but she was not unwilling to have others deceived, or sorry to know her reputation for accomplishment often higher than it deserved.

There was merit in every drawing – in the least finished, perhaps the most; her style was spirited; but had there been much less, or had there been ten times more, the delight and admiration of her two companions would have been the same. They were both in extasies. A likeness pleases every body, and Miss Woodhouse's performances must be capital.

'No great variety of faces for you,' said Emma. 'I had only my own family to study from. There is my father – another of my father – but the idea of sitting for his picture made him so nervous, that I could only take him by stealth; neither of them very like therefore. Mrs Weston again, and again, and again, you see. Dear Mrs Weston! always my kindest friend on every occasion. She would sit whenever I asked her. There is my sister; and really quite her own little elegant figure! – and the face not unlike. I should have made a good likeness of her, if she would have sat longer, but she was in such a hurry to have me draw her four children that she would not be quiet. Then, here come all my attempts at three of those four children; – there they are, Henry and John and Bella, from one end of the sheet to the other; and any one of them might do for any of the rest. She was so eager to have them drawn that I could not refuse; but there is no making children of three or four years old stand still you know; nor can it be very easy to take any likeness of them, beyond the air and complexion, unless they are coarser featured than any mama's children ever were. Here is my sketch of the fourth, who was a baby. I took him, as he was sleeping on the sofa, and it is as strong a likeness of his cockade as you would wish to see. He had nestled down his head most conveniently. That's very like. I am rather proud of little George. The corner of the sofa is very good. Then here is my last' – unclosing a pretty sketch of a gentleman in small size, whole-length – 'my last and my best – my brother, Mr John Knightley. – This did not want much of being finished, when I put it away in a pet, and vowed I would never take another likeness. I could not help being provoked; for after all my pains, and when I had really made a very good likeness of it – (Mrs Weston and I were quite agreed in thinking if *very* like) – only too handsome – too flattering – but that was a fault on the right side – after all this, came poor dear Isabella's cold approbation of – 'Yes, it was a little like – but to be sure it did not do him justice.' We had had a great deal of trouble in persuading him to sit at all. It was made a great favour of; and altogether it was more than I could bear; and so I never would finish it, to have it apologized over as an unfavourable likeness, to every morning visitor in Brunswick-square; – and, as I said, I did then forswear ever drawing anybody again. But for Harriet's sake, or rather for my own, and as there are no husbands and wives in the case at present, I will break my resolution now.'

Mr Elton seemed very properly struck and delighted by the idea, and was repeating, 'No husbands and wives in the case *at present* indeed, as you observe. Exactly so. No husbands and wives,' with so interesting a consciousness, that Emma began to consider whether she had not better leave them together at once. But as she wanted to be drawing, the declaration must wait a little longer.

She had soon fixed on the size and sort of portrait. It was to be a whole-length in water-colours, like Mr John Knightley's, and was destined, if she could please herself, to hold a very honourable station over the mantlepiece.

The sitting began; and Harriet, smiling and blushing, and afraid of not keeping her attitude and countenance, presented a very sweet mixture of youthful expression to the steady eyes of the artist. But there was no doing anything, with Mr Elton fidgeting behind her and watching every touch. She gave him credit for stationing himself where he might gaze and gaze again without offence; but was really obliged to put an end to it, and request him to place himself elsewhere. It then occurred to her to employ him in reading.

'If he would be so good as to read to them, it would be a kindness indeed! It would amuse away the difficulties of her part, and lessen the irksomeness of Miss Smith's.'

Mr Elton was only too happy. Harriet listened, and Emma drew in peace. She must allow him to be still frequently coming to look; anything less would certainly have been too little in a lover; and he was ready at the smallest intermission of the pencil, to jump up and see the progress, and be charmed. – There was no being displeased with such an encourager, for his admiration made him discern a likeness almost before it was possible. She could not respect his eye, but his love and his complaisance were unexceptionable.

The sitting was altogether very satisfactory; she was quite enough pleased with the first day's sketch to wish to go on. There was no want of likeness, she had been fortunate in the attitude, and as she meant to throw in a little improvement to the figure, to give a little more height, and considerably more elegance, she had great confidence of its being in every way a pretty drawing at last, and of its filling its destined place with credit to them both – a standing memorial of the beauty of one, the skill of the other, and the friendship of both; with as many other agreeable associations as Mr Elton's very promising attachment was likely to add.

Ready to jump up and see the progress.

Harriet was to sit again the next day; and Mr Elton, just as he ought, entreated for the permission of attending and reading to them again.

'By all means. We shall be most happy to consider you as one of the party.'

The same civilities and courtesies, the same success and satisfaction, took place on the morrow, and accompanied the whole progress of the picture, which was rapid and happy. Every body who saw it was pleased, but Mr Elton was in continual raptures, and defended it through every criticism.

'Miss Woodhouse has given her friend the only beauty she wanted,' – observed Mrs Weston to him – not in the least suspecting that she was addressing a lover. – 'The expression of the eye is most correct, but Miss Smith has not those eye-brows and eye-lashes. It is the fault of her face that she has them not.'

'Do you think so?' replied he. 'I cannot agree with you. It appears to me a most perfect resemblance in every feature. I never saw such a likeness in my life. We must allow for the effect of shade, you know.'

'You have made her too tall, Emma,' said Mr Knightley.

Emma knew that she had, but would not own it, and Mr Elton warmly added,

'Oh, no! certainly not too tall; not in the least too tall. Consider, she is sitting down – which naturally presents a different – which in short gives exactly the idea – and the proportions must be preserved, you know. Proportions, fore-shortening. Oh, no! it gives one exactly the idea of such a height as Miss Smith's. Exactly so indeed!'

'It is very pretty,' said Mr Woodhouse. 'So prettily done! Just as your drawings always are, my dear. I do not know anybody who draws as well as you do. The only thing I do not thoroughly like is, that she seems to be sitting out of doors, with only a little shawl over her shoulders – and it makes one think she must catch cold.'

'But, my dear papa, it is supposed to be summer; a warm day in Summer. Look at the tree.'

'But it is never safe to sit out of doors, my dear.'

'You, sir, may say any thing,' cried Mr Elton; 'but I must confess that I regard it as a most happy thought, the placing of Miss Smith out of doors; and the tree is touched with such inimitable spirit! Any other situation would have been much less in character. The naïveté of Miss Smith's manners – and altogether – Oh, it is most admirable – I cannot keep my eyes from it. I never saw such a likeness.'

The next thing wanted was to get the picture framed; and here were a few difficulties. It must be done directly; it must be done in London; the order must go through the hands of some intelligent person whose taste could be depended on; and Isabella, the usual doer of all commissions, must not be applied to, because it was December, and Mr Woodhouse could not bear the idea of her stirring out of her house in the fogs of December. But no sooner was the distress known to Mr Elton, than it was removed. His gallantry was always on the alert. 'Might he be trusted with the commission, what infinite pleasure should he have in executing it! he could ride to London at any time. It was impossible to say how much he should be gratified by being employed on such an errand.'

'He was too good! – she could not endure the thought! – she would not give him such a troublesome office for the world' – brought on the desired repetition of entreaties and assurances, – and a very few minutes settled the business.

Mr Elton was to take the drawing to London, chuse the frame, and give the directions; and Emma thought she could so pack it as to ensure its safety without much incommoding him, while he seemed mostly fearful of not being incommoded enough.

'What a precious deposit!' said he with a tender sigh, as he received it.

'This man is almost too gallant to be in love,' thought Emma. 'I should say so, but that I suppose there may be a hundred different ways of being in love. He is an excellent young man, and will suit Harriet exactly; it will be an "Exactly so," as he says himself; but he does sigh and languish, and study for compliments rather more than I could endure as a principal. I come in for a pretty good share as a second. But it is his gratitude on Harriet's account.'

CHAPTER SEVEN

THE VERY DAY OF MR ELTON'S going to London produced a fresh occasion for Emma's services towards her friend. Harriet had been at Hartfield, as usual, soon after breakfast; and after a time, had gone home to return again to dinner: she returned, and sooner than had been talked of, and with an agitated, hurried look, announcing something extraordinary to have happened which she was longing to tell. Half a minute brought it all out. She had heard, as soon as she got back to Mrs Goddard's, that Mr Martin had been there an hour before, and finding she was not at home, nor particularly expected,.had left a little parcel for her from one of his sisters, and gone away; and on opening this parcel, she had actually found, besides the two songs which she had lent Elizabeth to copy, a letter to herself; and this letter was from him, from Mr Martin, and contained a direct proposal of marriage. 'Who could have thought it! She was so surprized she did not know what to do. Yes, quite a proposal of marriage; and a very good letter, at least she thought so. And he wrote as if he really loved her very much – but she did not know – and so, she was come as fast as she could to ask Miss Woodhouse what she should do.' – Emma was half ashamed of her friend for seeming so pleased and so doubtful.

'Upon my word,' she cried, 'the young man is determined not to lose any thing for want of asking. He will connect himself well if he can.'

'Will you read the letter?' cried Harriet. 'Pray do. I'd rather you would.'

Emma was not sorry to be pressed. She read, and was surprized. The style of the letter was much above her expectation. There were not merely no grammatical errors, but as a composition it would not have disgraced a gentleman; the language, though plain was strong and unaffected, and the sentiments it conveyed very much to the credit of the writer. It was short, but expressed good sense, warm attachment, liberality, propriety, even delicacy of feeling. She paused over it, while Harriet stood anxiously watching for her opinion, with a 'Well, well,' and was at last forced to add, 'Is it a good letter? or is it too short?'

'Yes, indeed, a very good letter,' replied Emma rather slowly – 'so good a letter, Harriet, that every thing considered, I think one of his sisters must have helped him. I can hardly imagine the young man whom I saw talking with you the other day could express himself so well, if left quite to his own powers, and yet it is not the style of a woman; no, certainly, it is too strong and concise; not diffuse enough for a woman. No doubt he is a sensible man, and I suppose may have a natural talent for – thinks strongly and clearly – and when he takes a pen in hand, his thoughts naturally find proper words. It is so with some men. Yes, I understand the sort of mind. Vigorous, decided, with sentiments to a certain point, not coarse. A better written letter, Harriet, (returning it,) than I had expected.'

'Well,' said the still waiting Harriet; – 'well – and – and what shall I do?'

'What shall you do! In what respect? Do you mean with regard to this letter?'

'Yes.'

'But what are you in doubt of? You must answer it of course – and speedily.'

'Yes. But what shall I say? Dear Miss Woodhouse, do advise me.'

'Oh, no, no! the letter had much better be all your own. You will express yourself very properly, I am sure. There is no danger of your not being intelligible, which is the first thing. Your meaning must be unequivocal; no doubts or demurs: and such expressions of gratitude and concern for the pain you are inflicting as propriety requires, will present themselves unbidden to *your* mind, I am persuaded. *You* need not be prompted to write with the appearance of sorrow for his disappointment.'

'You think I ought to refuse him then,' said Harriet, looking down.

'Ought to refuse him! My dear Harriet, what do you mean? Are you in any doubt as to that? I thought – but I beg your pardon, perhaps I have been under a mistake. I certainly have been misunderstanding you, if you feel in doubt as to the *purport* of your answer. I had imagined you were consulting me only as to the wording of it.'

Harriet was silent. With a little reserve of manner, Emma continued:

'You mean to return a favourable answer, I collect.'

'No, I do not; that is, I do not mean – What shall I do? What would you advise me to do? Pray, dear Miss Woodhouse, tell me what I ought to do?'

'I shall not give you any advice, Harriet, I will have nothing to do with it. This is a point which you must settle with your own feelings.'

'I had no notion that he liked me so very much,' said Harriet, contemplating the letter. For a little while Emma persevered in her silence; but beginning to apprehend the bewitching flattery of that letter might be too powerful, she thought it best to say.

'I lay it down as a general rule, Harriet, that if a woman *doubts* as to whether she should accept a man or not, she certainly ought to refuse him. If she can hesitate as to "Yes," she ought to say "No" directly. It is not a state to be safely entered into with doubtful feelings, with half a heart. I thought it my duty as a friend, and older than yourself, to say thus much to you. But do not imagine that I want to influence you.'

'Oh! no, I am sure you are a great deal too kind to – but if you

would just advise me what I had best do – No, no, I do not mean
that – As you say, one's mind ought to be quite made up – One
should not be hesitating – It is a very serious thing, It will be safer
to say "No", perhaps. – Do you think I had better say "No?" '

'Not for the world,' said Emma, smiling graciously, 'would I
advise you either way. You must be the best judge of your own
happiness. If you prefer Mr Martin to every other person; if you
think him the most agreeable man you have ever been in company
with, why should you hesitate? You blush, Harriet. – Does any
body else occur to you at this moment under such a definition?
Harriet, Harriet, do not deceive yourself; do not be run away with
by gratitude and compassion. At this moment whom are you
thinking of?'

The symptoms were favourable. – Instead of answering, Harriet
turned away confused, and stood thoughtfully by the fire; and
though the letter was still in her hand, it was now mechanically
twisted about without regard. Emma waited the result with
impatience, but not without strong hopes. At last, with some hesitation, Harriet said –

'Miss Woodhouse, as you will not give me your opinion, I must
do as well as I can by myself; and I have now quite determined,
and really almost made up my mind – to refuse Mr Martin. Do you
think I am right?'

'Perfectly, perfectly right, my dearest Harriet; you are doing just
what you ought. While you were at all in suspense I kept my feelings
to myself, but now that you are so completely decided I have no
hesitation in approving. Dear Harriet, I give myself joy of this. It
would have grieved me to lose your acquaintance, which must have
been the consequence of your marrying Mr Martin. While you were
in the smallest degree wavering, I said nothing about it, because I
would not influence; but it would have been the loss of a friend to
me. I could not have visited Mrs Robert Martin, of Abbey-Mill
Farm. Now I am secure of you for ever.'

Harriet had not surmised her own danger, but the idea of it struck
her forcibly.

'You could not have visited me!' she cried, looking aghast. 'No,
to be sure you could not; but I never thought of that before. That
would have been too dreadful! – What an escape! – Dear Miss
Woodhouse, I would not give up the pleasure and honour of being
intimate with you for any thing in the world.'

'Indeed, Harriet, it would have been a severe pang to lose you;
but it must have been. You would have thrown yourself out of all
good society. I must have given you up.'

'Dear me! – How should I ever have borne it! It would have killed me never to come to Hartfield any more!'

'Dear affectionate creature! – *You* banished to Abbey-Mill Farm! – *You* confined to the society of the illiterate and vulgar all your life! I wonder how the young man could have the assurance to ask it. He must have a pretty good opinion of himself.'

'I do not think he is conceited either, in general,' said Harriet, her conscience opposing such censure; 'at least he is very good natured, and I shall always feel much obliged to him, and have a great regard for – but that is quite a different thing from – and you know, though he may like me, it does not follow that I should – and certainly I must confess that since my visiting here I have seen people – and if one comes to compare them, person and manners, there is no comparison at all, *one* is so very handsome and agreeable. However, I do really think Mr Martin a very amiable young man, and have a great opinion of him; and his being so much attached to me – and his writing such a letter – but as to leaving you, it is what I would not do upon any consideration.'

'Thank you, thank you, my own sweet little friend. We will not be parted. A woman is not to marry a man merely because she is asked, or because he is attached to her, and can write a tolerable letter.'

'Oh! no; – and it is but a short letter too.'

Emma felt the bad taste of her friend, but let it pass with a 'very true; and it would be a small consolation to her, for the clownish manner which might be offending her every hour of the day, to know that her husband could write a good letter.'

'Oh! yes, very. Nobody cares for a letter; the thing is, to be always happy with pleasant companions. I am quite determined to refuse him. But how shall I do? What shall I say?'

Emma assured her there would be no difficulty in the answer, and advised its being written directly, which was agreed to, in the hope of her assistance; and though Emma continued to protest against any assistance being wanted, it was in fact given in the formation of every sentence. The looking over his letter again, in replying to it, had such a softening tendency, that it was particularly necessary to brace her up with a few decisive expressions; and she was so very much concerned at the idea of making him unhappy, and thought so much of what his mother and sisters would think and say, and was so anxious that they should not fancy her ungrateful that Emma believed if the young man had come in her way at that moment, he would have been accepted after all.

This letter, however, was written, and sealed, and sent. The business was finished, and Harriet safe. She was rather low all the evening, but Emma could allow for her amiable regrets, and sometimes relieved them by speaking of her own affection, sometimes by bringing forward the idea of Mr Elton.

'I shall never be invited to Abbey-Mill again,' was said in rather a sorrowful tone.

'Nor if you were, could I ever bear to part with you, my Harriet. You are a great deal too necessary at Hartfield, to be spared to Abbey-Mill.'

'And I am sure I should never want to go there; for I am never happy but at Hartfield.'

Some time afterwards it was, 'I think Mrs Goddard would be very much surprized if she knew what had happened. I am sure Miss Nash would – for Miss Nash thinks her own sister very well married, and it is only a linen-draper.'

'One should be sorry to see greater pride or refinement in the teacher of a school, Harriet. I dare say Miss Nash would envy you such an opportunity as this of being married. Even this conquest would appear valuable in her eyes. As to anything superior for you, I suppose she is quite in the dark. The attentions of a certain person can hardly be among the tittle-tattle of Highbury yet. Hitherto I fancy you and I are the only people to whom his looks and manners have explained themselves.'

Harriet blushed and smiled, and said something about wondering that people should like her so much. The idea of Mr Elton was certainly cheering; but still, after a time, she was tender-hearted again towards the rejected Mr Martin.

'Now he has got my letter,' said she softly. 'I wonder what they are all doing – whether his sisters know – if he's unhappy, they will be unhappy too. I hope he will not mind it so very much.'

'Let us think of those among our absent friends who are more cheerfully employed,' cried Emma. 'At this moment, perhaps, Mr Elton is shewing your picture to his mother and sisters, telling how much more beautiful is the original, and after being asked for it five or six times, allowing them to hear your name, your own dear name.'

'My picture! – But he has left my picture in Bond-street.'

'Has he so! – Then I know nothing of Mr Elton. No, my dear little modest Harriet, depend upon it the picture will not be in Bond-street till just before he mounts his horse to-morrow. It is his companion all this evening, his solace, his delight. It opens his designs to his family, it introduces you among them, it diffuses through the party those pleasantest feelings of our nature, eager

Shewing your picture to his mother and sisters.

curiosity and warm prepossession. How cheerful, how animated, how suspicious, how busy their imaginations all are!'

Harriet smiled again, and her smiles grew stronger.

CHAPTER EIGHT

HARRIET SLEPT AT Hartfield that night. For some weeks past she had been spending more than half her time there, and gradually getting to have a bed-room appropriated to herself; and Emma judged it best in every respect, safest and kindest, to keep her with them as much as possible just at present. She was obliged to go the next morning for an hour or two to Mrs Goddard's, but it was then to be settled that she should return to Hartfield, to make a regular visit of some days.

While she was gone, Mr Knightley called, and sat some time with Mr Woodhouse and Emma, till Mr Woodhouse, who had previously made up his mind to walk out, was persuaded by his daughter not to defer it, and was induced by the entreaties of both, though against the scruples of his own civility, to leave Mr Knightley for that purpose. Mr Knightley, who had nothing of ceremony about him, was offering by his short, decided answers, an amusing contrast to the protracted apologies and civil hesitations of the other.

'Well, I believe, if you will excuse me, Mr Knightley, if you will not consider me as doing a very rude thing, I shall take Emma's advice and go out for a quarter of an hour. As the sun is out, I believe I had better take my three turns while I can. I treat you without ceremony, Mr Knightley. We invalids think we are privileged people.'

'My dear sir, do not make a stranger of me.'

'I leave an excellent substitute in my daughter. Emma will be happy to entertain you. And therefore I think I will beg your excuse and take my three turns – my winter walk.'

'You cannot do better, sir.'

'I would ask for the pleasure of your company, Mr Knightley, but I am a very slow walker, and my pace would be tedious to you; and besides, you have another long walk before you, to Donwell Abbey.'

'Thank you, sir, thank you; I am going this moment myself; and I think the sooner *you* go the better. I will fetch your great coat and open the garden door for you.'

Mr Woodhouse at last was off; but Mr Knightley, instead of being immediately off likewise, sat down again, seemingly inclined for more chat. He began speaking of Harriet, and speaking of her with more voluntary priase than Emma had ever heard before.

'I cannot rate her beauty as you do,' said he; 'but she is a pretty little creature, and I am inclined to think very well of her disposition. Her character depends upon those she is with; but in good hands she will turn out a valuable woman.'

'I am glad you think so; and the good hands, I hope, may not be wanting.'

'Come,' said he, 'you are anxious for a compliment, so I will tell you that you have improved her. You have cured her of her schoolgirl's giggle; she really does you credit.'

'Thank you. I should be mortified indeed if I did not believe I had been of some use; but it is not every body who will bestow praise where they may. *You* do not often overpower me with it.'

'You are expecting her again, you say, this morning?'

'Almost every moment. She has been gone longer already than she intended.'

'Something has happened to delay her; some visitors perhaps.'

'Highbury gossips! – Tiresome wretches!'

'Harriet may not consider every body tiresome that you would.'

Emma knew this was too true for contradiction, and therefore said nothing. He presently added, with a smile,

'I do not pretend to fix on times or places, but I must tell you that I have good reason to believe your little friend will soon hear of something to her advantage.'

'Indeed! how so? of what sort?'

'A very serious sort, I assure you,' still smiling.

'Very serious! I can think of but one thing – Who is in love with her? Who makes you their confidant?'

Emma was more than half in hopes of Mr Elton's having dropt a hint. Mr Knightley was a sort of general friend and adviser, and she knew Mr Elton looked up to him.

'I have reason to think,' he replied, 'that Harriet Smith will soon have an offer of marriage, and from a most unexceptionable quarter: – Robert Martin is the man. Her visit to Abbey-Mill, this summer, seems to have done his business. He is desperately in love and means to marry her.'

'He is very obliging,' said Emma; 'but is he sure that Harriet means to marry him?!'

'Well, well, means to make her an offer then. Will that do? He came to the Abbey two evenings ago, on purpose to consult me about it. He knows I have a thorough regard for him and all his family, and, I believe, considers me as one of his best friends. He came to ask me whether I thought it would be imprudent in him to settle so early; whether I thought her too young: in short, whether I approved his choice altogether; having some apprehension perhaps of her being considered (especially since *your* making so much of her) as in a line of society above him. I was very much pleased with all that he said. I never hear better sense from anyone than Robert Martin. He always speaks to the purpose; open, straight forward, and very well judging. He told me every thing; his circumstances and plans, and what they all proposed doing in the event of his marriage. He is an excellent young man, both as son and brother. I had no hesitation in advising him to marry. He proved to me that he could afford it; and that being the case, I was convinced he could not do better. I praised the fair lady too, and altogether sent him away very happy. If he had never esteemed my opinion before, he would have thought highly of me then; and, I dare say, left the house thinking me the best friend and counsellor man ever had. This happened the night before last. Now, as we may fairly suppose, he would not allow much time to pass before he spoke to the lady, and as he does not appear to have spoken yesterday, it is not unlikely that he should be at Mrs Goddard's today; and she may be detained by a visitor, without thinking him at all a tiresome wretch.'

'Pray, Mr Knightley,' said Emma, who had been smiling to herself through a great part of this speech, 'how do you know that Mr Martin did not speak yesterday?'

'Certainly,' replied he, surprised, 'I do not absolutely know it; but it may be inferred. Was not she the whole day with you?'

'Come,' said she, 'I will tell you something, in return for what you have told me. He did speak yesterday – that is, he wrote, and was refused.'

This was obliged to be repeated before it could be believed; and Mr Knightley actually looked red with surprize and displeasure, as he stood up, in tall indignation, and said,

'Then she is a greater simpleton than I ever believed her. What is the foolish girl about?'

'Oh! to be sure,' cried Emma, 'it is always incomprehensible to a man that a woman should ever refuse an offer of marriage. A man always imagines a woman to be ready for anybody who asks her.'

'Nonsense! a man does not imagine any such thing. But what is the meaning of this? Harriet Smith refuse Robert Martin? madness, if it is so; but I hope you are mistaken.'

'I saw her answer, nothing could be clearer.'

'You saw her answer! you wrote her answer too. Emma, this is your doing. You persuaded her to refuse him.'

'And if I did, (which, however, I am far from allowing,) I should not feel that I had done wrong. Mr Martin is a very respectable young man, but I cannot admit him to be Harriet's equal; and am rather surprised indeed that he should have ventured to address her. By your account, he does seem to have had some scruples. It is a pity that they were ever got over.'

'Not Harriet's equal!' exclaimed Mr Knightley loudly and warmly; and with calmer asperity, added, a few moments after-wards, 'No, he is not her equal indeed, for he is as much her superior in sense as in situation. Emma, your infatuation about that girl blinds you. What are Harriet Smith's claims, either of birth, nature or education, to any connection higher than Robert Martin? She is the natural daughter of nobody knows whom, with probably no settled provision at all, and certainly no respectable relations. She is known only as parlour-boarder at a common school. She is not a sensible girl, nor a girl of any information. She has been taught nothing useful, and is too young and too simple to have acquired any thing herself. At her age she can have no experience, and with her little wit, is not very likely ever to have any that can avail her. She is pretty, and she is good tempered, and that is all. My only scruple in advising the match was on his account, as being beneath his deserts, and a bad connexion for him. I felt, that as to fortune, in all probability he might do much better; and that as to a rational companion or useful helpmate, he could not do worse. But I could not reason so to a man in love, and was willing to trust to there being no harm in her, to her having that sort of disposition, which, in good hands, like his, might be easily led aright and turn out very well. The advantage of the match I felt to be all on her side; and had not the smallest doubt (nor have I now) that there would be a general cry-out upon her extreme good luck. Even *your* satisfaction I made sure of. It crossed my mind immediately that you would not regret your friend's leaving Highbury, for the sake of her being settled so well. I remember saying to myself, "Even Emma, with all her partiality for Harriet will think this a good match." '

'I cannot help wondering at your knowing so little of Harriet as to say any such thing. What! think a farmer, (and with all his sense and all his merit Mr Martin is nothing more,) a good match for my intimate friend! Not regret her leaving Highbury for the sake of marrying a man whom I could never admit as an acquaintance of my own! I wonder you should think it possible for me to have such feelings. I assure you mine are very different. I must think your statement by no means fair. You are not just to Harriet's claims. They would be estimated very differently by others as well as myself; Mr Martin may be the richest of the two, but he is undoubtedly her inferior as to rank in society. – The sphere in which she moves is much above his. – It would be a degradation.'

'A degradation to illegitimacy and ignorance, to be married to a respectable, intelligent gentleman-farmer!'

'As to the circumstances of her birth, though in a legal sense she may be called Nobody, it will not hold in common sense. She is not to pay for the offence of others, by being held below the level of those with whom she is brought up. – There can scarcely be a doubt that her father is a gentleman – and a gentleman of fortune. – Her allowance is very liberal; nothing has ever been grudged for her improvement or comfort. – That she is a gentleman's daughter, is indubitable to me; that she associates with gentlemen's daughters, no one, I apprehend, will deny. – She is superior to Mr Robert Martin.'

'Whoever might be her parents,' said Mr Knightley, 'whoever may have had the charge of her, it does not appear to have been any part of their plan to introduce her into what you would call good society. After receiving a very indifferent education she is left in Mrs Goddard's hands to shift as she can; – to move, in short, in Mrs Goddard's line, to have Mrs Goddard's acquaintance. Her friends evidently thought this good enough for her; and it *was* good enough. She desired nothing better herself. Till you chose to turn her into a friend, her mind had no distaste for her own set, nor any ambition beyond it. She was as happy as possible with the Martins in the summer. She had no sense of superiority then. If she has it now, you have given it. You have been no friend to Harriet Smith, Emma. Robert Martin would never have proceeded so far if he had not felt persuaded of her not being disinclined to him. I know him well. He has too much real feeling to address any woman on the hap-hazard of selfish passion. And as to conceit, he is the farthest from it of any man I know. Depend upon it he had encouragement.'

It was most convenient to Emma not to make a direct reply to this assertion; she chose rather to take up her own line of the subject again.

'You are a very warm friend to Mr Martin; but, as I said before, are unjust to Harriet. Harriet's claims to marry well are not so contemptible as you represent them. She is not a clever girl, but she has better sense than you are aware of, and does not deserve to have her understanding spoken of so slightingly. Waving that point, however, and supposing her to be, as you describe her, only pretty and good-natured, let me tell you, that in the degree she possesses them, they are not trivial recommendations to the world in general, for she is, in fact, a beautiful girl, and must be thought so by ninety-nine people out of an hundred; and till it appears that men are much more philosophic on the subject of beauty than they are generally supposed; till they do fall in love with well-informed minds instead of handsome faces, a girl, with such loveliness as Harriet, has a certainty of being admired and sought after, of having the power of choosing from among many, consequently a claim to be nice. Her good-nature, too, is not so very slight a claim, comprehending, as it does, real, thorough sweetness of temper and manner, a very humble opinion of herself, and a great readiness to be pleased with other people. I am very much mistaken if your sex in general would not think such beauty, and such temper, the highest claims a woman could possess.'

'Upon my word, Emma, to hear you abusing the reason you have, is almost enough to make me think so too. Better be without sense, than misapply it as you do.'

'To be sure!' cried she playfully. 'I know *that* is the feeling of you all. I know that such a girl as Harriet is exactly what every man delights in – what at once bewitches his senses and satisfies his judgment. Oh! Harriet may pick and choose. Were you, yourself, ever to marry, she is the very woman for you. And is she, at seventeen, just entering into life, just beginning to be known, to be wondered at because she does not accept the first offer she receives? no – pray let her have time to look about her.'

'I have always thought it a very foolish intimacy,' said Mr Knightley presently, 'though I have kept my thoughts to myself; but I now perceive that it will be a very unfortunate one for Harriet. You will puff her up with such ideas of her own beauty, and of what she has a claim to, that, in a little while, nobody within her reach will be good enough for her. Vanity working on a weak head, produces every sort of mischief. Nothing so easy as for a young lady to raise her expectations too high. Miss Harriet Smith may not find offers of marriage flow in so fast, though she is a very pretty girl. Men of sense, whatever you may chuse to say, do not want silly wives. Men of family would not be very fond of connecting themselves with a girl of such obscurity – and most prudent men would be afraid of the inconvenience and disgrace they might be involved in, when the mystery of her parentage came to be revealed. Let her marry Robert Martin, and she is safe, respectable, and happy for ever; but if you encourage her to expect to marry greatly, and teach her to be satisfied with nothing less than a man of consequence and large fortune, she may be a parlour-boarder at Mrs Goddard's all the rest of her life – or, at least, (for Harriet Smith is a girl who will marry somebody or other,) till she grows desperate, and is glad to catch at the old writing master's son.'

'We think so very differently on this point, Mr Knightley, that there can be no use in canvassing it. We shall only be making each other more angry. But as to my *letting* her marry Robert Martin, it is impossible; she has refused him, and so decidedly, I think, as must prevent any second application. She must abide by the evil of having refused him, whatever it may be; and as to the refusal itself, I will not pretend to say that I might not influence her a little; but I assure you there was very little for me or for anybody to do. His appearance is so much against him, and his manner so bad, that if she ever were disposed to favour him, she is not now. I can imagine, that before she had seen anybody superior, she might tolerate him. He was the brother of her friends, and he took pains to please her; and altogether, having seen nobody better (that must have been his great assistant) she might not, while she was at Abbey-Mill, find him disagreeable. But the case is altered now. She knows now what gentlemen are; and nothing but a gentleman in eduation and manner has any chance with Harriet.'

'Nonsense, errant nonsense, as ever was talked!' cried Mr Knightley. – 'Robert Martin's manners have sense, sincerity, and good-humour to recommend them; and his mind has more true gentility than Harriet Smith could understand.'

Emma made no answer, and tried to look cheerfully unconcerned, but was really feeling uncomfortable and wanting him very much to be gone. She did not repent what she had done; she still thought herself a better judge of such a point of female right and refinement than he could be; but yet she had a sort of habitual respect for his judgment in general, which made her dislike having it so loudly against her; and to have him sitting just opposite to her in angry state, was very disagreeable. Some minutes passed in this unpleasant silence, with only one attempt on Emma's side to talk of the weather, but he made no answer. He was thinking. The result of his thoughts appeared at last in these words.

'Robert Martin has no great loss – if he can but think so; and I hope it will not be long before he does. Your views for Harriet are best known to yourself; but as you make no secret of your love of match-making, it is fair to suppose that views, and plans, and projects you have; – and as a friend I shall just hint to you that if Elton is the man, I think it will be all labour in vain.'

Emma laughed and disclaimed. He continued,

'Depend upon it, Elton will not do. Elton is a very good sort of man, and a very respectable vicar of Highbury, but not at all likely to make an imprudent match. He knows the value of a good income as well as anybody. Elton may talk sentimentally, but he will act rationally. He is as well acquainted with his own claims, as you can be with Harriet's. He knows that he is a very handsome young man, and a great favourite wherever he goes; and from his general way of talking in unreserved moments, when there are only men present, I am convinced that he does not mean to throw himself away. I have heard him speak with great animation of a large family of young ladies that his sisters are intimate with, who have all twenty thousand pounds apiece.'

'I am very much obliged to you,' said Emma, laughing again. 'If

I had set my heart on Mr Elton's marrying Harriet, it would have been very kind to open my eyes, but at present I only want to keep Harriet to myself. I have done with match-making indeed. I could never hope to equal my own doings at Randalls. I shall leave off while I am well.'

'Good morning to you,' – said he, rising and walking off abruptly. He was very much vexed. He felt the disappointment of the young man, and was mortified to have been the means of promoting it, by the sanction he had given; and the part which he was persuaded Emma had taken in the affair, was provoking him exceedingly.

Emma remained in a state of vexation too; but there was more indistinctness in the causes of her's, than in his. She did not always feel so absolutely satisfied with herself, so entirely convinced that her opinions were right and her adversary's wrong, as Mr Knightley. He walked off in more complete self-approbation than he left for her. She was not so materially cast down, however, but that a little time and the return of Harriet were very adequate restoratives. Harriet's staying away so long was beginning to make her uneasy. The possibility of the young man's coming to Mrs Goddard's that morning, and meeting with Harriet and pleading his own cause, gave alarming idea. The dread of such a failure after all became the prominent uneasiness; and when Harriet appeared, and in very good spirits, and without having any such reason to give for her long absence, she felt a satisfaction which settled her with her own mind, and convinced her, that let Mr Knightley think or say what he would, she had done nothing which woman's friendship and woman's feelings would not justify.

He had frightened her a little about Mr Elton; but when she considered that Mr Knightley could not have observed him as she had done, neither with the interest, nor (she must be allowed to tell herself, in spite of Mr Knightley's pretensions) with the skill of such an observer on such a question as herself, that he had spoken it hastily and in anger, she was able to believe, that he had rather said what he wished resentfully to be true, than what he knew anything about. He certainly might have heard Mr Elton speak with more unreserve than she had ever done, and Mr Elton might not be of an imprudent, inconsiderate disposition as to money-matters; he might naturally be rather attentive than otherwise to them; but then, Mr Knightley did not make due allowance for the influence of a strong passion at war with all interested motives. Mr Knightley saw no such passion, and of course thought nothing of its effects; but she saw too much of it, to feel a doubt of its overcoming any hesitations that a reasonable prudence might originally suggest; and more than a reasonable, becoming degree of prudence, she was very sure did not belong to Mr Elton.

Harriet's cheerful look and manner established her's: she came back, not to think of Mr Martin, but to talk of Mr Elton. Miss Nash had been telling her something, which she repeated immediately with great delight. Mr Perry had been to Mrs Goddard's to attend a sick child, and Miss Nash had seen him, and he had told Miss Nash, that as he was coming back yesterday from Clayton Park, he had met Mr Elton, and found to his great surprize that Mr Elton was actually on his road to London, and not meaning to return till the morrow, though it was the whist-club night, which he had been never known to miss before; and Mr Perry had remonstrated with him about it, and told him how shabby it was in him, their best player, to absent himself, and tried very much to persuade him to put off his journey only one day; but it would not do; Mr Elton had been determined to go on, and had said in a *very particular* way indeed, that he was going on business which he would not put off for any inducement in the world; and something about a very enviable commission, and being the bearer of something exceedingly precious. Mr Perry could not quite understand him, but he was very sure there must be a *lady* in the case, and he told him so; and Mr Elton only looked very conscious and smiling, and rode off in great spirits. Miss Nash had told her all this, and had talked a great deal more about Mr Elton; and said, looking so very significantly at her, 'that she did not pretend to understand what his business might be, but she only knew that any woman whom Mr Elton could prefer, she should think the luckiest woman in the world; for, beyond a doubt, Mr Elton had not his equal for beauty or agreeableness.'

Northanger Abbey

Seventeen-year-old Catherine Morland, the daughter of a village clergy-man, is visiting Bath for the first time, chaperoned by her wealthy neighbours, the Allens. One of ten children, Catherine finds the social whirl very different to life in a country parsonage.

EVERY MORNING NOW brought its regular duties; – shops were to be visited; some new part of the town to be looked at; and the Pump-room to be attended, where they paraded up and down for an hour, looking at every body and speaking to no one. The wish of a numerous acquaintance in Bath was still uppermost with Mrs Allen, and she repeated it after every fresh proof, which every morning brought, of her knowing nobody at all.

They made their appearance in the Lower Rooms; and here fortune was more favourable to our heroine. The master of the ceremonies introduced to her a very gentlemanlike young man as a partner; – his name was Tilney. He seemed to be about four or five and twenty, was rather tall, had a pleasing countenance, a very intelligent and lively eye, and, if not quite handsome, was very near it. His address was good, and Catherine felt herself in high luck. There was little leisure for speaking while they danced; but when they were seated at tea, she found him as agreeable as she had already given him credit for being. He talked with fluency and spirit – and there was an archness and pleasantry in his manner which interested, though it was hardly understood by her. After chatting for some time on such matters as naturally arose from the objects around them, he suddenly addressed her with – 'I have hitherto been very remiss, madam, in the proper attentions of a partner here; I have not yet asked you how long you have been in Bath; whether you were ever here before; whether you have been at the Upper Rooms, the theatre, and the concert; and how you like the place altogether. I have been very negligent – but are you now at leisure to satisfy me in these particulars? If you are I will begin directly.'

'You need not give yourself that trouble, sir.'

'No trouble I assure you, madam.' Then forming his features into a set smile, and affectedly softening his voice, he added, with a simpering air, 'Have you been long in Bath, madam?'

'About a week, sir,' replied Catherine, trying not to laugh.

'Really!' with affected astonishment.

'Why should you be surprized, sir?'

'Why, indeed!' said he, in his natural tone – 'but some emotion must appear to be raised by your reply, and surprize is more easily assumed, and not less reasonable than any other. – Now let us go on. Were you never here before, madam?'

'Never, sir.'

'Indeed! Have you yet honoured the Upper Rooms?'

'Yes, sir, I was there last Monday.'

'Have you been to the theatre?'

'Yes, sir, I was at the play on Tuesday.'

'To the concert?'

'Yes, sir, on Wednesday.'

'And are you altogether pleased with Bath?'

'Yes – I like it very well.'

'Now I must give one smirk, and then we may be rational again.' Catherine turned away her head, not knowing whether she might venture to laugh.

'I see what you think of me,' said he gravely – 'I shall make but a poor figure in your journal to-morrow.'

'My journal!'

'Yes, I know exactly what you will say: Friday, went to the Lower Rooms; wore my sprigged muslin robe with blue trimmings – plain black shoes – appeared to much advantage; but was strangely harassed by a queer, half-witted man, who would make me dance with him, and distressed me by his nonsense.'

'Indeed I shall say no such thing.'

'Shall I tell you what you ought to say?'

'If you please.'

'I danced with a very agreeable young man, introduced by Mr King; had a great deal of conversation with him – seems a most extraordinary genius – hope I may know more of him. *That*, madam, is what I *wish* you to say.'

'But, perhaps, I keep no journal.'

'Perhaps you are not sitting in this room, and I am not sitting by you. These are points in which a doubt is equally possible. Not keep a journal! How are your absent cousins to understand the tenour of your life in Bath without one? How are the civilities and compliments of every day to be related as they ought to be, unless noted down every evening in a journal? How are your various dresses to be remembered, and the particular state of your complexion, and curl of your hair to be described in all their diversities, without having constant recourse to a journal? – My dear madam, I am not so ignorant of young ladies' ways as you wish to believe me; it is this delightful habit of journalizing which largely contributes to form the easy style of writing for which ladies are so generally celebrated. Every body allows that the talent of writing

agreeable letters is peculiarly female. Nature may have done something, but I am sure it must be essentially assisted by the practice
of keeping a journal.'

'I have sometimes thought,' said Catherine, doubtingly, 'whether
ladies do write so much better letters than gentlemen! This is – I
should not think the superiority was always on our side.'

'As far as I have had opportunity of judging, it appears to me
that the usual style of letter-writing among women is faultless,
except in three particulars.'

'And what are they?'

'A general deficiency of subject, a total inattention to stops, and
a very frequent ignorance of grammar.'

'Upon my word! I need not have been afraid of disclaiming the
compliment. You do not think too highly of us in that way.'

'I should no more lay it down as a general rule that women write
better letters than men, than that they sing better duets, or draw
better landscapes. In every power, of which taste is the foundation,
excellence is pretty fairly divided between the sexes.'

They were interrupted by Mrs Allen: – 'My dear Catherine,' said
she, 'do take this pin out of my sleeve; I am afraid it has torn a hole
already; I shall be quite sorry if it has, for this is a favourite gown,
though it cost but nine shillings a yard.'

'That is exactly what I should have guessed it, madam,' said Mr
Tilney, looking at the muslin.

'Do you understand muslins, sir?'

'Particularly well; I always buy my own cravats, and am allowed
to be an excellent judge; and my sister has often trusted me in the
choice of a gown. I bought one for her the other day, and it was
pronounced to be a prodigious bargain by every lady who saw it.
I gave but five shillings a yard for it, and a true Indian muslin.'

Mrs Allen was quite struck by his genius. 'Men commonly take
so little notice of those things,' said she: 'I can never get Mr Allen
to know one of my gowns from another. You must be a great
comfort to your sister, sir.'

'I hope I am, madam.'

'And pray, sir, what do you think of Miss Morland's gown?'

'It is very pretty, madam,' said he, gravely examining it; but I do
not think it will wash well; I am afraid it will fray.'

'How can you,' said Catherine, laughing, 'be so – ' she had almost
said, strange.

'I am quite of your opinion, sir,' replied Mrs Allen; 'and so I told
Miss Morland when she bought it.'

'But then you know, madam, muslin always turns to some

account or other; Miss Morland will get enough out of it for a handkerchief, or a cap, or a cloak. – Muslin can never be said to be wasted. I have heard my sister say so forty times, when she has been extravagant in buying more than she wanted, or careless in cutting it to pieces.'

'Bath is a charming place, sir; there are so many good shops here. – We are sadly off in the country; not but what we have very good shops in Salisbury, but it is so far to go; – eight miles is a long way; Mr Allen says it is nine, measured nine; but I am sure it cannot be more than eight; and it is such a fag – I come back tired to death. Now here one can step out of doors and get a thing in five minutes.'

Mr Tilney was polite enough to seem interested in what she said; and she kept him on the subject of muslins till the dancing recommenced. Catherine feared, as she listened to their discourse, that he indulged himself a little too much with the foibles of others. – 'What are you thinking of so earnestly?' said he, as they walked back to the ball-room; – 'not of your partner, I hope, for, by that shake of the head, your meditations are not satisfactory.'

Catherine coloured, and said, 'I was not thinking of any thing.'

'That is artful and deep, to be sure; but I had rather be told at once that you will not tell me.'

'Well then, I will not.'

'Thank you; for now we shall soon be acquainted, as I am authorized to tease you on this subject whenever we meet, and nothing in the world advances intimacy so much.'

They danced again; and, when the assembly closed, parted, on the lady's side at least, with a strong inclination for continuing the acquaintance. Whether she thought of him so much, while she drank her warm wine and water, and prepared herself for bed, as to dream of him when there, cannot be ascertained; but I hope it was no more than in a slight slumber, or a morning doze at most; for if it be true, as a celebrated writer has maintained, that no young lady can be justified in falling in love before the gentleman's love is declared, it must be very improper that a young lady should dream of a gentleman before the gentleman is first known to have dreamt of her. How proper Mr Tilney might be as a dreamer or a lover, had not yet perhaps entered Mr Allen's head, but that he was not objectionable as a common acquaintance for his young charge he was on inquiry satisfied; for he had early in the evening taken pains to know who her partner was, and had been assured of Mr Tilney's being a clergyman, and of a very respectable family in Gloucestershire.

CHAPTER FOUR

WITH MORE THAN USUAL eagerness did Catherine hasten to the Pump-room the next day, secure within herself of seeing Mr Tilney there before the morning were over, and ready to meet him with a smile: – but no smile was demanded – Mr Tilney did not appear. Every creature in Bath, except himself, was to be seen in the room at different periods of the fashionable hours; crowds of people were every moment passing in and out, up the steps and down; people whom nobody cared about, and nobody wanted to see; and he only was absent. 'What a delightful place Bath is,' said Mrs Allen, as they sat down near the great clock, after parading the room till they were tired; 'and how pleasant it would be if we had any acquaintance here.'

This sentiment had been uttered so often in vain, that Mrs Allen had no particular reason to hope it would be followed with more advantage now; but we are told to 'despair of nothing we would attain,' as 'unwearied diligence our point would gain;' and the unwearied diligence with which she had every day wished for the same thing was at length to have its just reward, for hardly had she been seated ten minutes before a lady of about her own age, who was sitting by her, and had been looking at her attentively for several minutes, addressed her with great complaisance in these words: – 'I think, madam, I cannot be mistaken; it is a long time since I had the pleasure of seeing you, but is not your name Allen?' This question answered, as it readily was, the stranger pronounced her's to be Thorpe; and Mrs Allen immediately recognized the features of a former schoolfellow and intimate, whom she had seen only once since their respective marriages, and that many years ago. Their joy on this meeting was very great, as well it might, since they had been contented to know nothing of each other for the last fifteen years. Compliments on good looks now passed; and, after observing how time had slipped away since they were last together, how little they had thought of meeting in Bath, and what a pleasure it was to see an old friend, they proceeded to make inquiries and give intelligence as to their families, sisters, and cousins, talking both together, far more ready to give than to receive information, and each hearing very little of what the other said. Mrs Thorpe, however, had one great advantage as a talker, over Mrs Allen, in a family of children; and when she expatiated on the talents of her sons, and the beauty of her daughters, – when she related their different situations and views, – that John was at Oxford, Edward at Merchant-Taylors', and William at sea, – and all of them more beloved and respected in their different station than any other three beings ever were, Mrs Allen had no similar information to give, no similar triumphs to press on the unwilling and unbelieving ear of her friend, and was forced to sit and appear to listen to all these maternal effusions, consoling herself, however, with the discovery, which her keen eye soom made, that the lace of Mrs Thorpe's pelisse was not half so handsome as that on her own.

'Here come my dear girls,' cried Mrs Thorpe, pointing at three smart looking females, who, arm in arm, were then moving towards her. 'My dear Mrs Allen, I long to introduce them; they will be so delighted to see you: the tallest is Isabella, my eldest; is not she a fine young woman? The others are very much admired too, but I believe Isabella is the handsomest.'

The Miss Thorpes were introduced; and Miss Morland, who had been for a short time forgotten, was introduced likewise. The name seemed to strike them all; and, after speaking to her with great civility, the eldest young lady observed aloud to the rest, 'How excessively like her brother Miss Morland is!'

'The very picture of him indeed!' cried the mother – and 'I should have known her any where for his sister!' was repeated by them all, two or three times over. For a moment Catherine was surprized; but Mrs Thorpe and her daughters had scarcely begun the history of their acquaintance with Mr James Morland, before she remembered that her eldest brother had lately formed an intimacy with a young man of his own college, of the name of Thorpe; and that he had spent the last week of the Christmas vacation with his family, near London.

The whole being explained, many obliging things were said by the Miss Thorpes of their wish of being better acquainted with her; of being considered as already friends, through the friendship of their brothers, &c. which Catherine heard with pleasure, and answered with all the pretty expressions she could command; and, as the first proof of amity, she was soon invited to accept an arm of the eldest Miss Thorpe, and take a turn with her about the room. Catherine was delighted with this extension of her Bath acquaintance, and almost forgot Mr Tilney while she talked to Miss Thorpe.

Friendship is certainly the finest balm for the pangs of disappointed love.

Their conversation turned upon those subjects, of which the free discussion has generally much to do in perfecting a sudden intimacy between two young ladies; such as dress, balls, flirtations, and quizzes. Miss Thorpe, however, being four years older than Miss Morland, and at least four years better informed, had a very decided advantage in discussing such points; she could compare the balls of Bath with those of Tunbridge; its fashions with the fashions of London; could rectify the opinions of her new friend in many articles of tasteful attire; could discover a flirtation between any gentleman and lady who only smiled on each other; and point out a quiz through the thickness of a crowd. These powers received due admiration from Catherine, to whom they were entirely new; and the respect which they naturally inspired might have been too great for familiarity, had not the easy gaiety of Miss Thorpe's manners, and her frequent expressions of delight on this acquaintance with her, softened down every feeling of awe, and left nothing but tender affection. Their increasing attachment was not to be satisfied with half a dozen turns in the Pump-room, but required, when they all quitted it together, that Miss Thorpe should accompany Miss Morland to the very door of Mr Allen's house; and that they should there part with a most affectionate and lengthened shake of hands, after learning, to their mutual relief, that they should see each other across the theatre at night, and say their prayers in the same chapel the next morning. Catherine then ran directly up stairs, and watched Miss Thorpe's progress down the street from the drawing-room window; admired the graceful spirit of her walk, the fashionable air of her figure and dress, and felt grateful, as well she might, for the chance which had procured her such a friend.

Mrs Thorpe was a widow, and not a very rich one; she was a good-humoured, well-meaning woman, and a very indulgent mother. Her eldest daughter had great personal beauty, and the younger ones, by pretending to be as handsome as their sister, imitating her air, and dressing in the same style, did very well.

This brief account of the family is intended to supersede the necessity of a long and minute detail from Mrs Thorpe herself, of her past adventures and sufferings, which might otherwise be expected to occupy the three or four following chapters; in which the worthlessness of lords and attornies might be set forth, and conversations, which had passed twenty years before, be minutely repeated.

CHAPTER FIVE

CATHERINE WAS NOT SO much engaged at the theatre that evening, in returning the nods and smiles of Miss Thorpe, though they certainly claimed much of her leisure, as to forget to look with an inquiring eye for Mr Tilney in every box which her eye could reach; but she looked in vain. Mr Tilney was no fonder of the play than the Pump-room. She hoped to be more fortunate the next day; and when her wishes for fine weather were answered by seeing a beautiful morning, she hardly felt a doubt of it; for a fine Sunday in Bath empties every house of its inhabitants, and all the world appears on such an occasion to walk about and tell their acquaintance what a charming day it is.

As soon as divine service was over, the Thorpes and Allens eagerly joined each other; and after staying long enough in the Pump-room to discover that the crowd was insupportable, and that there was not a genteel face to be seen, which every body discovers every Sunday throughout the season, they hastened away to the Crescent, to breathe the fresh air of better company. Here Catherine and Isabella, arm in arm, again tasted the sweets of friendship in an unreserved conversation; – they talked much, and with much enjoyment; but again was Catherine disappointed in her hope of re-seeing her partner. He was no where to be met with; every search for him was equally unsuccessful in morning lounges or evening assemblies; neither at the upper nor lower rooms, at dressed or undressed balls, was he perceivable; nor among the walkers, the horsemen, or the curricle-drivers of the morning. His name was not in the Pump-room book, and curiosity could do no more. He must be gone from Bath. Yet he had not mentioned that his stay would be so short! This sort of mysteriousness, which is always so becoming in a hero, threw a fresh grace in Catherine's imagination around his person and manners, and increased her anxiety to know more of him. From the Thorpes she could learn nothing, for they had been only two days in Bath before they met with Mrs Allen. It was a subject, however, in which she often indulged with her friend, from whom she received every possible encouragement to continue to think of him; and his impression of her fancy was not suffered therefore to weaken. Isabella was very sure that he must be a charming young man; and was equally sure that he must have been delighted with her dear Catherine, and would therefore shortly return. She liked him the better for being a clergyman, 'for she must confess herself very partial to the profession;' and something like a sigh escaped her as she said it. Perhaps Catherine was wrong in not demanding the cause of that gentle emotion – but she was not experienced enough in the finesse of love, or the duties of friendship, to know when delicate raillery was properly called for, or when a confidence should be forced.

Mrs Allen was now quite happy – quite satisfied with Bath. She had found some acquaintance, had been so lucky too as to find in them the family of a most worthy old friend; and, as the completion of good fortune, had found these friends by no means so expensively dressed as herself. Her daily expressions were no longer, 'I wish we had some acquaintance in Bath!' They were changed into – 'How glad I am we have met with Mrs Thorpe!' – and she was as eager in promoting the intercourse of the two families, as her young charge and Isabella themselves could be; never satisfied with the day unless she spent the chief of it by the side of Mrs Thorpe, in what they called conversation, but in which there was scarcely ever any exchange of opinion, and not often any resemblance of subject, for Mrs Thorpe talked chiefly of her children, and Mrs Allen of her gowns.

The progress of the friendship between Catherine and Isabella was quick as its beginning had been warm, and they passed so rapidly through every gradation of increasing tenderness, that there was shortly no fresh proof of it to be given to their friends or themselves. They called each other by their Christian name, were always arm in arm when they walked, pinned up each other's train for the dance, and were not to be divided in the set; and if a rainy morning deprived them of other enjoyments, they were still resolute in meeting in defiance of wet and dirt, and shut themselves up, to read novels together. Yes, novels; – for I will not adopt that ungenerous and impolitic custom so common with novel writers, of degrading by their contemptuous censure the very performances, to the number of which they are themselves adding – joining with their greatest enemies in bestowing the harshest epithets on such works, and scarcely ever permitting them to be read by their own heroine, who, if she accidentally take up a novel, is sure to turn over its insipid pages with disgust. Alas! if the heroine of one novel be not patron-ized by the heroine of another, from whom can she expect protection and regard? I cannot approve of it. Let us leave it to the Reviewers to abuse such effusions of fancy at their leisure, and over every new novel to talk in threadbare strains of the trash with which the press

Pinned up each other's train for the dance.

now groans. Let us not desert one another; we are an injured body. Although our productions have afforded more extensive and unaffected pleasure than those of any other literary corporation in the world, no species of composition has been so much decried. From pride, ignorance, or fashion, our foes are almost as many as our readers. And while the abilities of the nine-hundredth abridger of the History of England, or of the man who collects and publishes in a volume some dozen lines of Milton, Pope, and Prior, with a paper from the Spectator, and a chapter from Sterne, are eulogized

by a thousand pens, – there seems almost a general wish of decrying
the capacity and undervaluing the labour of the novelist, and of
slighting the performances which have only genius, wit, and taste
to recommend them. 'I am no novel reader – I seldom look into
novels – Do not imagine that *I* often read novels – It is really very
well for a novel.' – Such is the common cant. – 'And what are you
reading, Miss – ?' 'Oh! it is only a novel!' replies the young lady;
while she lays down her book with affected indifference, or momentary shame. – 'It is only Cecilia, or Camilla, or Belinda;' or, in
short, only some work in which the greatest powers of the mind
are displayed, in which the most thorough knowledge of human
nature, the happiest delineation of its varieties, the liveliest effusions
of wit and humour are conveyed to the world in the best chosen
language. Now, had the same young lady been engaged with a
volume of the Spectator, instead of such a work, how proudly
would she have produced the book, and told its name; though the
chances must be against her being occupied by any part of that
voluminous publication, of which either the matter or manner
would not disgust a young person of taste: the substance of its papers
so often consisting in the statement of improbable circumstances,
unnatural characters, and topics of conversation, which no longer
concern any one living; and their language, too, frequently so coarse
as to give no very favourable idea of the age that could endure it.

CHAPTER SIX

THE FOLLOWING CONVERSATION, which took place between the two
friends in the Pump-room one morning, after an acquaintance of
eight or nine days, is given as a specimen of their very warm
attachment, and of the delicacy, discretion, originality of thought,
and literary taste which marked the reasonableness of that
attachment.

They met by appointment; and as Isabella had arrived nearly five
minutes before her friend, her first address naturally was – 'My
dearest creature, what can have made you so late? I have been
waiting for you at least this age!'

'Have you, indeed! – I am very sorry for it; but really I thought
I was in very good time. It is but just one. I hope you have not
been here long?'

'Oh! these ten ages at least. I am sure I have been here this half hour. But now, let us go and sit down at the other end of the room, and enjoy ourselves. I have an hundred things to say to you. In the first place, I was so afraid it would rain this morning, just as I wanted to set off; it looked very showery, and that would have thrown me into agonies! Do you know, I saw the prettiest hat you can imagine, in a shop window in Milsom-street just now – very like yours, only with coquelicot ribbons instead of green; I quite longed for it. But, my dearest Catherine, what have you been doing with yourself all this morning? – Have you gone on with Udolpho?'

'Yes, I have been reading it ever since I woke; and I am got to the black veil.'

'Are you, indeed? How delightful! Oh! I would not tell you what is behind the black veil for the world! Are not you wild to know?'

'Oh! yes, quite; what can it be? – But do not tell me – I would not be told upon any account. I know it must be a skeleton, I am sure it is Laurentina's skeleton. Oh! I am delighted with the book! I should like to spend my whole life in reading it. Assure you, if it had not been to meet you, I would not have come away from it for all the world.'

'Dear creature! how much I am obliged to you; and when you have finished Udolpho, we will read the Italian together; and I have made out a list of ten or twelve more of the same kind for you.'

'Have you, indeed! How glad I am! – What are they all?'

'I will read you their names directly; here they are, in my pocket-book. Castle of Wolfenbach, Clermont, Mysterious Warnings, Necromancer of the Black Forest, Midnight Bell, Orphan of the Rhine, and Horrid Mysteries. Those will last us some time.'

'Yes, pretty well; but are they all horrid, are you sure they are all horrid?'

'Yes, quite sure; for a particular friend of mine, a Miss Andrews, a sweet girl, one of the sweetest creatures in the world, has read every one of them. I wish you knew Miss Andrews, you would be delighted with her. She is netting herself the sweetest cloak you can conceive. I think her as beautiful as an angel, and I am so vexed with the men for not admiring her! – I scold them all amazingly about it.'

'Scold them! Do you scold them for not admiring her?'

'Yes, that I do. There is nothing I would not do for those who are really my friends. I have no notion of loving people by halves, it is not my nature. My attachments are always excessively strong. I told Capt. Hunt at one of our assemblies this winter, that if he was to tease me all night, I would not dance with him, unless he would allow Miss Andrews to be as beautiful as an angel The men think us incapable of real friendship you know, and I am determined to shew them the difference. Now, if I were to hear any body speak slightingly of you, I should fire up in a moment: – but that is not at all likely, for *you* are just the kind of girl to be a great favourite with the men.'

'Oh! dear,' cried Catherine, colouring, 'how can you say so?'

'I know you very well; you have so much animation, which is exactly what Miss Andrews wants, for I must confess there is something amazingly insipid about her. Oh! I must tell you, that just after we parted yesterday, I saw a young man looking at you so earnestly – I am sure he is in love with you.' Catherine coloured, and disclaimed again. Isabella laughed. 'It is very true, upon my honour, but I see how it is; you are indifferent to every body's admiration, except that of one gentleman, who shall be nameless. Nay, I cannot blame you – (speaking more seriously) – your feelings are easily understood. Where the heart is really attached, I know very well how little one can be pleased with the attention of any body else. Every thing is so insipid, so uninteresting, that does not relate to the beloved object! I can perfectly comprehend your feelings.'

'But you should not persuade me that I think so very much about Mr Tilney, for perhaps I may never see him again.'

'Not see him again! My dearest creature, do not talk of it. I am sure you would be miserable if you thought so.'

'No, indeed, I should not. I do not pretend to say that I was not very much pleased with him; but while I have Udolpho to read, I feel as if nobody could make me miserable. Oh! the dreadful black veil! My dear Isabella, I am sure there must be Laurentina's skeleton behind it.'

'It is so odd to me, that you should never have read Udolpho before; but I suppose Mrs Morland objects to novels.'

'No, she does not. She very often reads Sir Charles Grandison herself; but new books do not fall in our way.'

'Sir Charles Grandison! That is an amazing horrid book, is it not? – I remember Miss Andrews could not get through the first volume.'

'It is not like Udolpho at all; but yet I think it is very entertaining.'

'Do you indeed! – you surprize me; I thought it had not been readable. But, my dearest Catherine, have you settled what to wear on your head to-night? I am determined at all events to be dressed exactly like you. The men take notice of *that* sometimes you know.'

'But it does not dignify if they do;' said Catherine, very innocently.

'Signify! Oh, heavens! I make it a rule never to mind what they

say. They are very often amazingly impertinent if you do not treat
them with spirit, and make them keep their distance.'

'Are they? – Well, I never observed *that*. They always behave very
well to me.'

'Oh! they give themselves such airs. They are the most conceited
creatures in the world, and think themselves of so much importance!
– By the bye, though I have thought of it a hundred times. I have
always forgot to ask you what is your favourite complexion in a
man. Do you like them best dark or fair?'

'I hardly know. I never much thought about it. Something
between both, I think. Brown – not fair, and not very dark.'

'Very well, Catherine. That is exactly he. I have not forgot your
description of Mr Tilney; – "a brown skin, with dark eyes, and
rather dark hair." – Well, my taste is different. I prefer light eyes,
and as to complexion – do you know – I like a sallow better than
any other. You must not betray me, if you should ever meet with
one of your acquaintance answering that description.'

'Betray you! – What do you mean?'

'Nay, do not distress me. I believe I have said too much. Let us
drop the subject.'

Catherine, in some amazement, complied; and after remaining a
few moments silent, was on the point of reverting to what interested
her at that time rather more than any thing else in the world,
Laurentina's skeleton; when her friend prevented her, by saying, –
'For Heaven's sake! let us move away from this end of the room.
Do you know, there are two odious young men who have been
staring at me this half hour. They really put me quite out of countenance. Let us go and look at the arrivals. They will hardly follow us
there.'

Away they walked to the book; and while Isabella examined the
names, it was Catherine's employment to watch the proceedings of
these alarming young men.

'They are not coming this way, are they? I hope they are not so
impertinent as to follow us. Pray let me know if they are coming.
I am determined I will not look up.'

In a few moments Catherine, with unaffected pleasure, assured
her that she need not be longer uneasy, as the gentlemen had just
left the Pump-room.

'And which way are they gone?' said Isabella, turning hastily
round. 'One was a very good-looking young man.'

'They went towards the churchyard.'

'Well, I am amazingly glad I have got rid of them! And now,

what say you to going to Edgar's Buildings with me, and looking at my new hat? You said you should like to see it.'

Catherine readily agreed, 'Only,' she added, 'perhaps we may overtake the two young men.'

'Oh! never mind that. If we make haste, we shall pass by them presently, and I am dying to shew you my hat.'

'But if we only wait a few minutes, there will be no danger of our seeing them at all.'

'I shall not pay them any such compliment, I assure you. I have no notion of treating men with such respect. *That* is the way to spoil them.'

Catherine had nothing to oppose against such reasoning; and therefore, to shew the independence of Miss Thorpe, and her resolution of humbling the sex, they set off immediately as fast as they could walk, in pursuit of the two young men.

CHAPTER SEVEN

HALF A MINUTE CONDUCTED them through the Pump-yard to the archway, opposite Union-passage; but here they were stopped. Every body acquainted with Bath may remember the difficulties of crossing Cheap-street at this point; it is indeed a street of so impertinent a nature, so unfortunately connected with the great London and Oxford roads, and the principal inn of the city, that a day never passes in which parties of ladies, however important their business, whether in quest of pastry, millinery, or even (as in the present case) of young men, are not detained on one side or other by carriages, horsemen, or carts. This evil had been felt and lamented, at least three times a day, by Isabella since her residence in Bath; and she was now fated to feel and lament it once more, for at the very moment of coming opposite to Union-passage, and within view of the two gentlemen who were proceeding through the crowds, and threading the gutters of that interesting alley, they were prevented crossing by the approach of a gig, drive along on bad pavement by a most knowing-looking coachman with all the vehemence that could most fitly endanger the lives of himself, his companion, and his horse.

'Oh, these odious gigs!' said Isabella, looking up, 'how I detest them.' But this detestation, though so just, was of short duration, for she looked again and exclaimed, 'Delightful! Mr Morland and my brother!'

'Good heaven! 'tis James!' was uttered at the same moment by Catherine; and, on catching the young men's eyes, the horse was immèdiately checked with a violence which almost threw him on his haunches, and the servant having now scampered up, the gentlemen jumped out, and the equipage was delivered to his care.

Catherine, by whom this meeting was wholly unexpected, received her brother with the liveliest pleasure; and he, being of a very amiable disposition, and sincerely attached to her, gave every proof on his side of equal satisfaction, which he could have leisure to do, while the bright eyes of Miss Thorpe were incessantly challenging his notice; and to her his devoirs were speedily paid, with a mixture of joy and embarrassment which might have informed Catherine, had she been more expert in the development of other people's feelings, and less simply engrossed by her own, that her brother thought her friend quite as pretty as she could do herself.

John Thorpe, who in the mean time had been giving orders about the horses, soon joined them, and from him she directly received the amends which were her due; for while he slightly and carelessly touched the hand of Isabella, on her he bestowed a whole scrape and half a short bow. He was a stout young man of middling height, who, with a plain face and ungraceful form, seemed fearful of being too handsome unless he wore the dress of a groom, and too much like a gentleman unless he were easy where he ought to be civil, and impudent where he might be allowed to be easy. He took out his watch: 'How long do you think we have been running it from Tetbury, Miss Morland?'

'I do not know the distance.' Her brother told her that it was twenty-three miles.

'*Three*-and twenty!' cried Thorpe; 'five-and-twenty if it is an inch.' Morland remonstrated, pleaded the authority of road-books, innkeepers, and milestones; but his friend disregarded them all; he had a surer test of distance. 'I know it must be five-and-twenty,' said he, 'by the time we have been doing it. It is now half after one; we drove out of the inn-yard at Tetbury as the town-clock struck eleven; and I defy any man in England to make my horse go less than ten miles an hour in harness; that makes it exactly twenty-five.'

'You have lost an hour,' said Morland; 'it was only ten o'clock when we came from Tetbury.'

'Ten o'clock! it was eleven, upon my soul! I counted every stroke. This brother of yours would persuade me out of my senses, Miss

Morland; do but look at my horse; did you ever see an animal so made for speed in your life?' (The servant had just mounted the carriage and was driving off.) 'Such true blood! Three hours and a half indeed coming only three-and-twenty miles! look at that creature, and suppose it possible if you can.'

'He *does* look very hot to be sure.'

'Hot! he had not turned a hair till we came to Walcot Church: but look at his forehand; look at his loins; only see how he moves; that horse *cannot* go less than ten miles an hour: tie his legs and he will get on. What do you think of my gig, Miss Morland? a neat one, is not it? Well hung; town built; I have not had it a month. It was built for a Christ-church man, a friend of mine, a very good sort of fellow; he ran it a few weeks, till, I believe, it was convenient to have done with it. I happened just then to be looking out for some light thing of the kind, though I had pretty well determined on a curricle too; but I chanced to meet him on Magdalen Bridge, as he was driving into Oxford, last term: "Ah! Thorpe," says he, "do you happen to want such a little thing as this? it is a capital one of the kind, but I am cursed tired of it." "Oh! d—," said I, "I am your man; what do you ask?" And how much do you think he did, Miss Morland?'

'I am sure I cannot guess at all.'

'Curricle-hung you see; seat, trunk, sword-case, splashing-board, lamps, silver moulding, all you see complete; the iron-work as good as new, or better. He asked fifty guineas; I closed with him directly, threw down the money, and the carriage was mine.'

'And I am sure,' said Catherine, 'I know so little of such things that I cannot judge whether it was cheap or dear.'

'Neither one nor t'other; I might have got it for less I dare say; but I hate haggling, and poor Freeman wanted cash.'

'That was very good-natured of you,' said Catherine, quite pleased.

'Oh! d— it, when one has the means of doing a kind thing by a friend, I hate to be pitiful.'

An inquiry now took place into the intended movements of the young ladies; and, on finding whither they were going, it was decided that the gentlemen should accompany them to Edgar's Buildings, and pay their respects to Mrs Thorpe. James and Isabella led the way; and so well satisfied was the latter with her lot, so contentedly was she endeavouring to ensure a pleasant walk to him who brought the double recommendation of being her brother's friend, and her friend's brother, so pure and uncoquettish were her feelings, that, though they overtook and passed the two offending young men in Milsom-street, she was so far from seeking to attract their notice, that she looked back at them only three times.

John Thorpe kept of course with Catherine, and, after a few minutes' silence, renewed the conversation about his gig – 'You will find, however, Miss Morland, it would be reckoned a cheap thing by some people, for I might have sold it for ten guineas more the next day; Jackson, of Oriel, bid me sixty at once; Morland was with me at the time.'

'Yes,' said Morland, who overheard this; 'but you forget that your horse was included.'

'My horse! oh, d— it! I would not sell my horse for a hundred. Are you fond of an open carriage, Miss Morland?'

'Yes, very; I have hardly ever had an opportunity of being in one; but I am particularly fond of it.'

'I am glad of it; I will drive you out in mine every day.'

'Thank you,' said Catherine, in some distress, from a doubt of the propriety of accepting such an offer.

'I will drive you up Lansdown Hill to-morrow.'

'Thank you; but will not your horse want rest?'

'Rest! he has only come three-and-twenty miles today; all nonsense; nothing ruins horses so much as rest; nothing knocks them up so soon. No, no; I shall exercise mine at the average of four hours every day while I am here.'

'Shall you indeed!' said Catherine very seriously, 'that will be forty miles a day.'

'Forty! aye fifty, for what I care. Well, I will drive you up Lansdown to-morrow; mind, I am engaged.'

'How delightful that will be!' cried Isabella, turning round; 'my dearest Catherine, I quite envy you; but I am afraid, brother, you will not have room for a third.'

'A third indeed! no, no; I did not come to Bath to drive my sisters about; that would be a good joke, faith! Morland must take care of you.'

This brought on a dialogue of civilities between the other two; but Catherine heard neither the particulars nor the result. Her companion's discourse now sunk from its hitherto animated pitch, to nothing more than a short decisive sentence of praise or condemnation on the face of every woman they met; and Catherine, after listening and agreeing as long as she could, with all the civility and deference of the youthful female mind, fearful of hazarding an opinion of its own in opposition to that of a self-assured man, especially where the beauty of her own sex is concerned, ventured at length to vary the subject by a question which had been long uppermost in her thoughts; it was, 'Have you ever read Udolpho, Mr Thorpe?'

'Udolpho! Oh, Lord! not I; I never read novels; I have something else to do.'

Catherine, humbled and ashamed, was going to apologize for her question, but he prevented her by saying, 'Novels are all so full of nonsense and stuff; there has not been a tolerably decent one come out since Tom Jones, except the Monk; I read that t'other day; but as for all the others, they are the stupidest things in creation.'

'I think you must like Udolpho, if you were to read it; it is so very interesting.'

'Not I, faith! No, if I read any, it shall be Mrs Radcliff's; her novels are amusing enough; they are worth reading; some fun and nature in *them*.'

'Udolpho was written by Mrs Radcliff,' said Catherine, with some hesitation, from the fear of mortifying him.

'No sure; was it? Aye, I remember, so it was; I was thinking of that other stupid book, written by that woman they make such a fuss about, she who married the French emigrant.'

'I suppose you mean Camilla?'

'Yes, that's the book; such unnatural stuff! – An old man playing at see-saw! I took up the first volume once and looked it over, but I soon found it would not do; indeed I guessed what sort of stuff it must be before I saw it: as soon as I heard she had married an emigrant, I was sure I should never be able to get through it.'

'I have never read it.'

'You had no loss I assure you; it is the horridest nonsense you can imagine; there is nothing in the world in it but an old man's playing at see-saw and learning Latin; upon my soul there is not.'

This critique, the justness of which was unfortunately lost on poor Catherine, brought them to the door of Mrs Thorpe's lodgings, and the feelings of the discerning and unprejudiced reader of Camilla gave way to the feelings of the dutiful and affectionate son, as they met Mrs Thorpe, who had described them from above, in the passage. 'Ah, mother! how do you do?' said he, giving her a hearty shake of the hand: 'where did you get that quiz of a hat, it makes you look like an old witch? Here is Morland and I come to stay a few days with you, so you must look out for a couple of good beds some where near.' And this address seemed to satisfy all the fondest wishes of the mother's heart, for she received him with the most delighted and exulting affection. On his two younger sisters he then bestowed an equal portion of his fraternal tenderness, for he asked

each of them how they did, and observed that they both looked
very ugly.

These manners did not please Catherine; but he was James's friend
and Isabella's brother; and her judgment was further bought off by
Isabella's assuring her, when they withdrew to see the new hat, that
John thought her the most charming girl in the world, and by John's
engaging her before they parted to dance with him that evening.
Had she been older or vainer, such attacks might have done little;
but, where youth and diffidence are united, it requires uncommon
steadiness of reason to resist the attraction of being called the most
charming girl in the world, and of being so very early engaged as
a partner; and the consequence was, that, when the two Morlands,
after sitting an hour with the Thorpes, set off to walk together to
Mr Allen's, and James, as the door was closed on them, said, 'Well,
Catherine, how do you like my friend Thorpe?' instead of
answering, as she probably would have done, had there been no
friendship and no flattery in the case. 'I do not like him at all;' she
directly replied, 'I like him very much; he seems very agreeable.'

'He is as good-natured a fellow as ever lived; a little of a rattle;
but that will recommend him to your sex I believe: and how do
you like the rest of the family?'

'Very, very much indeed: Isabella particularly.'

'I am very glad to hear you say so; she is just the kind of young
woman I could wish to see you attached to; she has so much good
sense, and is so thoroughly unaffected and amiable; I always wanted
you to know her; and she seems very fond of you. She said the
highest things in your praise that could possibly be; and the praise
of such a girl as Miss Thorpe even you, Catherine,' taking her hand
with affection, 'may be proud of.'

'Indeed I am,' she replied; 'I love her exceedingly, and am
delighted to find that you like her too. You hardly mentioned any
thing of her, when you wrote to me after your visit there.'

'Because I thought I should soon see you myself. I hope you will
be a great deal together while you are in Bath. She is a most amiable
girl; such a superior understanding! How fond all the family are of
her; she is evidently the general favourite; and how much she must
be admired in such a place as this – is not she?'

'Yes, very much indeed, I fancy; Mr Allen thinks her the prettiest
girl in Bath.'

'I dare say he does; and I do not know any man who is a better
judge of beauty than Mr Allen. I need not ask you whether you are
happy here, my dear Catherine; with such a companion and friend

as Isabella Thorpe, it would be impossible for you to be otherwise; and the Allens I am sure are very kind to you?'

'Yes, very kind; I never was so happy before; and now you are come it will be more delightful than ever; how good it is of you to come so far on purpose to see *me*.'

James accepted this tribute of gratitude, and qualified his conscience for accepting it too, by saying with perfect sincerity, 'Indeed, Catherine, I love you dearly.'

Inquiries and communications concerning brothers and sisters, the situation of some, the growth of the rest, and other family matters, now passed between them, and continued, with only one small digression on James's part, in praise of Miss Thorpe, till they reached Pulteney-street, where he was welcomed with great kindness by Mr and Mrs Allen, invited by the former to dine with them, and summoned by the latter to guess the price and weigh the merits of a new muff and tippet. A pre-engagement in Edgar's Buildings prevented his accepting the invitation of one friend, and obliged him to hurry away as soon as he had satisfied the demands of the other. The time of the two parties uniting in the Octagon Room being correctly adjusted, Catherine was then left to the luxury of a raised, restless, and frightened imagination over the pages of Udolpho, lost from all worldly concerns of dressing and dinner, incapable of soothing Mrs Allen's fears on the delay of an expected dress-maker, and having only one minute in sixty to bestow even on the reflection of her own felicity, in being already engaged for the evening.

CHAPTER EIGHT

IN SPITE OF UDOLPHO and the dress-maker, however, the party from Pulteney-street reached the Upper-rooms in very good time. The Thorpes and James Morland were there only two minutes before them; and Isabella having gone through the usual ceremonial of meeting her friend with the most smiling and affectionate haste, of admiring the set of her gown, and envying the curl of her hair, they followed their chaperons, arm in arm into the ball-room, whispering to each other whenever a thought occurred, and supplying the place of many ideas by a squeeze of the hand or a smile of affection.

The dancing began within a few minutes after they were seated; and James, who had been engaged quite as long as his sister, was very importunate with Isabella to stand up; but John was gone into the card-room to speak to a friend, and nothing, she declared, should induce her to join the set before her dear Catherine could join it too: 'I assure you,' said she, 'I would not stand up without your dear sister for all the world; for if I did we should certainly be separated the whole evening.' Catherine accepted this kindness with gratitude, and they continued as they were for three minutes longer, when Isabella, who had been talking to James on the other side of her, turned again to his sister and whispered, 'My dear creature, I am afraid I must leave you, your brother is so amazingly impatient to begin; I know you will not mind my going away, and I dare say John will be back in a moment, and then you may easily find me out.' Catherine, though a little disappointed, had too much good-nature to make any opposition, and the others rising up, Isabella had only time to press her friend's hand and say, 'Good bye, my dear love,' before they hurried off. The younger Miss Thorpes being also dancing, Catherine was left to the mercy of Mrs Thorpe and Mrs Allen, between whom she now remained. She could not help being vexed at the non-appearance of Mr Thorpe, for she not only longed to be dancing, but was likewise aware that, as the real dignity of her situation could not be known, she was sharing with the scores of other young ladies still sitting down all the discredit of wanting a partner. To be disgraced in the eye of the world, to wear the appearance of infamy while her heart is all purity, her actions all innocence, and the misconduct of another the true source of her debasement, is one of those circumstances which peculiarly belong to the heroine's life, and her fortitude under it what particularly dignifies her character. Catherine had fortitude too; she suffered, but no murmur passed her lips.

From this state of humiliation, she was roused, at the end of ten minutes, to a pleasanter feeling, by seeing, not Mr Thorpe, but Mr Tilney, within three yards of the place where they sat; he seemed to be moving that way, but he did not see her, and therefore the smile and the blush, which his sudden reappearance raised in Catherine, passed away without sullying her heroic importance. He looked as handsome and as lively as ever, and was talking with interest to a fashionable and pleasing-looking young woman, who leant on his arm, and whom Catherine immediately guessed to be his sister; thus unthinkingly throwing away a fair opportunity of considering him lost to her for ever, by being married already. But guided only by what was simple and probable, it had never entered her head that Mr Tilney could be married; he had not behaved, he had not talked, like the married men to whom she had been used;

he had never mentioned a wife, and he had acknowledged a sister. From these circumstances sprang the instant conclusion of his sister's now being by his side; and therefore, instead of turning of a deathlike paleness, and falling in a fit on Mrs Allen's bosom, Catherine sat erect, in the perfect use of her senses, and with cheeks only a little redder than usual.

Mr Tilney and his companion, who continued, though slowly, to approach, were immediately preceded by a lady, an acquaintance of Mrs Thorpe; and this lady stopping to speak to her, they, as belonging to her, stopped likewise, and Catherine, catching Mr Tilney's eye, instantly received from him the smiling tribute of recognition. She returned it with pleasure, and then advancing still nearer, he spoke both to her and Mrs Allen, by whom he was very civilly acknowledged. 'I am very happy to see you again, sir indeed; I was afraid you had left Bath.' He thanked her for her fears, and said that he had quitted it for a week, on the very morning after his having had the pleasure of seeing her.

'Well, sir, and I dare say you are not sorry to be back again, for it is just the place for young people – and indeed for every body else too. I tell Mr Allen, when he talks of being sick of it, that I am sure he should not complain, for it is so very agreeable a place, that it is much better to be here than at home at this dull time of year. I tell him he is quite in luck to be sent here for his health.'

'And I hope, madam, that Mr Allen will be obliged to like the place, from finding it of service to him.'

'Thank you, sir. I have no doubt that he will. – A neighbour of ours, Dr Skinner, was here for his health last winter, and came away quite stout.'

'That circumstance must give great encouragement.'

'Yes, sir – and Dr Skinner and his family were here three months; so I tell Mr Allen he must not be in a hurry to get away.'

Here they were interrupted by a request from Mrs Thorpe to Mrs Allen, that she would move a little to accommodate Mrs Hughes and Miss Tilney with seats, as they had agreed to join their party. This was accordingly done, Mr Tilney still continuing standing before them; and after a few minutes consideration, he asked Catherine to dance with him. This compliment, delightful as it was, produced severe mortification to the lady; and in giving her denial, she expressed her sorrow on the occasion so very much as if she really felt it, that had Thorpe, who joined her just afterwards, been half a minute earlier, he might have thought her sufferings rather too acute. The very easy manner in which he then told her that he had kept her waiting, did not by any means reconcile her more to

her lot; nor did the particulars which he entered into while they
were standing up, of the horses and dogs of the friend whom he
had just left, and of a proposed exchange of terriers between them,
interest her so much as to prevent her looking very often towards
that part of the room where she had left Mr Tilney. Of her dear
Isabella, to whom she particularly longed to point out that
gentleman, she could see nothing. They were in different sets. She
was separated from all her party, and away from all her acquaintance;

'I beg your pardon, Miss Morland,'

– one mortification succeeded another, and from the whole she deduced this useful lesson, that to go previously engaged to a ball, does not necessarily increase either the dignity or enjoyment of a young lady. From such a moralizing strain as this, she was suddenly roused by a touch on the shoulder, and turning round, perceived Mrs Hughes directly behind her, attended by Miss Tilney and a gentleman. 'I beg your pardon, Miss Morland,' said she, 'for this liberty, – but I cannot any how get to Miss Thorpe, and Mrs Thorpe said she was sure you would not have the least objection to letting in this young lady by you.' Mrs Hughes could not have applied to any creature in the room more happy to oblige her than Catherine. The young ladies were introduced to each other, Miss Tilney expressing a proper sense of such goodness, Miss Morland with the real delicacy of a generous mind making light of the obligation; and Mrs Hughes, satisfied with having so respectably settled her young charge, returned to her party.

Miss Tilney had a good figure, a pretty face, and a very agreeable countenance; and her air, though it had not all the decided pretention, the resolute stilishness of Miss Thorpe's, had more real elegance. Her manners shewed good sense and good breeding; they were neither shy, nor affectedly open; and she seemed capable of being young, attractive, and at a ball, without wanting to fix the attention of every man near her, and without exaggerated feelings of extatic delight or inconceivable vexation on every little trifling occurrence. Catherine, interested at once by her appearance and her relationship to Mr Tilney, was desirous of being acquainted with her, and readily talked therefore whenever she could think of any thing to say, and had courage and leisure for saying it. but the hindrance thrown in the way of a very speedy intimacy, by the frequent want of one or more of these requisites, prevented their doing more than going through the first rudiments of an acquaintance, by informing themselves how well the other liked Bath, how much she admired its buildings and surrounding country, whether she drew, or played or sang, and whether she was fond of riding on horseback.

The two dances were scarcely concluded before Catherine found her arm gently seized by her faithful Isabella, who in great spirits exclaimed – 'At last I have got you. My dearest creature, I have been looking for you this hour. What could induce you to come into this set, when you knew I was in the other? I have been quite wretched without you.'

'My dear Isabella, how was it possible for me to get at you? I could not even see where you were.'

'So I told your brother all the time – but he would not believe me. Do you go and see for her, Mr Morland, said I – but all in vain – he would not stir an inch. Was not it so, Mr Morland? but you men are all so immoderately lazy! I have been scolding him to such a degree, my dear Catherine, you would be quite amazed. – You know I never stand upon ceremony with such people.'

'Look at that young lady with the white beads round her head,' whispered Catherine, detaching her friend from James – 'It is Mr Tilney's sister.'

'Oh! heavens! You don't say so! Let me look at her this moment. What a delightful girl! I never saw any thing half so beautiful! But where is her all-conquering brother? Is he in the room? Point him out to me this instant, if he is. I die to see him. Mr Morland, you are not to listen. We are not talking about you.'

'But what is all this whispering about? What is going on?'

'There now, I knew how it would be. You men have such restless curiosity! Talk of the curiosity of women, indeed! – 'tis nothing. But be satisfied, for you are not to know any thing at all of the matter.'

'And is that likely to satisfy me, do you think?'

'Well, I declare I never knew any thing like you. What can it signify to you, what we are talking of? Perhaps we are talking about you, therefore I would advise you not to listen, or you may happen to hear something not very agreeable.'

In this common-place chatter, which lasted some time, the original subject seemed entirely forgotten; and though Catherine was very well pleased to have it dropped for awhile, she could not avoid a little suspicion at the total suspension of all Isabella's impatient desire to see Mr Tilney. When the orchestra struck up a fresh dance, James would have led his fair partner away, but she resisted. 'I tell you, Mr Morland,' she cried, 'I would not do such a thing for all the world. How can you be so teasing; only conceive, my dear Catherine, what your brother wants me to do. He wants me to dance with him again, though I tell him that it is a most improper thing, and entirely against the rules. It would make us the talk of the place, if we were not to change partners.'

'Upon my honour,' said James, 'in these public assemblies, it is as often done as not.'

'Nonsense, how can you say so? But when you men have a point to carry, you never stick at any thing. My sweet Catherine, do support me, persuade your brother how impossible it is. Tell him, that it would quite shock you to see me do such a thing; now would not it?'

'No, not at all; but if you think it wrong, you had much better change.'

'There,' cried Isabella, 'you hear what your sister says, and yet you will not mind her. Well, remember that it is not my fault, if we set all the old ladies in Bath in a bustle. Come along, my dearest Catherine, for heaven's sake, and stand by me.' And off they went, to regain their former place. John Thorpe, in the meanwhile, had walked away; and Catherine, ever willing to give Mr Tilney an opportunity of repeating the agreeable request which had already flattered her once, made her way to Mrs Allen and Mrs Thorpe as fast as she could, in the hope of finding him still with them – a hope which, when it proved to be fruitless, she felt to have been highly unreasonable. 'Well, my dear,' said Mrs Thorpe, impatient for praise of her son, 'I hope you have had an agreeable partner.'

'Very agreeable, madam.'

'I am glad of it. John has charming spirits, has not he?'

'Did you meet Mr Tilney, my dear?' said Mrs Allen.

'No, where is he?'

'He was with us just now, and said he was so tired of lounging about, that he was resolved to go and dance; so I thought perhaps he would ask you, if he met with you.'

'Where can he be?' said Catherine, looking round; but she had not looked round long before she saw him leading a young lady to the dance.

'Ah! he has got a partner, I wish he had asked *you*,' said Mrs Allen; and after a short silence, she added, 'he is a very agreeable young man.'

'Indeed he is, Mrs Allen,' said Mrs Thorpe, smiling complacently; 'I must say it, though I *am* his mother, that there' is not a more agreeable young man in the world.'

This inapplicable answer might have been too much for the comprehension of many; but it did not puzzle Mrs Allen, for after only a moment's consideration, she said, in a whisper to Catherine, 'I dare say she thought I was speaking of her son.'

Catherine was disappointed and vexed. She seemed to have missed by so little the very object she had had in view; and this persuasion did not incline her to a very gracious reply, when John Thorpe came up to her soon afterwards, and said, 'Well, Miss Morland, I suppose you and I are to stand up and jig it together again.'

'Oh, no; I am much obliged to you, our two dances are over; and, besides, I am tired, and do not mean to dance any more.'

'Do not you? – then let us walk about and quiz people. Come along with me, and I will shew you the four greatest quizzers in the room; my two younger sisters and their partners. I have been laughing at them this half hour.'

Again Catherine excused herself; and at last he walked off to quiz his sisters by himself. The rest of the evening she found very dull; Mr Tilney was drawn away from their party at tea, to attend that of his partner; Miss Tilney, though belonging to it, did not sit near her, and James and Isabella were so much engaged in conversing together, that the latter had no leisure to bestow more on her friend than one smile, one squeeze, and one 'dearest Catherine.'

CHAPTER NINE

THE PROGRESS OF CATHERINE'S unhappiness from the events of the evening, was as follows. It appeared first in a general dissatisfaction with every body about her, while she remained in the rooms, which speedily brought on considerable weariness and a violent desire to go home. This, on arriving in Pulteney-street, took the direction of extraordinary hunger, and when that was appeased, changed into an earnest longing to be in bed; such was the extreme point of her distress; for when there she immediately fell into a sound sleep which lasted nine hours, and from which she awoke perfectly revived, in excellent spirits, with fresh hopes and fresh schemes. The first wish of her heart was to improve her acquaintance with Miss Tilney, and almost her first resolution, to seek her for that purpose, in the Pump-room at noon. In the Pump-room, one so newly arrived in Bath must be met with, and that building she had already found so favourable for the discovery of female excellence, and the completions of female intimacy, so admirably adapted for secret discourses and unlimited conficence, that she was most reasonably encouraged to expect another friend from within its walls. Her plan for the morning thus settled, she sat quietly down to her book after breakfast, resolving to remain in the same place and the same employment till the clock struck one; and from habitude very little incommoded by the remarks and ejaculations of Mrs Allen, whose vacancy of mind and incapacity for thinking were such, that as she never talked a great deal, so she could never be entirely silent; and, therefore, while she sat at her work, if she lost her needle or broke her thread, if she heard a carriage in the street, or saw a speck upon her gown, she must observe it aloud, whether there were any one at leisure to answer her or not. At about half past twelve, a remarkably loud rap drew her in haste to the window, and scarcely had she time to inform Catherine of there being two open carriages at the door, in the first only a servant, her brother driving Miss Thorpe in the second, before John Thorpe came running up stairs, calling out, 'Well, Miss Morland, here I am. Have you been waiting long? We could not come before; the old devil of a coachmaker was such an eternity finding out a thing fit to be got into, and now it is ten thousand to one, but they break down before we are out of the street. How do you do, Mrs Allen? a famous ball last night, was not it? Come, Miss Morland, be quick, for the others are in a confounded hurry to be off. They want to get their tumble over.'

'What do you mean?' said Catherine, 'where are you all going to?'

'Going to? why, you have not forgot our engagement! Did not we agree together to take a drive this morning? What a head you have! We are going up Claverton Down.'

'Something was said about it, I remember,' said Catherine, looking at Mrs Allen for her opinion; 'but really I did not expect you.'

'Not expect me! that's a good one! And what a dust you would have made, if I had not come.'

Catherine's silent appeal to her friend, meanwhile, was entirely thrown away, for Mrs Allen, not being at all in the habit of conveying any expression herself by a look, was not aware of its being ever intended by any body else; and Catherine, whose desire of seeing Miss Tilney again could at that moment bear a short delay in favour of a drive, and who thought there could be no impropriety in her going with Mr Thorpe, as Isabella was going at the same time with James, was therefore obliged to speak plainer. 'Well, ma'am, what do you say to it? Can you spare me for an hour or two? shall I go?'

'Do just as you please, my dear,' replied Mrs Allen, with the most placid indifference. Catherine took the advice, and ran off to get ready. In a very few minutes she reappeared, having scarcely allowed the two others time enough to get through a few short sentences in her praise, after Thorpe had procured Mrs Allen's admiration of his gig; and then receiving her friend's parting good wishes, they both hurried down stairs. 'My dearest creature,' cried Isabella, to whom the duty of friendship immediately called her before she could get into the carriage, 'you have been at least three hours getting ready. I was afraid you were ill. What a delightful

Off they went, without a plunge or a caper.

ball we had last night. I have a thousand things to say to you; but make haste and get in, for I long to be off.'

Catherine followed her orders and turned away, but not too soon to hear her friend exclaim aloud to James, 'What a sweet girl she is! I quite doat on her.'

'You will not be frightened, Miss Morland,' said Thorpe, as he handed her in, 'if my horse should dance about a little at first setting off. He will, most likely, give a plunge or two, and perhaps take the rest for a minute; but he will soon know his master. He is full of spirits, playful as can be, but there is no vice in him.'

Catherine did not think the portrait a very inviting one, but it was too late to retreat, and she was too young to own herself frightened; so, resigning herself to her fate, and trusting to the animal's boasted knowledge of its owner, she sat peaceably down, and saw Thorpe sit down by her. Every thing being then arranged, the servant who stood at the horse's head was bid in an important voice 'to let him go,' and off they went in the quietest manner imaginable, without a plunge or a caper, or any thing like one. Catherine, delighted at so happy an escape, spoke her pleasure aloud with grateful surprize; and her companion immediately made the matter perfectly simple by assuring her that it was entirely owing to the peculiarly judicious manner in which he had then held the reins, and the singular discernment and dexterity with which he had directed his whip. Catherine, though she could not help wondering that with such perfect command of his horse, he should think it necessary to alarm her with a relation of its tricks, congratulated herself sincerely on being under the care of so excellent a coachman; and perceiving that the animal continued to go on in the same quiet manner, without shewing the smallest propensity towards any unpleasant vivacity, and (considering its inevitable pace was ten miles an hour) by no means alarmingly fast, gave herself up to all the enjoyment of air and exercise of the most invigorating kind, in a fine mild day of February, with the consciousness of safety. A silence of several minutes succeeded their first short dialogue; – it was broken by Thorpe's saying very abruptly, 'Old Allen is as rich as a Jew – is not he?' Catherine did not understand him – and he repeated his question, adding in explanation, 'Old Allen, the man you are with.'

'Oh! Mr Allen, you mean, Yes, I believe, he is very rich.'

'And no children at all?'

'No – not any.'

'A famous thing for his next heirs. He is *your* godfather, is not he?'

'My godfather! – no.'

'But you are always very much with them.'

'Yes, very much.'

'Aye, that is what I meant. He seems a good kind of old fellow enough, and has lived very well in his time, I dare say; he is not gouty for nothing. Does he drink his bottle a-day now?'

'His bottle a-day! – no. Why should you think of such a thing? He is a very temperate man, and you could not fancy him in liquor last night?'

'Lord help you! – You women are always thinking of men's being in liquor. Why you do not suppose a man is overset by a bottle? I am sure of *this* – that if every body was to drink their bottle a-day, there would not be half the disorders in the world there are now. It would be a famous good thing for us all.'

'I cannot believe it.'

'Oh! lord, it would be the saving of thousands. There is not the hundredth part of the wine consumed in this kingdom, that there ought to be. Our foggy climate wants help.'

'And yet I have heard that there is a great deal of wine drank in Oxford.'

'Oxford! There is no drinking at Oxford now, I assure you. Nobody drinks there. You hardly meet with a man who goes beyond his four pints at the utmost. Now, for instance, it was reckoned a remarkable thing at the last party in my rooms, that upon an average we cleared about five pints a head. It was looked upon as something out of the common way. *Mine* is famous good stuff to be sure. You would not often meet with any thing like it in Oxford – and that may account for it. But this will just give you a notion of the general rate of drinking there.'

'Yes, it does give a notion,' said Catherine, warmly, 'and that is, that you all drink a great deal more wine than I thought you did. However, I am sure James does not drink so much.'

This declaration brought on a loud and overpowering reply, of which no part was very distinct, except the frequent exclamations, amounting almost to oaths, which adorned it, and Catherine was left, when it ended, with rather a strengthened belief of there being a great deal of wine drank in Oxford, and the same happy conviction of her brother's comparative sobriety.

Thorpe's ideas then all reverted to the merits of his own equipage, and she was called on to admire the spirit and freedom with which his horse moved along, and the ease which his paces, as well as the excellence of the springs, gave the motion of the carriage. She followed him in all his admiration as well as she could. To go before, or beyond him was impossible. His knowledge and her ignorance of the subject, his rapidity of expression, and her diffidence of herself put that out of her power; she could strike out nothing new in commendation, but she readily echoed whatever he chose to assert, and it was finally settled between them without any difficulty, that his equipage was altogether the most complete of its kind in England, his carriage the neatest, his horse the best goer, and himself the best coachman. – 'You do not really think, Mr Thorpe,' said Catherine, venturing after some time to consider the matter as entirely decided, and to offer some little variation on the subject, 'that James's gig will break down?'

'Break down! Oh! lord! Did you ever see such a little tittuppy thing in your life? There is not a sound piece of iron about it. The wheels have been fairly worn out these ten years at least – and as for the body! Upon my soul, you might shake it to pieces yourself with a touch. It is the most devilish little ricketty business I ever beheld! – Thank God! we have got a better. I would not be bound to go two miles in it for fifty thousand pounds.'

'Good heavens!' cried Catherine, quite frightened, 'then pray let us turn back; they will certainly meet with an accident if we go on. Do let us turn back, Mr Thorpe; stop and speak to my brother, and tell him how very unsafe it is.'

'Unsafe! Oh, lord! what is there in that? they will only get a roll if it does break down; and there is plenty of dirt, it will be excellent falling. Oh, curse it! the carriage is safe enough, if a man knows how to drive it; a thing of that sort in good hands will last above twenty years after it is fairly worn out. Lord bless you! I would undertake for five pounds to drive it to York and back again, without losing a nail.'

Catherine listened with astonishment; she knew not how to reconcile two such different accounts of the same thing; for she had not been brought up to understand the propensities of a rattle, nor to know to how many idle assertions and impudent falsehoods the excess of vanity will lead. Her own family were plain matter-of-fact people, who seldom aimed at wit of any kind; her father, at the utmost, being contented with a pun, and her mother with a proverb; they were not in the habit therefore of telling lies to increase their importance, or of asserting at one moment what they would contradict the next. She reflected on the affair for some time in much perplexity, and was more than once on the point of requesting from Mr Thorpe a clearer insight into his real opinion on the subject; but she checked herself, because it appeared to her that he did not excel in giving those clearer insights, in making those things plain which he had before made ambiguous; and, joining to this, the consideration, that he would not really suffer his sister and his friend to be exposed to a danger from which he might easily preserve them, she concluded at last, that he must know the carriage to be in fact perfectly safe, and therefore would alarm herself no longer. By him the whole matter seemed entirely forgotten; and all the rest of his conversation, or rather talk, began and ended with himself and his own concerns. He told her of horses which he had bought for a trifle and sold for incredible sums; of racing matches, in which his judgment had infallibly foretold the winner; of shooting parties, in which he had killed more birds (though without having one good shot) than all his companions together; and described to her some famous day's sport, with the fox-hounds, in which his foresight and skill in directing the dogs had repaired the mistakes of the most experienced huntsman, and in which the boldness of his riding, though it had never endangered his own life for a moment, had been constantly leading others into difficulties, which he calmly concluded had broken the necks of many.

Little as Catherine was in the habit of judging for herself, and unfixed as were her general notions of what men ought to be, she could not entirely repress a doubt, while she bore with the effusions of his endless conceit, of his being altogether completely agreeable. It was a bold surmise, for he was Isabella's brother; and she had been assured by James, that his manners would recommend him to all her sex; but in spite of this, the extreme weariness of his company, which crept over her before they had been out an hour, and which continued unceasingly to increase till they stopped in Pulteney-street again, induced her, in some small degree, to resist high authority, and to distrust his powers of giving universal pleasure.

When they arrived at Mrs Allen's door, the astonishment of Isabella was hardly to be expressed, on finding that it was too late in the day for them to attend her friend into the house: – 'Past three o'clock!' it was inconceivable, incredible, impossible! and she would neither believe her own watch, nor her brother's, nor the servant's; she would believe no assurance of it founded on reason or reality, till Morland produced his watch, and ascertained the fact; to have doubted a moment longer *then*, would have been equally inconceivable, incredible, and impossible; and she could only protest, over and over again, that no two hours and a half had ever gone off so swiftly before, as Catherine was called on to confirm; Catherine could not tell a falsehood even to please Isabella; but the latter was spared the misery of her friend's dissenting voice, by not waiting for her answer. Her own feelings entirely engrossed her; her wretchedness was most acute on finding herself obliged to go directly home. – It was ages since she had had a moment's conversation with her dearest Catherine, and, though she had such thousands of things to say to her, it appeared as if they were never to be together again; so, with smiles of most exquisite misery, and the laughing eye of utter despondency, she bade her friend adieu and went on.

Catherine found Mrs Allen just returned from all the busy idleness of the morning, and was immediately greeted with, 'Well, my dear, here you are;' a truth which she had no greater inclination than power to dispute; 'and I hope you have had a pleasant airing?'

'Yes, ma'am, I thank you; we could not have had a nicer day.'

'So Mrs Thorpe said; she was vastly pleased at your all going.'

'You have seen Mrs Thorpe then?'

'Yes, I went to the Pump-room as soon as you were gone, and there I met her, and we had a great deal of talk together. She says there was hardly any veal to be got at market this morning, it is so uncommonly scarce.'

'Did you see any body else of our acquaintance?'

'Yes; we agreed to take in the Crescent, and there we met Mrs Hughes, and Mr and Miss Tilney walking with her.'

'Did you indeed? and did they speak to you?'

'Yes, we walked along the Crescent together for half an hour. They seem very agreeable people. Miss Tilney was in a very pretty spotted muslin, and I fancy, by what I can learn, that she always dresses very handsomely. Mrs Hughes talked to me a great deal about the family.'

'And what did she tell you of them?'

'Oh! a vast deal indeed; she hardly talked of any thing else.'

'Did she tell you what part of Gloucestershire they come from?'

'Yes, she did; but I cannot recollect now. But they are very good kind of people, and very rich. Mrs Tilney was a Miss Drummond, and she and Mrs Hughes were school fellows; and Miss Drummond had a very large fortune; and when she married, her father gave her twenty thousand pounds, and five hundred to buy wedding-clothes. Mrs Hughes saw all the clothes after they came from the warehouse.'

'And are Mr and Mrs Tilney in Bath?'

'Yes, I fancy they are, but I am not quite certain. Upon recollection, however, I have a notion they are both dead; at least the mother is; yes, I am sure Mrs Tilney is dead, because Mrs Hughes told me there was a very beautiful set of pearls that Mr Drummond gave his daughter on her wedding-day and that Miss Tilney has got now, for they were put by for her when her mother died.'

'And is Mr Tilney, my partner, the only son?'

'I cannot be quite positive about that, my dear; I have some idea he is; but, however, he is a very fine young man Mrs Hughes says, and likely to do well.'

Catherine enquired no further; she had heard enough to feel that Mrs Allen had no real intelligence to give, and that she was most particularly unfortunate herself in having missed such a meeting with both brother and sister. Could she have forseen such a circumstance, nothing should have persuaded her to go out with the others; and, as it was, she could only lament her ill-luck, and think over what she had lost, till it was clear to her, that the drive had by no means been very pleasant and that John Thorpe himself was quite disagreeable.

CHAPTER TEN

THE ALLENS, THORPES, and Morlands, all met in the evening at the theatre; and, as Catherine and Isabella sat together, there was then an opportunity for the latter to utter some few of the many thousand things which had been collecting within her for communication, in the immeasurable length of time which had divided them. – 'Oh, heavens! my beloved Catherine, have I got you at last?' was her address on Catherine's entering the box and sitting by her. 'Now, Mr Morland,' for he was close to her on the other side, 'I shall not speak another word to you all the rest of the evening; so I charge you not to expect it. My sweetest Catherine, how have you been this long age? but I need not ask you, for you look delightfully. You really have done your hair in a more heavenly style than ever: you mischievous creature, do you want to attract every body? I assure you, my brother is quite in love with you already; and as for Mr Tilney – but *that* is a settled thing – even *your* modesty cannot doubt his attachment now; his coming back to Bath makes it too plain. Oh! what would not I give to see him! I really am quite wild with impatience. My mother says he is the most delightful young man in the world, she saw him this morning you know: you must introduce him to me. Is he in the house now? – Look about for heaven's sake! I assure you, I can hardly exist till I see him.'

'No,' said Catherine, 'he is not here; I cannot see him any where.'

'Oh, horrid! am I never to be acquainted with him? How do you like my gown? I think it does not look amiss; the sleeves were entirely my own thought. Do you know I get so immoderately sick of Bath; your brother and I were agreeing this morning that, though it is vastly well to be here for a few weeks, we would not live here for millions. We soon found out that our tastes were exactly alike in preferring the country to every other place; really, our opinions were so exactly the same, it was quite ridiculous! There was not a single point in which we differed; I would not have had you by for the world; you are such a sly thing, I am sure you would have made some droll remark or other about it.'

'No, indeed I should not.'

'Oh, yes you would indeed; I know you better than you know

yourself. You would have told us that we seemed born for each other, or some nonsense of that kind, which would have distressed me beyond conception; my cheeks would have been as red as your roses; I would not have had you by for the world.'

'Indeed you do me injustice; I would not have made so improper a remark upon any account; and besides, I am sure it would never have entered my head.'

Isabella smiled incredulously, and talked the rest of the evening to James.

Catherine's resolution of endeavouring to meet Miss Tilney again continued in full force the next morning; and till the usual moment of going to the Pump-room, she felt some alarm from the dread of a second prevention. But nothing of that kind occurred, no visitors appeared to delay them, and they all three set off in good time for the Pump-room, where the ordinary course of events and conversation took place; Mr Allen, after drinking his glass of water, joined some gentlemen to talk over the politics of the day and compare the accounts of their newspapers; and the ladies walked about together, noticing every new face, and almost every new bonnet in the room. The female part of the Thorpe family, attended by James Morland, appeared among the crowd in less than a quarter of an hour, and Catherine immediately took her usual place by the side of her friend. James, who was now in constant attendance, maintained a similar position, and separating themselves from the rest of their party, they walked in that manner for some time, till Catherine began to doubt the happiness of a situation which confining her entirely to her friend and brother, gave her very little share in the notice of either. They were always engaged in some sentimental discussion or lively dispute, but their sentiment was conveyed in such whispering voices, and their vivacity attended with so much laughter, that though Catherine's supporting opinion was not unfrequently called for by one or the other, she was never able to give any, from not having heard a word of the subject. At length however she was empowered to disengage herself from her friend by the avowed necessity of speaking to Miss Tilney, whom she most joyfully saw just entering the room with Mrs Hughes, and whom she instantly joined, with a firmer determination to be acquainted, than she might have had courage to command, had she not been urged by the disappointment of the day before. Miss Tilney met her with great civility, returned her advances with equal good will, and they continued talking together as long as both parties remained in the room: and though in all probability not an observation was made, nor an expression used by either which had not been made and used some thousands of times before, under that roof, in every Bath season, yet the merit of their being spoken with simplicity and truth, and without personal conceit, might be something uncommon. –

'How well your brother dances!' was an artless exclamation of Catherine's towards the close of their conversation, which at once surprized and amused her companion.

'Henry!' she replied with a smile. 'Yes, he does dance very well.'

'He must have thought it very odd to hear me say I was engaged the other evening, when he saw me sitting down. But I really had been engaged the whole day to Mr Thorpe.' Miss Tilney could only

'Rid out this morning with my father.'

bow. 'You cannot think' added Catherine after a moment's silence, 'how surprized I was to see him again. I felt so sure of his being quite gone away.'

'When Henry had the pleasure of seeing you before, he was in Bath but for a couple of days. He came only to engage lodging for us.'

'*That* never occurred to me; and of course, not seeing him any where, I thought he must be gone. Was not the young lady he danced with on Monday a Miss Smith?'

'Yes, an acquaintance of Mrs Hughes.'

'I dare say she was very glad to dance. Do you think her pretty?'

'Not very.'

'He never comes to the Pump-room, I suppose?'

'Yes, sometimes; but he has rid out this morning with my father.'

Mrs Hughes now joined them, and asked Miss Tilney if she was ready to go. 'I hope I shall have the pleasure of seeing you again soon,' said Catherine. 'Shall you be at the cotillion ball to-morrow?'

'Perhaps we – yes, I think we certainly shall.'

'I am glad of it, for we shall all be there.' – This civility was duly returned; and they parted – on Miss Tilney's side with some knowledge of her new acquaintance's feelings, and on Catherine's, without the smallest consciousness of having explained them.

She went hor   very happy. The morning had answered all her hopes, and the evening of the following day was now the object of expectation, the future good. What gown and what head-dress she should wear on the occasion became her chief concern. She cannot be justified in it. Dress is at all times a frivolous distinction, and excessive solicitude about it often destroys its own aim. Catherine knew all this very well; her great aunt had read her a lecture on the subject only the Christmas before; and yet she lay awake ten minutes on Wednesday night debating between her spotted and her tamboured muslin, and nothing but the shortness of the time prevented her buying a new one for the evening. This would have been an error in judgment, great though not uncommon, from which one of the other sex rather than her own, a brother rather than a great aunt might have warned her, for man only can be aware of the insensibility of man towards a new gown. It would be mortifying to the feelings of many ladies, could they be made to understand how little the heart of man is affected by what is costly or new in their attire; how little it is biassed by the texture of their muslin, and how unsusceptible of peculiar tenderness towards the spotted, the sprigged, the mull or the jackonet. Woman is fine for her own satisfaction alone. No man will admire her the more, no woman will like her the better for it. Neatness and fashion are enough for the former, and a something of shabbiness or impropriety will be most endearing to the latter. – But not one of these grave reflections troubled the tranquillity of Catherine.

She entered the rooms on Thursday evening with feelings very different from what had attended her thither the Monday before. She had then been exulting in her engagement to Thorpe, and was now chiefly anxious to avoid his sight, lest he should engage her again; for though she could not, dared not expect that Mr Tilney should ask her a third time to dance, her wishes, hopes and plans all centred in nothing less. Every young lady may feel for my heroine in this critical moment, for every young lady has at some time or other known the same agitation. All have been, or at least all have believed themselves to be, in danger from the pursuit of some one whom they wished to avoid; and all have been anxious for the attentions of some one whom they wished to please. As soon as they were joined by the Thorpes, Catherine's agony began; she fidgetted about if John Thorpe came towards her, and hid herself as much as possible from his view, and when he spoke to her pretended not to hear him. The cotillions were over, the country-dancing beginning, and she saw nothing of the Tilneys. 'Do not be frightened, my dear Catherine,' whispered Isabella, 'but I am really going to dance with your brother again. I declare positively it is quite shocking. I tell him he ought to be ashamed of himself, but you and John must keep us in countenance. Make haste, my dear creature, and come to us. John is just walked off, but he will be back in a moment.'

Catherine had neither time nor inclination to answer. The others walked away, John Thorpe was still in view, and she gave herself up for lost. That she might not appear, however, to observe or expect him, she kept her eyes intently fixed on her fan; and a self-condemnation for her folly, in supposing that among such a crowd they should even meet with the Tilneys in any reasonable time, had just passed through her mind, when she suddenly found herself addressed and again solicited to dance, by Mr Tilney himself. With what sparkling eyes and ready motion she granted his request, and with how pleasing a flutter of heart she went with him to the set, may be easily imagined. To escape, and, as she believed, so narrowly escape John Thorpe, and to be asked, so immediately on his joining her, asked by Mr Tilney, as if he had sought her on purpose! – it did not appear to her that life could supply any greater felicity.

Scarcely had they worked themselves into the quiet possession of a place, however, when her attention was claimed by John Thorpe, who stood behind her, 'Heyday, Miss Morland!' said he, 'what is the meaning of this? – I thought you and I were to dance together.'

'I wonder you should think so, for you never asked me.' 'That is a good one, by Jove! – I asked you as soon as I came into the room, and I was just going to ask you again, but when I turned round, you were gone! – this is a cursed shabby trick! I only came for the sake of dancing with *you*, and I firmly believe you were engaged to me ever since Monday. Yes; I remember, I asked you while you were waiting in the lobby for your cloak. And here have I been telling all my acquaintance that I was going to dance with the prettiest girl in the room; and when they see you standing up with somebody else, they will quiz me famously.'

'Qh, no; they will never think of *me*, after such a description as that.'

'By heavens, if they do not, I will kick them out of the room for blockheads. What chap have you there?' Catherine satisfied his curiosity. 'Tilney,' he repeated, 'Hum – I do not know him. A good figure of a man; well put together. – Does he want a horse? – Here is a friend of mine, Sam Fletcher, has got one to sell that would suit any body. A famous clever animal for the road – only forty guineas. I had fifty minds to buy it myself, for it is one of my maxims always to buy a good horse when I meet with one; but it would not answer my purpose, it would not do for the field. I would give any money for a real good hunter. I have three now, the best that ever were back'd. I would not take eight hundred guineas for them. Fletcher and I mean to get a house in Leicestershire, against the next season It is so d— uncomfortable, living at an inn.'

This was the last sentence by which he could weary Catherine's attention, for he was just then born off by the resistless pressure of a long string of passing ladies. Her partner now drew near, and said, 'That gentleman would have put me out of patience, had he staid with you half a minute longer. He has no business to withdraw the attention of my partner from me. We have entered into a contract of mutual agreeableness for the space of an evening, and all our agreeableness belongs solely to each other for that time. Nobody can fasten themselves on the notice of one, without injuring the rights of the other. I consider a country-dance as an emblem of marriage. Fidelity and complaisance are the principal duties of both; and those men who do not chuse to dance or marry themselves, have no business with the partners or wives of their neighbours.'

'But they are such very different things! – '

'– That you think they cannot be compared together.'

'To be sure not. People that marry can never part, but must go and keep house together. People that dance, only stand opposite each other in a long room for half an hour.'

'And such is your definition of matrimony and dancing. Taken in that light certainly, their resemblance is not striking; but I think I could place them in such a view. – You will allow, that in both, man has the advantage of choice, woman only the power of refusal; that in both, it is an engagement between man and woman, formed for the advantage of each; and that when once entered into, they belong exclusively to each other till the moment of its dissolution; that it is their duty, each to endeavour to give the other no cause for wishing that he or she had bestowed themselves elsewhere, and their best interest to keep their own imaginations from wandering towards the perfections of their neighbours, or fancying that they should have been better off with any one else. You will allow all this?'

'Yes, to be sure, as you state it, all this sounds very well; but still they are so very different. – I cannot look upon them at all in the same light, nor think the same duties belong to them.'

'In one respect, there certainly is a difference. In marriage, the man is supposed to provide for the support of the woman; the woman to make the home agreeable to the man; he is to purvey, and she is to smile. But in dancing, their duties are exactly changed; the agreeableness, the compliance are expected from him, while she furnishes the fan and the lavender water. *That*, I suppose, was the difference of duties which struck you, as rendering the conditions incapable of comparison.'

'No, indeed, I never thought of that.'

'Then I am quite at a loss. One thing, however, I must observe. This disposition on your side is rather alarming. You totally disallow any similarity in the obligations; and may I not thence infer, that your notions of the duties of the dancing state are not so strict as your partner might wish? Have I not reason to fear, that if the gentleman who spoke to you just now were to return, or if any other gentleman were to address you, there would be nothing to restrain you from conversing with him as long as you chose?'

'Mr Thorpe is such a very particular friend of my brother's, that if he talks to me, I must talk to him again, but there are hardly three young men in the room besides him, that I have any acquaintance with.'

'And is that to be my only security? alas, alas!'

'Nay, I am sure you cannot have a better; for if I do not know any body, it is impossible for me to talk to them; and, besides, I do not *want* to talk to any body.'

'Now you have given me a security worth having; and I shall proceed with courage. Do you find Bath as agreeable as when I had the honour of making the enquiry before?'

'Yes; quite – more so, indeed.'

'More so! – Take care, or you will forget to be tired of it at the proper time. – You ought to be tired at the end of six weeks.'

'I do not think I should be tired, if I were to stay here six months.'

'Bath, compared with London, has little variety, and so every body finds out every year. "For six weeks, I allow Bath is pleasant enough; but beyond *that*, it is the most tiresome place in the world." You would be told so by people of all descriptions, who come regularly every winter, lengthen their six weeks into ten or twelve, and go away at last because they can afford to stay no longer.'

'Well, other people must judge for themselves, and those who go to London may think nothing of Bath. But I, who live in a small retired village in the country, can never find greater sameness in such a place as this, than in my own home; for here are a variety of amusements, a variety of things to be seen and done all day long, which I can know nothing of there.'

'You are not fond of the country.'

'Yes, I am. I have always lived there, and always been very happy. But certainly there is much more sameness in a country life than in a Bath life. One day in the country is exactly like another.'

'But then you spend your time so much more rationally in the country.'

'Do I?'

'Do you not?'

'I do not believe there is much difference.'

'Here you are in pursuit only of amusement all day long.'

'And so I am at home – only I do not find so much of it. I walk about here, and so I do there; – but here I see a variety of people in every street, and there I can only go and call on Mrs Allen.'

Mr Tilney was very much amused. 'Only go and call on Mrs Allen!' he repeated. 'What a picture of intellectual poverty! However, when you sink into this abyss again, you will have more to say. You will be able to talk of Bath, and of all that you did here.'

'Oh! yes. I shall never be in want of something to talk of again to Mrs Allen, or any body else. I really believe I shall always be talking of Bath, when I am at home again – I *do* like it so very much. If I could but have papa and mamma, and the rest of them here. I suppose I should be too happy! James's coming (my eldest brother) is quite delightful – and especially as it turns out, that the very family we are just got so intimate with, are his intimate friends already. Oh! who can ever be tired of Bath?'

'Not those who bring such fresh feelings of every sort to it, as you do. But papas and mammas, and brothers and intimate friends are a good deal gone by, to most of the frequenters of Bath – and the honest relish of balls and plays, and every-day sights, is past with them.'

Here their conversation closed; the demands of the dance becoming now too importunate for a divided attention.

Soon after their reaching the bottom of the set, Catherine perceived herself to be earnestly regarded by a gentleman who stood among the lookers-on, immediately behind her partner. He was a very handsome man, of a commanding aspect, past the bloom, but not past the vigour of life; and with his eye still directed towards her, she saw him presently address Mr Tilney in a familiar whisper. Confused by his notice, and blushing from the fear of its being excited by something wrong in her appearance, she turned away her head. But while she did so, the gentleman retreated, and her partner coming nearer, said, 'I see that you guess what I have just been asked. That gentleman knows your name, and you have a right to know his. It is General Tilney, my father.'

Catherine's answer was only 'Oh!' – but it was an 'Oh!' expressing every thing needful; attention to his words, and perfect reliance on their truth. With real interest and strong admiration did her eye now follow the General, as he moved through the crowd, and 'How handsome a family they are!' was her secret remark.

In chatting with Miss Tilney before the evening concluded, a new source of felicity arose to her. She had never taken a country walk since her arrival in Bath. Miss Tilney, to whom all the commonly-frequented environs were familiar, spoke of them in terms which made her all eagerness to know them too; and on her openly fearing that she might find nobody to go with her, it was proposed by the brother and sister that they should join in a walk, some morning or other. 'I shall like it,' she cried, 'beyond any thing in the world; and do not let us put it off – let us go to-morrow.' This was readily agreed to, with only a proviso of Miss Tilney's, that it did not rain, which Catherine was sure it would not. At twelve o'clock, they were to call for her in Pulteney-street – and 'remember – twelve o'clock,' was her parting speech to her new friend. Of her other, her older, her more established friend, Isabella, of whose fidelity and worth she had enjoyed a fortnight's experience, she scarcely saw any thing during the evening. Yet, though longing to make her acquainted with her happiness, she cheerfully submitted to the wish of Mr Allen, which took them rather early away, and her spirits danced within her, as she danced in her chair all the way home.

CHAPTER ELEVEN

THE MORROW BROUGHT a very sober looking morning; the sun making only a few efforts to appear; and Catherine augured from it, every thing most favourable to her wishes. A bright morning so early in the year, she allowed would generally turn to rain, but a cloudy one foretold improvement as the day advanced. She applied to Mr Allen for confirmation of her hopes, but Mr Allen not having his own skies and barometer about him, declined giving any absolute promise of sunshine. She applied to Mrs Allen, and Mrs Allen's opinion was more positive. 'She had no doubt in the world of its being a very fine day, if the clouds would only go off, and the sun keep out.'

At about eleven o'clock however, a few specks of small rain upon the windows caught Catherine's watchful eye, and 'Oh! dear, I do believe it will be wet,' broke from her in a most desponding tone.

'I thought how it would be,' said Mrs Allen.

'No walk for me to-day,' sighed Catherine; – 'but perhaps it may come to nothing, or it may hold up before twelve.'

'Perhaps it may, but then, my dear, it will be so dirty.'

'Oh! that will not signify; I never mind dirt.'

'No,' replied her friend very placidly, 'I know you never mind dirt.'

After a short pause, 'It comes on faster and faster!' said Catherine, as she stood watching at a window.

'So it does indeed. If it keeps raining, the streets will be very wet.'

'There are four umbrellas up already. How I hate the sight of an umbrella!'

'They are disagreeable things to carry. I would much rather take a chair at any time.'

'It was such a nice looking morning! I felt so convinced it would be dry!'

'Any body would have thought so indeed. There will be very few people in the Pump-room, if it rains all the morning. I hope Mr Allen will put on his great coat when he goes, but I dare say he will not, for he had rather do any thing in the world than walk out in a great coat; I wonder he should dislike it, it must be so comfortable.'

The rain continued – fast, though not heavy. Catherine went every five minutes to the clock, threatening on each return that, if it still kept on raining another five minutes, she would give up the matter as hopeless. The clock struck twelve, and it still rained. – 'You will not be able to go, my dear.'

'I do not quite despair yet. I shall not give it up till a quarter after twelve. This is just the time of day for it to clear up, and I do think it looks a little lighter. There, it is twenty minutes after twelve, and now I *shall* give it up entirely. Oh! that we had such weather here as they had at Udolpho, or at least in Tuscany and the South of France! – the night that poor St Aubin died! – such beautiful weather!'

At half past twelve, when Catherine's anxious attention to the weather was over, and she could no longer claim any merit from its amendment, the sky began voluntarily to clear. A gleam of sunshine took her quite by surprise; she looked round; the clouds were parting, and she instantly returned to the window to watch over and encourage the happy appearance. Ten minutes more made it certain that a bright afternoon would succeed, and justified the opinion of Mrs Allen, who had 'always thought it would clear up.' But whether Catherine might still expect her friends, whether there had not been too much rain for Miss Tilney to venture, must yet be a question.

It was too dirty for Mrs Allen to accompany her husband to the Pump-room; he accordingly set off by himself, and Catherine had barely watched him down the street, when her notice was claimed by the approach of the same two open carriages, containing the same three people that had surprised her so much a few mornings back.

'Isabella, my brother, and Mr Thorpe, I declare! They are coming for me perhaps – but I shall not go – I cannot go indeed, for you know Miss Tilney may still call.' Mrs Allen agreed to it. John Thorpe was soon with them, and his voice was with them yet sooner, for on the stairs he was calling out to Miss Morland to be quick. 'Make haste! make haste!' as he threw open the door – 'put on your hat this moment – there is no time to be lost – we are going to Bristol. – How d'ye do, Mrs Allen?'

'To Bristol! Is not that a great way off? – But, however, I cannot go with you today, because I am engaged, I expect some friends every moment.' This was of course vehemently talked down as no reason at all; Mrs Allen was called on to second him, and the two others walked in, to give their assistance. 'My sweetest Catherine, is not this delightful? We shall have a most heavenly drive. You are to thank your brother and me for the scheme; it darted into our heads at breakfast-time, I verily believe at the same instant; and we should have been off two hours ago if it had not been for this detestable rain. But it does not signify, the nights are moonlight, and we shall do delightfully. Oh! I am in such extasies at the thoughts of a little country air and quiet! – so much better than going to the Lower Rooms. We shall drive directly to Clifton and dine there; and, as soon as dinner is over, if there is time for it, go on to Kingsweston.'

'I doubt our being able to do so much,' said Morland.

'You croaking fellow!' cried Thorpe, 'we shall be able to do ten times more. Kingsweston! aye, and Blaize Castle too, and any thing else we can hear of; but here is your sister says she will not go.'

'Blaize Castle!' cried Catherine; 'what is that?'

'The finest place in England – worth going fifty miles at any time to see.'

'What, is it really a castle, an old castle?'

'The oldest in the kingdom.'

'But is it like what one reads of?'

'Exactly – the very same.'

'But now really – are there towers and long galleries?'

'By dozens.'

'Then I should like to see it; but I cannot – I cannot go.'

'Not go! – my beloved creature, what do you mean?'

'I cannot go, because' – (looking down as she spoke, fearful of Isabella's smile) 'I expect Miss Tilney and her brother to call on me to take a country walk. They promised to come at twelve, only it rained; but now, as it is so fine, I dare say they will be here soon.'

'Not they indeed,' cried Thorpe; 'for, as we turned into Broad-street, I saw them – does he not drive a phaeton with bright chestnuts?'

'I do not know indeed.'

'Yes, I know he does; I saw him. You are talking of the man you danced with last night, are not you?'

'Yes.'

'Well, I saw him at that moment turn up the Lansdown Road, – driving a smart-looking girl.'

'Did you indeed?'

'Did upon my soul; knew him again directly, and he seemed to have got some very pretty cattle too.'

'It is very odd! but I suppose they thought it would be too dirty for a walk.'

'And well they might, for I never saw so much dirt in my life. Walk! you could no more walk than you could fly! it has not been so dirty the whole winter; it is ancle-deep every where.'

Isabella corroborated it: – 'My dearest Catherine, you cannot form an idea of the dirt; come, you must go; you cannot refuse going now.'

'I should like to see the castle; but may we go all over it? may we go up every staircase, and into every suite of rooms?'

'Yes, yes, every hole and corner.'

'But then, – if they should only be gone out for an hour till it is drier, and call by and bye?'

'Make yourself easy, there is no danger of that, for I heard Tilney hallooing to a man who was just passing by on horseback, that they were going as far as Wick Rocks.'

'Then I will. Shall I go, Mrs Allen?'

'Just as you please, my dear.'

'Mrs Allen, you must persuade her to go,' was the general cry. Mrs Allen was not inattentive to it: – 'Well, my dear,' said she, 'suppose you go.' – And in two minutes they were off.

Catherine's feelings, as she got into the carriage, were in a very unsettled state; divided between regret for the loss of one great pleasure, and the hope of soon enjoying another, almost its equal in degree, however unlike in kind. She could not think the Tilneys had acted quite well by her, in so readily giving up their engagement, without sending her any message of excuse. It was now but an hour later than the time fixed on for the beginning of their walk; and, in spite of what she had heard of the prodigious accumulation of dirt in the course of that hour, she could not from her own observation help thinking, that they might have gone with very little inconvenience. To feel herself slighted by them was very painful. On the other hand, the delight of exploring an edifice like Udolpho, as her fancy represented Blaize Castle to be, was such a counterpoise of good, as might console her for almost any thing.

They passed briskly down Pulteney-street, and through Laura-place, without the exchange of many words. Thorpe talked to his horse, and she meditated, by turns, on broken promises and broken arches, phaetons and false hangings, Tilneys and trap-doors. As they entered Argyle-buildings, however, she was roused by this address from her companion, 'Who is that girl who looked at you so hard as she went by?'

'Who? – where?'

'Stop, stop, Mr Thorpe.'

'On the right-hand pavement – she must be almost out of sight now.' Catherine looked round and saw Miss Tilney leaning on her brother's arm, walking slowly down the street. She saw them both looking back at her. 'Stop, stop, Mr Thorpe,' she impatiently cried, 'it is Miss Tilney; it is indeed. – How could you tell me they were gone? – Stop, stop, I will get out this moment and go to them.' But to what purpose did she speak?: – Thorpe only lashed his horse into a brisker trot; the Tilneys, who had soon ceased to look after her, were in a moment out of sight round the corner of Laura-place, and in another moment she was herself whisked into the Marketplace. Still, however, and during the length of another street, she intreated him to stop. 'Pray, pray stop, Mr Thorpe. – I cannot go on. – I will not go on. – I must go back to Miss Tilney.' But Mr Thorpe only laughed, smacked his whip, encouraged his horse, made odd noises, and drove on; and Catherine, angry and vexed as she was, having no power of getting away, was obliged to give up the point and submit. Her reproaches, however, were not spared. 'How could you deceive me so, Mr Thorpe? – How could you say, that you saw them driving up the Lansdown-road? – I would not have had it happen so for the world. – They must think it so strange; so rude of me! to go by them, too, without saying a word! You do not know how vexed I am – I shall have no pleasure at Clifton, nor in any thing else. I had rather, ten thousand times rather get out now, and walk back to them. How could you say, you saw them driving out in a phaeton?' Thorpe defended himself very stoutly, declared he had never seen two men so much alike in his life, and would hardly give up the point of its having been Tilney himself.

Their drive, even when this subject was over, was not likely to be very agreeable. Catherine's complaisance was no longer what it had been in their former airing. She listened reluctantly, and her replies were short. Blaize Castle remained her only comfort; towards *that*, she still looked at intervals with pleasure; though rather than be disappointed of the promised walk, and especially rather than be thought ill of by the Tilneys, she would willingly have given up all the happiness which its walls could supply – the happiness of a progress through a long suite of lofty rooms, exhibiting the remains of magnificent furniture, though now for many years deserted – the happiness of being stopped in their way along narrow, winding vaults, by a low, grated door; or even of having their lamp, their only lamp, extinguished by a sudden gust of wind, and of being left in total darkness. In the meanwhile, they proceeded on their journey without any mischance; and were within view of the town of Keynsham, when a halloo from Morland, who was behind them, made his friend pull up to know what the matter. The others then came close enough for conversation, and Morland said, 'We had better go back, Thorpe; it is too late to go on to-day; your sister thinks so as well I. We have been exactly an hour coming from Pulteney-street, very little more than seven miles; and, I suppose, we have at least eight more to go. It will never do. We set out a great deal too late. We had much better put it off another day, and turn round.'

'It is all one to me,' replied Thorpe rather angrily; and instantly turning his horse, they were on their way back to Bath.

'If your brother had not got such a d— beast to drive,' said he soon afterwards, 'we might have done it very well. My horse would have trotted to Clifton within the hour, if left to himself, and I have almost broke my arm with pulling him in to that cursed broken-winded jade's pace. Morland is a fool for not keeping a horse and gig of his own.'

'No, he is not,' said Catherine warmly, 'for I am sure he could not afford it.'

'And why cannot he afford it?'

'Because he has not money enough.'

'And whose fault is that?'

'Nobody's, that I know of.' Thorpe then said something in the loud, incoherent way to which he had often recourse, about its being a d— thing to be miserly; and that if people who rolled in money could not afford things; he did not know who could; which Catherine did not even endeavour to understand. Disappointed of what was to have been the consolation for her first disappointment, she was less and less disposed either to be agreeable herself, or to find her companion so; and they returned to Pulteney-street without her speaking twenty words.

As she entered the house, the footman told her, that a gentleman and lady had called and enquired for her a few minutes after her setting off; that, when he told them she was gone out with Mr Thorpe, the lady had asked whether any message had been left for her; and on his saying no, had felt for a card, but said she had none about her, and went away. Pondering over these heart-rending tidings, Catherine walked slowly up stairs. At the head of them she was met by Mr Allen, who, on hearing the reason of their speedy return, said 'I am glad your brother had so much sense, I am glad you are come back. It was a strange, wild scheme.'

They all spent the evening together at Thorpe's. Catherine was disturbed and out of spirits; but Isabella seemed to find a pool of commerce, in the fate of which she shared, by private partnership with Morland, a very good equivalent for the quiet and country air of an inn at Clifton. Her satisfaction too, in not being at the Lower Rooms, was spoken more than once. 'How I pity the poor creatures that are going there! How glad I am that I am not amongst them! I wonder whether it will be a full ball or not! They have not begun dancing yet. I would not be there for all the world. It is so delightful to have an evening now and then to one-self. I dare say, Mr Morland, you long to be at it, do not you? I am sure you do. Well, pray do not let any body here be a restraint on you. I dare say we could do very well without you; but you men think yourselves of such consequence.'

Catherine could almost have accused Isabella of being wanting in tenderness towards herself and her sorrows; so very little did they appear to dwell on her mind, and so very inadequate was the comfort she offered. 'Do not be so dull, my dearest creature,' she whispered. 'You will quite break my heart. It was amazingly shocking to be sure; but the Tilneys were entirely to blame. Why were not they more punctual? It was dirty, indeed, but what did that signify? I am sure John and I should not have minded it. I never mind going through any thing, where a friend is concerned; this is my disposition, and John is just the same; he has amazing strong feelings. Good heavens! what a delightful hand you have got! Kings, I vow! I never was so happy in my life! I would fifty times rather you should have them than myself.'

And now I may dismiss my heroine to the sleepless couch, which is the true heroine's portion; to a pillow strewed with thorns and wet with tears. And lucky may she think herself, if she get another good night's rest in the course of the next three months.

CHAPTER TWELVE

'MRS ALLEN,' SAID CATHERINE the next morning, 'will there be any harm in my calling on Miss Tilney to-day? I shall not be easy till I have explained every thing.'

'Go by all means, my dear; only put on a white gown, Miss Tilney always wears white.'

Catherine cheerfully complied; and being properly equipped, was more impatient than ever to be at the Pump-room, that she might inform herself of General Tilney's lodging, for though she believed they were in Milsom-street, she was not certain of the house, and Mrs Allen's wavering convictions only made it more doubtful. To Milsom-street she was directed; and having made herself perfect in the number, hastened away with eager steps and a beating heart to pay her visit, explain her conduct, and be forgiven; tripping lightly through the church-yard, and resolutely turning away her eyes, that she might not be obliged to see her beloved Isabella and her dear family, who, she had reason to believe, were in a shop hard by. She reached the house without any impediment, looked at the number, knocked at the door, and inquired for Miss Tilney. The man believed

Miss Tilney to be at home, but was not quite certain. Would she be pleased to send up her name? She gave her card. In a few minutes the servant returned, and with a look which did not quite confirm his words, said he had been mistaken, for that Miss Tilney was walked out. Catherine, with a blush of mortification, left the house. She felt almost persuaded that Miss Tilney *was* at home, and too much offended to admit her; and as she retired down the street, could not withhold one glance at the drawing-room windows, in expectation of seeing her there, but no one appeared at them. At the bottom of the street, however, she looked back again, and then, not at a window, but issuing from the door, she saw Miss Tilney herself. She was followed by a gentleman, whom Catherine believed to be her father, and they turned up towards Edgar's-buildings. Catherine, in deep mortification, proceeded on her way. She could almost be angry herself at such angry incivility; but she checked the resentful sensation; she remembered her own ignorance. She knew not how much an offence as her's might be classed by the laws of worldly politeness, to what a degree of unforgivingness it might with propriety lead, nor to what rigours of rudeness in return it might justly make her amenable.

Dejected and humbled, she had even some thoughts of not going with the others to the theatre that night; but it must be confessed that they were not of long continuance: for she soon recollected, in the first place, that she was without any excuse for staying at home; and, in the second, that it was a play she wanted very much to see. To the theatre accordingly they all went; no Tilneys appeared to plague or please her; she feared that, amongst the many perfections of the family, a fondness for plays was not to be ranked; but perhaps it was because they were habituated to the finer performances of the London stage, which she knew, on Isabella's authority, rendered ever thing else of the kind 'quite horrid.' She was not deceived in her own expectation of pleasure; the comedy so well suspended her care, that no one, observing her during the first four acts, would have supposed she had any wretchedness about her. On the beginning of the fifth, however, the sudden view of Mr Henry Tilney and his father, joining a party in the opposite box, recalled her to anxiety and distress. The stage could no longer excite genuine merriment – no longer keep her whole attention. Every other look upon an average was directed towards the opposite box; and, for the space of two entire scenes, did she thus watch Henry Tilney, without being once able to catch his eye. No longer could he be suspected of indifference for a play; his notice was never withdrawn from the stage during two whole scenes. At length, however, he did look towards her, and he bowed – but such a bow! no smile, no continued observance attended it; his eyes were immediately returned to their former direction. Catherine was restlessly miserable; she could almost have run round to the box in which he sat, and forced him to hear her explanation. Feelings rather natural than heroic possessed her; instead of considering her own dignity injured by this ready condemnation – instead of proudly resolving, in conscious innocence, to shew her resentment towards him who could harbour a doubt of it, to leave to him all the trouble of seeking an explanation, and to enlighten him on the past only by avoiding his sight, or flirting with somebody else, she took to herself all the shame of misconduct, or at least of its appearance, and was only eager for an opportunity of explaining its cause.

The play concluded – the curtain fell – Henry Tilney was no longer to be seen where he had hitherto sat, but his father remained, and perhaps he might be now coming round to their box. She was right; in a few minutes he appeared, and, making his way through the then thinning rows, spoke with like calm politeness to Mrs Allen and her friend. – Not with such calmness was he answered by the latter: 'Oh! Mr Tilney, I have been quite wild to speak to you, and make my apologies. You must have thought me so rude; but indeed it was not my own fault, – was it, Mrs Allen? Did not they tell me that Mr Tilney and his sister were gone out in a phaeton together? and then what could I do? But I had ten thousand times rather have been with you; now had not I, Mrs Allen?'

'My dear, you tumble my gown,' was Mrs Allen's reply.

Her assurance, however, standing sole as it did, was not thrown away; it brought a more cordial, more natural smile into his countenance, and he replied in a tone which retained only a little affected reserve: – 'We were much obliged to you at any rate for wishing us a pleasant walk after our passing you in Argyle-street; you were so kind as to look back on purpose.'

'But indeed I did not wish you a pleasant walk; I never thought of such a thing; but I begged Mr Thorpe so earnestly to stop; I called out to him as soon as ever I saw you; now, Mrs Allen, did not – Oh! you were not there; but indeed I did; and, if Mr Thorpe would only have stopped, I would have jumped out and run after you.'

Is there a Henry in the world who could be insensible to such a declaration? Henry Tilney at least was not. With a yet sweeter smile, he said every thing that need be said of his sister's concern, regret, and dependence on Catherine's honour. – 'Oh! do not say Miss Tilney was not angry,' cried Catherine, 'because I know she was;

for she would not see me this morning when I called; I saw her walk out of the house the next minute after my leaving it; I was hurt, but I was not affronted. Perhaps you did not know I had been there.'

'I was not within at the time; but I heard of it from Eleanor, and she has been wishing ever since to see you, to explain the reason of such incivility; but perhaps I can do it as well. It was nothing more than that my father – they were just preparing to walk out, and he being hurried for time, and not caring to have it put off, made a point of her being denied. That was all, I do assure you. She was very much vexed, and meant to make her apology as soon as possible.'

Catherine's mind was greatly eased by this information, yet a something of solicitude remained, from which sprang the following question, thoroughly artless in itself, though rather distressing to the gentleman: – 'But, Mr Tilney, why were *you* less generous than your sister? If she felt such confidence in my good intentions, and could suppose it to be only a mistake, why should *you* be so ready to take offence?'

'Me! – I take offence!'

'Nay, I am sure by your look, when you came into the box, you were angry.'

'I angry! I could have no right.'

'Well, nobody would have thought you had no right who saw your face.' He replied by asking her to make room for him, and talking of the play.

He remained with them some time, and was only too agreeable for Catherine to be contented when he went away. Before they parted, however, it was agreed that the projected walk should be taken as soon as possible; and, setting aside the misery of his quitting their box, she was, upon the whole, left one of the happiest creatures in the world.

While talking to each other, she had observed with some surprize, that John Thorpe, who was never in the same part of the house for ten minutes together, was engaged in conversation with General Tilney; and she felt something more than surprize, when she thought she could perceive herself the object of their attention and discourse. What could they have to say of her? She feared General Tilney did not like her appearance: she found it was implied in his preventing her admittance to his daughter, rather than postpone his own walk a few minutes. 'How came Mr Thorpe to know your father?' was her anxious inquiry, as she pointed them out to her companion. He

knew nothing about it; but his father, like every military man, had
a very large acquaintance.

When the entertainment was over, Thorpe came to assist them in
getting out. Catherine was the immediate object of his gallantry;
and, while they waited in the lobby for a chair, he prevented the
inquiry which had travelled from her heart almost to the tip of her
tongue, by asking, in a consequential manner, whether she had seen
him talking with General Tilney: – 'He is a fine old fellow, upon
my soul! – stout, active – looks as young as his son. I have a great
regard for him, I assure you: a gentlemanlike, good sort of fellow
as ever lived.'

'But how came you to know him?'

'Know him! – There are few people much about town that I do
not know. I have met him for ever at the Bedford; and I knew his
face again to-day the moment he came into the billiard-room. One

The same kind of delicate flattery.

of the best players we have, by the bye; and we had a little touch together, though I was almost afraid of him at first: the odds were five to four against me; and, if I had not made one of the cleanest strokes that perhaps ever was made in his world – I took his ball exactly – but I could not make you understand it without a table; – however I *did* beat him. A very fine fellow; as rich as a Jew. I should like to dine with him; I dare say he gives famous dinners. But what do you think we have been talking of? – You. Yes, by heavens! – and the General thinks you the finest girl in Bath.'

'Oh! nonsense! how can you say so?'

'And what do you think I said?' (lowering his voice) 'Well done, General, said I, I am quite of your mind.'

Here Catherine, who was much less gratified by his admiration than by General Tilney's, was not sorry to be called away by Mr Allen. Thorpe, however, would see her to her chair, and, till she entered it, continued the same kind of delicate flattery, in spite of her entreating him to have done.

That General Tilney, instead of disliking, should admire her, was very delightful; and she joyfully thought, that there was not one of the family whom she need now fear to meet. – The evening had done more, much more, for her, than could have been expected.

CHAPTER THIRTEEN

MONDAY, TUESDAY, WEDNESDAY, Thursday, Friday and Saturday have now passed in review before the reader; the events of each day, its hopes and fears, mortifications and pleasures have been separately stated, and the pangs of Sunday only now remain to be described and close the week. The Clifton scheme had been deferred, not relinquished, and on the afternoon's Crescent of this day, it was brought forward again. In a private consultation between Isabella and James, the former of whom had particularly set her heart upon going, and the latter no less anxiously placed his upon pleasing her, it was agreed that, provided the weather were fair, the party should take place on the following morning; and they were to set off very early, in order to be at home in good time. The affair thus determined, and Thorpe's approbation secured, Catherine only remained to be apprized of it. She had left them for a few minutes to speak to Miss Tilney. In that interval the plan was completed, and as soon as she came again, her agreement was demanded; but instead of the gay acquiescence expected by Isabella, Catherine looked grave, was very sorry, but could not go. The engagement which ought to have kept her from joining in the former attempt, would make it impossible for her to accompany them now. She had that moment settled with Miss Tilney to take their promised walk to-morrow; it was quite determined, and she would not, upon any account, retract. But that she *must* and *should* retract, was instantly the eager cry of both the Thorpes; they must go to Clifton to-morrow, they would not go without her, it would be nothing to put off a mere walk for one day longer, and they would not hear of a refusal. Catherine was distressed, but not subdued. 'Do not urge me, Isabella. I am engaged to Miss Tilney. I cannot go.' This availed nothing. The same arguments assailed her again; she must go, she should go, and they would not hear of a refusal. 'It would be so easy to tell Miss Tilney that you had just been reminded of a prior engagement, and must only beg to put off the walk till Tuesday.'

'No, it would not be easy. I could not do it. There has been no prior engagement.' But Isabella became only more and more urgent; calling on her in the most affectionate manner; addressing her by the most endearing names. She was sure her dearest, sweetest Catherine would not seriously refuse such a trifling request to a friend who loved her so dearly. She knew her beloved Catherine to have so feeling a heart, so sweet a temper, to be so easily persuaded by those she loved. But all in vain; Catherine felt herself to be in the right, and though pained by such tender, such flattering supplication, could not allow it to influence her. Isabeela then tried another method. She reproached her with having more affection for Miss Tilney, though she had known her so little a while, than for her best and oldest friends; with being grown cold and indifferent, in short, towards herself. 'I cannot help being jealous, Catherine, when I see myself slighted for strangers, I, who love you so excessively! When once my affections are placed, it is not in the power of any thing to change them. But I believe my feelings are stronger than any body's; I am sure they are too strong for my own peace; and to see myself supplanted in your friendship by strangers, does cut me to the quick, I own. These Tilneys seem to swallow up every thing else.'

Catherine thought this reproach equally strange and unkind. Was it the part of a friend thus to expose her feelings to the notice of others? Isabella appeared to her ungenerous and selfish, regardless of every thing but her own gratification. These painful ideas crossed her mind, though she said nothing. Isabella, in the meanwhile, had applied her handkerchief to her eyes; and Morland, miserable at such a sight, could not help saying, 'Nay, Catherine. I think you cannot stand out any longer now. The sacrifice is not much; and to oblige such a friend – I shall think you quite unkind, if you will refuse.'

This was the first time of her brother's openly siding against her, and anxious to avoid his displeasure, she proposed a compromise. If they would only put off their scheme till Tuesday, which they might easily do, as it depended only on themselves, she could go with them, and every body might then be satisfied. But 'No, no, no!' was the immediate answer; 'that could not be, for Thorpe did not know that he might not go to town on Tuesday.' Catherine was sorry, but could do no more; and a short silence ensued, which was broken by Isabella; who in a voice of cold resentment said, 'Very well, then there is an end of the party. If Catherine does not go, I cannot. I cannot be the only woman. I would not, upon any account in the world, do so improper a thing.'

'Catherine, you must go,' said James.

'But why cannot Mr Thorpe drive one of his other sisters? I dare say either of them would like to go.'

'Thank ye,' cried Thorpe, 'but I did not come to Bath to drive my sisters about, and look like a fool. No, if you do not go, d— me if I do. I only go for the sake of driving you.'

'That is a compliment which gives me no pleasure.' But her words were lost on Thorpe, who had turned abruptly away.

The three others still continued together, walking in a most uncomfortable manner to poor Catherine; sometimes not a word was said, sometimes she was again attacked with supplications or reproaches, and her arm was still linked within Isabella's, though their hearts were at war. At one moment she was softened, at another irritated; always distressed, but always steady.

'I did not think you had been so obstinate, Catherine,' said James; 'you were not used to be so hard to persuade; you once were the kindest, best-tempered of my sisters.'

'I hope I am not less so now,' she replied, very feelingly; 'but indeed I cannot go. If I am wrong, I am doing what I believe to be right.'

'I suspect,' said Isabella, in a low voice, 'there is no great struggle.'

Catherine's heart swelled; she drew away her arm, and Isabella made no opposition. Thus passed a long ten minutes, till they were again joined by Thorpe, who coming to them with a gayer look, said, 'Well, I have settled the matter, and now we may all go to-morrow with a safe conscience. I have been to Miss Tilney, and made your excuses.'

'You have not!' cried Catherine.

'I have, upon my soul. Left her this moment. Told her you had sent me to say, that having just recollected a prior engagement of going to Clifton with us to-morrow, you could not have the pleasure of walking with her till Tuesday. She said very well, Tuesday was just as convenient to her; so there is an end of all our difficulties. – A pretty good thought of mine – hey?'

Isabella's countenance was once more all smiles and good-humour, and James too looked happy again.

'A most heavenly thought indeed! Now, my sweet Catherine, all our distresses are over; you are honourably acquitted, and we shall have a most delightful party.'

'This will not do,' said Catherine; 'I cannot submit to this. I must run after Miss Tilney directly and set her right.'

Isabella, however, caught hold of one hand; Thorpe of the other; and remonstrances poured in from all three. Even James was quite angry. When every thing was settled, when Miss Tilney herself said that Tuesday would suit her as well, it was quite ridiculous, quite absurd to make any further objection.

'I do not care. Mr Thorpe had no business to invent any such message. If I had thought it right to put if off, I could have spoken to Miss Tilney myself. This is only doing it in a ruder way; and how do I know that Mr Thorpe has – he may be mistaken again perhaps; he led me into one act of rudeness by the mistake on Friday. Let me go, Mr Thorpe; Isabella, do not hold me.'

Thorpe told her it would be in vain to go after the Tilneys; they were turning the corner into Brock-street, when he had overtaken them, and were at home by this time.

'Then I will go after them,' said Catherine; 'wherever they are I will go after them. It does not signify talking. If I could not be persuaded into doing what I thought wrong, I never will be tricked into it.' And with these words she broke away and hurried off. Thorpe would have darted after her, but Morland withheld him. 'Let her go, let her go, if she will go.'

'She is as obstinate as – '

Thorpe never finished the simile, for it could hardly have been a proper one.

Away walked Catherine in great agitation, as fast as the crowd would permit her, fearful of being pursued, yet determined to persevere. As she walked, she reflected on what had passed. It was painful to her to disappoint and displease them, particularly to displease her brother; but she could not repent her resistance. Setting her own inclination apart, to have failed a second time in her engagement to Miss Tilney, to have retracted a promise voluntarily made

'Let me go, Mr Thorpe.'

only five minutes before, and on a false pretence too, must have been wrong. She had not been withstanding them on selfish principles alone, she had not consulted merely her own gratification; *that* might have been ensured in some degree by the excursion itself, by seeing Blaize Castle; no, she had attended to what was due to others, and to her own character in their opinion. Her conviction of being right however was not enough to restore her composure, till she had spoken to Miss Tilney she could not be at ease; and quickening her pace when she got clear of the Crescent, she almost ran over the remaining ground till she gained the top of Milsom-street. So rapid had been her movements, that in spite of the Tilneys' advantage in the outset, they were but just turning into their lodgings as she came within view of them; and the servant still remaining at the open door, she used only the ceremony of saying that she must speak with Miss Tilney that moment, and hurrying by him proceeded up stairs. Then, opening the first door before her, which happened to be the right, she immediately found herself in the drawing-room with General Tilney, his son and daughter. Her explanation, defective only in being – from her irritation of nerves and shortness of breath – no explanation at all, was instantly given. 'I am come in a great hurry – It was all a mistake – I never promised to go – I told them from the first I could not go. – I ran away in a great hurry to explain it. – I did not care what you thought of me. – I would not stay for the servant.'

The business however, though not perfectly elucidated by this speech, soon ceased to be a puzzle. Catherine found that John Thorpe *had* given the message; and Miss Tilney had no scruple in owning herself greatly surprized by it. But whether her brother had still exceeded her in resentment, Catherine, though she instinctively addressed herself as much to one as to the other in her vindication, had no means of knowing. Whatever might have been felt before her arrival, her eager declarations immediately made every look and sentence as friendly as she could desire.

The affair thus happily settled, she was introduced by Miss Tilney to her father, and received by him with such ready, such solicitous politeness as recalled Thorpe's information to her mind, and made her think with pleasure that he might be sometimes depended on. To such anxious attention was the general's civility carried, that not aware of her extraordinary swiftness in entering the house, he was quite angry with the servant whose neglect had reduced her to open the door of the apartment herself. 'What did William mean by it? He should make a point of inquiring into the matter.' And if Catherine had not most warmly asserted his innocence, it seemed likely that William would lose the favour of his master for ever, if not his place, by her rapidity.

After sitting with them a quarter of an hour, she rose to take leave, and was then most agreeably surprised by General Tilney's asking her if she would do his daughter the honour of dining and spending the rest of the day with her. Miss Tilney added her own wishes. Catherine was greatly obliged; but it was quite out of her power. Mr and Mrs Allen would expect her back every moment.

The general declared he could say no more; the claims of Mr and Mrs Allen were not to be superseded; but on some other day he trusted, when longer notice could be given, they would not refuse to spare her to her friend. 'Oh, no; Catherine was sure they would not have the least objection, and she should have great pleasure in coming.' The general attended her himself to the street-door, saying every thing gallant as they went down stairs, admiring the elasticity of her walk, which corresponded exactly with the spirit of her dancing, and making her one of the most graceful bows she had ever beheld, when they parted.

Catherine, delighted by all that had passed, proceeded gaily to Pulteney-street; walking, as she concluded, with great elasticity, though she had never thought of it before. She reached home without seeing any thing more of the offended party; and now that she had been triumphant throughout, had carried her point and was secure of her walk, she began (as the flutter of her spirits subsided) to doubt whether she had been perfectly right. A sacrifice was always noble; and if she had given way to their entreaties, she should have been spared the distressing idea of a friend displeased, a brother angry, and a scheme of great happiness to both destroyed, perhaps through her means. To ease her mind, and ascertain by the opinion of an unprejudiced person what her own conduct had really been, she took occasion to mention before Mr Allen the half-settled scheme of her brother and the Thorpes for the following day. Mr Allen caught at it directly. 'Well,' said he, 'and do you think of going too?'

'No; I had just engaged myself to walk with Miss Tilney before they told me of it; and therefore you know I could not go with them, could I?'

'No, certainly not; and I am glad you do not think of it. These schemes are not at all the thing. Young men and women driving about the country in open carriages! Now and then it is very well; but going to inns and public places together! It is not right; and I wonder Mrs Thorpe should allow it. I am glad you do not think of going; I am sure Mrs Morland would not be pleased. Mrs Allen, are not you of my way of thinking? Do not you think these kind of projects objectionable?'

'Yes, very much so indeed. Open carriages are nasty things. A clean gown is not five minutes wear in them. You are splashed getting in and getting out; and the wind takes your hair and your bonnet in every direction. I hate an open carriage myself.'

'I know you do; but that is not the question. Do not you think it has an odd appearance, if young ladies are frequently driven about in them by young men, to whom they are not even related?'

'Yes, my dear, a very odd appearance indeed. I cannot bear to see it.'

'Dear madam,' cried Catherine, 'then why did not you tell me so before? I am sure if I had known it to be improper, I would not have gone with Mr Thorpe at all; but I always hoped you would tell me, if you thought I was doing wrong.'

'And so I should, my dear, you may depend on it; for as I told Mrs Morland at parting, I would always do the best for you in my power. But one must not be over particular. Young people *will* be young people, as your good mother says herself. You know I wanted you, when we first came, not to buy that sprigged muslin, but you would. Young people do not like to be always thwarted.'

'But this was something of real consequence; and I do not think you would have found me hard to persuade.'

'As far as it has gone hitherto, there is no harm done,' said Mr Allen; 'and I would only advise you, my dear, not to go out with Mr Thorpe any more.'

'That is just what I was going to say,' added his wife.

Catherine, relieved for herself, felt uneasy for Isabella; and after a moment's thought, asked Mr Allen whether it would not be both proper and kind in her to write to Miss Thorpe, and explain the indecorum of which she must be as insensible as herself; for she considered that Isabella might otherwise perhaps be going to Clifton the next day, in spite of what had passed. Mr Allen however discouraged her from doing any such thing. 'You had better leave her alone, my dear, she is old enough to know what she is about; and if not, has a mother to advise her. Mrs Thorpe is too indulgent beyond a doubt; but however you had better not interfere. She and your brother chuse to go, and you will be only getting ill-will.'

Catherine submitted; and though sorry to think that Isabella should be doing wrong, felt greatly relieved by Mr Allen's approbation of her own conduct, and truly rejoiced to be preserved by his advice from the danger of falling into such an error herself. Her escape from being one of the party of Clifton was now an escape indeed; for what would the Tilneys have thought of her, if she had broken her promise to them in order to do what was wrong in itself? if she had been guilty of one breach of propriety, only to enable her to be guilty of another?

Pride
and
Prejudice

The Bennets have five daughters and an entailed estate, which passes to the nearest male relative, a Mr Collins, on Mr Bennet's death. Mrs Bennet is a silly woman, obsessed with marrying off her daughters despite their lack of fortunes. Mr Bennet retreats to his study whenever possible. The younger sisters are giddy and flirt with the militiamen stationed nearby. The elder girls, Jane and Elizabeth are sometimes embarrassed by their family's improper behaviour. The arrival of a rich bachelor, Mr Bingley, in the neighbourhood causes great excitement, especially as he seems very partial to Jane. His friend, Mr Darcy, however, has a proud, arrogant manner. He provokes in the lively, unconventional Elizabeth an instant dislike.

'I HOPE, MY DEAR,' SAID MR BENNET to his wife, as they were at breakfast the next morning, 'that you have ordered a good dinner to-day, because I have reason to expect an addition to our family party.'

'Who do you mean, my dear? I know of nobody that is coming I am sure, unless Charlotte Lucas should happen to call in, and I hope *my* dinners are good enough for her. I do not believe she often sees such at home.'

'The person of whom I speak, is a gentleman and a stranger.' Mrs Bennet's eyes sparkled. – 'A gentleman and a stranger! It is Mr Bingley I am sure. Why Jane – you never dropt a word of this; you sly thing! Well, I am sure I shall be extremely glad to see Mr Bingley. – But – good lord! how unlucky! there is not a bit of fish to be got to-day. Lydia, my love, ring the bell. I must speak to Hill, this moment.'

'It is *not* Mr Bingley,' said her husband; 'it is a person whom I never saw in the whole course of my life.'

This roused a general astonishment; and he had the pleasure of being eagerly questioned by his wife and five daughters at once.

After amusing himself some time with their curiosity, he thus explained. 'About a month ago I received this letter, and about a fortnight ago I answered it, for I thought it a case of some delicacy, and required early attention. It is from my cousin, Mr Collins, who, when I am dead, may turn you all out of this house as soon as he pleases.'

'Oh! my dear,' cried his wife, 'I cannot bear to hear that mentioned. Pray do not talk of that odious man. I do think it is the hardest thing in the world, that your estate should be entailed away from your own children; and I am sure if I had been you, I should have tried long ago to do something or other about it.'

Jane and Elizabeth attempted to explain to her the nature of an entail.

They had often attempted it before, but it was a subject on which Mrs Bennet was beyond the reach of reason; and she continued to rail bitterly against the cruelty of settling an estate away from a family of five daughters, in favour of a man whom nobody cared anything about.

'It certainly is a most iniquitous affair,' said Mr Bennet, 'and nothing can clear Mr Collins from the guilt of inheriting Longbourn. But if you will listen to his letter, you may perhaps be a little softened by his manner of expressing himself.'

'No, that I am sure I shall not; and I think it was very impertinent of him to write to you at all, and very hypocritical. I hate such false friends. Why could not he keep on quarrelling with you, as his father did before him?'

'Why, indeed, he does seem to have some filial scruples on that head, as you will hear.'

> *Hunsford, near Westerham, Kent.*
> *15th October.*

DEAR SIR,

The disagreement subsisting between yourself and my late honoured father, always gave me much uneasiness, and since I have had the misfortune to lose him, I have frequently wished to heal the breach; but for some time I was kept back by my own doubts, fearing lest it might seem disrespectful to his memory for me to be on good terms with any one, with whom it had always pleased him to be at variance. – 'There, Mrs Bennet.' – My mind however is now made up on the subject, for having received ordination at Easter, I have been so fortunate as to be distinguished by the patronage of the Right Honourable Lady Catherine de Bourgh, widow of Sir Lewis de Bourgh, whose bounty and beneficence has preferred me to the valuable rectory of this parish, where it shall be my earnest endeavour to demean myself with grateful respect towards her Ladyship, and be ever ready to perform those rites and ceremonies which are instituted by the Church of England. As a clergyman, moreover, I feel it my duty to promote and establish the blessing of peace in all families within the reach of my influence; and on these grounds I flatter myself that my present overtures of good-will are highly commendable, and that the circumstance of my being next in the entail of Longbourn estate, will be kindly overlooked on your side, and not lead you to reject the offered olive branch. I cannot be otherwise than concerned at being the means of injuring your amiable daughters, and beg leave to apologise for it, as well as to assure you of my readiness to make them every possible amends, – but of this hereafter. If you should have no objection to receive me into your house, I propose myself the satisfaction of waiting on you and your family, Monday, November 18th, by four o'clock, and shall probably trespass on your hospitality till the Saturday se'night following, which I can do without any inconvenience, as Lady

Catherine is far from objecting to my occasional absence on a Sunday, provided that some other clergyman is engaged to do the duty of the day. I remain, dear sir, with respectful compliments to your lady and daughters, your well-wisher and friend.

WILLIAM COLLINS

'At four o'clock, therefore, we may expect this peace-making gentleman,' said Mr Bennet, as he folded up the letter. 'He seems to be a most conscientious and polite young man, upon my word; and I doubt not will prove a valuable acquaintance, especially if Lady Catherine should be so indulgent as to let him come to us again.'

'There is some sense in what he says about the girls however; and if he is disposed to make them any amends, I shall not be the person to discourage him.'

'Though it is difficult,' said Jane, 'to guess in what way he can mean to make us the atonement he thinks our due, the wish is certainly to his credit.'

Elizabeth was chiefly struck with his extraordinary deference for Lady Catherine, and his kind intention of christening, marrying, and burying his parishioners whenever it were required.

'He must be an oddity, I think,' said she. 'I cannot make him out. – There is something very pompous in his stile. – And what can he mean by apologizing for being next in the entail? – We cannot suppose he would help it, if he could. – Can he be a sensible man, sir?'

'No, my dear; I think not. I have great hopes of finding him quite the reverse. There is a mixture of servility and self-importance in his letter, which promises well. I am impatient to see him.'

'In point of composition,' said Mary, 'his letter does not seem defective. The idea of the olive branch perhaps is not wholly new, yet I think it is well expressed.'

To Catherine and Lydia, neither the letter nor its writer were in any degree interesting. It was next to impossible that their cousin should come in a scarlet coat, and it was now some weeks since they had received pleasure from the society of a man in any other colour. As for their mother, Mr Collins's letter had done away much of her ill-will, and she was preparing to see him with a degree of composure, which astonished her husband and daughters.

Mr Collins was punctual to his time, and was received with great politeness by the whole family. Mr Bennet indeed said little; but the ladies were ready enough to talk, and Mr Collins seemed neither in need of encouragement, nor inclined to be silent himself. He was a tall, heavy looking young man of five and twenty. His air was grave and stately, and his manners were very formal. He had not been long seated before he complimented Mrs Bennet on having so fine a family of daughters, said he had heard much of their beauty, but that, in this instance, fame had fallen short of the truth; and added, that he did not doubt her seeing them all in due time well disposed of in marriage. This gallantry was not much to the taste of some of his hearers, but Mrs Bennet, who quarrelled with no compliments, answered most readily,

'You are very kind, sir, I am sure; and I wish with all my heart it may prove so; for else they will be destitute enough. Things are settled so oddly.'

'You allude perhaps to the entail of this estate.'

'Ah! sir, I do indeed. It is a grevious affair to my poor girls, you must confess. Not that I mean to find fault with *you*, for such things I know are all chance in this world. There is no knowing how estates will go when once they come to be entailed.'

'I am very sensible, madam, of the hardship to my fair cousins, – and could say much on the subject, but that I am cautious of appearing forward and precipitate. But I can assure the young ladies that I come prepared to admire them. At present I will not say more, but perhaps when we are better acquainted –'

He was interrupted by a summons to dinner; and the girls smiled on each other. They were not the only objects of Mr Collins's admiration. The hall, the dining-room, and all its furniture were examined and praised; and his commendation of every thing would have touched Mrs Bennet's heart, but for the mortifying supposition of his viewing it all as his own future property. The dinner too in its turn was highly admired; and he begged to know to which of his fair cousins, the excellence of its cookery was owing. But here he was set right by Mrs Bennet, who assured him with some asperity that they were very well able to keep a good cook, and that her daughters had nothing to do in the kitchen. He begged pardon for having displeased her. In a softened tone she declared herself not at all offended; but he continued to apologise for about a quarter of an hour.

CHAPTER FOURTEEN

DURING DINNER, MR BENNET SCARCELY spoke at all; but when the servants were withdrawn, he thought it time to have some conversation with his guest, and therefore started a subject in which he expected him to shine, by observing that he seemed very fortunate in his patroness. Lady Catherine de Bourgh's attention to his wishes, and consideration for his comfort, appeared very remarkable. Mr Bennet could not have chosen better. Mr

Collins was eloquent in her praise. The subject elevated him to more than usual solemnity of manner, and with a most important aspect he protested that he had never in his life witnessed such behaviour in a person of rank – such affability and condescension, as he had himself experienced from Lady Catherine. She had been graciously pleased to approve of both the discourses, which he had already had the honour of preaching before her. She had also asked him twice to dine at Rosings; and had sent for him only the Saturday before, to make up her pool of quadrille in the evening. Lady Catherine was reckoned proud by many people he knew, but *he* had never seen any thing but affability in her. She had always spoken to him as she would to any other gentleman; she made not the smallest objection to his joining in the society of the neighbourhood, nor to his leaving his parish occasionally for a week or two, to visit his relations. She had even condescended to advise him to marry as soon as he could, provided he chose with discretion; and had once paid him a visit in his humble parsonage; where she had perfectly approved all the alterations he had been making, and had even vouchsafed to suggest some herself, – some shelves in the closets up stairs.

'That is all very proper and civil, I am sure,' said Mrs Bennet, 'and I dare say she is a very agreeable woman. It is a pity that great ladies in general are not more like her. Does she live near you, sir?'

'The garden in which stands my humble abode, is separated only by a lane from Rosings Park, her ladyship's residence.'

'I think you said she was a widow, sir? has she any family?'

'She has only one daughter, the heiress of Rosings, and of very extensive property.'

'Ah!' cried Mrs Bennet, shaking her head, 'then she is better off than many girls. And what sort of young lady is she? is she handsome?'

'She is a most charming young lady indeed. Lady Catherine herself says that in point of true beauty, Miss de Bourgh is far superior to the handsomest of her sex; because there is that in her features which marks the young woman of distinguished birth. She is unfortunately of a sickly constitution, which has prevented her making that progress in many accomplishments, which she could not otherwise have failed of; as I am informed by the lady who superintended her education, and who still resides with them. But she is perfectly amiable, and often condescends to drive by my humble abode in her little phaeton and ponies.'

'Has she been presented? I do not remember her name among the ladies at court.'

'Her indifferent state of health unhappily prevents her being in town; and by that means, as I told Lady Catherine myself one day, has deprived the British court of its brightest ornament. Her ladyship seemed pleased with the idea, and you may imagine that I am happy on every occasion to offer

Protested that he never read novels

those little delicate compliments which are always acceptable to ladies. I have more than once observed to Lady Catherine, that her charming daughter seemed born to be a duchess, and that the most elevated rank, instead of giving her consequence, would be adorned by her. – These are the kind of little things which please her ladyship, and it is a sort of attention which I conceive myself peculiarly bound to pay.'

'You judge very properly,' said Mr Bennet, 'and it is happy for you that you possess the talent of flattering with delicacy. May I ask whether these pleasing attentions proceed from the impulse of the moment, or are the result of previous study?'

'They arise chiefly from what is passing at the time, and though I sometimes amuse myself with suggesting and arranging such little elegant compliments as may be adapted to ordinary occasions, I always wish to give them as unstudied an air as possible.'

Mr Bennet's expectations were fully answered. His cousin was as absurd as he had hoped, and he listened to him with the keenest enjoyment, maintaining at the same time the most resolute composure of countenance, and except in an occasional glance at Elizabeth, requiring no partner in his pleasure.

By tea-time however the dose had been enough, and Mr Bennet was glad to take his guest into the drawing-room again, and when tea was over, glad to invite him to read aloud to the ladies. Mr Collins readily assented, and a book was produced; but on beholding it, (for every thing announced it to be from a circulating library,) he started back, and begging pardon, protested that he never read novels. – Kitty stared at him, and Lydia exclaimed. – Other books were produced, and after some deliberation he chose Fordyce's Sermons. Lydia gaped as he opened the volume, and before he had, with very monotonous solemnity, read three pages, she interrupted him with,

'Do you know, mama, that my uncle Philips talks of turning away Richard, and if he does, Colonel Forster will hire him. My aunt told me so herself on Saturday. I shall walk to Meryton to-morrow to hear more about it, and to ask when Mr Denny comes back from town.'

Lydia was bid by her two eldest sisters to hold her tongue; but Mr Collins, much offended, laid aside his book, and said,

'I have often observed how little young ladies are interested by books of a serious stamp, though written solely for their benefit. It amazes me, I confess; – for certainly, there can be nothing so advantageous to them as instruction. But I will no longer importune my young cousin.'

Then turning to Mr Bennet, he offered himself as his antagonist at backgammon. Mr Bennet accepted the challenge, observing that he acted very wisely in leaving the girls to their own trifling amusements. Mrs Bennet and her daughters apologized most civilly for Lydia's interruption, and promised that it should not occur again, if he would resume his book; but Mr Collins, after assuring them that he bore his young cousin no ill will, and should never resent her behaviour as any affront, seated himself at another table with Mr Bennet, and prepared for backgammon.

CHAPTER FIFTEEN

MR COLLINS WAS NOT A SENSIBLE man, and the deficiency of nature had been but little assisted by education or society; the greatest part of his life having been spent under the guidance of an illiterate and miserly father; and though he belonged to one of the universities, he had merely kept the necessary terms, without forming at it any useful acquaintance. The subjection in which his father had brought him up, had given him originally great humility of manner, but it was now a good deal counteracted by the self-conceit of a weak head, living in retirement, and the consequential feelings of early and unexpected prosperity. A fortunate chance had recommended him to Lady Catherine de Bourgh when the living of Hunsford was vacant; and the respect which he felt for her high rank, and his veneration for her as his patroness, mingling with a very good opinion of himself, of his authority as a clergyman, and his rights as a rector, made him altogether a mixture of pride and obsequiousness, self-importance and humility.

Having now a good house and very sufficient income, he intended to marry; and in seeking a reconciliation with the Longbourn family he had a wife in view, as he meant to chuse one of the daughters, if he found them as handsome and amiable as they were represented by common report. This was his plan of amends – of atonement – for inheriting their father's estate; and he thought it an excellent one, full of eligibility and suitableness, and excessively generous and disinterested on his own part.

His plan did not vary on seeing them. – Miss Bennet's lovely face confirmed his views, and established all his strictest notions of what was due to seniority; and for the first evening *she* was his settled choice. The next morning, however, made an alteration; for in a quarter of an hour's tête-à-tête with Mrs Bennet before breakfast, a conversation beginning with his parsonage-house, and leading naturally to the avowal of his hopes, that a mistress for it might be found at Longbourn, produced from her, amid very complaisant smiles and general encouragement, a caution against the very Jane he had fixed on. – 'As to her *younger* daughters she could not take upon her to say – she could not positively answer – but she did not *know* of any prepossession; – her *eldest* daughter, she must just mention – she felt incumbent on her to hint, was likely to be very soon engaged.'

Mr Collins had only to change from Jane to Elizabeth – and it was soon done – done while Mrs Bennet was stirring the fire. Elizabeth, equally next to Jane in birth and beauty, succeeded her of course.

Mrs Bennet treasured up the hint, and trusted that she might soon have two daughters married; and the man whom she could not bear to speak of the day before, was now high in her good graces.

Lydia's intention of walking to Meryton was not forgotten; every sister except Mary agreed to go with her; and Mr Collins was to attend them, at the request of Mr Bennet, who was most anxious to get rid of him, and have his library to himself; for thither Mr Collins had followed him after breakfast, and there he would continue, nominally engaged with one of the largest folios in the collection, but really talking to Mr Bennet, with little cessation, of his house and garden at Hunsford. Such doings discomposed Mr Bennet exceedingly. In his library he had been always sure of leisure and tranquillity; and though prepared, as he told Elizabeth, to meet with folly and conceit in every other room in the house, he was used to be free from them there; his civility, therefore, was most prompt in inviting Mr Collins to join his daughters in their walk; and Mr Collins, being in fact much better fitted for a walker than a reader, was extremely well pleased to close his large book, and go.

In pompous nothings on his side, and civil assents on that of his cousins, their time passed till they entered Meryton. The attention of the younger ones was then no longer to be gained by *him*. Their eyes were immediately wandering up in the street in quest of the officers, and nothing less than a very smart bonnet indeed, or a really new muslin in a shop window, could recall them.

But the attention of every young lady was soon caught by a young man, whom they had never seen before, of most gentlemanlike appearance, walking with an officer on the other side of the way. The officer was the very Mr Denny, concerning whose return from London Lydia came to enquire, and he bowed as they passed. All were struck with the stranger's air, all wondered who he could be, and Kitty and Lydia, determined if possible to find out, led the way across the street, under pretence of wanting something in an opposite shop, and fortunately had just gained the pavement when the two gentlemen turning back had reached the same spot. Mr Denny addressed them directly, and entreated permission to introduce his friend, Mr Wickham, who had returned with him the day before from town, and he was happy to say had accepted a commission in their corps. This was exactly as it should be; for the young man wanted only regimentals to make him completely charming. His appearance was greatly in his favour; he had all the best part of beauty, a fine countenance, a good figure, and very pleasing address. The introduction was followed up on his side by a happy readiness of conversation – a readiness at the same time perfectly correct and unassuming; and the whole party were still standing and talking together very agreeably, when the sound of horses drew their notice, and Darcy and Bingley were seen riding down the street. On distinguishing the ladies of the group, the two gentlemen came directly towards them, and began the usual civilities. Bingley was the principal spokesman, and Miss Bennet the principal object. He was then, he said, on his way to Longbourn on purpose to enquire after her. Mr Darcy corroborated it with a bow, and was beginning to determine not to fix his eyes on Elizabeth, when they were suddenly arrested by the sight of the stranger, and Elizabeth happening to see the countenance of both as they looked at each other, was all astonishment at the effect of the meeting. Both changed colour, one looked white, the other red. Mr Wickham, after a few moments, touched his hat – a salutation which Mr Darcy just deigned to return. What could be the meaning of it? – It was impossible to imagine; it was impossible not to long to know.

In another minute Mr Bingley, but without seeming to have noticed what passed, took leave and rode on with his friend.

Mr Denny and Mr Wickham walked with the young ladies to the door of Mr Philip's house, and then made their bows, in spite of Miss Lydia's pressing entreaties that they would come in, and even in spite of Mrs Philips' throwing up the parlour window, and loudly seconding the invitation.

Mrs Philips was always glad to see her nieces, and the two eldest, from their recent absence, were particularly welcome, and she was eagerly expressing her surprise at their sudden return home, which, as their own carriage had not fetched them, she should have known nothing about, if she had not happened to see Mr Jones's shop boy in the street, who had told her that they were not to send any more draughts to Netherfield because the Miss Bennets were come away, when her civility was claimed towards Mr Collins by Jane's introduction of him. She received him with her very best politeness, which he returned with as much more, apologising for his intrusion, without any previous acquaintance with her, which he could not help flattering himself however might be justified by his relationship to the young ladies who introduced him to her notice. Mrs Philips was quite awed by such an excess of good breeding; but her contemplation of one stranger was soon put an end to by exclamations and inquiries about the other, of whom, however, she could only tell her nieces what they already knew, that Mr Denny had brought him from London, and that he was to have a lieutenant's commission in the –shire. She had been watching him the last hour, she said, as he walked up and down the street, and had Mr Wickham appeared Kitty and Lydia would certainly have continued the occupation, but unluckily no one passed the windows now except a few of the officers, who in comparison with the stranger, were become 'stupid, disagreeable fellows'. Some of them were to dine with the Philipses the next day, and their aunt promised to make her husband call on Mr Wickham, and give him an invitation also, if the family from Longbourn would come in the evening. This was agreed to, and Mrs Philips protested that they would have a nice comfortable noisy game of lottery tickets, and a little bit of hot supper afterwards. The prospect of such delights was very cheering, and they parted in mutual good spirits. Mr Collins repeated his apologies in quitting the room, and was assured with unwearying civility that they were perfectly needless.

As they walked home, Elizabeth related to Jane what she had seen pass between the two gentlemen; but though Jane would have defended either or both, had they appeared to be wrong, she could no more explain such behaviour than her sister.

Mr Collins on his return highly gratified Mrs Bennet by admiring Mrs Philips's manners and politeness. He protested that except Lady Catherine and her daughter, he had never seen a more elegant woman; for she had not only received him with the utmost civility, but had even pointedly included him in her invitation for the next evening, although utterly unknown to her before. Something he supposed might be attributed to his connection with them, but yet he had never met with so much attention in the whole course of his life.

CHAPTER SIXTEEN

AS NO OBJECTION WAS MADE TO THE young people's engagement with their aunt, and all Mr Collins's scruples of leaving Mr and Mrs Bennet for a single evening during his visit were most steadily resisted, the coach conveyed him and his five cousins at a suitable hour to Meryton; and the girls had the pleasure of hearing, as they entered the drawing-room, that Mr Wickham had accepted their uncle's invitation, and was then in the house.

When this information was given, and they had all taken their seats, Mr Collins was at leisure to look around him and admire, and he was so much struck with the size and furniture of the apartment, that he declared he might almost have supposed himself in the smaller summer breakfast parlour at Rosings; a comparison that did not at first convey much gratification; but when Mrs Philips understood from him what Rosings was, and who was its proprietor, when she had listened to the description of only one of Lady Catherine's drawing-rooms, and found that the chimney-piece alone had cost eight hundred pounds, she felt all the force of the compliment, and would hardly have resented a comparison with the housekeeper's room.

In describing to her all the grandeur of Lady Catherine and her mansion, with occasional digressions in praise of his own humble abode, and the improvements it was receiving, he was happily employed until the gentlemen joined them; and he found in Mrs Philips a very attentive listener, whose opinion of his consequence increased with what she heard, and who was resolving to retail it all among her neighbours as soon as she could. To the girls, who could not listen to their cousin, and who had nothing to do but wish for an instrument, and examine their own indifferent imitations of china on the mantelpiece, the interval of waiting appeared very long. It was over at last however. The gentlemen did approach; and when Mr Wickham walked into the room, Elizabeth felt that she had neither been seeing him before, nor thinking of him since, with the smallest degree of unreasonable admiration. The officers of the —shire were in general a very creditable, gentlemanlike set, and the best of them were of

The officers of the —shire

the present party; but Mr Wickham was as far beyond them all in person, countenance, air, and walk, as *they* were superior to the broad-faced stuffy uncle Philips, breathing port wine, who followed them into the room.

Mr Wickham was the happy man towards whom almost every female eye was turned, and Elizabeth was the happy woman by whom he finally seated himself; and the agreeable manner in which he immediately fell into conversation, though it was only on its being a wet night, and on the probability of a rainy season, made her feel that the commonest, dullest, most threadbare topic might be rendered interesting by the skill of the speaker.

With such rivals for the notice of the fair, as Mr Wickham and the officers, Mr Collins seemed likely to sink into insignificance; to the young ladies he certainly was nothing; but he had still at intervals a kind listener in Mrs Philips, and was, by her watchfulness, most abundantly supplied with coffee and muffin.

When the card tables were placed, he had an opportunity of obliging her in return, by sitting down to whist.

'I know little of the game, at present,' said he, 'but I shall be glad to improve myself, for in my situation of life –' Mrs Philips was very thankful of his compliance, but could not wait for his reason.

Mr Wickham did not play at whist, and with ready delight was he received at the other table between Elizabeth and Lydia. At first there seemed danger of Lydia's engrossing him entirely, for she was a most determined talker; but being likewise extremely fond of lottery tickets, she soon grew too much interested in the game, too eager in making bets and exclaiming after prizes, to have attention for any one in particular. Allowing for the common demands of the game, Mr Wickham was therefore at leisure to talk to Elizabeth, and she was very willing to hear him, though what she chiefly wished to hear she could not hope to be told, the history of his acquaintance with Mr Darcy. She dared not even mention that gentleman. Her curiosity however was unexpectedly relieved. Mr Wickham began the subject himself. He inquired how far Netherfield was from Meryton; and, after receiving her answer, asked in an hesitating manner how long Mr Darcy had been staying there.

'About a month,' said Elizabeth; and then, unwilling to let the subject drop, added, 'He is a man of very large property in Derbyshire, I understand.'

'Yes,' replied Wickham; – 'his estate there is a noble one. A clear ten thousand per annum. You could not have met with a person more capable of giving you certain information on that head than myself – for I have been connected with his family in a particular manner from my infancy.'

Elizabeth could not but look surprised.

'You may well be surprised, Miss Bennet, at such an assertion, after seeing, as you probably might, the very cold manner of our meeting yesterday. – Are you much acquainted with Mr Darcy?'

'As much as I ever wish to be,' cried Elizabeth warmly, – 'I have spent four days in the same house with him, and I think him very disagreeable.'

'I have no right to give *my* opinion,' said Wickham, 'as to his being agreeable or otherwise. I am not qualified to form one. I have known him too long and too well to be a fair judge. It is impossible for *me* to be impartial. But I believe your opinion of him would in general astonish – and perhaps you would not express it quite so strongly anywhere else. – Here you are in your own family.'

'Upon my word I say no more *here* than I might say in any house in the neighbourhood, except Netherfield. He is not at all liked in Hertfordshire. Every body is disgusted with his pride. You will not find him more favourably spoken of by any one.'

'I cannot pretend to be sorry,' said Wickham, after a short interruption, 'that he or that any man should not be estimated beyond their deserts; but with *him* I believe it does not often happen. The world is blinded by his fortune and consequence, or frightened by his high and imposing manners, and sees him only as he chuses to be seen.'

'I should take him, even on *my* slight acquaintance, to be an ill-tempered man.' Wickham only shook his head.

'I wonder,' said he, at the next opportunity of speaking, 'whether he is likely to be in this country much longer.'

'I do not at all know; but I *heard* nothing of his going away when I was at Netherfield. I hope your plans in favour of the –shire will not be affected by his being in the neighbourhood.'

'Oh! no – it is not for *me* to be driven away by Mr Darcy. If *he* wishes to avoid seeing *me*, he must go. We are not on friendly terms, and it always gives me pain to meet him, but I have no reason for avoiding *him* but what I might proclaim to all the world; a sense of very great ill usage, and most painful regrets at his being what he is. His father, Miss Bennet, the late Mr Darcy, was one of the best men that ever breathed, and the truest friend I ever had; and I can never be in company with this Mr Darcy without being grieved to the soul by a thousand tender recollections. His behaviour to myself has been scandalous; but I verily believe I could forgive him any thing and every thing, rather than his disappointing the hopes and disgracing the memory of his father.'

Elizabeth found the interest of the subject increase, and listened with all her heart; but the delicacy of it prevented farther enquiry.

Mr Wickham began to speak on more general topics, Meryton, the neighbourhood, the society, appearing highly pleased with all that he had yet seen, and speaking of the latter especially, with gentle but very intelligible gallantry.

'It was the prospect of constant society, and good society,' he added, 'which was my chief inducement to enter the —shire. I knew it to be a most respectable, agreeable corps, and my friend Denny tempted me farther by his account of their present quarters, and the very great attentions and excellent acquaintance Meryton had procured them. Society, I own, is necessary to me. I have been a disappointed man, and my spirits will not bear solitude. I *must* have employment and society. A military life is not what I was intended for, but circumstances have now made it eligible. The church *ought* to have been my profession – I was brought up for the church and I should at this time have been in possession of a most valuable living, had it pleased the gentleman we were speaking of just now.'

'Indeed!'

'Yes – the late Mr Darcy bequeathed me the next presentation of the best living in his gift. He was my godfather, and excessively attached to me. I cannot do justice to his kindness. He meant to provide for me amply, and thought he had done it; but when the living fell, it was given elsewhere.'

'Good heavens!' cried Elizabeth; 'but how could *that* be? – How could his will be disregarded? – Why did not you seek legal redress?'

'There was just such an informality in the terms of the bequest as to give me no hope from law. A man of honour could not have doubted the intention, but Mr Darcy chose to doubt it – or to treat it as a merely conditional recommendation, and to assert that I had forfeited all claim to it by extravagance, imprudence, in short any thing or nothing. Certain it is, that the living became vacant two years ago, exactly as I was of an age to hold it, and that it was given to another man; and no less certain is it, that I cannot accuse myself of having really done any thing to deserve to lose it. I have a warm, unguarded temper, and I may perhaps have sometimes spoken my opinion *of* him, and *to* him, too freely. I can recall nothing worse. But the fact is, that we are very different sort of men, and that he hates me.'

'This is quite shocking! – He deserves to be publicly disgraced.'

'Some time or other he *will* be – but it shall not be by *me*. Till I can forget his father, I can never defy or expose *him*.'

Elizabeth honoured him for such feelings, and thought him handsomer than ever as he expressed them.

'But what,' said she, after a pause, 'can have been his motive? – what can have induced him to behave so cruelly?'

'A thorough, determined dislike of me – a dislike which I cannot but attribute in some measure to jealousy. Had the late Mr Darcy liked me less, his son might have borne with me better; but his father's uncommon attachment to me, irritated him I believe very early in life. He had not a temper to bear the sort of competition in which we stood – the sort of preference which was often given me.'

'I had not thought Mr Darcy so bad as this – though I have never liked him, I had not thought so very ill of him – I had supposed him to be despising his fellow-creatures in general, but did not suspect him of descending to such malicious revenge, such injustice, such inhumanity as this!'

After a few minutes reflection, however, she continued, 'I *do* remember his boasting one day, at Netherfield, of the implacability of his resentments, of his having an unforgiving temper. His disposition must be dreadful.'

'I will not trust myself on the subject,' replied Wickham, '*I* can hardly be just to him.'

Elizabeth was again deep in thought, and after a time exclaimed, 'To treat in such a manner, the godson, the friend, the favourite of his father!' – She could have added, 'A young man too, like *you*, whose very countenance may vouch for your being amiable' – but she contented herself with 'And one, too, who had probably been his own companion from childhood, connected together, as I think you said, in the closest manner!'

'We were born in the same parish, within the same park, the greatest part of our youth was passed together; inmates of the same house, sharing the same amusements, objects of the same parental care. *My* father began life in the profession which your uncle, Mr Philips, appears to do so much credit to – but he gave up every thing to be of use to the late Mr Darcy, and devoted all his time to the care of the Pemberley property. He was most highly esteemed by Mr Darcy, a most intimate, confidential friend. Mr Darcy often acknowledged himself to be under the greatest obligations to my father's active superintendance, and when immediately before my father's death, Mr Darcy gave him a voluntary promise of providing for me, I am convinced that he felt it to be as much of a debt of gratitude to *him*, as of affection to myself.'

'How strange!' cried Elizabeth. 'How abominable! – I wonder that the very pride of this Mr Darcy has not made him just to you! – If from no better motive, that he should not have been too proud to be dishonest, – for dishonesty I must call it.'

'It *is* wonderful,' – replied Wickham, – 'for almost all his actions may be traced to pride; – and pride has often been his best friend. It has connected him nearer with virtue than any other feeling. But we are none of us consistent; and in his behaviour to me, there were stronger impulses even than pride.'

'Can such abominable pride as his, have ever done him good?'

'Yes. It has often led him to be liberal and generous, – to give his money freely, to display hospitality, to assist his tenants, and relieve the poor. Family pride, and *filial* pride, for he is very proud of what his father was, have done this. Not to appear to disgrace his family, to degenerate from the popular qualities, or lose the influence of the Pemberley House, is a powerful motive. He has also *brotherly* pride, which with *some* brotherly affection, makes him a very kind and careful guardian of his sister; and you will hear him generally cried up as the most attentive and best of brothers.'

'What sort of a girl is Miss Darcy?'

He shook his head. – 'I wish I could call her amiable. It gives me pain to speak ill of a Darcy. But she is too much like her brother, – very, very proud. – As a child, she was affectionate and pleasing, and extremely fond of me; and I have devoted hours and hours to her amusement. But she is nothing to me now. She is a handsome girl, about fifteen or sixteen, and I understand highly accomplished. Since her father's death, her home has been London, where a lady lives with her, and superintends her education.'

After many pauses and many trials of other subjects, Elizabeth could not help reverting once more to the first, and saying,

'I am astonished at his intimacy with Mr Bingley! How can Mr Bingley, who seems good humour itself, and is, I really believe, truly amiable, be in friendship with such a man? How can they suit each other? – Do you know Mr Bingley?'

'Not at all.'

'He is a sweet tempered, amiable, charming man. He cannot know what Mr Darcy is.'

'Probably not; – but Mr Darcy can please where he chuses. He does not want abilities. He can be a conversible companion if he thinks it worth his while. Among those who are at all his equals in consequence, he is a very different man from what he is to the less prosperous. His pride never deserts him; but with the rich, he is liberal-minded, just, sincere, rational, honourable, and perhaps agreeable, – allowing something for fortune and figure.'

The whist party soon afterwards breaking up, the players gathered round the other table, and Mr Collins took his station between his cousin Elizabeth and Mrs Philips. – The usual inquiries as to his success were made by the latter. It had not been very great; he had lost every point; but when Mrs Philips began to express her concern thereupon, he assured her with much earnest gravity that it was not of the least importance, that he considered the money as a mere trifle, and begged she would not make herself uneasy.

'I know very well, madam,' said he, 'that when persons sit down to a card table, they must take their chance of these things, – and happily I am not in such circumstances as to make five shillings any object. There are undoubtedly many who could not say the same, but thanks to Lady Catherine de Bourgh, I am removed far beyond the necessity of regarding little matters.'

Mr Wickham's attention was caught; and after observing Mr Collins for a few moments, he asked Elizabeth in a low voice whether her relation were very intimately acquainted with the family of de Bourgh.

'Lady Catherine de Bourgh,' she replied, 'has very lately given him a living. I hardly know how Mr Collins was first introduced to her notice, but he certainly has not known her long.'

'You know of course that Lady Catherine de Bourgh and Lady Anne Darcy were sisters; consequently that she is aunt to the present Mr Darcy.'

'No, indeed, I did not. — I knew nothing at all of Lady Catherine's connections. I never heard of her existence till the day before yesterday.'

'Her daughter, Miss de Bourgh, will have a very large fortune, and it is believed that she and her cousin will unite the two estates.'

This information made Elizabeth smile, as she thought of poor Miss Bingley. Vain indeed must be all her attentions, vain and useless her affection for his sister and her praise of himself, if he were already self-destined to another.

'Mr Collins,' said she, 'speaks highly both of Lady Catherine and her daughter; but from some particulars that he has related of her ladyship, I suspect his gratitude misleads him, and that in spite of her being his patroness, she is an arrogant, conceited woman.'

'I believe her to be both in a great degree,' replied Wickham; 'I have not seen her for many years, but I very well remember that I never liked her, and that her manners were dictatorial and insolent. She has the reputation of being remarkably sensible and clever; but I rather believe she derives part of her abilities from her rank and fortune, part from her authoritative manner, and the rest from the pride of her nephew, who chuses that every one connected with him should have an understanding of the first class.'

Elizabeth allowed that he had given a very rational account of it, and they continued talking together with mutual satisfaction till supper put an end to cards; and gave the rest of the ladies their share of Mr Wickham's attentions. There could be no conversation in the noise of Mrs Philips's supper party, but his manners recommended him to every body. Whatever he said, was said well; and whatever he did, done gracefully. Elizabeth went away with her head full of him. She could think of nothing but of Mr Wickham, and of what he had told her, all the way home; but there was not time for her even to mention his name as they went, for neither Lydia nor Mr Collins were once silent. Lydia talked incessantly of lottery tickets, of the fish she had lost and the fish she had won, and Mr Collins, in describing the civility of Mr and Mrs Philips, protesting that he did not in the least regard his losses at whist, enumerating all the dishes at supper, and repeatedly fearing that he crouded his cousins, had more to say than he could well manage before the carriage stopped at Longbourn House.

Delighted to see their dear friend again

CHAPTER SEVENTEEN

ELIZABETH RELATED TO JANE THE NEXT day, what had passed between Mr Wickham and herself. Jane listened with astonishment and concern; – she knew not how to believe that Mr Darcy could be so unworthy of Mr Bingley's regard; and yet, it was not in her nature to question the veracity of a young man of such amiable appearance as Wickham. – The possibility of his having really endured such unkindness, was enough to interest all her tender feelings; and nothing therefore remained to be done, but to think well of them both, to defend the conduct of each, and throw into the account of accident or mistake, whatever could not be otherwise explained.

'They have both,' said she, 'been deceived, I dare say, in some way or other, of which we can form no idea. Interested people have perhaps misrepresented each to the other. It is, in short, impossible for us to conjecture the causes or circumstances which may have alienated them, without actual blame on either side.'

'Very true, indeed; – and now, my dear Jane, what have you got to say in behalf of the interested people who have probably been concerned in the business? – Do clear *them* too, or we shall be obliged to think ill of somebody.'

'Laugh as much as you chuse, but you will not laugh me out of my opinion. My dearest Lizzy, do but consider in what a disgraceful light it places Mr Darcy, to be treating his father's favourite in such a manner, – one, whom his father had promised to provide for. – It is impossible. No man of common humanity, no man who had any value for his character, could be capable of it. Can his most intimate friends be so excessively deceived in him? oh! no.'

'I can much more easily believe Mr Bingley's being imposed on, than that Mr Wickham should invent such a history of himself as he gave me last night; names, facts, every thing mentioned without ceremony. – If it be not so, let Mr Darcy contradict it. Besides, there was truth in his looks.'

'It is difficult indeed – it is distressing. – One does not know what to think.'

'I beg your pardon; – one knows exactly what to think.'

But Jane could think with certainty on only one point, – that Mr Bingley, if he *had been* imposed on, would have much to suffer when the affair became public.

The two young ladies were summoned from the shrubbery where this conversation passed, by the arrival of some of the very persons of whom they had been speaking; Mr Bingley and his sisters came to give their personal invitation for the long expected ball at Netherfield, which was fixed for the following Tuesday. The two ladies were delighted to see their dear friend again, called it an age since they had met, and repeatedly asked what she had been doing with herself since their separation. To the rest of the family they paid little attention; avoiding Mrs Bennet as much as possible, saying not much to Elizabeth, and nothing at all to the others. They were soon gone again, rising from their seats with an activity which took their brother by surprise, and hurrying off as if eager to escape from Mrs Bennet's civilities.

The prospect of the Netherfield ball was extremely agreeable to every female of the family. Mrs Bennet chose to consider it as given in compliment to her eldest daughter, and was particularly flattered by receiving the invitation from Mr Bingley himself, instead of a ceremonious card. Jane pictured to herself a happy evening in the society of her two friends, and the attentions of their brother; and Elizabeth thought with pleasure of dancing a great deal with Mr Wickham, and of seeing a confirmation of every thing in Mr Darcy's looks and behaviour. The happiness anticipated by Catherine and Lydia, depended less on any single event, or any particular person, for though they each, like Elizabeth, meant to dance half the evening with Mr Wickham, he was by no means the only partner who could satisfy them, and a ball was at any rate, a ball. And even Mary could assure her family that she had no disinclination for it.

'While I can have my mornings to myself,' said she, 'it is enough. – I think it no sacrifice to join occasionally in evening engagements. Society has claims on us all; and I profess myself one of those who consider intervals of recreation and amusement as desirable for every body.'

Elizabeth's spirits were so high on the occasion, that though she did not often speak unnecessarily to Mr Collins, she could not help asking him whether he intended to accept Mr Bingley's invitation, and if he did, whether he would think it proper to join in the evening's amusement; and she was rather surprised to find that he entertained no scruple whatever on that head, and was very far from dreading a rebuke either from the Archbishop, or Lady Catherine de Bourgh, by venturing to dance.

'I am by no means of opinion, I assure you,' said he, 'that a ball of this kind, given by a young man of character, to respectable people, can have any evil tendency; and I am so far from objecting to dancing myself that I shall hope to be honoured with the hands of all my fair cousins in the course of the evening, and I take this opportunity of soliciting yours, Miss Elizabeth, for the two first dances especially, – a preference which I trust my cousin Jane will attribute to the right cause, and not to any disrespect for her.'

Elizabeth felt herself completely taken in. She had fully proposed being engaged by Wickham for those very dances: – and to have Mr Collins instead! her liveliness had been never worse timed. There was no help for it however. Mr Wickham's happiness and her own was per force delayed a little longer, and Mr Collins's proposal accepted with as good a grace as she could. She was not the better pleased with his gallantry, from the idea it suggested of something more. – It now first struck her, that *she* was selected from among her sisters as worthy of being the mistress of Hunsford Parsonage, and of assisting to form a quadrille table at Rosings, in the absence of more eligible visitors. The idea soon reached to conviction, as she observed his increasing civilities toward herself, and heard his frequent attempt at a compliment on her wit and vivacity; and though more astonished than gratified herself, by this effect of her charms, it was not long before her mother gave her to understand that the probability of their marriage was exceedingly agreeable to *her*. Elizabeth however did not chuse to take the hint, being well aware that a serious dispute must be the consequence of any reply. Mr Collins might never make the offer, and till he did, it was useless to quarrel about him.

If there had not been a Netherfield ball to prepare for and talk of, the younger Miss Bennets would have been in a pitiable state at this time, for from the day of the invitation, to the day of the ball, there was such a succession of rain as prevented their walking to Meryton once. No aunt, no officers, no news could be sought after; – the very shoe-roses for Netherfield were got by proxy. Even Elizabeth might have found some trial of her patience in weather, which totally suspended the improvement of her acquaintance with Mr Wickham; and nothing less than a dance on Tuesday, could have made such a Friday, Saturday, Sunday and Monday, endurable to Kitty and Lydia.

CHAPTER EIGHTEEN

TILL ELIZABETH ENTERED THE DRAWING-ROOM at Netherfield and looked in vain for Mr Wickham among the cluster of red coats there assembled, a doubt of his being present had never occurred to her. The certainty of meeting him had not been checked by any of those recollections that might not unreasonably have alarmed her. She had dressed with more than usual care, and prepared in the highest spirits for the conquest of all that remained unsubdued of his heart, trusting that it was not more than might be won in the course of the evening. But in an instant arose the dreadful suspicion of his being purposely omitted for Mr Darcy's pleasure in the Bingleys' invitation to the officers; and though this was not exactly the case, the absolute fact of his absence was pronounced by his friend Mr Denny, to whom Lydia eagerly applied, and who told them that Wickham had been obliged to go to town on business the day before, and was not yet returned; adding, with a significant smile,

'I do not imagine his business would have called him away just now, if he had not wished to avoid a certain gentleman here.'

This part of his intelligence, though unheard by Lydia, was caught by Elizabeth, and as it assured her that Darcy was not less answerable for Wickham's absence than if her first surmise had been just, every feeling of displeasure against the former was so sharpened by immediate disappointment, that she could hardly reply with tolerable civility to the polite inquiries which he directly afterwards approached to make. – Attention, forbearance, patience with Darcy, was injury to Wickham. She was resolved against any sort of conversation with him, and turned away with a degree of ill humour, which she could not wholly surmount even in speaking to Mr Bingley, whose blind partiality provoked her.

But Elizabeth was not formed for ill-humour; and though every prospect of her own was destroyed for the evening, it could not dwell long on her spirits; and having told all her griefs to Charlotte Lucas, whom she had not seen for a week, she was soon able to make a voluntary transition to the oddities of her cousin, and to point him out to her particular notice. The two first dances, however, brought a return of distress; they were dances of mortification. Mr Collins, awkward and solemn, apologising instead of attending, and often moving wrong without being aware of it, gave her all the shame and misery which a disagreeable partner for a couple of dances can give. The moment of her release from him was ecstasy.

She danced next with an officer, and had the refreshment of talking of Wickham, and of hearing that he was universally liked. When those dances were over she returned to Charlotte Lucas, and was in conversation with her, when she found herself suddenly addressed by Mr Darcy, who took her so much by surprise in his application for her hand, that, without knowing what she did, she accepted him. He walked away again immediately, and she was left to fret over her own want of presence of mind; Charlotte tried to console her.

'I dare say you will find him very agreeable.'

'Heaven forbid! – *That* would be the greatest misfortune of all! – To find a man agreeable whom one is determined to hate! – Do not wish me such an evil.'

When the dancing recommenced, however, and Darcy approached to claim her hand, Charlotte could not help cautioning her in a whisper not to be a simpleton and allow her fancy for Wickham to make her appear unpleasant in the eyes of a man of ten times his consequence. Elizabeth made no answer, and took her place in the set, amazed at the dignity to which she was arrived in being allowed to stand opposite to Mr Darcy, and reading in her neighbours' looks their equal amazement in beholding it. They stood for some time without speaking a word; and she began to imagine that their silence was to last through the two dances, and at first was resolved not to break it; till suddenly fancying that it would be the greater punishment to her partner to oblige him to talk, she made some slight observation on the dance. He replied, and was again silent. After a pause of some minutes she addressed him a second time with

'It is *your* turn to say something now, Mr Darcy. – *I* talked about the dance, and *you* ought to make some kind of remark on the size of the room, or the number of couples.'

He smiled, and assured her that whatever she wished him to say should be said.

'Very well. – That reply will do for the present. – Perhaps by and bye I may observe that private balls are much pleasanter than public ones. – But *now* we may be silent.'

'Do you talk by rule then, while you are dancing?'

'Sometimes. One must speak a little, you know. It would look odd to be entirely silent for half an hour together, and yet for the advantage of *some*, conversation ought to be so arranged as that they may have the trouble of saying as little as possible.'

'Are you consulting your own feelings in the present case, or do you imagine that you are gratifying mine?'

'Both,' replied Elizabeth archly; 'for I have always seen a great similarity in the turn of our minds. – We are each of an unsocial, taciturn disposition, unwilling to speak, unless we expect to say something that will amaze the whole room, and be handed down to posterity with all the eclat of a proverb.'

'This is no very striking resemblance of your own character, I am sure,' said he. 'How near it may be to *mine*, I cannot pretend to say. – *You* think it a faithful portrait undoubtedly.'

'I must not decide on my own performance.'

He made no answer, and they were again silent till they had gone down the dance, when he asked her if she and her sisters did not very often walk to Meryton. She answered in the affirmative, and, unable to resist the temptation, added, 'When you met us there the other day, we had just been forming a new acquaintance.'

The effect was immediate. A deeper shade of hauteur overspread his features, but he said not a word, and Elizabeth, though blaming herself for her own weakness, could not go on. At length Darcy spoke, and in a constrained manner said,

'Mr Wickham is blessed with such happy manners as may ensure his *making* friends – whether he may be equally capable of *retaining* them, is less certain.'

'He has been so unlucky as to lose *your* friendship,' replied Elizabeth with emphasis, 'and in a manner which he is likely to suffer from all his life.'

Darcy made no answer, and seemed desirous of changing the subject. At that moment Sir William Lucas appeared close to them, meaning to pass through the set to the other side of the room; but on perceiving Mr Darcy he stopt with a bow of superior courtesy to compliment him on his dancing and his partner.

'I have been most highly gratified indeed, my dear Sir. Such very superior dancing is not often seen. It is evident that you belong to the first circles. Allow me to say, however, that your fair partner does not disgrace you, and that I must hope to have this pleasure often repeated, especially when a certain desirable event, my dear Miss Eliza, (glancing at her sister and Bingley,) shall take place. What congratulations will then flow in! I appeal to Mr Darcy: – but let me not interrupt you, Sir. – You will not

'Such very superior dancing is not often seen'

thank me for detaining you from the bewitching converse of that young lady, whose bright eyes are also upbraiding me.'

The latter part of his address was scarcely heard by Darcy; but Sir William's allusion to his friend seemed to strike him forcibly, and his eyes were directed with a very serious expression towards Bingley and Jane, who were dancing together. Recovering himself, however, shortly, he turned to his partner, and said,

'Sir William's interruption has made me forget what we were talking of.'

'I do not think we were speaking at all. Sir William could not have interrupted any two people in the room who had less to say for themselves. — We have tried two or three subjects already without success, and what we are to talk of next I cannot imagine.'

'What think you of books?' said he, smiling.

'Books — Oh! no. — I am sure we never read the same, or not with the same feelings.'

'I am sorry you think so; but if that be the case, there can at least be no want of subject. – We may compare our different opinions.'

'No – I cannot talk of books in a ball-room; my head is always full of something else.'

'The *present* always occupies you in such scenes – does it?' said he, with a look of doubt.

'Yes, always,' she replied, without knowing what she said, for her thoughts had wandered far from the subject, as soon afterwards appeared by her suddenly exclaiming, 'I remember hearing you once say, Mr Darcy, that you hardly ever forgave, that your resentment once created was unappeasable. You are very cautious, I suppose, as to its *being created*.'

'I am,' said he, with a firm voice.

'And never allow yourself to be blinded by prejudice?'

'I hope not.'

'It is particularly incumbent on those who never change their opinion, to be secure of judging properly at first.'

'May I ask to what these questions tend?'

'Merely to the illustration of *your* character,' said she, endeavouring to shake off her gravity. 'I am trying to make it out.'

'And what is your success?'

She shook her head. 'I do not get on at all. I hear such different accounts of you as puzzle me exceedingly.'

'I can readily believe,' answered he gravely, 'that report may vary greatly with respect to me; and I could wish, Miss Bennet, that you were not to sketch my character at the present moment, as there is reason to fear that the performance would reflect no credit on either.'

'But if I do not take your likeness now, I may never have another opportunity.'

'I would by no means suspend any pleasure of yours,' he coldly replied. She said no more, and they went down the other dance and parted in silence; on each side dissatisfied, though not to an equal degree, for in Darcy's breast there was a tolerable powerful feeling towards her, which soon procured her pardon, and directed all his anger against another.

They had not long separated when Miss Bingley came towards her, and with an expression of civil disdain thus accosted her,

'So, Miss Eliza, I hear you are quite delighted with George Wickham! – Your sister has been talking to me about him, and asking me a thousand questions; and I find that the young man forgot to tell you, among his other communications, that he was the son of old Wickham, the late Mr Darcy's steward. Let me recommend you, however, as a friend, not to give implicit confidence to all his assertions; for as to Mr Darcy's using him ill, it is perfectly false; for, on the contrary, he has been always remarkably kind to him, though George Wickham has treated Mr Darcy in a most infamous manner. I do not know the particulars, but I know very well that Mr Darcy is not in the least to blame, that he cannot bear to hear George Wickham mentioned, and that though my brother thought he could not well avoid including him in his invitation to the officers, he was excessively glad to find that he had taken himself out of the way. His coming into the country at all, is a most insolent thing indeed, and I wonder how he could presume to do it. I pity you, Miss Eliza, for this discovery of your favourite's guilt; but really considering his descent, one could not expect much better.'

'His guilt and his descent appear by your account to be the same,' said Elizabeth angrily; 'for I have heard you accuse him of nothing worse than of being the son of Mr Darcy's steward, and of *that*, I can assure you, he informed me himself.'

'I beg your pardon,' replied Miss Bingley, turning away with a sneer. 'Excuse my interference. – It was kindly meant.'

'Insolent girl!' said Elizabeth to herself. – 'You are much mistaken if you expect to influence me by such a paltry attack as this. I see nothing in it but your own wilful ignorance and the malice of Mr Darcy.' She then sought her eldest sister, who had undertaken to make inquiries on the same subject of Bingley. Jane met her with a smile of such sweet complacency, a glow of such happy expression, as sufficiently marked how well she was satisfied with the occurrences of the evening. – Elizabeth instantly read her feelings, and at that moment solicitude for Wickham, resentment against his enemies, and every thing else gave way before the hope of Jane's being in the fairest way for happiness.

'I want to know,' said she, with a countenance no less smiling than her sister's, 'what you have learnt about Mr Wickham. But perhaps you have been too pleasantly engaged to think of any third person; in which case you may be sure of my pardon.'

'No,' replied Jane, 'I have not forgotten him; but I have nothing satisfactory to tell you. Mr Bingley does not know the whole of his history, and is quite ignorant of the circumstances which have principally offended Mr Darcy; but he will vouch for the good conduct, the probity and honour of his friend, and is perfectly convinced that Mr Wickham has deserved much less attention from Mr Darcy than he has received; and I am sorry to say that by his account as well as his sister's, Mr Wickham is by no means a respectable young man. I am afraid he has been very imprudent, and has deserved to lose Mr Darcy's regard.'

'Mr Bingley does not know Mr Wickham himself?'

'No; he never saw him till the other morning at Meryton.'

'This account then is what he has received from Mr Darcy. I am perfectly satisfied. But what does he say of the living?'

'He does not exactly recollect the circumstances, though he has heard them from Mr Darcy more than once, but he believes that it was left to him *conditionally* only.'

'I have not a doubt of Mr Bingley's sincerity,' said Elizabeth warmly; 'but you must excuse my not being convinced by assurances only. Mr Bingley's defence of his friend was a very able one I dare say, but since he is unacquainted with several parts of the story, and has learnt the rest from that friend himself, I shall venture still to think of both gentlemen as I did before.'

She then changed the discourse to one more gratifying to each, and on which there could be no difference of sentiment. Elizabeth listened with delight to the happy, though modest hopes which Jane entertained of Bingley's regard, and said all in her power to heighten her confidence in it. On their being joined by Mr Bingley himself, Elizabeth withdrew to Miss Lucas; to whose inquiry after the pleasantness of her last partner she had scarcely replied, before Mr Collins came up to them and told her with great exultation that he had just been so fortunate as to make a most important discovery.

'I have found out,' said he, 'by a singular accident, that there is now in the room a near relation of my patroness. I happened to overhear the gentleman himself mentioning to the young lady who does the honours of this house the names of his cousin Miss de Bourgh, and of her mother Lady Catherine. How wonderfully these sort of things occur! Who would have thought of my meeting with – perhaps – a nephew of Lady Catherine de Bourgh in this assembly! – I am most thankful that the discovery is made in time for me to pay my respects to him, which I am now going to do, and trust he will excuse my not having done it before. My total ignorance of the connection must plead my apology.'

'You are not going to introduce yourself to Mr Darcy?'

'Indeed I am. I shall intreat his pardon for not having done it earlier. I believe him to be Lady Catherine's *nephew*. It will be in my power to assure him that her ladyship was quite well yesterday se'nnight.'

Elizabeth tried hard to dissuade him from such a scheme; assuring him that Mr Darcy would consider his addressing him without introduction as an impertinent freedom, rather than a compliment to his aunt; that it was not in the least necessary there should be any notice on either side, and that if it were, it must belong to Mr Darcy, the superior in consequence, to begin the acquaintance. – Mr Collins listened to her with the determined air of following his own inclination, and when she ceased speaking, replied thus,

'My dear Miss Elizabeth, I have the highest opinion in the world of your excellent judgment in all matters within the scope of your understanding, but permit me to say that there must be a wide difference between the established forms of ceremony amongst the laity, and those which regulate the clergy; for give me leave to observe that I consider the clerical office as equal in point of dignity with the highest rank in the kingdom – provided that a proper humility of behaviour is at the same time maintained. You must therefore allow me to follow the dictates of my conscience on this occasion, which leads me to perform what I look on as a point of duty. Pardon me for neglecting to profit by your advice, which on every other subject shall be my constant guide, though in the case before us I consider myself more fitted by education and habitual study to decide on what is right than a young lady like yourself.' And with a low bow he left her to attack Mr Darcy, whose reception of his advances she eagerly watched, and whose astonishment at being so addressed was very evident. Her cousin prefaced his speech with a solemn bow, and though she could not hear a word of it, she felt as if hearing it all, and saw in the motion of his lips the words 'apology,' 'Hunsford' and 'Lady Catherine de Bourgh.' – It vexed her to see him expose himself to such a man. Mr Darcy was eyeing him with unrestrained wonder, and when at last Mr Collins allowed him time to speak, replied with an air of distant civility. Mr Collins, however, was not discouraged from speaking again, and Mr Darcy's contempt seemed abundantly increasing with the length of his second speech, and at the end of it he only made him a slight bow, and moved another way. Mr Collins then turned to Elizabeth.

'I have no reason, I assure you,' said he, 'to be dissatisfied with my reception. Mr Darcy seemed much pleased with the attention. He answered me with the utmost civility, and even paid me the compliment of saying, that he was so well convinced of Lady Catherine's discernment as to be certain she could never bestow a favour unworthily. It was really a very handsome thought. Upon the whole, I am much pleased with him.'

As Elizabeth had no longer any interest of her own to pursue, she turned her attention almost entirely on her sister and Mr Bingley, and the train of agreeable reflections which her observations gave birth to, made her perhaps almost as happy as Jane. She saw her in idea settled in that very house in all the felicity which a marriage of true affection could bestow; and she felt capable under such circumstances, of endeavouring even to like Bingley's two sisters. Her mother's thoughts she plainly saw were bent the same way, and she determined not to venture near her, lest she might hear too much. When they sat down to supper, therefore, she considered it a most unlucky perverseness which placed them within one of each other; and deeply was she vexed to find that her mother was talking to that one person (Lady Lucas) freely, openly, and of nothing else but of her expectation that Jane would be soon married to Mr Bingley. – It was an animating subject, and Mrs Bennet seemed incapable of fatigue while enumerating the advantages of the match. His being such a charming young man, and so rich, and living but three miles from them, were the first points of self-congratulation; and then it was such a comfort to think how fond the two sisters were of Jane, and to be certain that they must desire the connection as much as she could do. It was, moreover, such a promising thing for her younger daughters, as Jane's marrying so greatly must throw them in the way of other rich men; and lastly, it was so pleasant at her time of life to be able to consign her single daughters to the care of their sister, that she might not be obliged to go into company more than she liked. It was necessary to make this circumstance a matter of pleasure, because on such occasions it is the etiquette; but no one was less likely than Mrs Bennet to find comfort in staying at home at any period of her life. She concluded with many good wishes that Lady Lucas might soon be equally fortunate, though evidently and triumphantly believing there was no chance of it.

In vain did Elizabeth endeavour to check the rapidity of her mother's words, or persuade her to describe her felicity in a less audible whisper; for to her inexpressible vexation, she could perceive that the chief of it was overheard by Mr Darcy, who sat opposite to them. Her mother only scolded her for being nonsensical.

'What is Mr Darcy to me, pray, that I should be afraid of him? I am sure we owe him no such particular civility as to be obliged to say nothing *he* may not like to hear.'

'For heaven's sake, madam, speak lower. – What advantage can it be to you to offend Mr Darcy? – You will never recommend yourself to his friend by so doing.'

Nothing that she could say, however, had any influence. Her mother would talk of her views in the same intelligible tone. Elizabeth blushed and blushed again with shame and vexation. She could not help frequently glancing her eye at Mr Darcy, though every glance convinced her of what she dreaded; for though he was not always looking at her mother, she was convinced that his attention was invariably fixed by her. The expression of his face changed gradually from indignant contempt to a composed and steady gravity.

At length however Mrs Bennet had no more to say; and Lady Lucas, who had been long yawning at the repetition of delights which she saw no likelihood of sharing, was left to the comforts of cold ham and chicken. Elizabeth now began to revive. But not long was the interval of tranquillity; for when supper was over, singing was talked of, and she had the mortification of seeing Mary, after very little entreaty, preparing to oblige the company. By many significant looks and silent entreaties, did she endeavour to prevent such a proof of complaisance, – but in vain; Mary would not understand them; such an opportunity of exhibiting was delightful to her, and she began her song. Elizabeth's eyes were fixed on her

with most painful sensations; and she watched her progress through the
several stanzas with an impatience which was very ill rewarded at their
close; for Mary, on receiving amongst the thanks of the table, the hint of a
hope that she might be prevailed on to favour them again, after the pause of
half a minute began another. Mary's powers were by no means fitted for
such a display; her voice was weak, and her manner affected. – Elizabeth was
in agonies. She looked at Jane, to see how she bore it; but Jane was very
composedly talking to Bingley. She looked at his two sisters, and saw them
making signs of derision at each other, and at Darcy, who continued
however impenetrably grave. She looked at her father to entreat his
interference, lest Mary should be singing all night. He took the hint, and
when Mary had finished her second song, said aloud,

'That will do extremely well, child. You have delighted us long enough.
Let the other young ladies have time to exhibit.'

Mary, though pretending not to hear, was somewhat disconcerted; and
Elizabeth sorry for her, and sorry for her father's speech, was afraid her
anxiety had done no good. – Others of the party were now applied to.

'If I,' said Mr Collins, 'were so fortunate as to be able to sing, I should have
great pleasure, I am sure, in obliging the company with an air; for I consider
music as a very innocent diversion, and perfectly compatible with the
profession of a clergyman. – I do not mean however to assert that we can be
justified in devoting too much of our time to music, for there are certainly
other things to be attended to. The rector of a parish has much to do. – In the
first place, he must make such an agreement for tythes as may be beneficial
to himself and not offensive to his patron. He must write his own sermons;
and the time that remains will not be too much for his parish duties, and the
care and improvement of his dwelling, which he cannot be excused from
making as comfortable as possible. And I do not think it of light importance
that he should have attentive and conciliatory manners towards every body,
especially towards those to whom he owes his preferment. I cannot acquit
him of that duty; not could I think well of the man who should omit an
occasion of testifying his respect towards any body connected with the
family.' And with a bow to Mr Darcy, he concluded his speech, which had
been spoken so loud as to be heard by half the room. – Many stared. – Many
smiled; but no one looked more amused than Mr Bennet himself, while his
wife seriously commended Mr Collins for having spoken so sensibly, and
observed in a half-whisper to Lady Lucas, that he was a remarkably clever,
good kind of young man.

To Elizabeth it appeared, that had her family made an agreement to
expose themselves as much as they could during the evening, it would have
been impossible for them to play their parts with more spirit, or finer
success; and happy did she think it for Bingley and her sister that some of the

exhibition had escaped his notice, and that his feelings were not of a sort to be much distressed by the folly which he must have witnessed. That his two sisters and Mr Darcy, however, should have such an opportunity of ridiculing her relations was bad enough, and she could not determine whether the silent contempt of the gentleman, or the insolent smiles of the ladies, were more intolerable.

The rest of the evening brought her little amusement. She was teased by Mr Collins, who continued most perseveringly by her side, and though he could not prevail with her to dance with him again, put it out of her power to dance with others. In vain did she entreat him to stand up with somebody else, and offer to introduce him to any young lady in the room. He assured her that as to dancing, he was perfectly indifferent to it; that his chief object was by delicate attentions to recommend himself to her, and that he should therefore make a point of remaining close to her the whole evening. There was no arguing upon such a project. She owed her greatest relief to her friend Miss Lucas, who often joined them, and good-naturedly engaged Mr Collins's conversation to herself.

She was at least free from the offence of Mr Darcy's farther notice; though often standing within a very short distance of her, quite disengaged, he never came near enough to speak. She felt it to be the probable consequence of her allusions to Mr Wickham, and rejoiced in it.

The Longbourn party were the last of all the company to depart; and by a manoeuvre of Mrs Bennet had to wait for their carriages a quarter of an hour after every body else was gone, which gave them time to see how heartily they were wished away by some of the family. Mrs Hurst and her sister scarcely opened their mouths except to complain of fatigue, and were evidently impatient to have the house to themselves. They repulsed every attempt of Mrs Bennet at conversation, and by so doing, threw a langour over the whole party, which was very little relieved by the long speeches of Mr Collins, who was complimenting Mr Bingley and his sisters on the elegance of their entertainment, and the hospitality and politeness which had marked their behaviour to their guests. Darcy said nothing at all. Mr Bennet, in equal silence, was enjoying the scene. Mr Bingley and Jane were standing together, a little detached from the rest, and talked only to each other. Elizabeth preserved as steady a silence as either Mrs Hurst or Miss Bingley; and even Lydia was too much fatigued to utter more than the occasional exclamation of 'Lord, how tired I am!' accompanied by a violent yawn.

When at length they arose to take leave, Mrs Bennet was most pressingly civil in her hope of seeing the whole family soon at Longbourn; and adressed herself particularly to Mr Bingley, to assure him how happy he would make them, by eating a family dinner with them at any time, without the ceremony of a formal invitation. Bingley was all grateful pleasure, and he readily engaged for taking the earliest opportunity of waiting on her, after his return from London, whither he was obliged to go the next day for a short time.

Mrs Bennet was perfectly satisfied; and quitted the house under the delightful persuasion that, allowing for the necessary preparations of settlements, new carriages and wedding clothes, she should undoubtedly see her daughter settled at Netherfield, in the course of three or four months. Of having another daughter married to Mr Collins, she thought with equal certainty, and with considerable, though not equal, pleasure. Elizabeth was the least dear to her of all her children; and though the man and the match were quite good enough for *her*, the worth of each was eclipsed by Mr Bingley and Netherfield.

'To assure you in the most animated language'

CHAPTER NINETEEN

THE NEXT DAY OPENED A NEW SCENE at Longbourn. Mr Collins made his declaration in form. Having resolved to do it without loss of time, as his leave of absence extended only to the following Saturday, and having no feelings of diffidence to make it distressing to himself even at the moment, he set about it in a very orderly manner, with all the observances which he supposed a regular part of the business. On finding Mrs Bennet, Elizabeth, and one of the younger girls together, soon after breakfast, he addressed the mother in these words,

'May I hope, Madam, for your interest with your fair daughter Elizabeth, when I solicit for the honour of a private audience with her in the course of this morning?'

Before Elizabeth had time for any thing but a blush of surprise, Mrs Bennet instantly answered,

'Oh dear! – Yes – certainly. – I am sure Lizzy will be very happy – I am sure she can have no objection. – Come, Kitty, I want you up stairs.' And gathering her work together, she was hastening away, when Elizabeth called out,

'Dear Ma'am, do not go. – I beg you will not go. – Mr Collins must excuse me. – He can have nothing to say to me that any body need not hear. I am going away myself.'

'No, no, nonsense, Lizzy. – I desire you will stay where you are.' – And upon Elizabeth's seeming really, with vexed and embarrassed looks, about to escape, she added, 'Lizzy, I *insist* upon your staying and hearing Mr Collins.'

Elizabeth would not oppose such an injunction – and a moment's consideration making her also sensible that it would be wisest to get it over as soon and as quietly as possible, she sat down again, and tried to conceal by incessant employment the feelings which were divided between distress and diversion. Mrs Bennet and Kitty walked off, and as soon as they were gone Mr Collins began.

'Believe me, my dear Miss Elizabeth, that your modesty, so far from doing you any disservice, rather adds to your other perfections. You would have been less amiable in my eyes had there *not* been this little unwillingness; but allow me to assure you that I have your respected mother's permission for this address. You can hardly doubt the purport of my discourse, however your natural delicacy may lead you to dissemble; my attentions have been too marked to be mistaken. Almost as soon as I entered the house I singled you out as the companion of my future life. But before I am run away with by my feelings on this subject, perhaps it will be advisable for me to state my reasons for marrying – and moreover for coming into Hertfordshire with the design of selecting a wife, as I certainly did.'

The idea of Mr Collins, with all his solemn composure, being run away with by his feelings, made Elizabeth so near laughing that she could not use the short pause he allowed in any attempt to stop him farther, and he continued:

'My reasons for marrying are, first, that I think it a right thing for every clergyman in easy circumstances (like myself) to set the example of matrimony in his parish. Secondly, that I am convinced it will add very greatly to my happiness; and thirdly – which perhaps I ought to have mentioned earlier, that it is the particular advice and recommendation of the very noble lady whom I have the honour of calling patroness. Twice has she condescended to give me her opinion (unasked too!) on this subject; and it was but the very Saturday night before I left Hunsford – between our pools at quadrille, while Mrs Jenkinson was arranging Miss de Bourgh's foot-stool, that she said, "Mr Collins, you must marry. A clergyman like you must marry. – Chuse properly, chuse a gentlewoman for *my* sake; and for your *own*, let her be an active, useful sort of person, not brought up high, but able to make a small income go a good way. This is my advice. Find such a woman as soon as you can, bring her to Hunsford, and I will visit her." Allow me, by the way to observe, my fair cousin, that I do not reckon the notice and kindness of Lady Catherine de Bourgh as among the least of the advantages in my power to offer. You will find her manners beyond any thing I can describe; and your wit and vivacity I think must be acceptable to her, especially when tempered with the silence and respect which her rank will inevitably excite. Thus much for my general intention in favour of matrimony; it remains to be told why my views were directed to Longbourn instead of my own neighbourhood, where I assure you there are many amiable young women. But the fact is, that being, as I am, to inherit this estate after the death of your honoured father, (who, however, may live many years longer), I could not satisfy myself without resolving to chuse a wife from among his daughters, that the loss to them might be as little as possible, when the melancholy event takes place – which, however, as I have already said, may not be for several years. This has been my motive, my fair cousin, and I flatter myself it will not sink me in your esteem. And now nothing remains for me but to assure you in the most animated language of the violence of my affection. To fortune I am perfectly indifferent, and shall make no demand of that nature on your father, since I am well aware that it could not be complied with; and that one thousand pounds in the 4 per cents. which will not be yours till after your mother's decease, is all that you may ever be entitled to. On that head, therefore, I shall be uniformly silent; and you may assure yourself that no ungenerous reproach shall ever pass my lips when we are married.'

It was absolutely necessary to interrupt him now.

'You are too hasty, Sir,' she cried. 'You forget that I have made no answer. Let me do it without farther loss of time. Accept my thanks for the compliment you are paying me. I am very sensible of the honour of your proposals, but it is impossible for me to do otherwise than decline them.'

'I am not now to learn,' replied Mr Collins, with a formal wave of the hand, 'that it is usual with young ladies to reject the addresses of the man whom they secretly mean to accept, when he first applies for their favour;

and that sometimes the refusal is repeated a second or even a third time. I am therefore by no means discouraged by what you have just said, and shall hope to lead you to the altar ere long.'

'Upon my word, Sir,' cried Elizabeth, 'your hope is rather an extraordinary one after my declaration. I do assure you that I am not one of those young ladies (if such young ladies there are) who are so daring as to risk their happiness on the chance of being asked a second time. I am perfectly serious in my refusal. – You could not make *me* happy, and I am convinced that I am the last woman in the world who would make *you* so. – Nay, were your friend Lady Catherine to know me, I am persuaded she would find me in every respect ill qualified for the situation.'

'Were it certain that Lady Catherine would think so,' said Mr Collins very gravely – 'but I cannot imagine that her ladyship would at all disapprove of you. And you may be certain that when I have the honour of seeing her again I shall speak in the highest terms of your modesty, economy, and other amiable qualifications.'

'Indeed, Mr Collins, all praise of me will be unnecessary. You must give me leave to judge for myself, and pay me the compliment of believing what I say. I wish you very happy and very rich, and by refusing your hand, do all in my power to prevent your being otherwise. In making me the offer, you must have satisfied the delicacy of your feelings with regard to my family, and may take possession of Longbourn estate whenever it falls, without any self-reproach. This matter may be considered, therefore, as finally settled.' And rising as she thus spoke, she would have quitted the room, had not Mr Collins thus addressed her.

'When I do myself the honour of speaking to you next in this subject I shall hope to receive a more favourable answer than you have now given me; though I am far from accusing you of cruelty at present, because I know it to be the established custom of your sex to reject a man on the first application, and perhaps you have even now said as much to encourage my suit as would be consistent with the true delicacy of the female character.'

'Really, Mr Collins,' cried Elizabeth with some warmth, 'you puzzle me exceedingly. If what I have hitherto said can appear to you in the form of encouragement, I know not how to express my refusal in such a way as may convince you of its being one.'

'You must give me leave to flatter myself, my dear cousin, that your refusal of my addresses is merely words of course. My reasons for believing it are briefly these: – It does not appear to me that my hand is unworthy your acceptance, or that the establishment I can offer would be any other than highly desirable. My situation in life, my connections with the family of de Bourgh, and my relationship to your own, are circumstances highly in my favour; and you should take it into farther consideration that in spite of your manifold attractions, it is by no means certain that another offer of marriage may ever be made you. Your portion is unhappily so small that it will in all likelihood undo the effects of your loveliness and amiable qualifications. As I must therefore conclude that you are not serious in your rejection of me, I shall chuse to attribute it to your wish of increasing my love by suspense, according to the usual practice of elegant females.'

'I do assure you, Sir, that I have no pretension whatever to that kind of elegance which consists in tormenting a respectable man. I would rather be paid the compliment of being believed. I thank you again and again for the honour you have done me in your proposals, but to accept them is absolutely impossible. My feelings in every respect forbid it. Can I speak plainer? Do not consider me now as an elegant female intending to plague you, but as a rational creature speaking the truth from her heart.'

'You are uniformly charming!' cried he, with an air of awkward gallantry; 'and I am persuaded that when sanctioned by the express authority of both your excellent parents, my proposals will not fail of being acceptable.'

To such perseverance in wilful self-deception Elizabeth would make no reply, and immediately and in silence withdrew; determined, if he persisted in considering her repeated refusals as flattering encouragement, to apply to her father, whose negative might be uttered in such a manner as must be decisive, and whose behaviour at least could not be mistaken for the affectation and coquetry of an elegant female.

CHAPTER TWENTY

MR COLLINS WAS NOT LEFT LONG to the silent contemplation of his successful love; for Mrs Bennet, having dawdled about in the vestibule to watch for the end of the conference, no sooner saw Elizabeth open the door and with quick step pass her towards the staircase, than she entered the breakfast-room, and congratulated both him and herself in warm terms on the happy prospect of their nearer connection. Mr Collins received and returned these felicitations with equal pleasure, and then proceeded to relate the particulars of their interview, with the result of which he trusted he had every reason to be satisfied, since the refusal which his cousin had steadfastly given him would naturally flow from her bashful modesty and the genuine delicacy of her character.

This information, however, startled Mrs Bennet; – she would have been glad to be equally satisfied that her daughter had meant to encourage him by protesting against his proposals, but she dared not to believe it, and could not help saying so.

'But depend upon it, Mr Collins,' she added, 'that Lizzy shall be brought to reason. I will speak to her about it myself directly. She is a very headstrong foolish girl, and does not know her own interest; but I will *make* her know it.'

'Pardon me for interrupting you, Madam,' cried Mr Collins; 'but if she is really headstrong and foolish, I know not whether she would altogether be a very desirable wife to a man in my situation, who naturally looks for happiness in the marriage state. If therefore she actually persists in rejecting my suit, perhaps it were better not to force her into accepting me, because if liable to such defects of temper, she could not contribute much to my felicity.'

'Sir, you quite misunderstand me,' said Mrs Bennet, alarmed. 'Lizzy is only headstrong in such matters as these. In every thing else she is as good natured a girl as ever lived. I will go directly to Mr Bennet, and we shall very soon settle it with her, I am sure.'

She would not give him time to reply, but hurrying instantly to her husband, called out as she entered the library,

'Oh! Mr Bennet, you are wanted immediately; we are all in an uproar. You must come and make Lizzy marry Mr Collins, for she vows she will not have him, and if you do not make haste he will change his mind and not have *her*.'

Mr Bennet raised his eyes from his book as she entered, and fixed them on her face with a calm unconcern which was not in the least altered by her communication.

'I have not the pleasure of understanding you,' said he, when she had finished her speech. 'Of what are you talking?'

'Of Mr Collins and Lizzy. Lizzy declares she will not have Mr Collins, and Mr Collins begins to say that he will not have Lizzy.'

'And what am I to do on the occasion? – It seems an hopeless business.'

'Speak to Lizzy about it yourself. Tell her that you insist upon her marrying him.'

'Let her be called down. She shall hear my opinion.'

Mrs Bennet rang the bell, and Miss Elizabeth was summoned to the library.

'Come here, child,' cried her father as she appeared. 'I have sent for you on an affair of importance. I understand that Mr Collins has made you an offer of marriage. Is it true?' Elizabeth replied that it was. 'Very well – and this offer of marriage you have refused?'

'I have, Sir.'

'Very well. We now come to the point. Your mother insists upon your accepting it. Is not it so, Mrs Bennet?'

'Yes, or I will never see her again.'

'An unhappy alternative is before you, Elizabeth. From this day you must be a stranger to one of your parents. – Your mother will never see you again if you do *not* marry Mr Collins, and I will never see you again if you *do*.'

Elizabeth could not but smile at such a conclusion of such a beginning; but Mrs Bennet, who had persuaded herself that her husband regarded the affair as she wished, was excessively disappointed.

'What do you mean, Mr Bennet, by talking in this way. You promised me to *insist* upon her marrying him.'

'My dear,' replied her husband. 'I have two small favours to request. First, that you will allow me the free use of my understanding on the present occasion; and secondly, of my room. I shall be glad to have the library to myself as soon as may be.'

Not yet, however, in spite of her disappointment in her husband, did Mrs Bennet give up the point. She talked to Elizabeth again and again; coaxed and threatened her by turns. She endeavoured to secure Jane in his interest, but Jane with all possible mildness declined interfering; – and Elizabeth sometimes with real earnestness and sometimes with playful gaiety replied to her attacks. Though her manner varied however, her determination never did.

Mr Collins, meanwhile, was meditating in solitude on what had passed. He thought too well of himself to comprehend on what motives his cousin could refuse him; and though his pride was hurt, he suffered in no other way. His regard for her was quite imaginary; and the possibility of her deserving her mother's reproach prevented his feeling any regret.

While the family were in this confusion, Charlotte Lucas came to spend the day with them. She was met in the vestibule by Lydia, who, flying to her, cried in a half whisper, 'I am glad you are come, for there is such fun here! – What do you think has happened this morning? – Mr Collins has made an offer to Lizzy, and she will not have him.'

Charlotte had hardly time to answer, before they were joined by Kitty, who came to tell the same news, and no sooner had they entered the breakfast-room, where Mrs Bennet was alone, than she likewise began on the subject, calling on Miss Lucas for her compassion, and entreating her to persuade her friend Lizzy to comply with the wishes of all her family. 'Pray do, my dear Miss Lucas,' she added in a melancholy tone, 'for nobody is on my side, nobody takes part with me, I am cruelly used, nobody feels for my poor nerves.'

Charlotte's reply was spared by the entrance of Jane and Elizabeth.

'Aye, there she comes,' continued Mrs Bennet, 'looking as unconcerned as may be, and caring no more for us than if we were at York, provided she

They entered the breakfast-room

can have her own way. But I tell you what, Miss Lizzy, if you take it into your head to go on refusing every offer of marriage in this way, you will never get a husband at all – and I am sure I do not know who is to maintain you when your father is dead. – *I* shall not be able to keep you – and so I warn you. – I have done with you from this very day. – I told you in the library, you know, that I should never speak to you again, and you will find me as good as my word. I have no pleasure in talking to undutiful children. – Not that I have much pleasure indeed in talking to any body. People who suffer as I do from nervous complaints can have no great inclination for talking. Nobody can tell what I suffer! – But it is always so. Those who do not complain are never pitied.'

Her daughters listened in silence to this effusion, sensible that any attempt to reason with or sooth her would only increase the irritation. She talked on, therefore, without interruption from any of them till they were joined by Mr Collins, who entered with an air more stately than usual, and on perceiving whom, she said to the girls,

'Now, I do insist upon it, that you, all of you, hold your tongues, and let Mr Collins and me have a little conversation together.'

Elizabeth passed quietly out of the room, Jane and Kitty followed, but Lydia stood her ground, determined to hear all she could; and Charlotte, detained first by the civility of Mr Collins, whose inquiries after herself and all her family were very minute, and then by a little curiosity, satisfied herself with walking to the window and pretending not to hear. In a doleful voice Mrs Bennet thus began the projected conversation. – 'Oh! Mr Collins!' –

'My dear Madam,' replied he, 'let us be for ever silent on this point. Far be it from me,' he presently continued in a voice that marked his displeasure, 'to resent the behaviour of your daughter. Resignation to inevitable evils is the duty of us all; the peculiar duty of a young man who has been so fortunate as I have been in early preferment; and I trust I am resigned. Perhaps not the less so from feeling a doubt of my positive happiness had my fair cousin honoured me with her hand; for I have often observed that resignation is never so perfect as when the blessing denied begins to lose somewhat of its value in our estimation. You will not, I hope, consider me as shewing any disrespect to your family, my dear Madam, by thus withdrawing my pretensions to your daughter's favour, without having paid yourself and Mr Bennet the compliment of requesting you to interpose your authority in my behalf. My conduct may I fear be objectionable in having accepted my dismission from your daughter's lips instead of your own. But we are all liable to error. I have certainly meant well through the whole affair. My object has been to secure an amiable companion for myself, with due consideration for the advantage of all your family, and if my *manner* has been at all reprehensible, I here beg leave to apologise.'

CHAPTER TWENTY ONE

THE DISCUSSION OF MR COLLINS'S offer was now nearly at an end, and Elizabeth had only to suffer from the uncomfortable feelings necessarily attending it, and occasionally from some peevish allusion of her mother. As for the gentleman himself, *his* feelings were chiefly expressed, not by embarrassment, or dejection, or by trying to avoid her, but by stiffness of manner and resentful silence. He scarcely ever spoke to her, and the assiduous attentions which he had been so sensible of himself, were transferred for the rest of the day to Miss Lucas, whose civility in listening to him, was a seasonable relief to them all, and especially to her friend.

The morrow produced no abatement of Mrs Bennet's ill humour or ill health. Mr Collins was also in the same state of angry pride. Elizabeth had hoped that his resentment might shorten his visit, but his plan did not appear in the least affected by it. He was always to have gone on Saturday, and to Saturday he still meant to stay.

After breakfast, the girls walked to Meryton to inquire if Mr Wickham were returned, and to lament over his absence from the Netherfield ball. He

joined them on their entering the town and attended them to their aunt's
where his regret and vexation, and the concern of every body was well
talked over. – To Elizabeth, however, he voluntarily acknowledged that
the necessity of his absence *had* been self imposed.

'I found,' said he, 'as the time drew near, that I had better not meet Mr
Darcy; – that to be in the same room, the same party with him for so many
hours together, might be more than I could bear, and that scenes might arise
unpleasant to more than myself.'

She highly approved his forbearance, and they had leisure for a full
discussion of it, and for all the commendation which they civilly bestowed
on each other, as Wickham and another officer walked back with them to
Longbourn, and during the walk, he particularly attended to her. His
accompanying them was a double advantage; she felt all the compliment it
offered to herself, and it was most acceptable as an occasion of introducing
him to her father and mother.

Soon after their return, a letter was delivered to Miss Bennet; it came
from Netherfield, and was opened immediately. The envelope contained a
sheet of elegant, little, hot pressed paper, well covered with a lady's fair,
flowing hand; and Elizabeth saw her sister's countenance change as she read
it, and saw her dwelling intently on some particular passages. Jane
recollected herself soon, and putting the letter away, tried to join with her
usual cheerfulness in the general conversation; but Elizabeth felt an anxiety
on the subject which drew off her attention even from Wickham; and no
sooner had he and his companion taken leave, than a glance from Jane
invited her to follow her up stairs. When they had gained their own room,
Jane taking out the letter said,

Walked back with them

'This is from Caroline Bingley; what it contains, has surprised me a good deal. The whole party have left Netherfield by this time, and are on their way to town; and without any intention of coming back again. You shall hear what she says.'

She then read the first sentence aloud, which comprised the information of their having just resolved to follow their brother to town directly, and of their meaning to dine that day in Grosvenor Street, where Mr Hurst had a house. The next was in these words. 'I do not pretend to regret any thing I shall leave in Hertfordshire, except your society, my dearest friend; but we will hope at some future period, to enjoy many returns of the delightful intercourse we have known, and in the mean while may lessen the pain of separation by a very frequent and most unreserved correspondence. I depend on you for that.' To these high flown expressions, Elizabeth listened with all the insensibility of distrust; and though the suddenness of their removal surprised her, she saw nothing in it really to lament; it was not to be supposed that their absence from Netherfield would prevent Mr Bingley's being there; and as to the loss of their society, she was persuaded that Jane must soon cease to regard it, in the enjoyment of his.

'It is unlucky,' she said, after a short pause, 'that you should not be able to see your friends before they leave the country. But may we not hope that the period of future happiness to which Miss Bingley looks forward, may arrive earlier than she is aware, and that the delightful intercourse you have known as friends, will be renewed with yet greater satisfaction as sisters? — Mr Bingley will not be detained in London by them.'

'Caroline decidedly says that none of the party will return into Hertfordshire this winter. I will read it to you —

'When my brother left us yesterday, he imagined that the business which took him to London, might be concluded in three or four days, but as we are certain it cannot be so, and at the same time convinced that when Charles gets to town, he will be in no hurry to leave it again, we have determined on following him thither, that he may not be obliged to spend his vacant hours in a comfortless hotel. Many of my acquaintance are already there for the winter; I wish I could hear that you, my dearest friend, had any intention of making one in the croud, but of that I despair. I sincerely hope your Christmas in Hertfordshire may abound in the gaieties which that season generally brings, and that your beaux will be so numerous as to prevent your feeling the loss of the three, of whom, we shall deprive you.'

'It is evident by this,' added Jane, 'that he comes back no more this winter.'

'It is only evident that Miss Bingley does not mean he *should*.'

'Why will you think so? It must be his own doing. — He is his own master. But you do not know *all*. I *will* read you the passage which particularly hurts me. I will have no reserves from *you*.' 'Mr Darcy is impatient to see his sister, and to confess the truth, *we* are scarcely less eager to meet her again. I really do not think Georgiana Darcy has her equal for beauty, elegance, and accomplishments; and the affection she inspires in Louisa and myself, is heightened into something still more interesting, from the hope we dare to entertain of her being hereafter our sister. I do not know whether I ever before mentioned to you my feelings on this subject, but I will not leave the country without confiding them, and I trust you will not esteem them unreasonable. My brother admires her greatly already, he will have frequent opportunity now of seeing her on the most intimate footing, her relations all wish the connection as much as his own, and a sister's partiality is not misleading me, I think, when I call Charles most capable of engaging any woman's heart. With all these circumstances to favour an attachment and nothing to prevent it, am I wrong, my dearest Jane, in indulging the hope of an event which will secure the happiness of so many?'

'What think you of *this* sentence, my dear Lizzy?' – said Jane as she finished it. 'Is it not clear enough? – Does it not expressly declare that Caroline neither expects nor wishes me to be her sister; that she is perfectly convinced of her brother's indifference, and that if she suspects the nature of my feelings for him, she means (most kindly!) to put me on my guard? Can there be any other opinion on the subject?'

'Yes, there can; for mine is totally different. – Will you hear it?'

'Most willingly.'

'You shall have it in few words. Miss Bingley sees that her brother is in love with you, and wants him to marry Miss Darcy. She follows him to town in the hope of keeping him there, and tries to persuade you that he does not care about you.'

Jane shook her head.

'Indeed, Jane, you ought to believe me. – No one who has ever seen you together, can doubt his affection. Miss Bingley I am sure cannot. She is not such a simpleton. Could she have seen half as much love in Mr Darcy for herself, she would have ordered her wedding clothes. But the case is this. We are not rich enough, or grand enough for them; and she is the more anxious to get Miss Darcy for her brother, from the notion that when there has been *one* intermarriage, she may have less trouble in achieving a second; in which there is certainly some ingenuity, and I dare say it would succeed, if Miss de Bourgh were out of the way. But, my dearest Jane, you cannot seriously imagine that because Miss Bingley tells you her brother greatly admires Miss Darcy, he is in the smallest degree less sensible of *your* merit than when he took leave of you on Tuesday, or that it will be in her power to persuade him that instead of being in love with you, he is very much in love with her friend.'

'If we thought alike of Miss Bingley,' replied Jane, 'your representation of all this, might make me quite easy. But I know the foundation is unjust. Caroline is incapable of wilfully deceiving any one; and all that I can hope in this case, is that she is deceived herself.'

'That is right. – You could not have started a more happy idea, since you will not take comfort in mine. Believe her to be deceived by all means. You have now done your duty by her, and must fret no longer.'

'But, my dear sister, can I be happy, even supposing the best, in accepting a man whose sisters and friends are all wishing him to marry elsewhere?'

'You must decide for yourself,' said Elizabeth, 'and if upon mature deliberation, you find that the misery of disobliging his two sisters is more than equivalent to the happiness of being his wife, I advise you by all means to refuse him.'

'How can you talk so?' – said Jane faintly smiling, – 'You must know that though I should be exceedingly grieved at this disapprobation, I could not hesitate.'

'I did not think you would; – and that being the case, I cannot consider your situation with much compassion.'

'But if he returns no more this winter, my choice will never be required. A thousand things may arise in six months!'

The idea of his returning no more Elizabeth treated with the utmost contempt. It appeared to her merely the suggestion of Caroline's interested wishes, and she could not for a moment suppose that those wishes, however openly or artfully spoken, could influence a young man so totally independent of every one.

She represented to her sister as forcibly as possible what she felt on the subject, and had soon the pleasure of seeing its happy effect. Jane's temper was not desponding, and she was gradually led to hope, though the diffidence of affection sometimes overcame the hope, that Bingley would return to Netherfield and answer every wish of her heart.

They agreed that Mrs Bennet should only hear of the departure of the family, without being alarmed on the score of the gentleman's conduct; but even this partial communication gave her a good deal of concern, and she bewailed it as exceedingly unlucky that the ladies should happen to go away, just as they were all getting so intimate together. After lamenting it however at some length, she had the consolation of thinking that Mr Bingley would be soon down again and soon dining at Longbourn, and the conclusion of all was the comfortable declaration that, though he had been invited only to a family dinner, she would take care to have two full courses.

CHAPTER TWENTY TWO

THE BENNETS WERE ENGAGED TO dine with the Lucases, and again during the chief of the day, was Miss Lucas so kind as to listen to Mr Collins. Elizabeth took an opportunity of thanking her. 'It keeps him in good humour,' said she, 'and I am more obliged to you than I can express.' Charlotte assured her friend of her satisfaction in being useful, and that it amply repaid her for the little sacrifice of her time. This was very amiable, but Charlotte's kindness extended farther than Elizabeth had any conception of; – its object was nothing less, than to secure her from any return of Mr Collins's addresses, by engaging them towards herself. Such was Miss Lucas's scheme; and appearances were so favourable that when they parted at night, she would have felt almost sure of success if he had not been to leave Hertfordshire so very soon. But here, she did injustice to the fire and independence of his character, for it led him to escape out of Longbourn House the next morning with admirable slyness, and hasten to Lucas Lodge to throw himself at her feet. He was anxious to avoid the notice of his cousins, from a conviction that if they saw him depart, they could not fail to conjecture his design, and he was not willing to have the attempt known till its success could be known likewise; for though feeling almost secure, and with reason, for Charlotte had been tolerably encouraging, he was comparatively diffident since the adventure of Wednesday. His reception however was of the most flattering kind. Miss Lucas perceived him from an upper window as he walked towards the house, and instantly set out to meet him accidentally in the lane. But little had she dared to hope that so much love and eloquence awaited her there.

In as short a time as Mr Collins's long speeches would allow, every thing was settled between them to the satisfaction of both; and as they entered the house, he earnestly entreated her to name the day that was to make him the happiest of men; and though such a solicitation must be waved for the present, the lady felt no inclination to trifle with his happiness. The stupidity with which he was favoured by nature, must guard his courtship from any charm that could make a woman wish for its continuance; and Miss Lucas, who accepted him solely from the pure and disinterested desire of an establishment, cared not how soon that establishment were gained.

Sir William and Lady Lucas were speedily applied to for their consent; and it was bestowed with a most joyful alacrity. Mr Collins's present circumstances made it a most eligible match for their daughter, to whom

So much love and eloquence

they could give little fortune; and his prospects of future wealth were exceedingly fair. Lady Lucas began directly to calculate with more interest than the matter had ever excited before, how many years longer Mr Bennet was likely to live; and Sir William gave it as his decided opinion, that whenever Mr Collins should be in possession of the Longbourn estate, it would be highly expedient that both he and his wife should make their appearance at St James's. The whole family in short were properly overjoyed on the occasion. The younger girls formed hopes of *coming out* a year or two sooner than they might otherwise have done; and the boys were relieved from their apprehension of Charlotte's dying an old maid. Charlotte herself was tolerably composed. She had gained her point, and had time to consider of it. Her reflections were in general satisfactory. Mr Collins to be sure was neither sensible nor agreeable; his society was irksome, and his attachment to her must be imaginary. But still he would be her husband. – Without thinking highly either of men or of matrimony, marriage had always been her object; it was the only honourable provision for well-educated young women of small fortune, and however uncertain of giving happiness, must be their pleasantest preservative from want. This preservative she had now obtained; and at the age of twenty-seven, without having ever been handsome, she felt all the good luck of it. The least agreeable circumstance in the business, was the surprise it must occasion to Elizabeth Bennet, whose friendship she valued beyond that of any other person. Elizabeth would wonder, and probably would blame her; and though her resolution was not to be shaken, her feelings must be hurt by such disapprobation. She resolved to give her the information herself, and therefore charged Mr Collins when he returned to Longbourn to dinner, to drop no hint of what had passed before any of the family. A promise of secrecy was of course very dutifully given, but it could not be kept without difficulty; for the curiosity excited by his long absence, burst forth in such very direct questions on his return, as required some ingenuity to evade, and he was at the same time exercising great self-denial, for he was longing to publish his prosperous love.

As he was to begin his journey too early on the morrow to see any of the family, the ceremony of leave-taking was performed when the ladies moved for the night; and Mrs Bennet with great politeness and cordiality said how happy they should be to see him at Longbourn again, whenever his other engagements might allow him to visit them.

'My dear Madam,' he replied, 'this invitation is particularly gratifying, because it is what I have been hoping to receive; and you may be very certain that I shall avail myself of it as soon as possible.'

They were all astonished; and Mr Bennet, who could by no means wish for so speedy a return, immediately said,

'But is there not danger of Lady Catherine's disapprobation here, my good sir? – You had better neglect your relations, than run the risk of offending your patroness.'

'My dear sir,' replied Mr Collins, 'I am particularly obliged to you for this friendly caution, and you may depend upon my not taking so material a step without her ladyship's concurrence.'

'You cannot be too much on your guard. Risk any thing rather than her displeasure; and if you find it likely to be raised by your coming to us again, which I should think exceedingly probable, stay quietly at home, and be satisfied that *we* shall take no offence.'

'Believe me, my dear sir, my gratitude is warmly excited by such affectionate attention; and depend upon it, you will speedily receive from me a letter of thanks for this, as well as for every other mark of your regard during my stay in Hertfordshire. As for my fair cousins, though my absence may not be long enough to render it necessary, I shall now take the liberty of wishing them health and happiness, not excepting my cousin Elizabeth.'

With proper civilities the ladies then withdrew; all of them equally surprised to find that he meditated a quick return. Mrs Bennet wished to understand by it that he thought of paying his addresses to one of her younger girls, and Mary might have been prevailed on to accept him. She rated his abilities much higher than any of the others; there was a solidity in his reflections which often struck her, and though by no means so clever as herself, she thought that if encouraged to read and improve himself by such an example as her's, he might become a very agreeable companion. But on the following morning, every hope of this kind was done away. Miss Lucas called soon after breakfast, and in a private conference with Elizabeth related the event of the day before.

The possibility of Mr Collins's fancying himself in love with her friend had once occurred to Elizabeth within the last day or two; but that Charlotte could encourage him, seemed almost as far from possibility as that she could encourage him herself, and her astonishment was consequently so great as to overcome at first the bounds of decorum, and she could not help crying out,

'Engaged to Mr Collins! my dear Charlotte, – impossible!'

The steady countenance which Miss Lucas had commanded in telling her story, gave way to a momentary confusion here on receiving so direct a reproach; though, as it was no more than she expected, she soon regained her composure, and calmly replied,

'Why should you be surprised, my dear Eliza? – Do you think it incredible that Mr Collins should be able to procure any woman's good opinion, because he was not so happy as to succeed with you?'

But Elizabeth had now recollected herself, and making a strong effort for it, was able to assure her with tolerable firmness that the prospect of their relationship was highly grateful to her, and that she wished her all imaginable happiness.

'I see what you are feeling,' replied Charlotte, – 'you must be surprised, very much surprised, – so lately as Mr Collins was wishing to marry you. But when you have had time to think it all over, I hope you will be satisfied with what I have done. I am not romantic you know. I never was. I ask only a comfortable home; and considering Mr Collins's character, connections, and situation in life, I am convinced that my chance of happiness with him is as fair, as most people can boast on entering the marriage state.'

Elizabeth quietly answered, 'Undoubtedly;' – and after an awkward pause, they returned to the rest of the family. Charlotte did not stay much longer, and Elizabeth was then left to reflect on what she had heard. It was a long time before she became at all reconciled to the idea of so unsuitable a match. The strangeness of Mr Collins's making two offers of marriage within three days, was nothing in comparison of his being now accepted. She had always felt that Charlotte's opinion of matrimony was not exactly like her own, but she could not have supposed it possible that when called into action, she would have sacrificed every better feeling to worldly advantage. Charlotte the wife of Mr Collins, was a most humiliating picture! — And to the pang of a friend disgracing herself and sunk in her esteem, was added the distressing conviction that it was impossible for that friend to be tolerably happy in the lot she had chosen.

Mansfield Park

Fanny Price is one of a large, impoverished family. She comes to Mansfield Park as a child; to be brought up with her wealthy cousins, Tom, Edmund, Maria and Julia Bertram. Sir Thomas, his wife Lady Bertram and her sister Mrs Norris act as her guardians. Most of the family regard Fanny as a poor relation, but her cousin Edmund is kind from the start, inspiring her devotion. Mrs Norris indulges the Bertram girls, but treats Fanny with open resentment. Fanny grows up quiet, delicate and diffident, aware of her lowly position. Some years later Mr Bertram goes to the Bahamas to look after the family estates there, and while he is away his children throw off his strict restraints on their behaviour. Maria, the eldest daughter, becomes engaged to the dull but rich Mr Rushworth, heir to the magnificent Sotherton estate.

Mrs Grant, the vicar's wife, invites her charming half-brother and sister Henry and Mary Crawford, to stay. Before long, both Maria and Julia Bertram imagine themselves in love with Henry. Mary tries briefly to attract the elder son, Tom, but soon turns her attention to Edmund. He is utterly enchanted by her. Only Fanny is unimpressed by the Crawfords.

Edmund lends his spare horse to Mary. As a result Fanny has no way of taking the exercise she needs for her health. Her aunts send her on strenuous errands in the summer heat, exhausting her. Edmund realizes he has been neglecting Fanny. Ashamed of himself, he vows to make amends.

FANNY'S RIDES RECOMMENCED THE very next day; and as it was a pleasant fresh-feeling morning, less hot than the weather had lately been, Edmund trusted that her losses both of health and pleasure would be soon made good. While she was gone, Mr Rushworth arrived, escorting his mother, who came to be civil and to show her civility especially, in urging the execution of the plan for visiting Sotherton, which had been started a fortnight before, and which, in consequence of her subsequent absence from home, had since lain dormant. Mrs Norris and her nieces were all well pleased with its revival, and an early day was named, and agreed to, provided Mr Crawford should be disengaged; the young ladies did not forget that stipulation, and though Mrs Norris would willingly have answered for his being so, they would neither authorise the liberty, nor run the risk; and at last, on a hint from Miss Bertram, Mr Rushworth discovered that the most proper thing to be done was for him to walk down to the Parsonage directly, and call on Mr Crawford, and inquire whether Wednesday would suit him or not.

Before his return, Mrs Grant and Miss Crawford came in. Having been out some time, and taken a different route to the house, they had not met him. Comfortable hopes, however, were given that he would find Mr Crawford at home. The Sotherton scheme was mentioned of course. It was hardly possible, indeed, that anything else should be talked of, for Mrs Norris was in high spirits about it; and Mrs Rushworth, a well-meaning, civil, prosing, pompous woman, who thought nothing of consequence but as it related to her own and her son's concerns, had not yet given over pressing Lady Bertram to be of the party. Lady Bertram constantly declined it; but her placid manner of refusal made Mrs Rushworth still think she wished to come, till Mrs Norris's more numerous words and louder tone convinced her of the truth.

'The fatigue would be too much for my sister, a great deal too much, I assure you, my dear Mrs Rushworth. Ten miles there, and ten back, you know. You must excuse my sister on this occasion, and accept of our two dear girls and myself without her. Sotherton is the only place that could give her a *wish* to go so far, but it cannot be, indeed. She will have a companion in Fanny Price, you know, so it will all do very well; and as for Edmund, as he is not here to speak for himself, I will answer for his being most happy to join the party. He can go on horseback, you know.'

Mrs Rushworth being obliged to yield to Lady Bertram's staying at home, could only be sorry. 'The loss of her ladyship's company would be a great drawback, and she should have been extremely happy to have seen the young lady too, Miss Price, who had never been at Sotherton yet, and it was a pity she should not see the place.'

'You are very kind, you are all kindness, my dear madam,' cried Mrs Norris; 'but as to Fanny, she will have opportunities in plenty of seeing Sotherton. She has time enough before her; and her going now is quite out of the question. Lady Bertram could not possibly spare her.'

'Oh no! I cannot do without Fanny.'

Mrs Rushworth proceeded next, under the conviction that everybody must be wanting to see Sotherton, to include Miss Crawford in the invitation; and though Mrs Grant, who had not been at the trouble of visiting Mrs Rushworth on her coming into the neighbourhood, civilly declined it on her own account, she was glad to secure any pleasure for her sister; and Mary, properly pressed and persuaded, was not long in accepting her share of the civility. Mr Rushworth came back from the Parsonage successful; and Edmund made his appearance just in time to learn what had been settled for Wednesday, to attend Mrs Rushworth to her carriage, and walk half-way down the park with the two other ladies.

On his return to the breakfast-room, he found Mrs Norris trying to make up her mind as to whether Miss Crawford's being of the party were desirable or not, or whether her brother's barouche would not be full without her. The Miss Bertrams laughed at the idea, assuring her that the barouche would hold four perfectly well, independent of the box, on which *one* might go with him.

'But why is it necessary,' said Edmund, 'that Crawford's carriage, or his *only*, should be employed? Why is no use to be made of my mother's chaise? I could not, when the scheme was first mentioned the other day, understand why a visit from the family were not to be made in the carriage of the family.'

'What!' cried Julia; 'go, boxed up three in a postchaise in this weather, when we may have seats in a barouche! No, my dear Edmund, that will not quite do.'

'Besides,' said Maria, 'I know that Mr Crawford depends upon taking us. After what passed at first, he would claim it as a promise.'

'And, my dear Edmund,' added Mrs Norris, 'taking out *two* carriages when *one* will do, would be trouble for nothing; and, between ourselves, coachman is not very fond of the roads between this and Sotherton; he always complains bitterly of the narrow lanes scratching his carriage, and you know one should not like to have dear Sir Thomas, when he comes home, find all the varnish scratched off.'

'That would not be a very handsome reason for using Mr Crawford's,' said Maria; 'but the truth is, that Wilcox is a stupid old fellow, and does not know how to drive. I will answer for it, that we shall find no inconvenience from narrow roads on Wednesday.'

'There is no hardship, I suppose, nothing unpleasant,' said Edmund, 'in going on the barouche box.'

'Unpleasant!' cried Maria; 'oh dear! I believe it would be generally thought the favourite seat. There can be no comparison as to one's view of the country. Probably Miss Crawford will choose the barouche box herself.'

'There can be no objection, then, to Fanny's going with you; there can be no doubt of your having room for her.'

'Fanny!' repeated Mrs Norris; 'my dear Edmund, there is no idea of her going with us. She stays with her aunt. I told her Mrs Rushworth so. She is not expected.'

'You can have no reason, I imagine, madam,' said he, addressing his mother, 'for wishing Fanny *not* to be of the party, but as it relates to yourself, to your own comfort. If you could do without her, you would not wish to keep her at home?'

'To be sure not, but I *cannot* do without her.'

'You can, if I stay at home with you, as I mean to do.'

There was a general cry out at this. 'Yes,' he continued, 'there is no necessity for my going, and I mean to stay at home. Fanny has a great desire to see Sotherton. I know she wishes it very much. She has not often a gratification of the kind, and I am sure, ma'am, you would be glad to give her the pleasure now?'

'Oh yes! very glad, if your aunt sees no objection.'

Mrs Norris was very ready with the only objection which could remain – their having positively assured Mrs Rushworth that Fanny could not go, and the very strange appearance there would consequently be in taking her, which seemed to her a difficulty quite impossible to be got over. It must have the strangest appearance! It would be something so very unceremonious, so bordering on disrespect for Mrs Rushworth, whose own manners were such a pattern of good breeding and attention, that she really did not feel equal to it. Mrs Norris had no affection for Fanny, and no wish of procuring her pleasure at any time; but her opposition to Edmund *now*, arose more from partiality for her own scheme, because it *was* her own, than from anything else. She felt that she had arranged everything extremely well, and that any alteration must be for the worse. When Edmund, therefore, told her in reply, as he did when she would give him the hearing, that she need not distress herself on Mrs Rushworth's account, because he had taken the opportunity as he walked with her through the hall of mentioning Miss Price as one who would probably be of the party, and had directly received a very sufficient invitation for his cousin, Mrs Norris was too much vexed to submit with a very good grace, and would only say, 'Very well, very well, just as you choose, settle it your own way, I am sure I do not care about it.'

'It seems very odd,' said Maria, 'that you should be staying at home instead of Fanny.'

'I am sure she ought to be very much obliged to you,' added Julia, hastily leaving the room as she spoke, from a consciousness that she ought to offer to stay at home herself.

'Fanny will feel quite as grateful as the occasion requires,' was Edmund's reply only, and the subject dropped.

Fanny's gratitude, when she heard the plan, was in fact much greater than her pleasure. She felt Edmund's kindness with all, and more than all, the sensibility which he, unsuspicious of her fond attachment, could be aware of; but that he should forego any enjoyment on her account gave her pain, and her own satisfaction in seeing Sotherton would be nothing without him.

The next meeting of the two Mansfield families produced another alteration in the plan, and one that was admitted with general approbation. Mrs Grant offered herself as companion for the day to Lady Bertram in lieu of her son, and Dr Grant was to join them at dinner. Lady Bertram was very well pleased to have it so, and the young ladies were in spirits again. Even Edmund was very thankful for an arrangement which restored him to his share of the party; and Mrs Norris thought it an excellent plan, and had it at her tongue's end, and was on the point of proposing it, when Mrs Grant spoke.

Wednesday was fine, and soon after breakfast the barouche arrived, Mr Crawford driving his sisters; and as everybody was ready, there was nothing to be done but for Mrs Grant to alight, and the others to take their places. The place of all places, the envied seat, the post of honour, was unappropriated. To whose happy lot was it to fall? While each of the Miss Bertrams were meditating how best, and with the most appearance of obliging the others, to secure it, the matter was settled by Mrs Grant's saying, as she stepped from the carriage, 'As there are five of you, it will be better that one should sit with Henry; and as you were saying lately that you wished you could drive, Julia, I think this will be a good opportunity for you to take a lesson.'

Happy Julia! Unhappy Maria! The former was on the barouche-box in a moment, the latter took her seat within, in gloom and mortification; and the carriage drove off amid the good wishes of the two remaining ladies, and the barking of pug in his mistress's arms.

Their road was through a pleasant country; and Fanny, whose rides had never been extensive, was soon beyond her knowledge, and was very happy in observing all that was new, and admiring all that was pretty. She was not often invited to join in the conversation of the others, nor did she desire it. Her own thoughts and reflections were habitually her best companions; and, in observing the appearance of the country, the bearings of the roads, the difference of soil, the state of the harvest, the cottages, the cattle, the children, she found entertainment that could only have been heightened by having Edmund to speak of what she felt. That was the only point of resemblance between her and the lady who sat by her; in everything but a value for Edmund, Miss Crawford was very unlike her. She had none of Fanny's delicacy of taste, of mind, of feeling; she saw Nature, inanimate Nature, with little observation; her attention was all for men and women, her talents for the light and lively. In looking back after Edmund, however, when there was any stretch of road behind them, or when he gained on them in ascending a considerable hill, they were united, and a 'there he is' broke at the same moment from them both, more than once.

For the first seven miles Miss Bertram had very little real comfort; her prospect always ended in Mr Crawford and her sister sitting side by side, full

Their road was through a pleasant country

of conversation and merriment; and to see only his expressive profile as he turned with a smile to Julia, or to catch the laugh of the other, was a perpetual source of irritation, which her own sense of propriety could but just smooth over. When Julia looked back, it was with a countenance of delight, and whenever she spoke to them, it was in the highest spirits: 'her view of the country was charming, she wished they could all see it,' etc.; but her only offer of exchange was addressed to Miss Crawford, as they gained the summit of a long hill, and was not more inviting than this: 'Here is a fine burst of country. I wish you had my seat, but I dare say you will not take it, let me press you ever so much'; and Miss Crawford could hardly answer, before they were moving again at a good pace.

When they came within the influence of Sotherton associations, it was better for Miss Bertram, who might be said to have two strings to her bow. She had Rushworth-feelings, and Crawford-feelings, and in the vicinity of Sotherton, the former had considerable effect. Mr Rushworth's consequence was hers. She could not tell Miss Crawford that 'those woods belonged to Sotherton'; she could not carelessly observe that 'she believed that it was now all Mr Rushworth's property on each side of the road,' without elation of heart; and it was a pleasure to increase with their approach to the capital freehold mansion, and ancient manorial residence of the family, with all its rights of court-leet and court-baron.

'Now, we shall have no more rough road, Miss Crawford; our difficulties are over. The rest of the way is such as it ought to be. Mr Rushworth has made it since he succeeded to the estate. Here begins the village. Those cottages are really a disgrace. The church spire is reckoned remarkably handsome. I am glad the church is not so close to the great house as often happens in old places. The annoyance of the bells must be terrible. There is the Parsonage; a tidy-looking house, and I understand the clergyman and his wife are very decent people. Those are almshouses, built by some of the family. To the right is the steward's house; he is a very respectable man. Now we are coming to the lodge-gates; but we have nearly a mile through the park still. It is not ugly, you see, at this end; there is some fine timber, but the situation of the house is dreadful. We go down hill to it for half a mile, and it is a pity, for it would not be an ill-looking place if it had a better approach.'

Miss Crawford was not slow to admire; she pretty well guessed Miss Bertram's feelings, and made it a point of honour to promote her enjoyment to the utmost. Mrs Norris was all delight and volubility; and even Fanny had something to say in admiration, and might be heard with complacency. Her eye was eagerly taking in every thing within her reach; and after being at some pains to get a view of the house, and observing that 'it was a sort of building which she could not look at but with respect,' she added: 'Now, where is the avenue? The house fronts the east, I perceive. The avenue, therefore, must be at the back of it. Mr Rushworth talked of the west front.'

'Yes, it is exactly behind the house; begins at a little distance, and ascends for half a mile to the extremity of the grounds. You may see something of it here – something of the more distant trees. It is oak entirely.'

Miss Bertram could now speak with decided information of what she had known nothing about when Mr Rushworth had asked her opinion; and her spirits were in as happy a flutter as vanity and pride could furnish, when they drove up to the spacious stone steps before the principal entrance.

CHAPTER NINE

MR RUSHWORTH WAS AT THE DOOR to receive his fair lady; and the whole party were welcomed by him with due attention. In the drawing-room they were met with equal cordiality by the mother, and Miss Bertram had all the distinction with each that she could wish. After the business of arriving was over, it was first necessary to eat, and the doors were thrown open to admit them through one or two intermediate rooms into the appointed dining-parlour, where a collation was prepared with abundance and elegance. Much was said, and much was ate, and all went well. The particular object of the day was then considered. How would Mr Crawford like, in what manner would he choose, to take a survey of the grounds? Mr Rushworth mentioned his curricle, Mr Crawford suggested the greater desirableness of some carriage which might convey more than two. 'To be depriving themselves of the advantage of other eyes and other judgments, might be an evil even beyond the loss of present pleasure.'

Mrs Rushworth proposed that the chaise should be taken also; but this was scarcely received as an amendment: the young ladies neither smiled nor spoke. Her next proposition, of showing the house to such of them as had not been before, was more acceptable, for Miss Bertram was pleased to have its size displayed, and all were glad to be doing something.

The whole party rose accordingly, and under Mrs Rushworth's guidance were shown through a number of rooms, all lofty, and many large, and amply furnished in the taste of fifty years back, with shining floors, solid mahogany, rich damask, marble, gilding and carving, each handsome in its way. Of pictures there were abundance, and some few good, but the larger part were family portraits, no longer anything to anybody except Mrs Rushworth, who had been at great pains to learn all that the housekeeper could teach, and was now almost equally well qualified to show the house. On the present occasion, she addressed herself chiefly to Miss Crawford and Fanny, but there was no comparison in the willingness of their attention; for Miss Crawford, who had seen scores of great houses, and cared for none of them, had only the appearance of civilly listening, while Fanny, to whom everything was almost as interesting as it was new, attended with unaffected earnestness to all that Mrs Rushworth could relate of the family in former times, its rise and grandeur, regal visits and loyal efforts, delighted to connect anything with history already known, or warm her imagination with scenes of the past.

The situation of the house excluded the possibility of much prospect from any of the rooms; and while Fanny and some of the others were attending Mrs Rushworth, Henry Crawford was looking grave and shaking his head at the windows. Every room on the west front looked across a lawn to the beginning of the avenue immediately beyond tall iron palisades and gates.

Having visited many more rooms than could be supposed to be of any other use than to contribute to the window tax, and find employment for housemaids, 'Now,' said Mrs Rushworth, 'we are coming to the chapel, which properly we ought to enter from above, and look down upon; but as we are quite among friends, I will take you in this way, if you will excuse me.'

They entered. Fanny's imagination had prepared her for something grander than a mere spacious, oblong room, fitted up for the purpose of devotion; with nothing more striking or more solemn than the profusion of mahogany, and the crimson velvet cushions appearing over the ledge of the family gallery above. 'I am disappointed,' said she, in a low voice to Edmund. 'This is not my idea of a chapel. There is nothing awful here, nothing melancholy, nothing grand. Here are no aisles, no arches, no inscriptions, no banners. No banners, cousin, to be "blown by the night wind of heaven." No signs that a "Scottish monarch sleeps below."'

'You forget, Fanny, how lately all this has been built, and for how confined a purpose, compared with the old chapels of castles and monasteries. It was only for the private use of the family. They have been buried, I suppose, in the parish church. *There* you must look for the banners and the achievements.'

'It was foolish of me not to think of all that; but I am disappointed.'

Mrs Rushworth began her relation. 'This chapel was fitted up as you see it, in James the Second's time. Before that period, as I understand, the pews were only wainscot; and there is some reason to think that the linings and cushions of the pulpit and family seat were only purple cloth; but this is not quite certain. It is a handsome chapel, and was formerly in constant use both morning and evening. Prayers were always read in it by the domestic chaplain, within the memory of many; but the late Mr Rushworth left it off.'

'Every generation has its improvements,' said Miss Crawford, with a smile, to Edmund.

Mrs Rushworth was gone to repeat her lesson to Mr Crawford; and Edmund, Fanny and Miss Crawford remained in a cluster together.

'It is a pity,' cried Fanny, 'that the custom should have been discontinued. It was a valuable part of former times. There is something in a chapel and chaplain so much in character with a great house, with one's ideas of what such a household should be! A whole family assembling regularly for the purpose of prayer is fine!'

'Very fine, indeed,' said Miss Crawford, laughing. 'It must do the heads of the family a great deal of good to force all the poor housemaids and foot-men to leave business and pleasure, and say their prayers here twice a day, while they are inventing excuses themselves for staying away.'

'*That* is hardly Fanny's idea of a family assembling,' said Edmund. 'If the master and mistress do *not* attend themselves, there must be more harm than good in the custom.'

'At any rate, it is safer to leave people to their own devices on such subjects. Everybody likes to go their own way – to choose their own time and manner of devotion. The obligation of attendance, the formality, the restraint, the length of time – altogether it is a formidable thing, and what nobody likes; and if the good people who used to kneel and gape in that gallery could have foreseen that the time would ever come when men and women might lie another ten minutes in bed when they woke with a headache, without danger of reprobation because chapel was missed, they would have jumped with joy and envy. Cannot you imagine with what unwilling feelings the former belles of the house of Rushworth did many a time repair to this chapel? The young Mrs Eleanors and Mrs Bridgets – starched up into seeming piety, but with heads full of something very different – especially if the poor chaplain were not worth looking at – and, in those days, I fancy parsons were very inferior even to what they are now.'

For a few moments she was unanswered. Fanny coloured and looked at Edmund, but felt too angry for speech; and *he* needed a little recollection before he could say, 'Your lively mind can hardly be serious even on serious subjects. You have given us an amusing sketch, and human nature cannot say it was not so. We must all feel *at times* the difficulty of fixing our thoughts as we could wish; but if you are supposing it a frequent thing, that is to say, a weakness grown into a habit from neglect, what could be expected from the *private* devotions of such persons? Do you think the minds which are suffered, which are indulged in wanderings in a chapel, would be more collected in a closet?'

'Yes, very likely. They would have two chances at least in their favour. There would be less to distract the attention from without, and it would not be tried so long.'

'The mind which does not struggle against itself under *one* circumstance, would find objects to distract it in the *other*, I believe; and the influence of the place and of example may often rouse better feelings than are begun with. The greater length of the service, however, I admit to be sometimes too hard a stretch upon the mind. One wishes it were not so; but I have not yet left Oxford long enough to forget what chapel prayers are.'

While this was passing, the rest of the party being scattered about the chapel, Julia called Mr Crawford's attention to her sister, by saying, 'Do look at Mr Rushworth and Maria, standing side by side, exactly as if the ceremony were going to be performed. Have not they completely the air of it?'

Mr Crawford smiled his acquiescence, and stepping forward to Maria, said, in a voice which she only could hear, 'I do not like to see Miss Bertram so near the altar.'

Starting, the lady instinctively moved a step or two, but recovering herself in a moment, affected to laugh, and asked him in a tone not much louder, 'If he would give her away?'

'I am afraid I should do it very awkwardly,' was his reply, with a look of meaning.

Julia, joining them at the moment, carried on the joke. 'Upon my word, it is really a pity that it should not take place directly, if we had but a proper licence, for here we are all together, and nothing in the world could be more snug and pleasant.' And she talked and laughed about it with so little caution, as to catch the comprehension of Mr Rushworth and his mother, and expose her sister to the whispered gallantries of her lover, while Mrs Rushworth spoke with proper smiles and dignity of its being a most happy event to her whenever it took place.

'If Edmund were but in orders!' cried Julia, and running to where he stood with Miss Crawford and Fanny: 'My dear Edmund, if you were but in orders now, you might perform the ceremony directly. How unlucky that you are not ordained; Mr Rushworth and Maria are quite ready.'

Miss Crawford's countenance, as Julia spoke, might have amused a disinterested observer. She looked almost aghast under the new idea she was receiving. Fanny pitied her. 'How distressed she will be at what she said just now,' passed across her mind.

'Ordained!' said Miss Crawford; 'what, are you to be a clergyman?'

'Yes; I shall take orders soon after my father's return; probably at Christmas.'

Miss Crawford rallying her spirits, and recovering her complexion, replied only, 'If I known this before, I would have spoken of the cloth with more respect,' and turned the subject.

The chapel was soon afterwards left to the silence and stillness which reigned in it, with few interruptions, throughout the year. Miss Bertram, displeased with her sister, led the way, and all seemed to feel that they had been there long enough.

The lower part of the house had been now entirely shown, and Mrs Rushworth, never weary in the cause, would have proceeded towards the principal staircase, and taken them through all the rooms above, if her son had not interposed with a doubt of there being time enough. 'For if,' said he, with a sort of self-evident proposition which many a clearer head does not always avoid, 'we are *too long* going over the house, we shall not have time for what is to be done out of doors. It is past two, and we are to dine at five.'

Mrs Rushworth submitted; and the question of surveying the grounds with the who and the how was likely to be more fully agitated, and Mrs Norris was beginning to arrange by what junction of carriages and horses most could be done, when the young people, meeting with an outward door, temptingly open on a flight of steps which led immediately to turf and shrubs, and all the sweets of pleasure-grounds, as by one impulse, one wish for air and liberty, all walked out.

'Suppose we turn down here for the present,' said Mrs Rushworth, civilly taking the hint and following them. 'Here are the greatest number of our plants, and here are the curious pheasants.'

'Query,' said Mr Crawford, looking round him, 'whether we may not find something to employ us here, before we go further? I see walls of great promise. Mr Rushworth, shall we summon a council on this lawn?'

'James,' said Mrs Rushworth to her son, 'I believe the wilderness will be new to all the party. The Miss Bertrams have never seen the wilderness yet.'

No objection was made, but for some time there seemed no inclination to move in any plan, or to any distance. All were attracted at first by the plants or the pheasants, and all dispersed about in happy independence. Mr Crawford was the first to move forward, to examine the capabilities of that end of the house. The lawn, bounded on each side by a high wall, contained beyond the first planted area a bowling-green, and beyond the bowling-green a long terrace walk, backed by iron palisades, and commanding a view over them into the tops of the trees of the wilderness immediately adjoining. It was a good spot for fault-finding. Mr Crawford was soon followed by Miss Bertram and Mr Rushworth; and when, after a little time, the others began to form into parties, these three were found in busy consultation on the terrace by Edmund, Miss Crawford, and Fanny, who seemed as naturally to unite, and who, after a short participation of their regrets and difficulties, left them and walked on. The remaining three, Mrs Rushworth, Mrs Norris, and Julia, were still far behind; for Julia, whose happy star no longer prevailed, was obliged to keep by the side of Mrs Rushworth, and restrain her impatient feet to that lady's slow pace, while her aunt, having fallen in with the housekeeper, who was come out to feed the pheasants, was lingering behind in gossip with her. Poor Julia, the only one out of the nine not tolerably satisfied with their lot, was now in a state of complete penance, and as different from the Julia of the barouche-box as could well be imagined. The politeness which she had been brought up to practise as a duty made it impossible for her to escape; while the want of that higher species of self-command, that just consideration of others, that knowledge of her own heart, that principle of right, which had not formed any essential part of her education, made her miserable under it.

'This is insufferably hot,' said Miss Crawford, when they had taken one turn on the terrace, and were drawing a second time to the door in the middle which opened to the wilderness. 'Shall any of us object to being comfortable? Here is a nice little wood, if one can but get into it. What happiness if the door should not be locked! But of course it is; for in these great places the gardeners are the only people who can go where they like.'

The door, however, proved not to be locked, and they were all agreed in turning joyfully through it, and leaving the unmitigated glare of day behind. A considerable flight of steps landed them in the wilderness, which was a planted wood of about two acres, and though chiefly of larch and laurel, and beech cut down, and though laid out with too much regularity, was darkness and shade, and natural beauty, compared with the bowling-green and the terrace. They all felt the refreshment of it, and for some time could only walk and admire. At length, after a short pause, Miss Crawford began with: 'So you are to be a clergyman, Mr Bertram. This is rather a surprise to me.'

'Why should it surprise you? You must suppose me designed for some profession, and might perceive that I am neither a lawyer, nor a soldier, nor a sailor.'

'Very true; but, in short, it had not occurred to me. And you know there is generally an uncle or a grandfather to leave a fortune to the second son.'

'A very praiseworthy practice,' said Edmund, 'but not quite universal. I am one of the exceptions, and *being* one, must do something for myself.'

'But why are you to be a clergyman? I thought *that* was always the lot of the youngest, where there were many to choose before him.'

'Do you think the church itself never chosen, then?'

'*Never* is a black word. But yes, in the *never* of conversation, which means *not very often*, I do think it. For what is to be done in the church? Men love to distinguish themselves, and in either of the other lines distinction may be gained, but not in the church. A clergyman is nothing.'

'The *nothing* of conversation has its gradations, I hope, as well as the *never*. A clergyman cannot be high in state or fashion. He must not head mobs, or set the tone in dress. But I cannot call that situation nothing which has the charge of all that is of the first importance to mankind individually or collectively considered, temporally and eternally, which has the guardianship of religion and morals, and consequently of the manners which result from their influence. No one here can call the *office* nothing. If the man who holds it is so, it is by the neglect of his duty, by foregoing its just importance, and stepping out of his place to appear what he ought not to appear.'

'*You* assign greater consequence to the clergyman than one has been used to hear given, or than I can quite comprehend. One does not see much of this influence and importance in society, and how can it be acquired where they are so seldom seen themselves? How can two sermons a week, even supposing them worth hearing, supposing the preacher to have the sense to prefer Blair's to his own, do all that you speak of – govern the conduct and fashion the manners of a large congregation for the rest of the week? One scarcely sees a clergyman out of his pulpit.'

'*You* are speaking of London, *I* am speaking of the nation at large.'

'The metropolis, I imagine, is a pretty fair sample of the rest.'

'Not, I should hope, of the proportion of virtue to vice throughout the kingdom. We do not look in great cities for our best morality. It is not there that respectable people of any denomination can do most good; and it certainly is not there that the influence of the clergy can be most felt. A fine preacher is followed and admired; but it is not in fine preaching only that a good clergyman will be useful in his parish and his neighbourhood, where the parish and neighbourhood are of a size capable of knowing his private character, and observing his general conduct, which in London can rarely be the case. The clergy are lost there in the crowds of their parishioners. They are known to the largest part only as preachers. And with regard to their influencing public matters, Miss Crawford must not misunderstand me, or suppose I mean to call them the arbiters of good breeding, the regulators of refinement and courtesy, the masters of the ceremonies of life. The *manners* I speak of might rather be called *conduct*, perhaps, the result of good principles; the effect, in short, of those doctrines which it is their duty to teach and recommend; and it will, I believe, be everywhere found, that as the clergy are, or are not what they ought to be, so are the rest of the nation.'

'Certainly,' said Fanny, with gentle earnestness.

'There,' cried Miss Crawford, 'you have quite convinced Miss Price already.'

'I wish I could convince Miss Crawford too.'

'I do not think you ever will,' said she, with an arch smile; 'I am just as much surprised now as I was at first that you should intend to take orders. You really are fit for something better. Come, do change your mind. It is not too late. Go into the law.'

'Go into the law! With as much ease as I was told to go into this wilderness.'

'Now you are going to say something about law being the worst wilderness of the two, but I forestall you; remember. I have forestalled you.'

'You need not hurry when the object is only to prevent my saying a bon-mot, for there is not the least wit in my nature. I am a very matter-of-fact, plain-spoken being, and may blunder on the borders of a repartee for half-an-hour together without striking it out.'

A general silence succeeded. Each was thoughtful. Fanny made the first interruption by saying: 'I wonder that I should be tired with only walking in this sweet wood; but the next time we come to a seat, if it is not disagreeable to you, I should be glad to sit down for a little while.'

'My dear Fanny,' cried Edmund, immediately drawing her arm within his, 'how thoughtless I have been! I hope you are not very tired. Perhaps,' turning to Miss Crawford, 'my other companion may do me the honour of taking an arm.'

'Thank you, but I am not at all tired.' She took it, however, as she spoke, and the gratification of having her do so, of feeling such a connection for the first time, made him a little forgetful of Fanny. 'You scarcely touch me,' said he. 'You do not make me of any use. What a difference in the weight of a woman's arm from that of a man! At Oxford I have been a good deal used to have a man lean on me for the length of a street, and you are only a fly in comparison.'

'I am really not tired, which I almost wonder at; for we must have walked at least a mile in this wood. Do not you think we have?'

'Not half a mile,' was his sturdy answer; for he was not yet so much in love as to measure distance, or reckon time, with feminine lawlessness.

'Oh! you do not consider how much we have wound about. We have taken such a very serpentine course, and the wood itself must be half a mile long in a straight line, for we have never seen the end of it yet since we left the first great path.'

'But if you remember, before we left that first great path, we saw directly to the end of it. We looked down the whole vista, and saw it closed by iron gates, and it could not have been more than a furlong in length.'

'Oh! I know nothing of your furlongs, but I am sure it is a very long wood, and that we have been winding in and out ever since we came into it; and therefore, when I say that we have walked a mile in it, I must speak within compass.'

'We have been exactly a quarter of an hour here,' said Edmund, taking out his watch. 'Do you think we are walking four miles an hour?'

'Oh! do not attack me with your watch. A watch is always too fast or too slow. I cannot be dictated to by a watch.'

A few steps further brought them out at the bottom of the very walk they had been talking of; and standing back, well shaded and sheltered, and looking over a ha-ha into the park, was a comfortable-sized bench on which they all sat down.

'I am afraid you are very tired, Fanny,' said Edmund, observing her; 'why would you not speak sooner? This will be a bad day's amusement for you if you are to be knocked up. Every sort of exercise fatigues her so soon, Miss Crawford, except riding.'

'How abominable in you, then, to let me engross her horse as I did all last week! I am ashamed of you and of myself, but it shall never happen again.'

'*Your* attentiveness and consideration make me more sensible of my own neglect. Fanny's interest seems in safer hands with you than with me.'

'That she should be tired now, however, gives me no surprise; for there is nothing in the course of one's duties so fatiguing as what we have been doing this morning: seeing a great house, dawdling from one room to another, straining one's eyes and one's attention, hearing what one does not understand, admiring what one does not care for. It is generally allowed to be the greatest bore in the world, and Miss Price has found it so, though she did not know it.'

'I shall soon be rested,' said Fanny; 'to sit in the shade on a fine day, and look upon verdure, is the most perfect refreshment.'

After sitting a little while, Miss Crawford was up again. 'I must move,' said she, 'resting fatigues me. I have looked across the ha-ha till I am weary. I must go and look through that iron gate at the same view, without being able to see it so well.'

Edmund left the seat likewise. 'Now, Miss Crawford, if you will look up the walk, you will convince yourself that it cannot be half a mile long, or or half half a mile.'

'It is an immense distance,' said she; 'I see *that* with a glance.'

He still reasoned with her, but in vain. She would not calculate, she would not compare. She would only smile and assert. The greatest degree of rational consistency could not have been more engaging, and they talked with mutual satisfaction. At last it was agreed that they should endeavour to determine the dimensions of the wood by walking a little more about it. They would go to the end of it, in the line they were then in (for there was a straight green walk along the bottom by the side of the ha-ha), and perhaps turn a little way in some other direction, if it seemed likely to assist them, and be back in a few minutes. Fanny said she was rested, and would have moved too, but this was not suffered. Edmund urged her remaining where she was with an earnestness which she could not resist, and she was left on the bench to think with pleasure of her cousin's care, but with great regret that she was not stronger. She watched them till they had turned the corner, and listened till all sound of them had ceased.

CHAPTER TEN

A QUARTER OF AN HOUR, TWENTY MINUTES, passed away, and Fanny was still thinking of Edmund, Miss Crawford, and herself, without interruption from anyone. She began to be surprised at being left so long, and to listen with an anxious desire of hearing their steps and their voices again. She listened, and at length she heard; she heard voices and feet approaching; but she had just satisfied herself that it was not those she wanted, when Miss Bertram, Mr Rushworth, and Mr Crawford, issued from the same path which she had trod herself, and were before her.

'Miss Price all alone!' and 'My dear Fanny, how comes this?' were the first salutations. She told her story. 'Poor dear Fanny,' cried her cousin, 'how ill you have been used by them! You had better have stayed with us.'

Then seating herself with a gentleman on each side, she resumed the conversation which had engaged them before, and discussed the possibility of improvements with much animation. Nothing was fixed on; but Henry Crawford was full of ideas and projects, and, generally speaking, whatever he proposed was immediately approved, first by her, and then by Mr Rushworth, whose principal business seemed to be to hear the others, and who scarcely risked an original thought of his own beyond a wish that they had seen his friend Smith's place.

After some minutes spent in this way, Miss Bertram, observing the iron gate, expressed a wish of passing through it into the park, that their views and their plans might be more comprehensive. It was the very thing of all others to be wished, it was the best, it was the only way of proceeding with any advantage, in Henry Crawford's opinion, and he directly saw a knoll not half a mile off, which would give them exactly the requisite command of the house. Go therefore they must to that knoll, and through that gate; but the gate was locked. Mr Rushworth wished he had brought the key; he had been very near thinking whether he should not bring the key; he was determined he would never come without the key again; but still this did not remove the present evil. They could not get through; and as Miss Bertram's inclination for so doing did by no means lessen, it ended in Mr

Rushworth's declaring outright that he would go and fetch the key. He set off accordingly.

'It is undoubtedly the best thing we can do now, as we are so far from the house already,' said Mr Crawford, when he was gone.

'Yes, there is nothing else to be done. But now, sincerely, do not you find the place altogether worse than you expected?'

'No, indeed, far otherwise. I find it better, grander, more complete in its style, though that style may not be the best. And to tell you the truth,' speaking rather lower, 'I do not think that *I* shall ever see Sotherton again with so much pleasure as I do now. Another summer will hardly improve it to me.'

After a moment's embarrassment the lady replied: 'You are too much a man of the world not to see with the eyes of the world. If other people think Sotherton improved, I have no doubt that you will.'

'I am afraid I am not quite so much the man of the world as might be good for me in some points. My feelings are not quite so evanescent, nor my memory of the past under such easy dominion as one finds to be the case with men of the world.'

This was followed by a short silence. Miss Bertram began again. 'You seemed to enjoy your drive here very much this morning. I was glad to see you so well entertained. You and Julia were laughing the whole way.'

'Were we? Yes, I believe we were; but I have not the least recollection at what. Oh! I believe I was relating to her some ridiculous stories of an old Irish groom of my uncle's. Your sister loves to laugh.'

'You think her more lighthearted than I am.'

'More easily amused,' he replied, 'consequently, you know,' smiling, 'better company. I could not have hoped to entertain *you* with Irish anecdotes during a ten miles' drive.'

'Naturally, I believe, I am as lively as Julia, but I have more to think of now.'

'You have, undoubtedly; and there are situations in which very high spirits would denote insensibility. Your prospects, however, are too fair to justify want of spirits. You have a very smiling scene before you.'

'Do you mean literally or figuratively? Literally, I conclude. Yes, certainly the sun shines, and the park looks very cheerful. But unluckily that iron gate, that ha-ha, give me a feeling of restraint and hardship. "I cannot get out," as the starling said.' As she spoke, and it was with expression, she walked to the gate: he followed her. 'Mr Rushworth is so long fetching this key!'

'And for the world you would not get out without the key and without Mr Rushworth's authority and protection, or I think you might with little difficulty pass round the edge of the gate, here, with my assistance; I think it might be done, if you really wished to be more at large, and could allow yourself to think it not prohibited.'

'Prohibited! Nonsense! I certainly can get out that way, and I will. Mr Rushworth will be here in a moment, you know; we shall not be out of sight.'

'Or if we are, Miss Price will be so good as to tell him he will find us near that knoll: the grove of oak on the knoll.'

Fanny, feeling all this to be wrong, could not help making an effort to prevent it. 'You will hurt yourself against those spikes; you will tear your gown; you will be in danger of slipping into the ha-ha. You had better not go.'

Her cousin was safe on the other side while these words were spoken, and, smiling with all the good humour of success, she said: 'Thank you, my dear Fanny, but I and my gown are alive and well, and so good-bye.'

Fanny was again left to her solitude, and with no increase of pleasant feelings, for she was sorry for almost all that she had seen and heard, astonished at Miss Bertram, and angry with Mr Crawford. By taking a circuitous route, and, as it appeared to her, very unreasonable direction to the knoll, they were soon beyond her eye; and for some minutes longer she remained without sight or sound of any companion. She seemed to have the little wood all to herself. She could almost have thought that Edmund and Miss Crawford had left it, but that it was impossible for Edmund to forget her so entirely.

She was again roused from disagreeable musings by sudden footsteps: somebody was coming at a quick pace down the principal walk. She expected Mr Rushworth, but it was Julia, who, hot and out of breath, and with a look of disappointment, cried out on seeing her: 'Heyday! Where are the others? I thought Maria and Mr Crawford were with you.'

Fanny explained.

'A pretty trick, upon my word! I cannot see them anywhere,' looking eagerly into the park. 'But they cannot be very far off, and I think I am equal to as much as Maria, even without help.'

'But, Julia, Mr Rushworth will be here in a moment with the key. Do wait for Mr Rushworth.'

'Not I, indeed. I have had enough of the family for one morning. Why, child, I have but this moment escaped from his horrible mother. Such a penance as I have been enduring, while you were sitting here so composed and so happy! It might have been as well, perhaps, if you had been in my place, but you always contrive to keep out of these scrapes.'

This was a most unjust reflection, but Fanny could allow for it, and let it pass: Julia was vexed, and her temper was hasty; but she felt that it would not last, and therefore taking no notice, only asked her if she had not seen Mr Rushworth.

'Yes, yes, we saw him. He was posting away as if upon life and death, and could but just spare time to tell us his errand, and where you all were.'

'It is a pity he should have so much trouble for nothing.'

'*That* is Miss Maria's concern. I am not obliged to punish myself for *her* sins. The mother I could not avoid, as long as my tiresome aunt was dancing about with the housekeeper, but the son I *can* get away from.'

And she immediately scrambled across the fence, and walked away, not attending to Fanny's last question of whether she had seen any thing of Miss Crawford and Edmund. The sort of dread in which Fanny now sat of seeing Mr Rushworth, prevented her thinking so much of their continued absence, however, as she might have done. She felt that he had been very ill used, and was quite unhappy in having to communicate what had passed. He joined her within five minutes after Julia's exit; though she made the best of the story, he was evidently mortified and displeased in no common degree. At first he scarcely said any thing; his looks only expressed his extreme surprise and vexation, and he walked to the gate and stood there, without seeming to know what to do.

'They desired me to stay; my cousin Maria charged me to say that you would find them at that knoll, or thereabouts.'

'I do not believe I shall go any further,' said he, sullenly; 'I see nothing of them. By the time I get to the knoll, they may be gone some where else. I have had walking enough.'

And he sat down with a most gloomy countenance by Fanny.

'I am very sorry,' said she; 'it is very unlucky.' And she longed to be able to say some thing more to the purpose.

After an interval of silence, 'I think they might as well have stayed for me,' said he.

'Miss Bertram thought you would follow her.'

'I should not have had to follow her if she had stayed.'

This could not be denied, and Fanny was silenced. After another pause, he went on: 'Pray, Miss Price, are you such a great admirer of this Mr Crawford as some people are? For my part, I can see nothing in him.'

'I do not think him at all handsome.'

'Handsome! Nobody can call such an undersized man handsome. He is not five foot nine. I should not wonder if he was not more than five foot eight. I think he is an ill-looking fellow. In my opinion, these Crawfords are no addition at all. We did very well without them.'

A small sigh escaped Fanny here, and she did not know how to contradict him.

'If I had made any difficulty about fetching the key, there might have been some excuse, but I went the very moment she said she wanted it.'

'Nothing could be more obliging than your manner, I am sure, and I dare say you walked as fast as you could; but still it is some distance, you know, from this spot, to the house, quite into the house; and when people are waiting they are bad judges of time, and every half minute seems like five.'

He got up and walked to the gate again, and 'wished he had had the key about him at the time.' Fanny thought she discerned in his standing there an indication of relenting, which encouraged her to another attempt, and she said, therefore: 'It is a pity you should not join them. They expected to have a better view of the house from that part of the park, and will be thinking how it may be improved; and nothing of that sort, you know, can be settled without you.'

She found herself more successful in sending away, than in retaining a companion. Mr Rushworth was worked on. 'Well,' said he, 'if you really think I had better go: it would be foolish to bring the key for nothing.' And letting himself out, he walked off without further ceremony.

Fanny's thoughts were now all engrossed by the two who had left her so long ago, and getting quite impatient, she resolved to go in search of them. She followed their steps along the bottom walk, and had just turned up into another, when the voice and the laugh of Miss Crawford once more caught her ear; the sound approached, and a few more windings brought them before her. They were just returned into the wilderness from the park, to which a side gate, not fastened, had tempted them very soon after their leaving her, and they had been across a portion of the park into the very avenue which Fanny had been hoping the whole morning to reach at last, and had been sitting down under one of the trees. This was their history. It was evident that they had been spending their time pleasantly, and were not aware of the length of their absence. Fanny's best consolation was in being assured that Edmund had wished for her very much, and that he should certainly have come back for her, had she not been tired already; but this was not quite sufficient to do away with the pain of having been left a whole hour, when he had talked of only a few minutes, nor to banish the sort of curiosity she felt, to know what they had been conversing about all that time; and the result of the whole was to her disappointment and depression, as they prepared by general agreement to return to the house.

On reaching the bottom of the steps to the terrace, Mrs Rushworth and Mrs Norris presented themselves at the top, just ready for the wilderness, at the end of an hour and a half from their leaving the house. Mrs Norris had been too well employed to move faster. Whatever cross accidents had occurred to intercept the pleasures of her nieces, she had found a morning of complete enjoyment; for the housekeeper, after a great many courtesies on

Convinced him it was an ague, and promised him a charm for it

the subject of pheasants, had taken her to the dairy, told her all about their cows, and given her the receipt for a famous cream cheese; and since Julia's leaving them, they had been met by the gardener, with whom she had made a most satisfactory acquaintance, for she had set him right as to his grandson's illness, convinced him that it was an ague, and promised him a charm for it; and he, in return, had shown her all his choicest nursery of plants, and actually presented her with a very curious specimen of heath.

On this rencontre they all returned to the house together, there to lounge away the time as they could with sofas, and chit-chat, and *Quarterly Reviews*, till the return of the others, and the arrival of dinner. It was late before the Miss Bertrams and the two gentlemen came in, and their ramble did not appear to have been more than partially agreeable, or at all productive of anything useful with regard to the object of the day. By their own accounts they had been all walking after each other, and the junction which had taken place at last seemed, to Fanny's observation, to have been as much too late for re-establishing harmony, as it confessedly had been for determining on any alteration. She felt, as she looked at Julia and Mr Rushworth, that hers was not the only dissatisfied bosom amongst them; there was gloom on the face of each. Mr Crawford and Miss Bertram were much more gay, and she thought that he was taking particular pains, during dinner, to do away any little resentment of the other two, and restore general good humour.

Dinner was soon followed by tea and coffee, a ten miles' drive home allowed no waste of hours; and from the time of their sitting down to table, it was a quick succession of busy nothings till the carriage came to the door, and Mrs Norris, having fidgeted about, and obtained a few pheasants' eggs and a cream cheese from the housekeeper, and made abundance of civil speeches to Mrs Rushworth, was ready to lead the way. At the same moment, Mr Crawford, approaching Julia, said: 'I hope I am not to lose my companion, unless she is afraid of the evening air in so exposed a seat.' The request had not been foreseen, but was very graciously received, and Julia's day was likely to end almost as well as it began. Miss Bertram had made up her mind to something different, and was a little disappointed; but her conviction of being really the one preferred comforted her under it, and enabled her to receive Mr Rushworth's parting attentions as she ought. He was certainly better pleased to hand her into the barouche than to assist her in ascending the box, and his complacency seemed confirmed by the arrangement.

'Well, Fanny, this has been a fine day for you, upon my word,' said Mrs Norris, as they drove through the park. 'Nothing but pleasure from beginning to end! I am sure you ought to be very much obliged to your Aunt Bertram and me, for contriving to let you go. A pretty good day's amusement you have had!'

Maria was just discontented enough to say directly: 'I think *you* have done pretty well yourself, ma'am. Your lap seems full of good things, and here is a basket of something between us, which has been knocking my elbow unmercifully.'

'My dear, it is only a beautiful little heath, which that nice old gardener would make me take; but if it is in your way, I will have it in my lap directly. There, Fanny, you shall carry that parcel for me; take great care of it; do not let it fall; it is a cream cheese, just like the excellent one we had at dinner. Nothing would satisfy that good old Mrs Whitaker, but my taking one of the cheeses. I stood out as long as I could, till the tears almost came into her eyes, and I knew it was just the sort that my sister would be delighted with.

That Mrs Whitaker is a treasure! She was quite shocked when I asked her whether wine was allowed at the second table, and she has turned away two housemaids for wearing white gowns. Take care of the cheese, Fanny. Now I can manage the other parcel and the basket very well.'

'What else have you been spunging?' said Maria, half pleased that Sotherton should be so complimented.

'Spunging, my dear! It is nothing but four of those beautiful pheasants' eggs, which Mrs Whitaker would quite force upon me; she would not take a denial. She said it must be such an amusement to me, as she understood I lived quite alone, to have a few living creatures of that sort; and so to be sure it will. I shall get the dairymaid to set them under the first spare hen, and if they come to good I can have them moved to my own house and borrow a coop; and it will be a great delight to me in my lonely hours to attend to them. And if I have good luck your mother shall have some.'

It was a beautiful evening, mild and still, and the drive was as pleasant as the serenity of Nature could make it; but when Mrs Norris ceased speaking, it was altogether a silent drive to those within. Their spirits were in general exhausted; and to determine whether the day had afforded most pleasure or pain, might occupy the meditations of almost all.

CHAPTER ELEVEN

THE DAY AT SOTHERTON, with all its imperfections, afforded the Miss Bertrams much more agreeable feelings than were derived from the letters from Antigua, which soon afterwards reached Mansfield. It was much pleasanter to think of Henry Crawford than of their father; and to think of their father in England again within a certain period, which these letters obliged them to do, was a most unwelcome exercise.

November was the black month fixed for his return. Sir Thomas wrote of it with as much decision as experience and anxiety could authorise. His business was so nearly concluded as to justify him in proposing to take his passage in the September packet, and he consequently looked forward with the hope of being with his beloved family again early in November.

Maria was more to be pitied than Julia; for to her the father brought a husband, and the return of the friend most solicitous for her happiness would unite her to the lover, on whom she had chosen that happiness should depend. It was a gloomy prospect, and all she could do was to throw a mist over it, and hope when the mist cleared away she should see some thing else. It would hardly be *early* in November, there were generally delays, a bad passage or *some thing*; that favouring *some thing* which everybody who shuts their eyes while they look, or their understandings while they reason, feels the comfort of. It would probably be the middle of November at least; the middle of November was three months off. Three months comprised thirteen weeks. Much might happen in thirteen weeks.

Sir Thomas would have been deeply mortified by a suspicion of half that his daughters felt on the subject of his return, and would hardly have found consolation in a knowledge of the interest it excited in the breast of another young lady. Miss Crawford, on walking up with her brother to spend the evening at Mansfield Park, heard the good news; and though seeming to have no concern in the affair beyond politeness, and to have vented all her feelings in a quiet congratulation, heard it with an attention not so easily satisfied. Mrs Norris gave the particulars of the letters, and the subject was dropped; but after tea, as Miss Crawford was standing at an open window with Edmund and Fanny looking out on a twilight scene, while the Miss Bertrams, Mr Rushworth, and Henry Crawford were all busy with candles at the pianoforte, she suddenly revived it by turning round towards the group, and saying, 'How happy Mr Rushworth looks! He is thinking of November.'

Edmund looked round at Mr Rushworth too, but had nothing to say.

'Your father's return will be a very interesting event.'

'It will, indeed, after such an absence; an absence not only long, but including so many dangers.'

'It will be the forerunner also of other interesting events; your sister's marriage, and your taking orders.'

'Yes.'

'Don't be affronted,' said she, laughing, 'but it does put me in mind of some of the old heathen heroes, who, after performing great exploits in a foreign land, offered sacrifices to the gods on their safe return.'

'There is no sacrifice in the case,' replied Edmund, with a serious smile, and glancing at the pianoforte again, 'it is entirely her own doing.'

'Oh yes! I know it is. I was merely joking. She has done no more than what every young woman would do; and I have no doubt of her being extremely happy. My other sacrifice of course you do not understand.'

'My taking orders, I assure you, is quite as voluntary as Maria's marrying.'

'It is fortunate that your inclination and your father's convenience should accord so well. There is a very good living kept for you, I understand, hereabouts.'

'Which you suppose has biassed me?'

'But *that* I am sure it has not,' cried Fanny.

'Thank you for your good word, Fanny, but it is more than I would affirm myself. On the contrary, the knowing that there was such provision for me probably did bias me. Nor can I think it wrong that it should. There was no natural disinclination to be overcome, and I see no reason why a man should make a worse clergyman for knowing that he will have a competence early in life. I was in safe hands. I hope I should not have been influenced myself in a wrong way, and I am sure my father was too conscientious to have allowed it. I have no doubt that I was biassed, but I think it was blamelessly.'

'It is the same sort of thing,' said Fanny, after short pause, 'as for the son of an admiral to go into the navy or the son of a general to be in the army, and nobody sees any thing wrong in that. Nobody wonders that they should

Busy at the pianoforte

prefer the line where their friends can serve them best, or suspects them to be less in earnest in it than they appear.'

'No, my dear Miss Price, and for reasons good. The profession, either navy or army, is its own justification. It has everything in its favour; heroism, danger, bustle, fashion. Soldiers and sailors are always acceptable in society. Nobody can wonder that men are soldiers and sailors.'

'But the motives of a man who takes orders with the certainty of preferment may be fairly suspected, you think?' said Edmund. 'To be justified in your eyes, he must do it in the most complete uncertainty of any provision.'

'What! take orders without a living! No; that is madness indeed; absolute madness.'

'Shall I ask you how the church is to be filled, if a man is neither to take orders with a living, nor without? No; for you certainly would not know what to say. but I must beg some advantage to the clergyman from your own argument. As he cannot be influenced by those feelings which you rank highly as temptation and reward to the soldier and sailor, in their choice of a profession, as heroism, and noise, and fashion, are all against him, he ought to be less liable to the suspicion of wanting sincerity or good intentions in the choice of his.'

'Oh! no doubt he is very sincere in preferring an income ready made, to the trouble of working for one: and has the best intentions of doing nothing all the rest of his days but eat, drink, and grow fat. It is indolence, Mr Bertram, indeed. Indolence and love of ease; a want of all laudable ambition, of taste for good company, or of inclination to take the trouble of being agreeable, which makes men clergymen. A clergyman has nothing to do but be slovenly and selfish; read the newspaper, watch the weather, and quarrel with his wife. His curate does all the work, and the business of his own life is to dine.'

'There are such clergymen, no doubt, but I think they are not so common as to justify Miss Crawford in esteeming it their general character. I suspect that in this comprehensive and (may I say) commonplace censure, you are not judging from yourself, but from prejudiced persons, whose opinions you have been in the habit of hearing. It is impossible that your own observation can have given you much knowledge of the clergy. You can have been personally acquainted with very few of a set of men you condemn so conclusively. You are speaking what you have been told at your uncle's table.'

'I speak what appears to me the general opinion; and where an opinion is general, it is usually correct. Though I have not seen much of the domestic lives of clergymen, it is seen by too many to leave any deficiency of information.'

'Where any one body of educated men, of whatever denomination, are condemned indiscriminately, there must be a deficiency of information, or (smiling) of some thing else. Your uncle, and his brother admirals, perhaps knew little of clergymen beyond the chaplains whom, good or bad, they were always wishing away.'

'Poor William! He has met with great kindness from the chaplain of the Antwerp,' was a tender apostrophe of Fanny's, very much to the purpose of her own feelings if not of the conversation.

'I have been so little addicted to take my opinions from my uncle,' said Miss Crawford, 'that I can hardly suppose – and since you push me so hard, I must observe, that I am not entirely without the means of seeing what clergymen are, being at this present time the guest of my own brother, Dr Grant. And though Dr Grant is most kind and obliging to me, and though he is really a gentlemen, and, I dare say, a good scholar and clever, and often preaches good sermons, and is very respectable, *I* see him to be an indolent, selfish bon vivant, who must have his palate consulted in every thing; who will not stir a finger for the convenience of any one; and who, moreover, if the cook makes a blunder, is out of humour with his excellent wife. To own the truth, Henry and I were partly driven out this very evening by a disappointment about a green goose, which he could not get the better of. My poor sister was forced to stay and bear it.'

'I do not wonder at your disapprobation, upon my word. It is a great defect of temper, made worse by a very faulty habit of self-indulgence; and to see your sister suffering from it must be exceedingly painful to such feelings as yours. Fanny, it goes against us. We cannot attempt to defend Dr Grant.'

'No,' replied Fanny, 'but we need not give up his profession for all that; because, whatever profession Dr Grant had chosen, he would have taken a – not a good temper into it; and as he must, either in the navy or army, have had a great many more people under his command than he has now, I think more would have been made unhappy by him as a sailor or soldier than as a clergyman. Besides, I cannot but suppose that whatever there may be to wish otherwise in Dr Grant, would have been in a greater danger of becoming worse in a more active and worldly profession, where he would have had less time and obligation – where he might have escaped that knowledge of himself, the *frequency*, at least, of that knowledge which it is impossible he should escape as he is now. A man – a sensible man like Dr Grant, cannot be in the habit of teaching others, their duty every week, cannot go to church twice every Sunday, and preach such very good sermons in so good a manner as he does, without being the better for it himself. It must make him think; and I have no doubt that he oftener endeavours to restrain himself than he would if he had been any thing but a clergyman.'

'We cannot prove to the contrary, to be sure; but I wish you a better fate, Miss Price, than to be the wife of a man whose amiableness depends upon his own sermons; for, though he may preach himself into a good humour every Sunday, it will be bad enough to have him quarrelling about green geese from Monday morning till Saturday night.'

'I think the man who could often quarrel with Fanny,' said Edmund, affectionately, 'must be beyond the reach of any sermons.'

Fanny turned further into the window; and Miss Crawford had only time to say, in a pleasant manner, 'I fancy Miss Price has been more used to deserve praise than to hear it;' when being earnestly invited by the Miss Bertrams to join in a glee, she tripped off to the instrument, leaving Edmund looking after her in an ecstasy of admiration of all her many virtues, from her obliging manners down to her light and graceful tread.

'There goes good humour, I am sure,' said he presently. 'There goes a temper which would never give pain! How well she walks! and how readily she falls in with the inclination of others! joining them the moment she is asked. What a pity,' he added, after an instant's reflection, 'that she should have been in such hands!'

Fanny agreed to it, and had the pleasure of seeing him continue at the window with her, in spite of the expected glee; and of having his eyes soon turned, like hers, towards the scene without, where all that was solemn, and soothing, and lovely, appeared in the brilliancy of an unclouded night, and the contrast of the deep shade of the woods. Fanny spoke her feelings. 'Here's harmony!' said she; 'here's repose! Here's what may leave all painting and all music behind, and what poetry can only attempt to describe! Here's what may tranquillise every care, and lift the heart to rapture! When I look out on such a night as this, I feel as if there could be neither wickedness nor sorrow in the world; and there certainly would be less of both if the sublimity of Nature were more attended to, and people were carried more out of themselves by contemplating such a scene.'

'I like to hear your enthusiasm, Fanny. It is a lovely night, and they are much to be pitied who have not been taught to feel, in some degree, as you do; who have not, at least, been given a taste for Nature in early life. They lose a great deal.'

'*You* taught me to think and feel on the subject, cousin.'

'I had a very apt scholar. There's Arcturus looking very bright.'

'Yes, and the Bear. I wish I could see Cassiopeia.'

'We must go out on the lawn for that. Should you be afraid?'

'Not in the least. It is a great while since we have had any star-gazing.'

'Yes, I do not know how it has happened.' The glee began. 'We will stay till this is finished, Fanny,' said he, turning his back on the window; and as it advanced, she had the mortification of seeing him advance too, moving forward by gentle degrees towards the instrument, and when it ceased, he was close by the singers, among the most urgent in requesting to hear the glee again.

Fanny sighed alone at the window till scolded away by Mrs Norris's threats of catching cold.

CHAPTER TWELVE

SIR THOMAS WAS TO RETURN IN November, and his eldest son had duties to call him earlier home. The approach of September brought tidings of Mr Bertram, first in a letter to the gamekeeper and then in a letter to Edmund; and by the end of August he arrived himself, to be gay, agreeable, and gallant again as occasion served, or Miss Crawford demanded; to tell of races and Weymouth, and parties and friends, to which she might have listened six weeks before with some interest, and altogether to give her the fullest conviction, by the power of actual comparison, of her preferring his younger brother.

It was very vexatious, and she was heartily sorry for it; but so it was; and so far from now meaning to marry the elder, she did not even want to attract him beyond what the simplest claims of conscious beauty required; his lengthened absence from Mansfield, without any thing but pleasure in view, and his own will to consult, made it perfectly clear that he did not care about her; and his indifference was so much more than equalled by her own, that, were he now to step forth the owner of Mansfield Park, the Sir Thomas complete, which he was to be in time, she did not believe she could accept him.

The season and duties which brought Mr Bertram back to Mansfield took Mr Crawford into Norfolk. Everingham could not do without him in the beginning of September. He went for a fortnight – a fortnight of such dullness to the Miss Bertrams as ought to have put them both on their guard, and made even Julia admit, in her jealousy of her sister, the absolute necessity of distrusting his attentions, and wishing him not to return; and a fortnight of sufficient leisure, in the intervals of shooting and sleeping, to have convinced the gentleman that he ought to keep longer away, had he been more in the habit of examining his own motives, and of reflecting to what the indulgence of his idle vanity was tending; but, thoughtless and selfish from prosperity and bad example, he would not look beyond the present moment. The sisters, handsome, clever, and encouraging, were an amusement to his sated mind; and finding nothing in Norfolk to equal the social pleasures of Mansfield, he gladly returned to it at the time appointed, and was welcomed thither quite as gladly by those whom he came to trifle with further.

Maria, with only Mr Rushworth to attend to her, and doomed to the repeated details of his day's sport, good or bad, his boast of his dogs, his jealousy of his neighbours, his doubts of their qualifications, and his zeal after poachers, subjects which will not find their way to female feelings without some talent on one side or some attachment on the other, had missed Mr Crawford grievously; and Julia, unengaged and unemployed, felt all the right of missing him much more. Each sister believed herself the favourite. Julia might be justified in so doing by the hints of Mrs Grant, inclined to credit what she wished, and Maria by the hints of Mr Crawford himself. Every thing returned into the same channel as before his absence; his manners being to each so animated and agreeable as to lose no ground with either, and just stopping short of the consistence, the steadiness, the solicitude, and the warmth which might excite general notice.

Fanny was the only one of the party who found anything to dislike; but since the day at Sotherton, she could never see Mr Crawford with either sister without observation, and seldom without wonder or censure; and had her confidence in her own judgment been equal to her exercise of it in every other respect, had she been sure that she was seeing clearly, and judging candidly, she would probably have made some important communications to her usual confidant. As it was, however, she only hazarded a hint, and the hint was lost. 'I am rather surprised,' said she, 'that Mr Crawford should come back again so soon, after being here so long before, full seven weeks; for I had understood he was so very fond of change and moving about, that I thought something would certainly occur when he was once gone, to take him elsewhere. He is used to much gayer places than Mansfield.'

'It is to his credit,' was Edmund's answer; 'and I dare say it gives his sister pleasure. She does not like his unsettled habits.'

'What a favourite he is with my cousins!'

'Yes, his manners to women are such as must please. Mrs Grant, I believe, suspects him of a preference for Julia; I have never seen much symptom of it, but I wish it may be so. He has no faults but what a serious attachment would remove.'

'If Miss Bertram were not engaged,' said Fanny, cautiously, 'I could sometimes almost think that he admired her more than Julia.'

'Which is, perhaps, more in favour of his liking Julia best, than you, Fanny, may be aware; for I believe it often happens, that a man, before he has quite made up his own mind, will distinguish the sister or intimate friend of the woman he is really thinking of, more than the woman herself. Crawford has too much sense to stay here if he found himself in any danger from Maria; and I am not at all afraid for her, after such a proof as she has given, that her feelings are not strong.'

Fanny supposed she must have been mistaken, and meant to think differently in future; but with all that submission to Edmund could do, and all the help of the coinciding looks and hints which she occasionally noticed in some of the others, and which seemed to say that Julia was Mr Crawford's choice, she knew not always what to think. She was privy, one evening, to the hopes of her Aunt Norris on the subject, as well as to her feelings, and the feelings of Mrs Rushworth, on a point of some similarity, and could not help wondering as she listened; and glad would she have been not to be obliged to listen, for it was while all the other young people were dancing, and she sitting, most unwillingly, among the chaperons at the fire, longing for the re-entrance of her elder cousin, on whom all her own hopes of a partner then depended. It was Fanny's first ball, though without the preparation or splendour of many a young lady's first ball, being the thought only of the afternoon, built on the late acquisition of a violin player in the servant's hall, and the possibility of raising five couples with the help of Mrs Grant and a new intimate friend of Mr Bertram's just arrived on a visit. It had, however, been a very happy one to Fanny through four dances, and she was quite grieved to be losing even a quarter of an hour. While waiting and wishing, looking now at the dancers and now at the door, this dialogue between the two above-mentioned ladies was forced on her:

'I think, ma'am,' said Mrs Norris – her eyes directed towards Mr Rushworth and Maria, who were partners for the second time, 'we shall see some happy faces again now.'

'Yes, ma'am, indeed,' replied the other with a stately simper, 'there will be some satisfaction in looking on *now*, and I think it was rather a pity they should have been obliged to part. Young folks in their situation should be excused complying with the common forms. I wonder my son did not propose it.'

'I dare say he did, ma'am. Mr Rushworth is never remiss. But dear Maria has such a strict sense of propriety, so much of that true delicacy which one seldom meets with now-a-days, Mrs Rushworth – that wish of avoiding particularity! Dear ma'am, only look at her face at this moment; how different from what it was the two last dances!'

Miss Bertram did indeed look happy, her eyes were sparkling with pleasure, and she was speaking with great animation, for Julia and her partner, Mr Crawford, were close to her; they were all in a cluster together. How she had looked before, Fanny could not recollect, for she had been dancing with Edmund herself, and had not thought about her.

Mrs Norris continued, 'It is quite delightful, ma'am, to see young people so properly happy, so well suited, and so much the thing! I cannot but think of dear Sir Thomas's delight. And what do you say, ma'am, to the chance of another match? Mr Rushworth has set a good example and such things are very catching.'

Mrs Rushworth, who saw nothing but her son, was quite at a loss. 'The couple above, ma'am. Do you see no symptoms there?'

'Oh dear! Miss Julia and Mr Crawford. Yes, indeed, a very pretty match. What is his property?'

'Four thousand a year.'

'Very well. Those who have not more, must be satisfied with what they have. Four thousand a year is a pretty estate, and he seems a very genteel, steady young man, so I hope Miss Julia will be very happy.'

'It is not a settled thing, ma'am, yet. We only speak of it among friends. But I have very little doubt it *will be*. He is growing extremely particular in his attentions.'

Fanny could listen no further. Listening and wondering were all suspended for a time, for Mr Bertram was in the room again; and though feeling it would be a great honour to be asked by him, she thought it must happen. He came towards their little circle; but instead of asking her to dance, drew a chair near her, and gave her an account of the present state of a sick horse, and the opinion of the groom, from whom he had just parted. Fanny found that it was not to be, and in the modesty of her nature immediately felt that she had been unreasonable in expecting it.

When he had told of his horse, he took a newspaper from the table, and looking over it, said in a languid way, 'If you want to dance, Fanny, I will stand up with you.' With more than equal civility the offer was declined; she did not wish to dance. 'I am glad of it,' said he, in a much brisker tone, and throwing down the newspaper again, 'for I am tired to death. I only wonder how the good people can keep it up so long. They had need be *all* in love, to find any amusement in such folly; and so they are, I fancy. If you look at them you may see they are so many couple of lovers – all but Yates and Mrs Grant – and, between ourselves, she, poor woman, must want a lover as much as any one of them. A desperate dull life hers must be with the doctor,' making a sly face as he spoke towards the chair of the latter, who proving, however, to be close at his elbow, made so instantaneous a change of expression and subject necessary, as Fanny, in spite of every thing, could hardly help laughing at. 'A strange business this in America, Dr Grant! What is your opinion? I always come to you to know what I am to think of public matters.'

'My dear Tom,' cried his aunt soon afterwards, 'as you are not dancing, I dare say you will have no objection to join us in a rubber; shall you?' Then leaving her seat, and coming to him to enforce the proposal, added in a whisper, 'We want to make a table for Mrs Rushworth, you know. Your mother is quite anxious about it, but cannot very well spare time to sit down herself, because of her fringe. Now, you, and I, and Dr Grant, will just do; and though *we* play but half-crowns, you know, you may bet half-guineas with *him*.'

'I should be most happy,' replied he aloud, and jumping up with alacrity, 'it would give me the greatest pleasure; but that I am this moment going to dance. Come, Fanny,' taking her hand, 'do not be dawdling any longer, or the dance will be over.'

Fanny was led off very willingly, though it was impossible for her to feel much gratitude towards her cousin, or distinguish, as he certainly did, between the selfishness of another person and his own.

'A pretty modest request upon my word,' he indignantly exclaimed as they walked away. 'To want to nail me to a card table for the next two hours with herself and Dr Grant, who are always quarrelling, and that poking old woman, who knows no more of whist than of algebra. I wish my good aunt would be a little less busy! And to ask me in such a way too! without ceremony, before them all, so as to leave me no possibility of refusing. *That* is what I dislike most particularly. It raises my spleen more than any thing to have the pretence of being asked, of being given a choice, and at the same time addressed in such a way as to oblige one to do the very thing, whatever it be! If I had not luckily thought of standing up with you I could not have got out of it. It is a great deal too bad. But when my aunt has got a fancy in her head, nothing can stop her.'

CHAPTER THIRTEEN

THE HONOURABLE JOHN YATES, this new friend, had not much to recommend him beyond habits of fashion and expense, and being the younger son of a lord with a tolerable independence; and Sir Thomas would probably have thought his introduction at Mansfield by no means desirable. Mr Bertram's acquaintance with him had begun at Weymouth, where they had spent ten days together in the same society, and the friendship, if friendship it might be called, had been proved and perfected by Mr Yates's being invited to take Mansfield in his way, whenever he could, and by his promising to come; and he did come rather earlier than had been expected, in consequence of the sudden breaking-up of a large party assembled for gaiety at the house of another friend, which he had left Weymouth to join. He came on the wings of disappointment, and with his head full of acting, for it had been a theatrical party; and the play in which he had borne a part was within two days of representation, when the sudden death of one of the nearest connections of the family had destroyed the scheme and dispersed the performers. To be so near happiness, so near fame, so near the long paragraph in praise of the private theatricals at Ecclesford, the seat of the

Right Hon Lord Ravenshaw, in Cornwall, which would of course have immortalised the whole party for at least a twelvemonth! and being so near, to lose it all, was an injury to be keenly felt, and Mr Yates could talk of nothing else. Ecclesford and its theatre, with its arrangements and dresses, rehearsals, and jokes, was his never-failing subject, and to boast of the past his only consolation.

Happily for him, a love of the theatre is so general, an itch for acting so strong among young people, that he could hardly out-talk the interest of his hearers. From the first casting of the parts, to the epilogue, it was all bewitching, and there were few who did not wish to have been a party concerned, or would have hesitated to try their skill. The play had been *Lovers' Vows*, and Mr Yates was to have been Count Cassel. 'A trifling part,' said he, 'and not at all to my taste, and such a one as I certainly would not accept again; but I was determined to make no difficulties. Lord Ravenshaw and the duke had appropriated the only two characters worth playing before I reached Ecclesford; and though Lord Ravenshaw offered to resign his to me, it was impossible to take it, you know. I was sorry for *him* that he should have so mistaken his powers, for he was no more equal to the Baron – a little man with a weak voice, always hoarse after the first ten minutes. It must have injured the piece materially; but *I* was resolved to make no difficulties. Sir Henry thought the duke not equal to Frederick, but that was because Sir Henry wanted the part himself; whereas it was certainly in the best hands of the two. I was surprised to see Sir Henry such a stick. Luckily the strength of the piece did not depend upon him. Our Agatha was inimitable, and the duke was thought very great by many. And upon the whole it would certainly have gone off wonderfully.'

'It was a hard case, upon my word;' and, 'I do think you were very much to be pitied,' were the kind responses of listening sympathy.

'It is not worth complaining about; but to be sure the poor old dowager could not have died at a worse time; and it is impossible to help wishing that the news could have been suppressed for just the three days we wanted. It was but three days; and being only a grandmother, and all happening two hundred miles off, I think there would have been no great harm, and it *was* suggested, I know; but Lord Ravenshaw, who I suppose is one of the most correct men in England, would not hear of it.'

'An afterpiece instead of a comedy,' said Mr Bertram. 'Lovers' vows were at an end, and Lord and Lady Ravenshaw left to act My Grandmother by themselves. Well, the jointure may comfort *him*; and perhaps, between friends, he began to tremble for his credit and his lungs in the Baron, and was not sorry to withdraw; and to make *you* amends. Yates, I think we must raise a little theatre at Mansfield, and ask you to be our manager.'

This, though the thought of the moment, did not end with the moment;

for the inclination to act was awakened, and in no one more strongly than in him who was now master of the house; and who having so much leisure as to make almost any novelty a certain good, had likewise such a degree of lively talents and comic taste, as were exactly adapted to the novelty of acting. The thought returned again and again. 'Oh, for the Ecclesford theatre and scenery to try something with!' Each sister could echo the wish; and Henry Crawford, to whom, in all the riot of his gratifications it was yet an untasted pleasure, was quite alive at the idea. 'I really believe,' said he, 'I could be fool enough at this moment to undertake any character that ever was written, from Shylock or Richard III down to the singing hero of a farce in his scarlet coat and cocked hat. I feel as if I could be any thing or every thing; as if I could rant and storm, or sigh, or cut capers in any tragedy or comedy in the English language. Let us be doing some thing. Be it only half a play, an act, a scene; what should prevent us? Not these countenances, I am sure,' looking towards the Miss Bertrams, 'and for a theatre, what signifies a theatre? We shall be only amusing ourselves. Any room in this house might suffice.'

'We must have a curtain,' said Tom Bertram; 'a few yards of green baize for a curtain, and perhaps that may be enough.'

'Oh, quite enough!' cried Mr Yates, 'with only just a side wing or two run up, doors in flat, and three or four scenes to be let down; nothing more would be necessary on such a plan as this. For mere amusement among ourselves, we should want nothing more.'

'I believe we must be satisfied with *less*,' said Maria. 'There would not be time, and other difficulties would arise. We must rather adopt Mr Crawford's views, and make the *performance*, not the *theatre*, our object. Many parts of our best plays are independent of scenery.'

'Nay,' said Edmund, who began to listen with alarm. 'Let us do nothing by halves. If we are to act, let it be in a theatre completely fitted up with pit, boxes, and gallery, and let us have a play entire from beginning to end; so as it be a German play, no matter what, with a good tricking, shifting afterpiece, and a figure-dance, and a hornpipe, and a song between the acts. If we do not outdo Ecclesford, we do nothing.'

'Now, Edmund, do not be disagreeable,' said Julia. 'Nobody loves a play better than you do, or can have gone much further to see one.'

'True, to see real acting, good hardened real acting; but I would hardly walk from this room to the next to look at the raw efforts of those who have not been bred to the trade: a set of gentlemen and ladies, who have all the disadvantages of education and decorum to struggle through.'

After a short pause, however, the subject still continued, and was discussed with unabated eagerness, every one's inclination increasing by the discussion, and a knowledge of the inclination of the rest; and though

nothing was settled but that Tom Bertram would prefer a comedy, and his
sisters and Henry Crawford a tragedy, and that nothing in the world could
be easier than to find a piece which would please them all, the resolution to
act something or other seemed so decided, as to make Edmund quite
uncomfortable. He was determined to prevent it, if possible, though his
mother, who equally heard the conversation, which passed at table, did not
evince the least disapprobation.

The same evening afforded him an opportunity of trying his strength.
Maria, Julia, Henry Crawford, and Mr Yates were in the billiard-room.
Tom returning from them into the drawing-room, where Edmund was
standing thoughtfully by the fire, while Lady Bertram was on the sofa at a
little distance, and Fanny close beside her, arranging her work, thus began as
he entered:

'Such a horribly vile billiard-table as ours is not to be met with, I believe,
above ground. I can stand it no longer, and I think, I may say, that nothing
shall ever tempt me to it again; but one good thing I have just ascertained; it
is the very room for a theatre, precisely the shape and length for it; and the
doors at the further end, communicating with each other, as they may be
made to do in five minutes, by merely moving the bookcase in my father's
room, is the very thing we could have desired, if we had set down to wish
for it; and my father's room will be an excellent green room. It seems to join
the billiard-room on purpose.'

'You are not serious, Tom, in meaning to act?' said Edmund, in a low
voice, as his brother approached the fire.

'Not serious! never more so, I assure you. What is there to surprise you in
it?'

'I think it would be very wrong. In a *general* light, private theatricals are
open to some objections, but as *we* are circumstanced, I must think it would
be highly injudicious, and more than injudicious, to attempt any thing of the
kind. It would show great want of feeling on my father's account, absent as
he is, and in some degree of constant danger; and it would be imprudent, I
think, with regard to Maria, whose situation is a very delicate one,
considering everything, extremely delicate.'

'You take up a thing so seriously! as if we were going to act three times a
week till my father's return, and invite all the country. But it is not to be a
display of that sort. We mean nothing but a little amusement among
ourselves, just to vary the scene, and exercise our powers in some thing new.
We want no audience, no publicity. We may be trusted, I think, in choosing
some play most perfectly unexceptionable; and I can conceive no greater
harm or danger to any of us in conversing in the elegant written language of
some respectable author than in chattering in words of our own. I have no
fears, and no scruples. And as to my father's being absent, it is so far from an

Just falling into a gentle doze

objection, that I consider it rather as a motive; for the expectation of his return must be a very anxious period to my mother; and if we can be the means of amusing that anxiety, and keeping up her spirits for the next few weeks, I shall think our time very well spent, and so, I am sure, will he. It is a *very* anxious period for her.'

As he said this, each looked towards their mother. Lady Bertram, sunk back in one corner of the sofa, the picture of health, wealth, ease, and tranquillity, was just falling into a gentle doze, while Fanny was getting through the few difficulties of her work for her.

Edmund smiled and shook his head.

'By jove! this won't do,' cried Tom, throwing himself into a chair with a hearty laugh. 'To be sure, my dear mother, your anxiety – I was unlucky there.'

'What is the matter?' asked her ladyship, in the heavy tone of one half roused, 'I was not asleep.'

'Oh, dear no, ma'am, nobody suspected you! Well, Edmund,' he continued, returning to the former subject, posture, and voice, as soon as Lady Bertram began to nod again, 'but *this* I *will* maintain, that we shall be doing no harm.'

'I cannot agree with you; I am convinced that my father would totally disapprove it.'

'And I am convinced to the contrary. Nobody is fonder of the exercise of talent in young people, or promotes it more than my father, and for any thing of the acting, spouting, reciting kind, I think he has always a decided taste. I am sure he encouraged it in us as boys. How many a time have we mourned over the dead body of Julius Cæsar, and *to be'd* and not *to be'd*, in this very room, for his amusement? And I am sure, *my name was Norval*, every evening of my life through one Christmas holidays.'

'It was a very different thing. You must see the difference yourself. My father wished us, as schoolboys, to speak well, but he would never wish his grown-up daughters to be acting plays. His sense of decorum is strict.'

'I know all that,' said Tom, displeased. 'I know my father as well as you do; and I'll take care that his daughters do nothing to distress him. Manage your own concerns, Edmund, and I'll take care of the rest of the family.'

'If you are resolved on acting,' replied the persevering Edmund, 'I must hope it will be in a very small and quiet way; and I think a theatre ought not to be attempted. It would be taking liberties with my father's house in his absence which could not be justified.'

'For everything of that nature, I will be answerable,' said Tom, in a decided tone. 'His house shall not be hurt. I have quite as great an interest in being careful of his house as you can have; and as to such alterations as I was suggesting just now, such as moving a bookcase, or unlocking a door; or even as using the billiard-room for the space of a week without playing at billiards in it, you might just as well suppose he would object to our sitting more in this room, and less in the breakfast-room, than we did before he went away, or to my sister's pianoforte being moved from one side of the room to the other. Absolute nonsense!'

'The innovation, if not wrong as an innovation, will be wrong as an expense.'

'Yes, the expense of such an undertaking would be prodigious! Perhaps it might cost a whole twenty pounds. Something of a theatre we must have undoubtedly, but it will be on the simplest plan; a green curtain and a little carpenter's work, and that's all; and as the carpenter's work may be all done at home by Christopher Jackson himself, it will be too absurd to talk of expense; and as long as Jackson is employed, everything will be right with Sir Thomas. Don't imagine that nobody in this house can see or judge but yourself. Don't act yourself, if you do not like it, but don't expect to govern every body else.'

'No, as to acting myself,' said Edmund, '*that* I absolutely protest against.'

Tom walked out of the room as he said it, and Edmund was left to sit down and stir the fire in thoughtful vexation.

Fanny, who had heard it all, and borne Edmund company in every feeling throughout the whole, now ventured to say, in her anxiety to suggest some comfort, 'Perhaps they may not be able to find any play to suit them. Your brother's taste, and your sisters', seem very different.'

'I have no hope there, Fanny. If they persist in the scheme, they will find some thing. I shall speak to my sisters and try to dissuade *them*, and that is all I can do.'

'I should think my Aunt Norris would be on your side.'

'I dare say she would, but she has no influence with either Tom or my sisters that could be of any use; and if I cannot convince them myself, I shall let things take their course, without attempting it through her. Family squabbling is the greatest evil of all, and we had better do any thing than be altogether by the ears.'

His sisters, to whom he had an opportunity of speaking the next morning, were quite as impatient of his advice, quite as unyielding to his representation, quite as determined in the cause of pleasure, as Tom. Their mother had no objection to the plan, and they were not in the least afraid of their father's disapprobation. There could be no harm in what had been done in so many respectable families, and by so many women of the first consideration; and it must be scrupulousness run mad, that could see anything to censure in a plan like theirs, comprehending only brothers and sisters, and intimate friends, and which would never be heard of beyond themselves. Julia *did* seem inclined to admit that Maria's situation might require particular caution and delicacy – but that could not extend to *her* – *she* was at liberty; and Maria evidently considered her engagement as only raising her so much more above restraint, and leaving her less occasion than Julia, to consult either father or mother. Edmund had little to hope, but he was still urging the subject, when Henry Crawford entered the room, fresh from the Parsonage. calling out, 'No want of hands in our theatre, Miss

Bertram. No want of understrappers; my sister desires her love, and hopes to be admitted into the company, and will be happy to take the part of any old duenna, or tame confidante, that you may not like to do yourselves.'

Maria gave Edmund a glance, which meant, 'What say you now? Can we be wrong if Mary Crawford feels the same?' And Edmund, silenced, was obliged to acknowledge that the charm of acting might well carry fascination to the mind of genius; and with the ingenuity of love, to dwell more on the obliging, accommodating purport of the message than on anything else.

The scheme advanced. Opposition was vain; and as to Mrs Norris, he was mistaken in supposing she would wish to make any. She started no difficulties that were not talked down in five minutes by her eldest nephew and niece, who were all-powerful with her; and, as the whole arrangement was to bring very little expense to anybody, and none at all to herself, as she foresaw in it all the comfort of hurry, bustle, and importance, and derived the immediate advantage of fancying herself obliged to leave her own house, where she had been living a month at her own cost, and take up her abode in theirs, that every hour might be spent in their service, she was, in fact, exceedingly delighted with the project.

CHAPTER FOURTEEN

FANNY SEEMED NEARER BEING RIGHT than Edmund had supposed. The business of finding a play that would suit every body proved to be no trifle; and the carpenter had received his orders and taken his measurements, had suggested and removed at least two sets of difficulties, and having made the necessity of an enlargement of plan and expense fully evident, was already at work, while a play was still to seek. Other preparations were also in hand. An enormous roll of green baize had arrived from Northampton, and been cut out by Mrs Norris (with a saving by her good management, of full three quarters of a yard), and was actually forming into a curtain by the housemaids, and still the play was wanting; and as two or three days passed away in this manner, Edmund began almost to hope that none might ever be found.

There were, in fact, so many things to be attended to, so many people to be pleased, so many best characters required, and above all, such a need that the play should be at once both tragedy and comedy, that there did seem as little chance of a decision as anything pursued by youth and zeal could hold out.

On the tragic side were the Miss Bertrams, Henry Crawford and Mr

Yates; on the comic, Tom Bertram, not *quite* alone, because it was evident that Mary Crawford's wishes, though politely kept back, inclined the same way: but his determinateness and his power seemed to make allies unnecessary; and, independent of this great irreconcilable difference, they wanted a piece containing very few characters in the whole, but every character first-rate, and three principal women. All the best plays were run over in vain. Neither *Hamlet*, nor *Macbeth*, nor *Othello*, nor *Douglas*, nor *The Gamester*, presented anything that could satisfy even the tragedians; and *The Rivals*, *The School for Scandal*, *Wheel of Fortune*, *Heir at Law*, and a long et cetera, were successively dismissed with yet warmer objections. No piece could be proposed that did not supply some body with a difficulty, and on one side or the other it was a continual repetition of, 'Oh no, *that* will never do! Let us have no ranting tragedies. Too many characters. Not a tolerable woman's part in the play. Anything but *that*, my dear Tom. It would be impossible to fill it up. One could not expect anybody to take such a part. Nothing but buffoonery from beginning to end. *That* might do, perhaps, but for the low parts. If I *must* give my opinion, I have always thought it the most insipid play in the English language, *I* do not wish to make objections; I shall be happy to be of any use, but I think we could not choose worse.'

Fanny looked on and listened, not unamused to observe the selfishness which, more or less disguised, seemed to govern them all, and wondering how it would end. For her own gratification she could have wished that some thing might be acted, for she had never seen even half a play, but every thing of higher consequence was against it.

'This will never do,' said Tom Bertram at last. 'We are wasting time most abominably. Some thing must be fixed on. No matter what, so that some thing is chosen. We must not be so nice. A few characters too many must not frighten us. We must *double* them. We must descend a little. If a part is insignificant, the greater our credit in making any thing of it. From this moment, *I* make no difficulties. I take any part you choose to give me, so as it be comic. Let it but be comic, I condition for nothing more.'

For about the fifth time he then proposed *The Heir at Law*, doubting only whether to prefer Lord Duberley or Dr Pangloss for himself; and very earnestly, but very unsuccessfully, trying to persuade the others that there were some fine tragic parts in the rest of the dramatis personæ.

The pause which followed this fruitless effort was ended by the same speaker, who taking up one of the many volumes of plays that lay on the table, and turning it over, suddenly exclaimed – '*Lovers' Vows*! And why should not *Lovers' Vows* do for *us* as well as for the Ravenshaws? How came it never to be thought of before? It strikes me as if it would do exactly. What say you all? Here are two capital tragic parts for Yates and Crawford, and here is the rhyming Butler for me, if nobody else wants it; a trifling part, but the sort of thing I should not dislike, and, as I said before, I am determined to take any thing and do my best. And as for the rest, they may be filled up by any body. It is only Count Cassel and Anhalt.'

The suggestion was generally welcome. Everybody was growing weary of indecision, and the first idea with everybody was, that nothing had been proposed before so likely to suit them all. Mr Yates was particularly pleased: he had been sighing and longing to do the Baron at Ecclesford, had grudged every rant of Lord Ravenshaw's and been forced to re-rant it all in his own room. To storm through Baron Wildenheim was the height of his theatrical ambition; and with the advantage of knowing half the scenes by heart already, he did now with the greatest alacrity, offer his services for the part. To do him justice, however, he did not resolve to appropriate it; for remembering that there was some very good ranting ground in Frederick, he professed an equal willingness for that. Henry Crawford was ready to take either. Whichever Mr Yates did not choose would perfectly satisfy him, and a short parley of compliment ensued. Miss Bertram, feeling all the interest of an Agatha in the question, took on her to decide it, by observing to Mr Yates, that this was a point in which height and figure ought to be considered, and that *his* being the tallest, seemed to fit him peculiarly for the Baron. She was acknowledged to be quite right, and the two parts being accepted accordingly, she was certain of the proper Frederick. Three of the characters were now cast, besides Mr Rushworth, who was always answered for by Maria as willing to do anything, when Julia, meaning, like her sister, to be Agatha, began to be scrupulous on Miss Crawford's account.

'This is not behaving well by the absent,' said she. 'Here are not women enough. Amelia and Agatha may do for Maria and me, but here is nothing for your sister, Mr Crawford.'

Mr Crawford desired *that* might not be thought of: he was very sure his sister had no wish of acting but as she might be useful, and that she would not allow herself to be considered in the present case. But this was immediately opposed by Tom Bertram, who asserted the part of Amelia to be in every respect the property of Miss Crawford, if she would accept it. 'It falls as naturally, as necessarily, to her,' said he, 'as Agatha does to one or other of my sisters. It can be no sacrifice on their side, for it is highly comic.'

A short silence followed. Each sister looked anxious; for each felt the best claim to Agatha, and was hoping to have it pressed on her by the rest. Henry Crawford, who meanwhile had taken up the play, and with seeming carelessness was turning over the first act, soon settled the business.

'I must entreat Miss *Julia* Bertram,' said he, 'not to engage in the part of Agatha, or it will be the ruin of all my solemnity. You must not, indeed you must not (turning to her). I could not stand your countenance dressed up in woe and paleness. The many laughs we have had together would infallibly come across me, and Frederick and his knapsack would be obliged to run away.'

Pleasantly, courteously, it was spoken; but the manner was lost in the matter to Julia's feelings. She saw a glance at Maria, which confirmed the injury to herself: it was a scheme, a trick; she was slighted, Maria was preferred; the smile of triumph which Maria was trying to suppress showed how well it was understood; and before Julia could command herself enough to speak, her brother gave his weight against her too, by saying, 'Oh yes! Maria must be Agatha. Maria will be the best Agatha. Though Julia fancies she prefers tragedy, I would not trust her in it. There is nothing of tragedy about her. She has not the look of it. Her features are not tragic features, and she walks too quick, and speaks too quick, and would not keep her countenance. She had better do the old country-woman: the Cottager's Wife; you had, indeed, Julia. Cottager's Wife is a very pretty part, I assure you. The old lady relieves the high-flown benevolence of her husband with a good deal of spirit. You shall be Cottager's Wife.'

'Cottager's Wife!' cried Mr Yates. 'What are you talking of? The most trivial, paltry, insignificant part; the merest commonplace; not a tolerable speech in the whole. Your sister do that! It is an insult to propose it. At Ecclesford the governess was to have done it. We all agreed that it could not be offered to any body else. A little more justice, Mr Manager, if you please. You do not deserve the office, if you cannot appreciate the talents of your company a little better.'

'Why, as to *that*, my good friend, till I and my company have really acted there must be some guess work; but I mean no disparagement to Julia. We cannot have two Agatha's, and we must have one Cottager's Wife; and I am sure I set her the example of moderation myself in being satisfied with the old Butler. If the part is trifling she will have more credit in making something of it; and if she is so desperately bent against every thing humorous, let her take Cottager's speeches instead of Cottager's Wife's and so change the parts all through; *he* is solemn and pathetic enough, I am sure. It could make no difference in the play, and as for Cottager himself, when he has got his wife's speeches, *I* would undertake him with all my heart.'

'With all your partiality for Cottager's Wife,' said Henry Crawford, 'it will be impossible to make anything of it fit for your sister, and we must not suffer her good nature to be imposed on. We must not *allow* her to accept the part. She must not be left to her own complaisance. Her talents will be wanted in Amelia. Amelia is a character more difficult to be well represented than even Agatha. I consider Amelia is the most difficult character in the whole piece. It requires great powers, great nicety, to give her playfulness and simplicity without extravagance. I have seen good actresses fail in the part. Simplicity, indeed, is beyond the reach of almost every actress by profession. It requires a delicacy of feeling which they have not. It requires a gentlewoman – a Julia Bertram. You *will* undertake it, I hope?' turning to her with a look of anxious entreaty, which softened her a little; but while she hesitated what to say, her brother again interposed with Miss Crawford's better claim.

'No, no, Julia must not be Amelia. It is not at all the part for her. She would not like it. She would not do well. She is too tall and robust. Amelia should be a small, light, girlish, skipping figure. It is fit for Miss Crawford, and Miss Crawford only. She looks the part, and I am persuaded will do it admirably.'

Without attending to this, Henry Crawford continued his supplication. 'You must oblige us,' said he, 'indeed you must. When you have studied the character, I am sure you will feel it suit you. Tragedy may be your choice, but it will certainly appear that comedy chooses *you*. You will be to visit me in prison with a basket of provisions; you will not refuse to visit me in prison? I think I see you coming in with your basket?'

The influence of his voice was felt. Julia wavered; but was he only trying to soothe and pacify her, and make her overlook the previous affront? She distrusted him. The slight had been most determined. He was, perhaps, but at treacherous play with her. She looked suspiciously at her sister; Maria's countenance was to decide it; if she were vexed and alarmed – but Maria looked all serenity and satisfaction, and Julia well knew that on this ground Maria could not be happy but at her expense. With hasty indignation, therefore, and a tremulous voice, she said to him, 'You do not seem afraid of not keeping your countenance when I come in with a basket of provisions – though one might have supposed – but it is only as Agatha that I was to be so overpowering!' She stopped, Henry Crawford looked rather foolish, and as if he did not know what to say. Tom Bertram began again:

'Miss Crawford must be Amelia. She will be an excellent Amelia.'

'Do not be afraid of *my* wanting the character,' cried Julia, with angry quickness: 'I am *not* to be Agatha, and I am sure I will do nothing else; and as to Amelia, it is of all parts in the world most disgusting to me. I quite detest her. An odious, little, pert, unnatural, impudent girl. I have always protested against comedy, and this is comedy in its worst form.' And so saying, she walked hastily out of the room, leaving awkward feelings to more than one, but exciting small compassion in any except Fanny, who had been a quiet auditor of the whole, and who could not think of her as under the agitations of *jealousy* without great pity.

A short silence succeeded her leaving them; but her brother soon returned to business and *Lovers' Vows*, and was eagerly looking over the play, with Mr Yates' help, to ascertain what scenery would be necessary, while Maria and Henry Crawford conversed together in an under voice, and the declaration with which she began of, 'I am sure I would give up the part of Julia most willingly, but that though I shall probably do it very ill, I feel persuaded *she* would do it worse,' was doubtless receiving all the compliments it called for.

When this had lasted some time, the division of the party was completed by Tom Bertram and Mr Yates walking off together to consult further in the room now beginning to be called *the Theatre*, and Miss Bertram's resolving to go down to the Parsonage herself with the offer of Amelia to Miss Crawford; and Fanny remained alone.

The first use she made of her solitude was to take up the volume which had been left on the table, and begin to acquaint herself with the play of which she had heard so much. Her curiosity was all awake, and she ran through it with an eagerness which was suspended only by intervals of astonishment, that it could be chosen in the present instance, that it could be proposed and accepted in a private theatre! Agatha and Amelia appeared to her in their different ways so totally improper for home representation; the situation of one, and the language of the other, so unfit to be expressed by any woman of modesty, that she could hardly suppose her cousins could be aware of what they were engaging in; and longed to have them roused as soon as possible by the remonstrance which Edmund would certainly make.

CHAPTER FIFTEEN

MISS CRAWFORD ACCEPTED THE PART very readily; and soon after Miss Bertram's return from the Parsonage, Mr Rushworth arrived, and another character was consequently cast. He had the offer of Count Cassel and Anhalt, and at first did not know which to choose, and wanted Miss Bertram to direct him; but upon being made to understand the different style of the characters, and which was which, and recollecting that he had once seen the play in London, and had thought Anhalt a very stupid fellow, he soon decided for the Count. Miss Bertram approved the decision, for the less he had to learn the better; and though she could not sympathise in his wish that the Count and Agatha might be to act together, nor wait very patiently while he was slowly turning over the leaves with the hope of still discovering such a scene, she very kindly took his part in hand, and curtailed every speech that admitted being shortened; besides pointing out the necessity of his being very much dressed, and choosing his colours. Mr

Rushworth liked the idea of his finery very well, though affecting to despise it; and was too much engaged with what his own appearance would be to think of the others, or draw any of those conclusions, or feel any of that displeasure which Maria had been half prepared for.

Thus much was settled before Edmund, who had been out all the morning, knew any thing of the matter; but when he entered the drawing-room before dinner, the buzz of discussion was high between Tom, Maria, and Mr Yates; and Mr Rushworth stepped forward with great alacrity to tell him the agreeable news.

'I am to have another fine fancy suit'

'We have got a play,' said he. 'It is to be *Lovers' Vows*; and I am to be Count Cassel, and am come in first with a blue dress, and a pink satin cloak, and afterwards am to have another fine fancy suit, by way of a shooting-dress. I do not know how I shall like it.'

Fanny's eyes followed Edmund, and her heart beat for him as she heard this speech, and saw his look and felt what his sensations must be.

'*Lovers' Vows*!' in a tone of the greatest amazement, was his only reply to Mr Rushworth, and he turned towards his brother and sisters as if hardly doubting a contradiction.

'Yes,' cried Mr Yates. 'After all our debatings and difficulties, we find there is nothing that will suit us altogether so well, nothing so unexceptionable as *Lovers' Vows*. The wonder is that it should not have been thought of before. My stupidity was abominable, for here we have all the advantage of what I saw at Ecclesford; and it is so useful to have anything of a model! We have cast almost every part.'

'But what do you do for women?' said Edmund gravely, and looking at Maria.

Maria blushed in spite of herself as she answered, 'I take the part which Lady Ravenshaw was to have done, and (with a bolder eye) Miss Crawford is to be Amelia.'

'I should not have thought it the sort of play to be so easily filled up, with *us*,' replied Edmund, turning away to the fire, where sat his mother, aunt, and Fanny, and seating himself with a look of great vexation.

Mr Rushworth followed him to say, 'I come in three times, and have two-and-forty speeches. That's something, is not it? But I do not much like the idea of being so fine. I shall hardly know myself in a blue dress, and a pink satin cloak.'

Edmund could not answer him. In a few minutes Mr Bertram was called out of the room to satisfy some doubts of the carpenter; and being accompanied by Mr Yates, and followed soon afterwards by Mr Rushworth, Edmund almost immediately took the opportunity of saying, 'I cannot before Mr Yates speak what I feel as to this play, without reflecting on his friends at Ecclesford; but I must now, my dear Maria, tell *you*, that I think it exceedingly unfit for private representation, and that I hope you will give it up. I cannot but suppose you *will* when you have read it carefully over. Read only the first act aloud to either mother or aunt, and see how you can approve it. It will not be necessary to send you to your *father*'s judgment, I am convinced.'

'We see things very differently,' cried Maria. 'I am perfectly acquainted with the play, I assure you; and with a very few omissions, and so forth, which will be made, of course, I can see nothing objectionable in it; and *I* am not the *only* young woman you find, who thinks it very fit for private representation.'

'I am sorry for it,' was his answer; 'but in this matter it is *you* who are to lead. *You* must set the example. If others have blundered, it is your place to put them right, and show them what true delicacy is. In all points of decorum, *your* conduct must be law to the rest of the party.'

This picture of her consequence had some effect, for no one loved better to lead than Maria; and with far more good humour she answered, 'I am much obliged to you, Edmund; you mean very well, I am sure; but I still think you see things too strongly; and I really cannot undertake to harangue all the rest upon a subject of this kind. *There* would be the greatest indecorum, I think.'

'Do you imagine that I could have such an idea in my head? No: let your conduct be the only harangue. Say that, on examining the part, you feel yourself unequal to it; that you find it requiring more exertion and confidence than you can be supposed to have. Say this with firmness, and it will be quite enough. All who can distinguish will understand your motive. The play will be given up, and your delicacy honoured as it ought.'

'Do not act anything improper, my dear,' said Lady Bertram. 'Sir Thomas would not like it. Fanny, ring the bell; I must have my dinner. To be sure Julia is dressed by this time.'

'I am convinced, madam,' said Edmund, preventing Fanny, 'that Sir Thomas would not like it.'

'There, my dear, do you hear what Edmund says?'

'If I were to decline the part,' said Maria, with renewed zeal, 'Julia would certainly take it.'

'What!' cried Edmund, 'if she knew your reasons!'

'Oh! she might think the difference between us – the difference in our situations – that *she* need not be so scrupulous as *I* might feel necessary. I am sure she would argue so. No: you must excuse me; I cannot retract my consent; it is too far settled, every body would be so disappointed, Tom would be quite angry; and if we are so very nice, we shall never act any thing.'

'I was just going to say the very same thing,' said Mrs Norris. 'If every play is to be objected to, you will act nothing, and the preparations will be all so much money thrown away, and I am sure *that* would be a discredit to us all. I do not know the play; but, as Maria says, if there is anything a little too warm (and it is so with most of them) it can be easily left out. We must not be over precise, Edmund. As Mr Rushworth is to act too, there can be no harm. I only wish Tom had known his own mind when the carpenters began, for there was the loss of half a day's work about the side-doors. The curtain will be a good job, however. The maids do their work very well, and I think we shall be able to send back some dozens of the rings. There is no occasion to put them so very close together. I *am* of some use, I hope, in preventing waste and making the most of things. There should always be one steady head to superintend so many young ones. I forgot to tell Tom of some thing that happened to me this very day. I had been looking about me in the poultry yard, and was just coming out, when who should I see but Dick Jackson, making up to the servants' hall-door with two bits of deal board in his hand, bringing them to father you may be sure; mother had chanced to send him on a message to father, and then father had bid him bring up them two bits of board, for he could not know how do without them. I knew what all this meant, for the servants' dinner-bell was ringing at the very moment over our heads; and as I hate such encroaching people (the Jacksons are very encroaching, I have always said so: just the sort of people to get all they can), I said to the boy directly (a great lubberly fellow of ten years old, you know, who ought to be ashamed of himself); '*I'll* take the boards to your father, Dick, so get you home again as fast as you can.' The boy looked very silly, and turned away without offering a word, for I believe I might speak pretty sharp; and I dare say it will cure him of coming marauding about the house for one while. I hate such greediness; so good as your father is to the family, employing the man all the year round!'

Nobody was at the trouble of an answer; the others soon returned; and Edmund found that to have endeavoured to set them right must be his only satisfaction.

Dinner passed heavily. Mrs Norris related again her triumph over Dick Jackson, but neither play nor preparation were otherwise much talked of, for Edmund's disapprobation was felt even by his brother, though he would not have owned it. Maria, wanting Henry Crawford's animating support, thought the subject better avoided. Mr Yates, who was trying to make himself agreeable to Julia, found her gloom less impenetrable on any topic than that of his regret at her secession from their company; and Mr Rushworth, having only his own part and his own dress in his head, had soon talked away all that could be said of either.

But the concerns of the theatre were suspended only for an hour or two: there was still a great deal to be settled; and the spirits of evening giving fresh courage, Tom, Maria, and Mr Yates, soon after their being reassembled in the drawing-room, seated themselves in committee at a separate table, with the play open before them, and were just getting deep in the subject, when a most welcome interruption was given by the entrance of Mr and Miss Crawford, who, late and dark and dirty as it was, could not help coming, and were received with the most grateful joy.

'Well, how do you go on?' and 'What have you settled?' and 'Oh! we can do nothing without you,' followed the first salutations; and Henry Crawford was soon seated with the other three at the table, while his sister made her way to Lady Bertram, and with pleasant attention was complimenting *her*. 'I must really contratulate your ladyship,' said she, 'on

A most welcome interruption

the play being chosen; for though you have borne it with exemplary patience, I am sure you must be sick of all our noise and difficulties. The actors may be glad, but the by-standers must be infinitely more thankful for a decision; and I do sincerely give you joy, madam, as well as Mrs Norris, and everybody else who is in the same predicament,' glancing half fearfully, half slyly, beyond Fanny to Edmund.

She was very civilly answered by Lady Bertram, but Edmund said nothing. His being only a by-stander was not disclaimed. After continuing in chat with the party round the fire a few minutes, Miss Crawford returned to the party round the table; and standing by them, seemed to interest herself in their arrangements till, as if struck by a sudden recollection, she exclaimed, 'My good friends, you are most composedly at work upon these cottages and ale-houses, inside and out; but pray, let me know my fate in the meanwhile. Who is to be Anhalt? What gentleman among you am I to have the pleasure of making love to?'

For a moment no one spoke; and then many spoke together to tell the same melancholy truth, that they had not yet got any Anhalt. 'Mr Rushworth was to be Count Cassel, but no one had yet undertaken Anhalt.'

'I had my choice of the parts,' said Mr Rushworth; 'but I thought I should like the Count best, though I do not much relish the finery I am to have.'

'You choose very wisely, I am sure,' replied Miss Crawford, with a brightened look; 'Anhalt is a heavy part.'

'*The Count* has two-and-forty speeches,' returned Mr Rushworth, 'which is no trifle.'

'I am not at all surprised,' said Miss Crawford, after a short pause, 'at this want of an Anhalt. Amelia deserves no better. Such a forward young lady might well frighten the men.'

'I should be but too happy in taking the part, if it were possible,' cried Tom; 'but, unluckily, the Butler and Anhalt are in together. I will not entirely give it up, however; I will try what can be done – I will look it over again.'

'Your *brother* should take the part,' said Mr Yates, in a low voice. 'Do you not think he would?'

'*I* shall not ask him,' replied Tom, in a cold determined manner.

Miss Crawford talked of some thing else, and soon afterwards rejoined the party at the fire.

'They do not want me at all,' said she, seating herself. 'I only puzzle them, and oblige them to make civil speeches. Mr Edmund Bertram, as you do not act yourself, you will be a disinterested adviser; and, therefore, I apply to *you*. What shall we do for an Anhalt? Is it practicable for any of the others to double it? What is your advice?'

'My advice,' said he calmly, 'is that you change the play.'

'*I* should have no objection,' she replied; 'for though I should not particularly dislike the part of Amelia, if well supported, that is, if every thing went well, I shall be sorry to be an inconvenience; but as they do not choose to hear your advice at *that table* (looking round), it certainly will not be taken.'

Edmund said no more.

'If *any* part could tempt *you* to act, I suppose it would be Anhalt,' observed the lady archly, after a short pause; 'for he is a clergyman, you know.'

'*That* circumstance would by no means tempt me,' he replied, 'for I should be sorry to make the character ridiculous by bad acting. It must be very difficult to keep Anhalt from appearing a formal solemn lecturer; and the man who chooses the profession itself, is, perhaps, one of the last who would wish to represent it on the stage.'

Miss Crawford was silenced, and with some feelings of resentment and mortification, moved her chair considerably nearer the tea-table, and gave all her attention to Mrs Norris, who was presiding there.

'Fanny,' cried Tom Bertram, from the other table, where the conference was eagerly carrying on, and the conversation incessant, 'we want your services.'

Fanny was up in a moment, expecting some errand; for the habit of employing her in that way was not yet overcome, in spite of all that Edmund could do.

'Oh! we do not want to disturb you from your seat. We do not want your *present* services. We shall only want you in our play. You must be Cottager's Wife.'

'Me!' cried Fanny, sitting down again with a most frightened look. 'Indeed, you must excuse me. I could not act any thing if you were to give me the world. No, indeed, I cannot act.'

'Indeed, but you must, for we cannot excuse you. It need not frighten you; it is a nothing of a part, a mere nothing, not above half-a-dozen speeches altogether, and it will not much signify if nobody hears a word you say, so you may be as creep-mouse as you like, but we must have you to look at.'

'If you are afraid of half-a-dozen speeches,' cried Mr Rushworth, 'what would you do with such a part as mine? I have forty-two to learn.'

'It is not that I am afraid of learning by heart,' said Fanny, shocked to find herself at that moment the only speaker in the room, and to feel that almost every eye was upon her; 'but I really cannot act.'

'Yes, yes, you can act well enough for *us*. Learn your part, and we will teach you all the rest. You have only two scenes, and as I shall be Cottager, I'll put you in and push you about, and you will do it very well, I'll answer for it.'

'No, indeed, Mr Bertram, you must excuse me. You cannot have an idea. It would be absolutely impossible for me. If I were to undertake it, I should only disappoint you.'

'Phoo! Phoo! Do not be so shamefaced. You'll do it very well. Every allowance will be made for you. We do not expect perfection. You must get a brown gown, and a white apron, and a mob cap, and we must make you a few wrinkles, and a little of the crowsfoot at the corner of your eyes, and you will be a very proper, little old woman.'

'You must excuse me, indeed you must excuse me,' cried Fanny, growing more and more red from excessive agitation, and looking distressfully at Edmund, who was kindly observing her; but unwilling to exasperate his brother by interference, gave her only an encouraging smile. Her entreaty had no effect on Tom; he only said again what he had said before, and it was not merely Tom, for the requisition was now backed by Maria, and Mr Crawford, and Mr Yates, with an urgency which differed from his but in being more gentle or more ceremonious, and which altogether was quite overpowering to Fanny; and before she could breathe after it, Mrs Norris completed the whole by thus addressing her in a whisper at once angry and audible: 'What a piece of work here is about nothing; I am quite ashamed of you, Fanny, to make such a difficulty of obliging your cousins in a trifle of this sort – so kind as they are to you! Take the part with a good grace, and let us hear no more of the matter, I entreat.'

'Do not urge her, madam,' said Edmund. 'It is not fair to urge her in this manner. You see she does not like to act. Let her choose for herself, as well as the rest of us. Her judgment may be quite as safely trusted. Do not urge her any more.'

'I am not going to urge her,' replied Mrs Norris sharply; 'but I shall think her a very obstinate, ungrateful girl, if she does not do what her aunt and cousins wish her; very ungrateful, indeed, considering who and what she is.'

Edmund was too angry to speak; but Miss Crawford looking for a moment with astonished eyes at Mrs Norris, and then at Fanny, whose tears were beginning to show themselves, immediately said, with some keenness, 'I do not like my situation; this *place* is too hot for me,' and moved away her chair to the opposite side of the table, close to Fanny, saying to her, in a kind, low whisper, as she placed herself, 'Never mind, my dear Miss Price, this is a cross evening; everybody is cross and teasing, but do not let us mind them'; and with pointed attention continued to talk to her and endeavour to raise her spirits, in spite of being out of spirits herself. By a look at her brother, she prevented any further entreaty from the theatrical board, and the really good feelings by which she was almost purely governed, were rapidly restoring her to all the little she had lost in Edmund's favour.

Fanny did not love Miss Crawford; but she felt very much obliged to her for her present kindness; and when, from taking notice of her work, and wishing *she* could work as well, and begging for the pattern, and supposing Fanny was now preparing for her *appearance*, as of course she would come out when her cousin was married, Miss Crawford proceeded to inquire if she had heard lately from her brother at sea, and said that she had quite a curiosity to see him, and imagined him a very fine young man, and advised Fanny to get his picture drawn before he went to sea again, she could not help admitting it to be very agreeable flattery, or help listening and answering with more animation than she had intended.

The consultation upon the play still went on, and Miss Crawford's attention was first called from Fanny, by Tom Bertram's telling her, with infinite regret, that he found it absolutely impossible for him to undertake the part of Anhalt in addition to the Butler: he had been most anxiously trying to make it out to be feasible, but it would not do; he must give it up. 'But there will not be the smallest difficulty in filling it,' he added. 'We have but to speak the word; we may pick and choose. I could name, at this moment, at least six young men within six miles of us, who are wild to be admitted into our company, and there are one or two that would not disgrace us; I should not be afraid to trust either of the Olivers or Charles Maddox. Tom Oliver is a very clever fellow, and Charles Maddox is as gentlemanlike a man as you will see anywhere, so I will take my horse early to-morrow morning and ride over to Stoke, and settle with one of them.'

While he spoke, Maria was looking apprehensively round at Edmund in full expectation that he must oppose such an enlargement of the plan as this: so contrary to all their first protestations; but Edmund said nothing. After a moment's thought, Miss Crawford calmly replied, 'As far as I am concerned, I can have no objection to anything that you all think eligible. Have I ever seen either of the gentlemen? Yes, Mr Charles Maddox dined at my sister's one day, did not he, Henry? A quiet looking young man. I remember him. Let *him* be applied to, if you please, for it will be less unpleasant for me than to have a perfect stranger.'

Charles Maddox was to be the man. Tom repeated his resolution of going to him early on the morrow; and though Julia, who had scarcely opened her lips before, observed in a sarcastic manner, and with a glance first at Maria, and then at Edmund, that 'the Mansfield theatricals would enliven the whole neighbourhood exceedingly,' Edmund still held his peace, and showed his feelings only by a determined gravity.

'I am not very sanguine as to our play,' said Miss Crawford, in an under voice to Fanny, after some consideration; 'and I can tell Mr Maddox that I shall shorten some of *his* speeches, and a great many of *my own* before we rehearse together. It will be very disagreeable, and by no means what I expected.'

CHAPTER SIXTEEN

IT WAS NOT IN MISS CRAWFORD's power to talk Fanny into any real forgetfulness of what had passed. When the evening was over, she went to bed, full of it, her nerves still agitated by the shock of such an attack from her cousin Tom, so public and so persevered in, and her spirits sinking under her aunt's unkind reflection and reproach. To be called into notice in such a manner, to hear that it was but the prelude to something so infinitely worse, to be told that she must do what was so impossible as to act; and then to have the charge of obstinacy and ingratitude follow it, enforced with such a hint at the dependence of her situation, had been too distressing at the time to make the remembrance when she was alone much less so, especially with the superadded dread of what the morrow might produce in continuation of the subject. Miss Crawford had protected her only for the time; and if she were applied to again among themselves with all the authoritative urgency that Tom and Maria were capable of, and Edmund perhaps away, what should she do? She fell asleep before she could answer the question, and found it quite as puzzling when she awoke the next morning. The little white attic, which had continued her sleeping room ever since her first entering the family, proving incompetent to suggest any reply, she had recourse, as soon as she was dressed, to another apartment more spacious and more meet for walking about in and thinking, and of which she had now for some time been almost equally mistress. It had been their schoolroom; so called till the Miss Bertrams would not allow it to be called so any longer, and inhabited as such to a later period. There Miss Lee had lived, and there they had read and written, and talked and laughed, till within the last three years, when she had quitted them. The room had then become useless, and for some time was quite deserted, except by Fanny, when she visited her plants, or wanted one of the books, which she was still glad to keep there, from the deficiency of space and accommodation in her little chamber above; but gradually, as her value for the comforts of it increased, she had added to her possessions, and spent more of her time there; and having nothing to oppose her, had so naturally and so artlessly worked herself into it, that it was now generally admitted to be hers. The East Room, as it had been called ever since Maria Bertram was sixteen, was now considered Fanny's, almost as decidedly as the white attic: the smallness of the one making the use of the other so evidently reasonable, that the Miss Bertrams, with every superiority in their own apartments which their own sense of superiority could demand, were entirely approving it; and Mrs Norris, having stipulated for there never being a fire in it on Fanny's account, was tolerably resigned to her having the use of what nobody else wanted, though the terms in which she sometimes spoke of the indulgence seemed to imply that it was the best room in the house.

The aspect was so favourable, that even without a fire it was habitable in many an early spring and late autumn morning, to such a willing mind as Fanny's; and while there was a gleam of sunshine, she hoped not to be driven from it entirely, even when winter came. The comfort of it in her hours of leisure was extreme. She could go there after any thing unpleasant below, and find immediate consolation in some pursuit, or some train of thought at hand. Her plants, her books – of which she had been a collector from the first hour of her commanding a shilling – her writing-desk and her works of charity and ingenuity, were all within her reach; or if indisposed for employment, if nothing but musing would do, she could scarcely see an object in that room which had not an interesting remembrance connected with it. Every thing was a friend, or bore her thoughts to a friend; and though there had been sometimes much of suffering to her, though her motives had often been misunderstood, her feelings disregarded; and her comprehension undervalued; though she had known the pains of tyranny, or ridicule, and neglect; yet almost every recurrence of either had led to something consolatory; her Aunt Bertram had spoken for her, or Miss Lee had been encouraging, or, what was yet more frequent or more dear, Edmund had been her champion and her friend; he had supported her cause or explained her meaning; he had told her not to cry, or had given her some proof of affection which made her tears delightful, and the whole was now so blended together, so harmonised by distance, that every former affliction had its charm. The room was most dear to her, and she would not have changed its furniture for the handsomest in the house, though what had been originally plain, had suffered all the ill-usage of children; and its greatest elegancies and ornaments were a faded footstool of Julia's work, too ill done for the drawing-room, three transparencies, made in a rage for transparencies, for the three lower panes of one window, where Tintern Abbey held its station between a cave in Italy and a moonlight lake in Cumberland, a collection of family profiles, thought unworthy of being any where else, over the mantelpiece, and by their side, and pinned against the wall, a small sketch of a ship sent four years ago from the Mediterranean by William, with H.M.S. *Antwerp* at the bottom, in letters as tall as the mainmast.

To this nest of comforts Fanny now walked down to try its influence on an agitated, doubting spirit, to see if by looking at Edmund's profile she could catch any of his counsel, or by giving air to her geraniums she might inhale a breeze of mental strength herself. But she had more than fears of her own perseverance to remove: she had begun to feel undecided as to what she *ought to do*; and as she walked round the room her doubts were increasing. Was she *right* in refusing what was so warmly asked, so strongly wished for – what might be so essential to a scheme on which some of those to whom she owed the greatest complaisance had set their hearts? Was it not ill-nature, selfishness, and a fear of exposing herself? And would Edmund's judgment, would his persuasion of Sir Thomas's disapprobation of the whole, be enough to justify her in a determined denial in spite of all the rest? It would be so horrible to her to act, that she was inclined to suspect the truth and purity of her own scruples; and as she looked around her, the claims of her cousins to being obliged were strengthened by the sight of present upon present that she had received from them. The table between the windows was covered with work-boxes and netting-boxes which had been given her at different times, principally by Tom; and she grew bewildered as to the amount of the debt which all these kind remembrances produced. A tap at the door roused her in the midst of this attempt to find her way to her duty, and her gentle 'come in' was answered by the appearance of one, before whom all her doubts were wont to be laid. Her eyes brightened at the sight of Edmund.

'Can I speak with you, Fanny, for a few minutes?' said he.

'Yes, certainly.'

'I want to consult. I want your opinion.'

'My opinion!' she cried, shrinking from such a compliment, highly as it gratified her.

'Yes, your advice and opinion. I do not know what to do. This acting scheme gets worse and worse, you see. They have chosen almost as bad a play as they could, and now, to complete the business, are going to ask the help of a young man very slightly known to any of us. This is the end of all the privacy and propriety which was talked about at first. I know no harm of Charles Maddox; but the excessive intimacy which must spring from his being admitted among us in this manner is highly objectionable, the *more* than intimacy – the familiarity. I cannot think of it with any patience; and it does appear to me an evil of such magnitude as must, *if possible*, be prevented. Do not you see it in the same light?'

'Yes; but what can be done? Your brother is so determined.'

'There is but *one* thing to be done, Fanny. I must take Anhalt myself. I am well aware that nothing else will quiet Tom.'

Fanny could not answer him.

'It is not at all what I like,' he continued. 'No man can like being driven into the *appearance* of such inconsistency. After being known to oppose the scheme from the beginning, there is absurdity in the face of my joining them *now*, when they are exceeding their first plan in every respect; but I can think of no other alternative. Can you, Fanny?'

'No,' said Fanny slowly, 'not immediately, but—'

'But what? I see your judgment is not with me. Think it a little over. Perhaps you are not so much aware as I am of the mischief that *may*, of the unpleasantness that *must* arise from a young man's being received in this manner; domesticated among us; authorised to come at all hours, and placed suddenly on a footing which must do away all restraints. To think only of the licence which every rehearsal must tend to create. It is all very bad! Put yourself in Miss Crawford's place, Fanny. Consider what it would be to act Amelia with a stranger. She has a right to be felt for, because she evidently feels for herself. I heard enough of what she said to you last night to understand her unwillingness to be acting with a stranger; and as she probably engaged in the part with different expectations – perhaps without considering the subject enough to know what was likely to be – it would be ungenerous, it would be really wrong to expose her to it. Her feelings ought to be respected. Does it not strike you so, Fanny? You hesitate.'

'I am sorry for Miss Crawford; but I am more sorry to see you drawn in to do what you had resolved against, and what you are known to think will be disagreeable to my uncle. It will be such a triumph to the others!'

'They will not have much cause of triumph when they see how infamously I act. But, however, triumph there certainly will be, and I must brave it. But if I can be the means of restraining the publicity of the business, of limiting the exhibition, of concentrating our folly, I shall be well repaid. As I am now, I have no influence, I can do nothing: I have offended them, and they will not hear me; but when I have put them in good humour by this concession, I am not without hopes of persuading them to confine the representation within a much smaller circle than they are now in the high road for. This will be a material gain. My object is to confine it to Mrs Rushworth and the Grants. Will not this be worth gaining?'

'Yes, it will be a great point.'

'But still it has not your approbation. Can you mention any other measure by which I have a chance of doing equal good?'

'No, I cannot think of any thing else.'

'Give me your approbation, then, Fanny. I am not comfortable without it.'

'Oh cousin!'

'If you are against me, I ought to distrust myself, and yet— But it is absolutely impossible to let Tom go on in this way, riding about the country in quest of any body who can be persuaded to act – no matter whom: the look of a gentleman is to be enough. I thought *you* would have entered more into Miss Crawford's feelings.'

'No doubt she will be very glad. It must be a great relief to her,' said Fanny, trying for greater warmth of manner.

'She never appeared more amiable than in her behaviour to you last night. It gave her a very strong claim on my goodwill.'

'She *was* very kind, indeed, and I am glad to have her spared —'

She could not finish the generous effusion. Her conscience stopped her in the middle, but Edmund was satisfied.

'I shall walk down immediately after breakfast,' said he, 'and am sure of giving pleasure there. And, now, dear Fanny, I will not interrupt you any longer. You want to be reading. But I could not be easy till I had spoken to you, and come to a decision. Sleeping or waking, my head has been full of this matter all night. It is an evil, but I am certainly making it less than it might be. If Tom is up, I shall go to him directly and get it over, and when we meet at breakfast we shall be all in high good humour at the prospect of acting the fool together with such unanimity. *You* in the meanwhile will be taking a trip into China, I suppose. How does Lord Macartney go on? (opening a volume on the table and then taking up some others). And here are Crabbe's *Tales*, and *The Idler*, at hand to relieve you, if you tire of your great book. I admire your little establishment exceedingly; and as soon as I am gone, you will empty your head of all this nonsense of acting, and sit comfortably down to your table. But do not stay here to be cold.'

He went; but there was no reading, no China, no composure for Fanny. He had told her the most extraordinary, the most inconceivable, the most unwelcome news; and she could think of nothing else. To be acting! After all his objections – objections so just and so public! After all that she had heard him say, and seen him look, and known him to be feeling. Could it be possible? Edmund so inconsistent! Was he not deceiving himself? Was he not wrong? Alas! it was all Miss Crawford's doing. She had seen her influence in every speech, and was miserable. The doubts and alarms as to her own conduct, which had previously distressed her, and which had all slept while she listened to him, were become of little consequence now. This deeper anxiety swallowed them up. Things should take their course; she cared not how it ended. Her cousins might attack, but could hardly teaze her. She was beyond their reach; and if at last obliged to yield – no matter – it was all misery *now*.

CHAPTER SEVENTEEN

IT WAS, INDEED, A TRIUMPHANT day to Mr Bertram and Maria. Such a victory over Edmund's discretion had been beyond their hopes, and was most delightful. There was no longer any thing to disturb them in their darling project, and they congratulated each other in private on the jealous weakness to which they attributed the change, with all the glee of feelings gratified in every way. Edmund might still look grave, and say he did not like the scheme in general, and must disapprove the play in particular; their point was gained; he was to act, and he was driven to it by force of selfish inclinations only. Edmund had descended from that moral elevation which he had maintained before, and they were both as much the better as the happier for the descent.

They behaved very well, however, to *him* on the occasion, betraying no exultation beyond the lines about the corners of the mouth, and seemed to think it as great an escape to be quit of the intrusion of Charles Maddox, as if they had been forced into admitting him against their inclination. 'To have it quite in their own family circle was what they had particularly wished. A stranger among them would have been the destruction of all their comfort'; and when Edmund, pursuing that idea, gave a hint of his hope as to the limitation of the audience, they were ready, in the complaisance of the moment, to promise any thing. It was all good humour and encouragement. Mrs Norris offered to contrive his dress, Mr Yates assured him that Anhalt's last scene with the Baron admitted a good deal of action and emphasis, and Mr Rushworth undertook to count his speeches.

'Perhaps,' said Tom, '*Fanny* may be more disposed to oblige us now. Perhaps you may persuade *her*.'

'No, she is quite determined. She certainly will not act.'

'Oh! very well.' And not another word was said; but Fanny felt herself again in danger, and her indifference to the danger was beginning to fail her already.

There were not fewer smiles at the Parsonage than at the Park on this change in Edmund; Miss Crawford looked very lovely in hers, and entered with such an instantaneous renewal of cheerfulness into the whole affair, as could have but one effect on him. 'He was certainly right in respecting such feelings; he was glad he had determined on it.' And the morning wore away in satisfactions very sweet, if not very sound. One advantage resulted from it to Fanny; at the earnest request of Miss Crawford, Mrs Grant had, with her usual good humour, agreed to undertake the part for which Fanny had been wanted; and this was all that occurred to gladden *her* heart during the day; and even this, when imparted by Edmund, brought a pang with it, for it was Miss Crawford to whom she was obliged; it was Miss Crawford whose kind exertions were to excite her gratitude, and whose merit in making them was spoken of with a glow of admiration. She was safe; but peace and safety were unconnected here. Her mind had been never farther from peace. She could not feel that she had done wrong herself, but she was disquieted in every other way. Her heart and her judgment were equally against Edmund's decision: she could not acquit his unsteadiness, and his happiness under it made her wretched. She was full of jealousy and agitation. Miss Crawford came with looks of gaiety which seemed an insult, with friendly expressions towards herself which she could hardly answer calmly. Everybody around her was gay and busy, prosperous and important; each had their object of interest, their part, their dress, their favourite scene, their friends and confederates: all were finding employment in consultations and comparisons, or diversion in the playful conceits they suggested. She alone was sad and insignificant; she had no share in any thing; she might go or stay; she might be in the midst of their noise, or retreat from it to the solitude of the East Room, without being seen or missed. She could almost think any thing would have been preferable to this. Mrs Grant was of consequence: *her* good nature had honourable mention: her taste and her time were considered; her presence was wanted; she was sought for, and attended, and praised; and Fanny was at first in some danger of envying her the character she had accepted. But reflection brought better feelings, and showed her that Mrs Grant was entitled to respect, which could never have belonged to *her*; and that, had she received even the greatest, she could never have been easy in joining a scheme which, considering only her uncle, she must condemn altogether.

Fanny's heart was not absolutely the only saddened one amongst them, as she soon began to acknowledge to herself. Julia was a sufferer, too, though not quite so blamelessly.

Henry Crawford had trifled with her feelings; but she had very long allowed, and even sought his attentions with a jealousy of her sister so reasonable as ought to have been their cure; and now that the conviction of his preference for Maria had been forced on her, she submitted to it without any alarm for Maria's situation, or any endeavour at rational tranquillity for herself. She either sat in gloomy silence, wrapped in such gravity as nothing could subdue, no curiosity touch, no wit amuse; or allowing the attentions of Mr Yates, was talking with forced gaiety to him alone, and ridiculing the acting of the others.

For a day or two after the affront was given Henry Crawford had endeavoured to do it away by the usual attack of gallantry and compliment, but he had not cared enough about it to persevere against a few repulses; and becoming soon too busy with his play to have time for more than one flirtation, he grew indifferent to the quarrel, or rather thought it a lucky occurrence, as quietly putting an end to what might ere long have raised expectations in more than Mrs Grant. She was not pleased to see Julia excluded from the play, and sitting by disregarded; but as it was not a matter which really involved her happiness, as Henry must be the best judge of his own, and as he did assure her, with a most persuasive smile, that neither he nor Julia had ever had a serious thought of each other, she could only renew her former caution as to the elder sister, entreat him not to risk his tranquillity by too much admiration there, and then gladly take her share in any thing that brought cheerfulness to the young people in general, and that did so particularly promote the pleasure of the two so dear to her.

'I rather wonder Julia is not in love with Henry,' was her observation to Mary.

'I dare say she is,' replied Mary coldly. 'I imagine both sisters are.'

'Both! No, no, that must not be. Do not give him a hint of it. Think of Mr Rushworth!'

'You had better tell Miss Bertram to think of Mr Rushworth. It may do *her* some good. I often think of Mr Rushworth's property and independence and wish them in other hands; but I never think of *him*. A man might represent the county with such an estate; a man might escape a profession and represent the county.'

'I dare say he *will* be in parliament soon. When Sir Thomas comes I dare say he will be in for some borough, but there has been nobody to put him in the way of doing any thing yet.'

'Sir Thomas is to achieve many mighty things when he comes home,' said Mary, after a pause. 'Do you remember Hawkins Browne's "Address to Tobacco," in imitation of Pope?

> Blest leaf! whose aromatic gales dispense
> To Templars modesty, to Parsons sense.

I will parody them:

> Blest Knight! whose dictatorial looks dispense
> To Children affluence, to Rushworth sense.

Will not that do, Mrs Grant? Everything seems to depend upon Sir Thomas's return.'

'You will find his consequence very just and reasonable when you see him in his family, I assure you. I do not think we do so well without him. He has a fine dignified manner, which suits the head of such a house, and keeps every body in their place. Lady Bertram seems more of a cipher now than when he is at home; and nobody else can keep Mrs Norris in order. But, Mary, do not fancy that Maria Bertram cares for Henry. I am sure *Julia* does not, or she would not have flirted as she did last night with Mr Yates; and though he and Maria are very good friends, I think she likes Sotherton too well to be inconstant.'

'I would not give much for Mr Rushworth's chance, if Henry stepped in before the articles were signed.'

'If you have such a suspicion, some thing must be done; and as soon as the play is all over, we will talk to him seriously, and make him know his own mind; and if he means nothing, we will send him off, though he is Henry, for a time.'

Julia *did* suffer, however, though Mrs Grant discerned it not, and though it escaped the notice of many of her own family likewise. She had loved, she did love still, and she had all the suffering which a warm temper and a high spirit were likely to endure under the disappointment of a dear, though irrational hope, with a strong sense of ill-usage. Her heart was sore and angry, and she was capable only of angry consolations. The sister with whom she was used to be on easy terms was now become her greatest enemy: they were alienated from each other; and Julia was not superior to the hope of some distressing end to the attentions which were still carrying on there, some punishment to Maria for conduct so shameful towards herself as well as towards Mr Rushworth. With no material fault of temper, or difference of opinion, to prevent their being very good friends while their interests were the same, the sisters, under such a trial as this, had not affection or principle enough to make them merciful or just, to give them honour or compassion. Maria felt her triumph, and pursued her purpose, careless of Julia; and Julia could never see Maria distinguished by Henry Crawford without trusting that it would create jealousy, and bring a public disturbance at last.

Fanny saw and pitied much of this in Julia; but there was no outward fellowship between them. Julia made no communication, and Fanny took no liberties. They were two solitary sufferers, or connected only by Fanny's consciousness.

The inattention of the two brothers and the aunt to Julia's discomposure, and their blindness to its true cause, must be imputed to the fullness of their own minds. They were totally preoccupied. Tom was engrossed by the concerns of his theatre, and saw nothing that did not immediately relate to it. Edmund, between his theatrical and his real part – between Miss Crawford's claims and his own conduct – between love and consistency, was equally unobservant; and Mrs Norris was too busy in contriving and directing the general little matters of the company, superintending their various dresses with economical expedience, for which nobody thanked her, and saving, with delighted integrity, half-a-crown here and there to the absent Sir Thomas, to have leisure for watching the behaviour, or guarding the happiness of his daughters.

CHAPTER EIGHTEEN

EVERYTHING WAS NOW IN A regular train; theatre, actors, actresses and dresses were all getting forward; but though no other great impediments arose, Fanny found, before many days were past, that it was not all uninterrupted enjoyment to the party themselves, and that she had not to witness the continuance of such unanimity and delight, as had been almost too much for her at first. Everybody began to have their vexation. Edmund had many. Entirely against *his* judgment, a scene painter arrived from town, and was at work, much to the increase of the expenses, and, what was worse, of the éclat of their proceedings; and his brother, instead of being really guided by him as to the privacy of the representation, was giving an invitation to every family who came in his way. Tom himself began to fret over the scene painter's slow progress, and to feel the miseries of waiting. He had learned his part – all parts, for he took every trifling one that could be united with the Butler, and began to be impatient to be acting; and every day thus unemployed was tending to increase his sense of the insignificance of all his parts together, and make him more ready to regret that some other play had not been chosen.

Fanny, being always a very courteous listener, and often the only listener at hand, came in for the complaints and the distresses of most of them. *She* knew that Mr Yates was in general thought to rant dreadfully; that Mr Yates was disappointed in Henry Crawford; that Tom Bertram spoke so quick he would be unintelligible; that Mrs Grant spoiled everything by laughing; that Edmund was behind-hand with his part, and that it was a misery to have any thing to do with Mr Rushworth, who was wanting a prompter through every speech. She knew, also, that poor Mr Rushworth could seldom get any body to rehearse with him; *his* complaint came before her as well as the rest; and so decided to her eye was her cousin Maria's avoidance of him and so needlessly often the rehearsal of the first scene between her and Mr Crawford, that she had soon all the terror of other complaints from *him*. So far from being all satisfied and all enjoying, she found every body requiring some thing they had not, and giving occasion of discontent to the others. Every body had a part either too long or too short; nobody would attend as they ought; nobody would remember on which side they were to come in; nobody but the complainer would observe any directions.

Fanny believed herself to derive as much innocent enjoyment from the play as any of them; Henry Crawford acted well, and it was a pleasure to her to creep into the theatre, and attend the rehearsal of the first act, in spite of the feelings it excited in some speeches for Maria. Maria, she also thought, acted well, too well; and after the first rehearsal or two, Fanny began to be their only audience, and sometimes as prompter, sometimes as spectator, was often very useful. As far as she could judge, Mr Crawford was considerably the best actor of all; he had more confidence then Edmund, more judgment than Tom, more talent and taste than Mr Yates. She did not like him as a man, but she must admit him to be the best actor, and on this point there were not many who differed from her. Mr Yates, indeed, exclaimed against his tameness and insipidity; and the day came at last when Mr Rushworth turned to her with a black look and said: 'Do you think there is any thing so very fine in all this? For the life and soul of me, I cannot admire him; and between ourselves, to see such an undersized, little, mean-looking man, set up for a fine actor, is very ridiculous in my opinion.'

From this moment there was a return of his former jealousy, which Maria, from increasing hopes of Crawford, was at little pains to remove, and the chances of Mr Rushworth's ever attaining to the knowledge of his two-and-forty speeches became much less. As to his ever making any thing *tolerable* of them, nobody had the smallest idea of that except his mother; *she*, indeed, regretted that his part was not more considerable, and deferred coming over to Mansfield till they were forward enough in their rehearsal to comprehend all his scenes; but the others aspired at nothing beyond his remembering the catch-word, and the first line of his speech, and being able to follow the prompter through the rest. Fanny, in her pity and kindheartedness, was at great pains to teach him how to learn, giving him all the helps and directions in her power, trying to make an artificial memory for him, and learning every word of his part herself, but without being much the forwarder.

Many uncomfortable, anxious, apprehensive feelings she certainly had; but with all these, and other claims on her time and attention, she was as far from finding herself without employment or utility amongst them, as without a companion in uneasiness; quite as far from having no demand on her leisure as on her compassion. The gloom of her first anticipations was proved to have been unfounded. She was occasionally useful to all; she was perhaps as much at peace as any.

There was a great deal of needlework to be done, moreover, in which her help was wanted; and that Mrs Norris thought her quite as well off as the rest was evident by the manner in which she claimed it: 'Come, Fanny,' she cried, 'these are fine times for you, but you must not be always walking from one room to the other, and doing the lookings-on at your ease, in this way; I want you here. I have been slaving myself till I can hardly stand, to contrive Mr Rushworth's cloak without sending for any more satin; and now I think you may give me your help in putting it together. There are but three seams, you may do them in a trice. It would be lucky for me if I had nothing but the executive part to do. *You* are best off, I can tell you; but if nobody did more than *you*, we should not get on very fast.'

Fanny took the work very quietly, without attempting any defence; but her kinder Aunt Bertram observed on her behalf:

'One cannot wonder, sister, that Fanny *should* be delighted; it is all new to her, you know; you and I used to be very fond of a play ourselves, and so am I still; and as soon as I am a little more at leisure, *I* mean to look in at their rehearsals too. What is the play about, Fanny, you have never told me?'

'Oh! sister, pray do not ask her now; for Fanny is not one of those who can talk and work at the same time. It is about lovers' vows.'

'I believe,' said Fanny to her Aunt Bertram, 'there will be three acts rehearsed to-morrow evening, and that will give you an opportunity of seeing all the actors at once.'

'You had better stay till the curtain is hung,' interposed Mrs Norris; 'the curtain will be hung in a day or two – there is very little sense in a play without a curtain – and I am much mistaken if you do not find it drawn up into very handsome festoons.'

Lady Bertram seemed quite resigned to waiting. Fanny did not share her aunt's composure; she thought of the morrow a great deal, for if the three acts were rehearsed, Edmund and Miss Crawford would then be acting together for the first time; the third act would bring a scene between them which interested her most particularly, and which she was longing and dreading to see how they would perform. The whole subject of it was love – a marriage of love was to be described by the gentleman, and very little short of a declaration of love be made by the lady.

She had read, and read the scene again with many painful, many wondering emotions, and looked forward to their representation of it as a circumstance almost too interesting. She did not *believe* they had yet rehearsed it, even in private.

The morrow came, the plan for the evening continued, and Fanny's consideration of it did not become less agitated. She worked very diligently under her aunt's directions, but her diligence and her silence concealed a very absent, anxious mind; and about noon she made her escape with her work to the East Room, that she might have no concern in another, and, as she deemed it, most unnecessary rehearsal of the first act, which Henry Crawford was just proposing, desirous at once of having her time to herself, and of avoiding the sight of Mr Rushworth. A glimpse, as she passed through the hall, of the two ladies walking up from the Parsonage, made no change in her wish of retreat, and she worked and meditated in the East Room, undisturbed, for a quarter of an hour, when a gentle tap at the door was followed by the entrance of Miss Crawford.

'Am I right? yes; this is the East Room. My dear Miss Price, I beg your pardon, but I have made my way to you on purpose to entreat your help.'

Fanny, quite surprised, endeavoured to show herself mistress of the room by her civilities, and looked at the bright bars of her empty grate with concern.

'Thank you; I am quite warm, very warm. Allow me to stay here a little while, and do have the goodness to hear my third act. I have brought my book, and if you would but rehearse it with me, I should be so obliged! I came here to-day intending to rehearse it with Edmund – by ourselves – against the evening, but he is not in the way; and if he *were*, I do not think I could go through it with *him*, till I have hardened myself a little; for really there *is* a speech or two— You will be so good, won't you?'

Fanny was most civil in her assurances, though she could not give them in a very steady voice.

'Have you ever happened to look at the part I mean?' continued Miss Crawford, opening her book. 'Here it is. I did not think much of it at first – but, upon my word— There, look at *that* speech, and *that*, and *that*. How am I ever to look him in the face and say such things? Could you do it? But then he is your cousin, which makes all the difference. You must rehearse it with me, that I may fancy *you* him, and get on by degrees. You *have* a look of *his* sometimes.'

'Have I? I will do my best with the greatest readiness; but I must *read* the part, for I can *say* very little of it.'

'None of it, I suppose. You are to have the book, of course. Now for it. We must have two chairs at hand for you to bring forward to the front of the stage. There – very good schoolroom chairs, not made for a theatre, I dare say; much more fitted for little girls to sit and kick their feet against when they are learning a lesson. What would your governess and your uncle say to see them used for such a purpose? Could Sir Thomas look in upon us just now, he would bless himself, for we are rehearsing all over the house. Yates is storming away in the dining-room. I heard him as I came upstairs, and the theatre is engaged of course by those indefatigable rehearsers, Agatha and Frederick. If *they* are not perfect, I *shall* be surprised. By the bye, I looked in upon them five minutes ago, and it happened to be exactly at one of the times when they were trying *not* to embrace, and Mr Rushworth was with me. I thought he began to look a little queer, so I turned it off as well as I could, by whispering to him, "We shall have an excellent Agatha, there is something so *maternal* in her manner, so completely *maternal* in her voice and countenance." Was not that well done of me? He brightened up directly. Now for my soliloquy.'

She began, and Fanny joined in with all the modest feeling which the idea of representing Edmund was so strongly calculated to inspire; but with looks and voice so truly feminine, as to be no very good picture of a man. With such an Anhalt, however, Miss Crawford had courage enough; and they had got through half the scene, when a tap at the door brought a pause, and the entrance of Edmund, the next moment, suspended it all.

Surprise, consciousness, and pleasure appeared in each of the three on this unexpected meeting; and as Edmund was come on the very same business that had brought Miss Crawford, consciousness and pleasure were likely to be more than momentary in *them*. He, too, had his book, and was seeking Fanny, to ask her to rehearse with him, and help him to prepare for the evening, without knowing Miss Crawford to be in the house; and great was the joy and animation of being thus thrown together, of comparing schemes, and sympathising in praise of Fanny's kind offices.

She could not equal them in their warmth. *Her* spirits sank under the glow of theirs, and she felt herself becoming too nearly nothing to both, to have any comfort in having been sought by either. They must now rehearse together. Edmund proposed, urged, entreated it, till the lady, not very unwilling at first, could refuse no longer, and Fanny was wanted only to prompt and observe them. She was invested, indeed, with the office of judge and critic, and earnestly desired to exercise it and tell them all their faults; but from doing so every feeling within her shrank – she could not, would not, dared not, attempt it; had she been otherwise qualified for criticism, her conscience must have restrained her from venturing at disapprobation. She believed herself to feel too much of it in the aggregate for honesty or safety in particulars. To prompt them must be enough for her; and it was sometimes *more* than enough; for she could not always pay attention to the book. In watching them she forgot herself; and, agitated by the increasing spirit of Edmund's manner, had once closed the page and turned away exactly as he wanted help. It was imputed to very reasonable weariness, and she was thanked and pitied; but she deserved their pity more than she hoped they would ever surmise. At last the scene was over, and Fanny forced herself to add her praise to the compliments each was giving the other; and when again alone, and able to recall the whole, she was inclined to believe their performance would indeed, have such nature and feeling in it as must ensure their credit, and make it a very suffering exhibition to herself. Whatever might be its effect, however, she must stand the brunt of it again that very day.

The first regular rehearsal of the three first acts was certainly to take place in the evening: Mrs Grant and the Crawfords were engaged to return for that purpose as soon as they could after dinner; and every one concerned was looking forward with eagerness. There seemed a general diffusion of cheerfulness on the occasion. Tom was enjoying such an advance towards the end; Edmund was in spirits from the morning's rehearsal, and little vexations seemed everywhere smoothed away. All were alert and impatient; the ladies moved soon, the gentlemen soon followed them, and with the exception of Lady Bertram, Mrs Norris and Julia, everybody was in the theatre at an early hour; and, having lighted it up as well as its unfinished state admitted, were waiting only the arrival of Mrs Grant and the Crawfords to begin.

They did not wait long for the Crawfords, but there was no Mrs Grant. She could not come. Dr Grant, professing an indisposition, for which he had little credit with his fair sister-in-law, could not spare his wife.

'Dr Grant is ill,' said she, with mock solemnity. 'He has been ill ever since he did not eat any of the pheasant to-day. He fancied it tough, sent away his plate, and has been suffering ever since.'

Here was disappointment! Mrs Grant's non-attendance was sad indeed. Her pleasant manners and cheerful conformity made her always valuable amongst them; but *now* she was absolutely necessary. They could not act, they could not rehearse with any satisfaction without her. The comfort of the whole evening was destroyed. What was to be done? Tom, as Cottager,

'My father is come!'

was in despair. After a pause of perplexity, some eyes began to be turned towards Fanny, and a voice or two to say, 'If Miss Price would be so good as to *read* the part.' She was immediately surrounded by supplications, everybody asked it, even Edmund said, 'Do, Fanny, if it is not *very* disagreeable to you.'

But Fanny still hung back. She could not endure the idea of it. Why was not Miss Crawford to be applied to as well? Or why had not she rather gone to her own room, as she had felt to be safest, instead of attending the rehearsal at all? She had known it would irritate and distress her; she had known it her duty to keep away. She was properly punished.

'You have only to *read* the part,' said Henry Crawford, with renewed entreaty.

'And I do believe she can say every word of it,' added Maria, 'for she could put Mrs Grant right the other day in twenty places. Fanny, I am sure you know the part.'

Fanny could not say she did *not*; and as they all persevered, as Edmund repeated his wish, and with a look of even fond dependence on her good nature, she must yield. She would do her best. Everybody was satisfied; and she was left to the tremors of a most palpitating heart, while the others prepared to begin.

They *did* begin; and being too much engaged in their own noise to be struck by an unusual noise in the other part of the house, had proceeded some way, when the door of the room was thrown open, and Julia, appearing at it, with a face all aghast, exclaimed, 'My father is come! He is in the hall at this moment.'

Persuasion

Eight years ago Anne Elliot rejected Captain Frederick Wentworth. Despite her love for him, she was swayed by her snobbish father and her well-meaning friend Lady Russell. Anne's youthful beauty has now faded, and she is generally ignored by her family. Forced by debt, her father lets his entailed estate, Kellynch to Admiral Croft, and goes to Bath with his elder daughter Elizabeth and her widowed friend, Mrs Clay. Anne gladly stays behind with her sister Mary, wife of the local squire, Mr Musgrove. Captain Wentworth is related to the Admiral and reappears, by now a well-to-do man. He seems indifferent to Anne and flirts with Mr Musgrove's spirited young sister, Louisa. On an outing to Lyme Louisa suffers a bad fall, and Anne witnesses Captain Wentworth's obvious distress. Before she leaves Lyme, a stranger stares admiringly at her. The stranger is her father's heir, Mr Elliot. Shortly after leaving Lyme, Anne travels to Bath with Lady Russell.

Every body has their taste in noises as well as in other matters; and sounds are quite innoxious, or most distressing, by their sort rather than their quantity. When Lady Russell, not long afterwards, was entering Bath on a wet afternoon, and driving through the long course of streets from the Old Bridge to Camden-place, amidst the dash of other carriages, the heavy rumble of carts and drays, the bawling of newsmen, muffin-men and milk-men, and the ceaseless clink of pattens, she made no complaint. No, these were noises which belonged to the winter pleasures; her spirits rose under their influence; and, like Mrs Musgrove, she was feeling, though not saying, that, after being long in the country, nothing could be so good for her as a little quiet cheerfulness.

Anne did not share these feelings. She persisted in a very determined, though very silent, disinclination for Bath; caught the first dim view of the extensive buildings, smoking in rain, without any wish of seeing them better; felt their progress through the streets to be, however disagreeable, yet too rapid; for who would be glad to see her when she arrived? And looked back, with fond regret, to the bustles of Uppercross and the seclusion of Kellynch.

Elizabeth's last letter had communicated a piece of news of some interest. Mr Elliot was in Bath. He had called in Camden-place; had called a second time, a third; had been pointedly attentive: if Elizabeth and her father did not deceive themselves, had been taking as much pains to seek the acquaintance, and proclaim the value of the connection, as he had formerly taken pains to shew neglect. This was very wonderful, if it were true; and

Lady Russell was in a state of very agreeable curiosity and perplexity about Mr Elliot, already recanting the sentiment she had so lately expressed to Mary, of his being 'a man whom she had no wish to see.' She had a great wish to see him. If he really sought to reconcile himself like a dutiful branch, he must be forgiven for having dismembered himself from the paternal tree.

Anne was not animated to an equal pitch by the circumstance; but she felt that she would rather see Mr Elliot again than not, which was more than she could say for many other persons in Bath.

She was put down in Camden-place; and Lady Russell then drove to her own lodgings, in Rivers-street.

CHAPTER FIFTEEN

SIR WALTER HAD TAKEN a very good house in Camden-place, a lofty, dignified situation, such as becomes a man of consequence; and both he and Elizabeth were settled there, much to their satisfaction.

Anne entered it with a sinking heart, anticipating an imprisonment of many months, and anxiously saying to herself, 'Oh! when shall I leave you again?' A degree of unexpected cordiality, however, in the welcome she received, did her good. Her father and sister were glad to see her, for the sake of shewing her the house and furniture, and met her with kindness. Her making a fourth, when they sat down to dinner, was noticed as an advantage.

Mrs Clay was very pleasant, and very smiling; but her courtesies and smiles were more a matter of course. Anne had always felt that she would pretend what was proper on her arrival; but the complaisance of the others was unlooked for. They were evidently in excellent spirits, and she was soon to listen to the causes. They had no inclination to listen to her. After laying out for some compliments of being deeply regretted in their old neighbourhood, which Anne could not pay, they had only a few faint enquiries to make, before the talk must be all their own. Uppercross excited no interest, Kellynch very little, it was all Bath.

They had the pleasure of assuring her that Bath more than answered their expectations in every respect. Their house was undoubtedly the best in Camden-place; their drawing-rooms had many decided advantages over all the others which they had either seen or heard of; and the superiority was not less in the style of the fitting-up, or the taste of the furniture. Their acquaintance was exceedingly sought after. Every body was wanting to visit them. They had drawn back from many introductions, and still were perpetually having cards left by people of whom they knew nothing.

Here were funds of enjoyment! Could Anne wonder that her father and sister were happy? She might not wonder, but she must sigh that her father should feel no degradation in his change; should see nothing to regret in the duties and dignity of the resident land-holder; should find so much to be vain of in the littleness of a town; and she must sigh, and smile, and wonder too, as Elizabeth threw open the folding-doors, and walked with exultation from one drawing-room to the other, boasting of their space, at the possibility of that woman, who had been mistress of Kellynch Hall, finding extent to be proud of between two walls, perhaps thirty feet asunder.

But this was not all which they had to make them happy. They had Mr Elliot, too. Anne had a great deal to hear of Mr Elliot. He was not only pardoned, they were delighted with him. He had been in Bath about a fortnight; (he had passed through Bath in November, in his way to London, when the intelligence of Sir Walter's being settled there had of course reached him, though only twenty-four hours in the place, but he had not been able to avail himself of it); but he had now been a fortnight in Bath, and his first object, on arriving, had been to leave his card in Camden-place, following it up by such assiduous endeavours to meet, and, when they did meet, by such great openness of conduct, such readiness to apologise for the past, such solicitude to be received as a relation again, that their former good understanding was completely re-established.

They had not a fault to find in him. He had explained away all the appearance of neglect on his own side. It had originated in misapprehension entirely. He had never had an idea of throwing himself off; he had feared that he was thrown off, but knew not why; and delicacy had kept him silent. Upon the hint of having spoken disrespectfully or carelessly of the family, and the family honours, he was quite indignant. He, who had ever boasted of being an Elliot, and whose feelings, as to connection, were only too strict to suit the unfeudal tone of the present day! He was astonished, indeed! But his character and general conduct must refute it. He could refer Sir Walter to all who knew him; and, certainly, the pains he had been taking on this, the first opportunity of reconciliation, to be restored to the footing of a relation and heir-presumptive, was a strong proof of his opinions on the subject.

The circumstances of his marriage too were found to admit of much extenuation. This was an article not to be entered on by himself; but a very intimate friend of his, a Colonel Wallis, a highly respectable man, perfectly the gentleman, (and not an ill-looking man, Sir Walter added) who was living in very good style in Marlborough Buildings, and had, at his own particular request, been admitted to their acquaintance through Mr Elliot, had mentioned one or two things relative to the marriage, which made a material difference in the discredit of it.

Colonel Wallis had known Mr Elliot long, had been well acquainted also with his wife, had perfectly understood the whole story. She was certainly not a woman of family, but well educated, accomplished, rich, and excessively in love with his friend. There had been the charm. She had sought him. Without that attraction, not all her money would have tempted Elliot, and Sir Walter was, moreover, assured of her having been a very fine woman. Here was a great deal to soften the business. A very fine woman, with a large fortune, in love with him! Sir Walter seemed to admit it as complete apology, and though Elizabeth could not see the circumstance in quite so favourable a light, she allowed it be a great extenuation.

Mr Elliot had called repeatedly, had dined with them once, evidently delighted by the distinction of being asked, for they gave no dinners in general; delighted, in short, by every proof of cousinly notice, and placing his whole happiness in being on intimate terms in Camden-place.

Anne listened, but without quite understanding it. Allowances, large allowances, she knew, must be made for the ideas of those who spoke. She heard it all under embellishment. All that sounded extravagant or irrational in the progress of the reconciliation might have no origin but in the language of the relators. Still, however, she had the sensation of there being something more than immediately appeared, in Mr Elliot's wishing, after an interval of so many years, to be well received by them. In a worldly view, he had nothing to gain by being on terms with Sir Walter, nothing to risk by a state of variance. In all probability he was already the richer of the two, and the Kellynch estate would as surely be his hereafter as the title. A sensible man! and he had looked like a *very* sensible man, why should it be an object to him? She could only offer one solution; it was, perhaps, for Elizabeth's sake. There might really have been a liking formerly, though convenience and accident had drawn him a different way, and now that he could afford to please himself, he might mean to pay his addresses to her. Elizabeth was certainly very handsome, with well-bred, elegant manners, and her character might never have been penetrated by Mr Elliot, knowing her but in public, and when very young himself. How her temper and understanding might bear the investigation of his present keener time of life was another concern, and rather a fearful one. Most earnestly did she wish that he might not be too nice, or too observant, if Elizabeth were his object; and that Elizabeth was disposed to believe herself so, and that her friend Mrs Clay was encouraging the idea, seemed apparent by a glance or two between them, while Mr Elliot's frequent visits were talked of.

Anne mentioned the glimpses she had had of him at Lyme, but without being much attended to. 'Oh! yes, perhaps, it had been Mr Elliot. They did not know. It might be him, perhaps.' They could not listen to her description of him. They were discribing him themselves; Sir Walter especially. He did justice to his very gentlemanlike appearance, his air of elegance and fashion, his good shaped face, his sensible eye, but, at the same time, 'must lament his being very much under-hung, a defect which time seemed to have increased; nor could he pretend to say that ten years had not altered almost every feature for the worse. Mr Elliot appeared to think that he (Sir Walter) was looking exactly as he had done when they last parted;' but Sir Walter had 'not been able to return the compliment entirely, which had embarrassed him. He did not mean to complain, however. Mr Elliot was better to look at than most men, and he had no objection to being seen with him any where.'

Mr Elliot, and his friends in Marlborough Buildings, were talked of the whole evening. 'Colonel Wallis had been so impatient to be introduced to them! and Mr Elliot so anxious that he should!' And there was a Mrs Wallis, at present only known to them by description, as she was in daily expectation of her confinement; but Mr Elliot spoke of her as 'a most charming woman, quite worthy of being known in Camden-place,' and as soon as she recovered, they were to be acquainted. Sir Walter thought much of Mrs Wallis; she was said to be an excessively pretty woman, beautiful. 'He longed to see her. He hoped she might make some amends for the many very plain faces he was continually passing in the streets. The worst of Bath was, the number of its plain women. He did not mean to say that there were no pretty women, but the number of the plain was out of all proportion. He had frequently observed, as he walked, that one handsome face would be followed by thirty, or five and thirty frights; and once, as he had stood in a shop in Bond-street he had counted eighty-seven women go by, one after another, without there being a tolerable face among them. It had been a frosty morning, to be sure, a sharp frost, which hardly one woman in a thousand could stand the test of. But still, there certainly were a dreadful multitude of ugly women in Bath; and as for the men! they were infinitely worse. Such scare-crows as the streets were full of! It was evident how little the women were used to the sight of any thing tolerable, by the effect which a man of decent appearance produced. He had never walked any where arm in arm with Colonel Wallis, (who was a fine military figure, though sandy-haired) without observing that every woman's eye was upon him; every woman's eye was sure to be upon Colonel Wallis.' Modest Sir Walter! He was not allowed to escape, however. His daughter and Mrs Clay united in hinting that Colonel Wallis's companion might have as good a figure as Colonel Wallis, and certainly was not sandy-haired.

'How is Mary looking?' said Sir Walter, in the height of his good humour, 'The last time I saw her, she had a red nose, but I hope that may not happen every day.'

'Oh! no, that must have been quite accidental. In general she has been in very good health, and very good looks since Michaelmas.'

'If I thought it would not tempt her to go out in sharp winds, and grow coarse, I would send her a new hat and pelisse.'

Anne was considering whether she should venture to suggest that a gown, or a cap, would not be liable to any such misuse, when a knock at the

Arm-in-arm with Colonel Wallis

door suspended every thing. 'A knock at the door! and so late! It was ten o'clock. Could it be Mr Elliot? They knew he was to dine in Lansdown Crescent. It was possible that he might stop in his way home, to ask them how they did. They could think of no one else. Mrs Clay decidedly thought it Mr Elliot's knock.' Mrs Clay was right. With all the state which a butler and foot-boy could give, Mr Elliot was ushered into the room.

It was the same, the very same man, with no difference but of dress. Anne drew a little back, while the others received his compliments, and her sister his apologies for calling at so unusual an hour, but 'he could not be so near without wishing to know that neither she nor her friend had taken cold the day before, &c. &c.' which was all as politely done, and as politely taken as possible, but her part must follow then. Sir Walter talked of his youngest daughter; 'Mr Elliot must give him leave to present him to his youngest daughter' – (there was no occasion for remembering Mary) and Anne, smiling and blushing, very becomingly shewed to Mr Elliot the pretty features which he had by no means forgotten, and instantly saw, with amusement at his little start of surprise, that he had not been at all aware of who she was. He looked completely astonished, but not more astonished than pleased; his eyes brightened, and with the most perfect alacrity he welcomed the relationship, alluded to the past, and entreated to be received as an acquaintance already. He was quite as good-looking as he had appeared at Lyme, his countenance improved by speaking, and his manners were so exactly what they ought to be, so polished, so easy, so particularly agreeable, that she could compare them in excellence to only one person's manners. They were not the same, but they were, perhaps, equally good.

He sat down with them, and improved their conversation very much. There could be no doubt of his being a sensible man. Ten minutes were enough to certify that. His tone, his expressions, his choice of subject, his knowing where to stop, – it was all the operation of a sensible, discerning mind. As soon as he could, he began to talk to her of Lyme, wanting to compare opinions respecting the place, but especially wanting to speak of the circumstance of their happening to be guests in the same inn at the same time, to give his own route, understand something of hers, and regret that he should have lost such an opportunity of paying his respects to her. She gave him a short account of her party, and business at Lyme. His regret increased as he listened. He had spent his whole solitary evening in the room adjoining theirs; had heard voices – mirth continually; thought they must be a most delightful set of people – longed to be with them; but certainly without the smallest suspicion of his possessing the shadow of a right to introduce himself. If he had but asked who the party were! The name of Musgrove would have told him enough. 'Well, it would serve to cure him of an absurd practice of never asking a question at an inn, which he had adopted, when quite a young man, on the principle of its being very ungenteel to be curious.

'The notions of a young man of one or two and twenty,' said he, 'as to what is necessary in manners to make him quite the thing, are more absurd, I believe, than those of any other set of beings in the world. The folly of the means they often employ is only to be equalled by the folly of what they have in view.'

But he must not be addressing his reflections to Anne alone; he knew it; he was soon diffused again among the others, and it was only at intervals that he could return to Lyme.

His enquiries, however, produced at length an account of the scene she had been engaged in there, soon after his leaving the place. Having alluded to 'an accident,' he must hear the whole. When he questioned, Sir Walter and Elizabeth began to question also; but the difference in their manner of doing it could not be unfelt. She could only compare Mr Elliot to Lady Russell, in the wish of really comprehending what had passed, and in the degree of concern for what she must have suffered in witnessing it.

He staid an hour with them. The elegant little clock on the mantelpiece had struck 'eleven with its silver sounds,' and the watchman was beginning to be heard at a distance telling the same tale, before Mr Elliot or any of them seemed to feel that he had been there long.

Anne could not have supposed it possible that her first evening in Camden-place could have passed so well!

CHAPTER SIXTEEN

THERE WAS ONE POINT WHICH Anne, on returning to her family, would have been more thankful to ascertain, even than Mr Elliot's being in love with Elizabeth, which was, her father's not being in love with Mrs Clay; and she was very far from easy about it, when she had been at home a few hours. On going down to breakfast the next morning, she found there had just been a decent pretence on the lady's side of meaning to leave them. She could imagine Mrs Clay to have said, that 'now Miss Anne was come, she could not suppose herself at all wanted;' for Elizabeth was replying, in a sort of whisper, 'That must not be any reason, indeed. I assure you I feel it none. She is nothing to me, compared with you;' and she was in full time to hear her father say, 'My dear Madam, this must not be. As yet, you have seen nothing of Bath. You have been here only to be useful. You must not run away from us now. You must stay to be acquainted with Mrs Wallis, the

beautiful Mrs Wallis. To your fine mind, I well know the sight of beauty is a
real gratification.'

He spoke and looked so much in earnest, that Anne was not surprised to
see Mrs Clay stealing a glance at Elizabeth and herself. Her countenance,
perhaps, might express some watchfulness; but the praise of the fine mind
did not appear to excite a thought in her sister. The lady could not but yield
to such joint entreaties, and promise to stay.

In the course of the same morning, Anne and her father chancing to be
alone together, he began to compliment her on her improved looks; he
thought her 'less thin in her person, in her cheeks; her skin, her complexion,
greatly improved – clearer, fresher. Had she been using any thing in
particular!' 'No, nothing.' 'Merely Gowland,' he supposed. 'No, nothing at
all.' 'Ha! he was surprised at that;' and added, 'Certainly you cannot do
better than continue as you are; you cannot be better than well; or I should
recommend Gowland, the constant use of Gowland, during the spring
months. Mrs Clay has been using it at my recommendation, and you see
what it has done for her. You see how it has carried away her freckles.'

If Elizabeth could but have heard this! Such personal praise might have
struck her, especially as it did not appear to Anne that the freckles were at all
lessened. But every thing must take its chance. The evil of the marriage
would be much diminished, if Elizabeth were also to marry. As for herself,
she might always command a home with Lady Russell.

Lady Russell's composed mind and polite manners were put to some trial
on this point, in her intercourse in Camden-place. The sight of Mrs Clay in
such favour, and of Anne so overlooked, was a perpetual provocation to her
there; and vexed her as much when she was away, as a person in Bath who
drinks the water, gets all the new publications, and has a very large
acquaintance, has time to be vexed.

As Mr Elliot became known to her, she grew more charitable, or more
indifferent, towards the others. His manners were an immediate recommendation; and on conversing with him she found the solid so fully
supporting the superficial, that she was at first, as she told Anne, almost
ready to exclaim, 'Can this be Mr Elliot?' and could not seriously picture to
herself a more agreeable or estimable man. Every thing united in him; good
understanding, correct opinions, knowledge of the world, and a warm
heart. He had strong feelings of family-attachment and family-honour,
without pride or weakness; he lived with the liberality of a man of
fortune, without display; he judged for himself in every thing essential,
without defying public opinion in any point of worldly decorum. He was
steady, observant, moderate, candid; never run away with by spirits or by
selfishness, which fancied itself strong feeling; and yet, with a sensibility to
what was amiable and lovely, and a value for all the felicities of domestic

He began to compliment her on her improved looks

life, which characters of fancied enthusiasm and violent agitation seldom really possess. She was sure that he had not been happy in marriage. Colonel Wallis said it, and Lady Russell saw it; but it had been no unhappiness to sour his mind, nor (she began pretty soon to suspect) to prevent his thinking of a second choice. Her satisfaction in Mr Elliot outweighed all the plague of Mrs Clay.

It was now some years since Anne had begun to learn that she and her excellent friend could sometimes think differently; and it did not surprise her, therefore, that Lady Russell should see nothing suspicious or inconsistent, nothing to require more motives than appeared, in Mr Elliot's great desire of a reconciliation. In Lady Russell's view, it was perfectly natural that Mr Elliot, at a mature time of life, should feel it a most desirable object, and what would very generally recommend him, among all sensible people, to be on good terms with the head of his family; the simplest process in the world of time upon a head naturally clear, and only erring in the heyday of youth. Anne presumed, however, still to smile about it; and at last to mention 'Elizabeth.' Lady Russell listened, and looked, and made only this cautious reply: 'Elizabeth! Very well. Time will explain.'

It was a reference to the future, which Anne, after a little observation, felt she must submit to. She could determine nothing at present. In that house Elizabeth must be first; and she was in the habit of such general observance as 'Miss Elliot,' that any particularity of attention seemed almost impossible. Mr Elliot, too, it must be remembered, had not been a widower seven months. A little delay on his side might be very excusable. In fact, Anne could never see the crape round his hat, without fearing that she was the inexcusable one, in attributing to him such imaginations; for though his marriage had not been very happy, still it had existed so many years that she could not comprehend a very rapid recovery from the awful impression of its being dissolved.

However it might end, he was without any question their pleasantest acquaintance in Bath; she saw nobody equal to him; and it was a great indulgence now and then to talk to him about Lyme, which he seemed to have as lively a wish to see again, and to see more of, as herself. They went through the particulars of their first meeting a great many times. He gave her to understand that he had looked at her with some earnestness. She knew it well; and she remembered another person's look also.

They did not always think alike. His value for rank and connexion she perceived to be greater than hers. It was not merely complaisance, it must be a liking to the cause, which made him enter warmly into her father and sister's solicitudes on a subject which she thought unworthy to excite them. The Bath paper one morning announced the arrival of the Dowager Viscountess Dalrymple, and her daughter, the Honourable Miss Carteret; and all the comfort of No. – , Camden-place, was swept away for many days; for the Dalrymples (in Anne's opinion, most unfortunately) were cousins of the Elliots; and the agony was, how to introduce themselves properly.

Anne had never seen her father and sister before in contact with nobility, and she must acknowledge herself disappointed. She had hoped better things from their high ideas of their own situation in life, and was reduced to form a wish which she had never foreseen – a wish that they had more pride; for 'our cousins Lady Dalrymple and Miss Carteret;' 'our cousins, the Dalrymples,' sounded in her ears all day long.

Sir Walter had once been in company with the late Viscount, but had never seen any of the rest of the family, and the difficulties of the case arose from there having been a suspension of all intercourse by letters of ceremony, ever since the death of that said late Viscount, when, in consequence of a dangerous illness of Sir Walter's at the same time, there had been an unlucky omission at Kellynch. No letter of condolence had been sent to Ireland. The neglect had been visited on the head of the sinner, for when poor Lady Elliot died herself, no letter of condolence was received at Kellynch, and, consequently, there was but too much reason to apprehend that the Dalrymples considered the relationship as closed. How to have this anxious business set to rights, and be admitted as cousins again, was the question; and it was a question which, in a more rational manner, neither Lady Russell nor Mr Elliot thought unimportant. 'Family connexions were always worth preserving, good company always worth seeking; Lady Dalrymple had taken a house, for three months, in Laura-place, and would be living in style. She had been at Bath the year before, and Lady Russell had heard her spoken of as a charming woman. It was very desirable that the connexion should be renewed, if it could be done, without any compromise of propriety on the side of the Elliots.'

Sir Walter, however, would choose his own means, and at last wrote a very fine letter of ample explanation, regret and entreaty, to his right honourable cousin. Neither Lady Russell nor Mr Elliot could admire the letter; but it did all that was wanted, in bringing three lines of scrawl from the Dowager Viscountess. 'She was very much honoured, and should be happy in their acquaintance.' The toils of the business were over, the sweets began. They visited in Laura-place, they had the cards of Dowager Viscountess Dalrymple, and the Hon. Miss Carteret, to be arranged wherever they might be most visible; and 'Our cousins in Laura-place,' – 'Our cousin, Lady Dalrymple and Miss Carteret,' were talked of to every body.

Anne was ashamed. Had Lady Dalrymple and her daughter even been very agreeable, she would still have been ashamed of the agitation they created, but they were nothing. There was no superiority of manner, accomplishment, or understanding. Lady Dalrymple had acquired the name of 'a charming woman,' because she had a smile and a civil answer for every body. Miss Carteret, with still less to say, was so plain and so awkward, that she would never have been tolerated in Camden-place but for her birth.

Lady Russell confessed that she had expected something better; but yet 'it was an acquaintance worth having,' and when Anne ventured to speak her opinion of them to Mr Elliot, he agreed to their being nothing in themselves, but still maintained that as a family connexion, as good company, as those who would collect good company around them, they had their value. Anne smiled and said,

'My idea of good company, Mr Elliot, is the company of clever, well-informed people, who have a great deal of conversation; that is what I call good company.'

'You are mistaken,' said he gently, 'that is not good company, that is the best. Good company requires only birth, education and manners, and with regard to education is not very nice. Birth and good manners are essential; but a little learning is by no means a dangerous thing in good company, on the contrary, it will do very well. My cousin, Anne, shakes her head. She is not satisfied. She is fastidious. My dear cousin, (sitting down by her) you have a better right to be fastidious than almost any other woman I know; but will it answer? Will it make you happy? Will it not be wiser to accept the society of these good ladies in Laura-place, and enjoy all the advantages of the connexion as far as possible? You may depend upon it, that they will move in the first set in Bath this winter, and as rank is rank, your being known to be related to them will have its use in fixing your family (our family let me say) in that degree of consideration which we must all wish for.'

'Yes,' sighed Anne, 'we shall, indeed, be known to be related to them!' – then recollecting herself, and not wishing to be answered, she added, 'I certainly do think there has been by far too much trouble taken to procure the acquaintance. I suppose (smiling) I have more pride than any of you; but I confess it does vex me, that we should be so solicitous to have the relationship acknowledged, which we may be very sure is a matter of perfect indifference to them.'

'Pardon me, dear cousin, you are unjust to your own claims. In London, perhaps, in your present quiet style of living, it might be as you say: but in Bath, Sir Walter Elliot and his family will always be worth knowing, always acceptable as acquaintance.'

'Well,' said Anne, 'I certainly am proud, too proud to enjoy a welcome which depends so entirely upon place.'

'I love your indignation,' said he; 'it is very natural. But here you are in Bath, and the object is to be established here with all the credit and dignity which ought to belong to Sir Walter Elliot. You talk of being proud, I am called proud I know, and I shall not wish to believe myself otherwise, for our pride, if investigated, would have the same object, I have no doubt, though the kind may seem a little different. In one point, I am sure, my dear cousin, (he continued, speaking lower, though there was no one else in the room) in one point, I am sure, we must feel alike. We must feel that every addition to your father's society, among his equals or superiors, may be of use in diverting his thoughts from those who are beneath him.'

He looked, as he spoke, to the seat which Mrs Clay had been lately occupying, a sufficient explanation of what he particularly meant; and though Anne could not believe in their having the same sort of pride, she was pleased with him for not liking Mrs Clay; and her conscience admitted that his wishing to promote her father's getting great acquaintance, was more than excusable in the view of defeating her.

CHAPTER SEVENTEEN

WHILE SIR WALTER AND Elizabeth were assiduously pushing their good fortune in Laura–place, Anne was renewing an acquaintance of a very different description.

She had called on her former governess, and had heard from her of there being an old school–fellow in Bath, who had the two strong claims on her attention, of past kindness and present suffering. Miss Hamilton, now Mrs Smith, had shewn her kindness in one of those periods of her life when it had been most valuable. Anne had gone unhappy to school, grieving for the loss of a mother whom she had dearly loved, feeling her separation from home, and suffering as a girl of fourteen, of strong sensibility and not high spirits, must suffer at such a time; and Miss Hamilton, three years older than herself, but still from the want of near relations and a settled home, remaining another year at school, had been useful and good to her in a way which had considerably lessened her misery, and could never be remembered with indifference.

Miss Hamilton had left school, and married not long afterwards, was said to have married a man of fortune, and this was all that Anne had known of her, till now that their governess's account brought her situation forward in a more decided but very different form.

She was a widow, and poor. Her husband had been extravagant; and at his death, about two years before, had left his affairs dreadfully involved. She had had difficulties of every sort to contend with, and in addition to these distresses, had been afflicted with a severe rheumatic fever, which finally settling in her legs, had made her for the present a cripple. She had come to Bath on that account, and was now in lodgings near the hot-baths, living in a very humble way, unable even to afford herself the comfort of a servant, and of course almost excluded from society.

Their mutual friend answered for the satisfaction which a visit from Miss Elliot would give Mrs Smith, and Anne therefore lost no time in going. She mentioned nothing of what she had heard, or what she intended, at home. It would excite no proper interest there. She only consulted Lady Russell, who entered thoroughly into her sentiments, and was most happy to convey her as near to Mrs Smith's lodgings in Westgate-buildings, as Anne chose to be taken.

The visit was paid, their acquaintance re-established, their interest in each other more than re-kindled. The first ten minutes had its awkwardness and its emotion. Twelve years were gone since they had parted, and each presented a somewhat different person from what the other had imagined. Twelve years had changed Anne from the blooming, silent, unformed girl of fifteen, to the elegant little woman of seven and twenty, with every beauty excepting bloom, and with manners as consciously right as they were invariably gentle; and twelve years had transformed the fine-looking, well-grown Miss Hamilton, in all the glow of health and confidence of superiority, into a poor, infirm, helpless widow, receiving the visit of her former protegée as a favour; but all that was uncomfortable in the meeting had soon passed away, and left only the interesting charm of remembering former partialities and talking over old times.

Anne found in Mrs Smith the good sense and agreeable manners which she had almost ventured to depend on, and a disposition to converse and be cheerful beyond her expectation. Neither the dissipations of the past – and she had lived very much in the world, nor the restrictions of the present; neither sickness nor sorrow seemed to have closed her heart or ruined her spirits.

In the course of a second visit she talked with great openness, and Anne's astonishment increased. She could scarcely imagine a more cheerless situation in itself than Mrs Smith's. She had been very fond of her husband, – she had buried him. She had been used to affluence, – it was gone. She had no child to connect her with life and happiness again, no relations to assist in the arrangement of perplexed affairs, no health to make all the rest supportable. Her accommodations were limited to a noisy parlour, and a dark bed-room behind, with no possibility of moving from one to the other without assistance, which there was only one servant in the house to afford, and she never quitted the house but to be conveyed into the warm bath. – Yet, in spite of all this, Anne had reason to believe that she had moments only of languor and depression, to hours of occupation and enjoyment. How could it be? – She watched – observed – reflected – and finally determined that this was not a case of fortitude or of resignation only. – A submissive spirit might be patient, a strong understanding would supply resolution, but here was something more: here was that elasticity of mind, that disposition to be comforted, that power of turning readily from evil to good, and of finding employment which carried her out of herself, which was from Nature alone. It was the choicest gift of Heaven; and Anne viewed her friend as one of those instances in which, by a merciful appointment, it seems designed to counterbalance almost every other want.

There had been a time, Mrs Smith told her, when her spirits had nearly failed. She could not call herself an invalid now, compared with her state on first reaching Bath. Then, she had indeed been a pitiable object – for she had caught cold on the journey, and had hardly taken possession of her lodgings, before she was again confined to her bed, and suffering under severe and constant pain; and all this among strangers – with the absolute necessity of having a regular nurse, and finances at that moment paricularly unfit to meet any extraordinary expense. She had weathered it however, and could truly say that it had done her good. It had increased her comforts by making her feel herself to be in good hands. She had seen too much of the world, to expect sudden or disinterested attachment any where, but her illness had proved to her that her landlady had a character to preserve, and would not use her ill; and she had been particularly fortunate in her nurse, as a sister of her landlady, a nurse by profession, and who had always a home in that house when unemployed, chanced to be at liberty just in time to attend her. – 'And she,' said Mrs Smith, 'Besides nursing me most admirably, has really proved an invaluable acquaintance. – As soon as I could use my hands, she taught me to knit, which has been a great amusement; and she put me in the way of making these little thread-cases, pin-cushions and card-racks, which you always find me so busy about, and which supply me with the means of doing a little good to one or two very poor families in this neighbourhood. She has a large acquaintance, of course professionally, among those who can afford to buy, and she disposes of my merchandize. She always takes the right time for applying. Every body's heart is open, you know, when they have recently escaped from severe pain, or are recovering the blessing of health, and nurse Rooke thoroughly understands when to speak. She is a shrewd, intelligent, sensible woman. Hers is a line for seeing human nature; and she has a fund of good sense and observation which, as a companion, make her infinitely superior to thousands of those who having only received "the best education in the world," know nothing worth attending to. Call it gossip if you will; but when nurse Rooke has half an hour's leisure to bestow on me, she is sure to have something to relate that is entertaining and profitable, something that makes one know one's species better. One likes to hear what is going on, to be *au fait* as to the newest modes of being trifling and silly. To me, who live so much alone, her conversation I assure you is a treat.'

Anne, far from wishing to cavil at the pleasure, replied, 'I can easily believe it. Women of that class have great opportunities, and if they are intelligent may be well worth listening to. Such varieties of human nature as they are in the habit of witnessing! And it is not merely in its follies, that they are well read; for they see it occasionally under every circumstance that can be most interesting or affecting. What instances must pass before them of ardent, disinterested, self-denying attachment, of heroism, fortitude, patience, resignation – of all the conflicts and all the sacrifices that ennoble us most. A sick chamber may often furnish the worth of volumes.'

'Yes,' said Mrs Smith more doubtingly, 'sometimes it may, though I fear its lessons are not often in the elevated style you describe. Here and there, human nature may be great in times of trial, but generally speaking it is its weakness and not its strength that appears in a sick chamber; it is selfishness and impatience rather than generosity and fortitude, that one hears of. There is so little real friendship in the world! – and unfortunately' (speaking low and tremulously) 'there are so many who forget to think seriously till it is almost too late.'

Anne saw the misery of such feelings. The husband had not been what he ought, and the wife had been led among that part of mankind which made her think worse of the world, than she hoped it deserved. It was but a passing emotion however with Mrs Smith, she shook it off, and soon added in a different tone,

'I do not suppose the situation my friend Mrs Rooke is in at present, will furnish much either to interest or edify me. – She is only nursing Mrs Wallis of Marlborough-buildings – a mere pretty, silly, expensive, fashionable woman, I believe – and of course will have nothing to report but of lace and finery. – I mean to make my profit of Mrs Wallis, however. She has plenty of money, and I intend she shall buy all the high-priced things I have in hand now.'

Anne had called several times on her friend, before the existence of such a person was known in Camden-place. At last, it became necessary to speak of her. – Sir Walter, Elizabeth and Mrs Clay returned one morning from Laura-place, with a sudden invitation from Lady Dalrymple for the same evening, and Anne was already engaged, to spend that evening in Westgate-buildings. She was not sorry for the excuse. They were only asked, she was sure, because Lady Dalrymple being kept at home by a bad cold, was glad to make use of the relationship which had been so pressed on her, – and she declined on her own account with great alacrity – 'She was engaged to spend the evening with an old schoolfellow.' They were not much interested in any thing relative to Anne, but still there were questions enough asked, to make it understood what this old schoolfellow was; and Elizabeth was disdainful, and Sir Walter severe.

'Westgate-buildings!' said he; 'and who is Miss Anne Elliot to be visiting in Westgate-buildings? – A Mrs Smith. A widow Mrs Smith, – and who was her husband? One of the five thousand Mr Smiths whose names are to be met with every where. And what is her attraction? That she is old and sickly. – Upon my word, Miss Anne Elliot, you have the most extraordinary taste! Every thing that revolts other people, low campany, paltry rooms, foul air, disgusting associations are inviting to you. But surely, you may put off this old lady till to-morrow. She is not so near her end, I presume, but that she may hope to see another day. What is her age? Forty?'

'No, Sir, she is not one and thirty; but I do not think I can put off my engagement, because it is the only evening for some time which will at once suit her and myself. – She goes into the warm bath to-morrow, and for the rest of the week you know we are engaged.'

'But what does Lady Russell think of this acquaintance?' asked Elizabeth.

'She sees nothing to blame in it,' replied Anne; 'on the contrary, she approves it; and has generally taken me, when I have called on Mrs Smith.'

'Westgate-buildings must have been rather surprised by the appearance of a carriage drawn up near its pavement!' observed Sir Walter. – 'Sir Henry Russell's widow, indeed, has no honours to distinguish her arms; but still, it is a handsome equipage, and no doubt is well known to convey a Miss Elliot. – A widow Mrs Smith, lodging in Westgate-buildings! – A poor widow, barely able to live, between thirty and forty – a mere Mrs Smith, an every day Mrs Smith, of all people and all names in the world, to be the chosen friend of Miss Anne Elliot, and to be preferred by her, to her own family connexions among the nobility of England and Ireland! Mrs Smith, such a name!'

Mrs Clay, who had been present while all this passed, now thought it advisable to leave the room, and Anne could have said much and did long to say a little, in defence of *her* friend's not very dissimilar claims to theirs, but her sense of personal respect to her father prevented her. She made no reply. She left it to himself to recollect, that Mrs Smith was not the only widow in Bath between thirty and forty, with little to live on, and no sirname of dignity.

Anne kept her appointment; the others kept theirs, and of course she heard the next morning that they had had a delightful evening. – She had been the only one of the set absent; for Sir Walter and Elizabeth had not only been quite at her ladyship's service themselves, but had actually been happy to be employed by her in collecting others, and had been at the trouble of inviting both Lady Russell and Mr Elliot; and Mr Elliot had made a point of leaving Colonel Wallis early, and Lady Russell had fresh arranged all her evening engagements in order to wait on her. Anne had the whole history of all that such an evening could supply, from Lady Russell. To her, its greatest interest must be, in having been very much talked of between her friend and Mr Elliot, in having been wished for, regretted, and at the same time honoured for staying away in such a cause. – Her kind, compassionate visits to this old schoolfellow, sick and reduced, seemed to have quite delighted Mr Elliot. He thought her a most extraordinary young woman; in her temper, manners, mind, a model of female excellence. He could meet even Lady Russell in a discussion of her merits; and Anne could not be given to understand so much by her friend, could not know herself to be so highly rated by a sensible man, without many of those agreeable sensations which her friend meant to create.

Lady Russell was now perfectly decided in her opinion of Mr Elliot. She was as much convinced of his meaning to gain Anne in time, as of his deserving her; and was beginning to calculate the number of weeks which would free him from all the remaining restraints of widowhood, and leave him at liberty to exert his most open powers of pleasing. She would not speak to Anne with half the certainty she felt on the subject, she would venture on little more than hints of what might be hereafter, of a possible attachment on his side, of the desirableness of the alliance, supposing such attachment to be real, and returned. Anne heard her, and made no violent exclamations. She only smiled, blushed, and gently shook her head.

'I am no match-maker, as you well know,' said Lady Russell, 'being much too well aware of the uncertainty of all human events and calculations. I only mean that if Mr Elliot should some time hence pay his addresses to you, and if you should be disposed to accept him, I think there would be every possibility of your being happy together. A most suitable connection every body must consider it – but I think it might be a very happy one.'

'Mr Elliot is an exceedingly agreeable man, and in many respects I think highly of him,' said Anne; 'but we should not suit.'

Lady Russell let this pass, and only said in rejoinder, 'I own that to be able to regard you as the future mistress of Kellynch, the future Lady Elliot – to look forward and see you occupying your dear mother's place, succeeding to all her rights, and all her popularity, as well as to all her virtues, would be the highest possible gratification to me. – You are your mother's self in countenance and disposition; and if I might be allowed to fancy you such as she was, in situation, and name, and home, presiding and blessing in the same spot, and only superior to her in being more highly valued! My dearest Anne, it would give me more delight than is often felt at my time of life!'

Anne was obliged to turn away, to rise, to walk to a distant table, and, leaning there in pretended employment, try to subdue the feeling this picture excited. For a few moments her imagination and her heart were bewitched. The idea of becoming what her mother had been; of having the precious name of 'Lady Elliot' first revived in herself; of being restored to Kellynch, calling it her home again, her home for ever, was a charm which she could not immediately resist. Lady Russell said not another word, willing to leave the matter to its own operation; and believing that, could Mr Elliot at that moment with propriety have spoken for himself! – She believed, in short, what Anne did not believe. The same image of Mr Elliot speaking for himself, brought Anne to composure again. The charm of Kellynch and of 'Lady Elliot' all faded away. She never could accept him. And it was not only that her feelings were still adverse to any man save one; her judgment, on a serious consideration of the possibilities of such a case, was against Mr Elliot.

Though they had now been acquainted a month, she could not be satisfied that she really knew his character. That he was a sensible man, an agreeable man, – that he talked well, professed good opinions, seemed to judge properly and as a man of principle, – this was all clear enough. He certainly knew what was right, nor could she fix on any one article of moral duty evidently transgressed; but yet she would have been afraid to answer for his conduct. She distrusted the past, if not the present. The names which occasionally dropt of former associates, the allusions to former practices and pursuits, suggested suspicions not favourable of what he had been. She saw that there had been bad habits; that Sunday-travelling had been a common thing; that there had been a period of his life (and probably not a short one) when he had been, at least, careless on all serious matters; and, though he might now think very differently, who could answer for the true sentiments of a clever, cautious man, grown old enough to appreciate a fair character? How could it ever be ascertained that his mind was truly cleansed?

Mr Elliot was rational, discreet, polished, – but he was not open. There was never any burst of feeling, any warmth of indignation or delight, at the evil or good of others. This, to Anne, was decided imperfection. Her early impressions were incurable. She prized the frank, the open-hearted, the eager character beyond all others. Warmth and enthusiasm did captivate her still. She felt that she could so much more depend upon the sincerity of those who sometimes looked or said a careless or a hasty thing, than of those whose presence of mind never varied, whose tongue never slipped.

Mr Elliot was too generally agreeable. Various as were the tempers in her father's house, he pleased them all. He endured too well, – stood too well with everybody. He had spoken to her with some degree of openness of Mrs Clay; had appeared completely to see what Mrs Clay was about, and to hold her in contempt; and yet Mrs Clay found him as agreeable as any body.

Lady Russell saw either less or more than her young friend, for she saw nothing to excite distrust. She could not imagine a man more exactly what he ought to be than Mr Elliot; nor did she ever enjoy a sweeter feeling than the hope of seeing him receive the hand of her beloved Anne in Kellynch church, in the course of the following autumn.

CHAPTER EIGHTEEN

IT WAS THE BEGINNING OF February; and Anne, having been a month in Bath, was growing very eager for news from Uppercross and Lyme. She wanted to hear much more than Mary communicated. It was three weeks since she had heard at all. She only knew that Henrietta was at home again; and that Louisa, though considered to be recovering fast, was still at Lyme; and she was thinking of them all very intently one evening, when a thicker letter than usual from Mary was delivered to her, and, to quicken the pleasure and surprise, with Admiral and Mrs Croft's compliments.

The Crofts must be in Bath! A circumstance to interest her. They were people whom her heart turned to very naturally.

'What is this?' cried Sir Walter. 'The Crofts arrived in Bath? The Crofts who rent Kellynch? What have they brought you?'

'A letter from Uppercross Cottage, Sir.'

'Oh! those letters are convenient passports. They secure an introduction. I should have visited Admiral Croft, however, at any rate. I know what is due to my tenant.'

Anne could listen no longer; she could not even have told how the poor Admiral's complexion escaped; her letter engrossed her. It had been begun several days back.

'February 1st,———.

'My dear Anne,

'I make no apology for my silence, because I know how little people think of letters in such a place as Bath. You must be a great deal too happy to care for Uppercross, which, as you well know, affords little to write about. We have had a very dull Christmas; Mr and Mrs Musgrove have not had one dinner-party all the holidays. I do not reckon the Hayters as any body. The holidays, however, are over at last: I believe no children ever had such long ones. I am sure I had not. The house was cleared yesterday, except of the little Harvilles; but you will be surprised to hear they have never gone home. Mrs Harville must be an odd mother to part with them so long. I do not understand it. They are not at all nice children, in my opinion; but Mrs Musgrove seems to like them quite as well, if not better, than her grandchildren. What dreadful weather we have had! It may not be felt in Bath, with your nice pavements; but in the country it is of some consequence. I have not had a creature call on me since the second week in January, except Charles Hayter, who has been calling much oftener than was welcome. Between ourselves, I think it a great

pity Henrietta did not remain at Lyme as long as Louisa; it would have kept her a little out his way. The carriage is gone to-day, to bring Louisa and the Harvilles to-morrow. We are not asked to dine with them, however, till the day after, Mrs Musgrove is so afraid of her being fatigued by the journey, which is not very likely, considering the care that will be taken of her; and it would be much more convenient to me to dine there to-morrow. I am glad you find Mr Elliot so agreeable, and wish I could be acquainted with him too; but I have my usual luck, I am always out of the way when any thing desirable is going on; always the last of my family to be noticed. What an immense time Mrs Clay has been staying with Elizabeth! Does she never mean to go away? But perhaps if she were to leave the room vacant we might now be invited. Let me know what you think of this. I do not expect my children to be asked, you know. I can leave them at the Great House very well, for a month or six weeks. I have this moment heard that the Crofts are going to Bath almost immediately; they think the admiral gouty. Charles heard it quite by chance: they have not had the civility to give me any notice, or offer to take any thing. I do not think they improve at all as neighbours. We see nothing of them, and this is really an instance of gross inattention. Charles joins me in love, and every thing proper.
Yours, affectionately,

'Mary M——.'

'I am sorry to say that I am very far from well; and Jemima has just told me that the butcher says there is a bad sore-throat very much about. I dare say I shall catch it; and my sore-throats, you know, are always worse than anybody's.'

So ended the first part, which had been afterwards put into an envelope, containing nearly as much more.

'I kept my letter open, that I might send you word how Louisa bore her journey, and now I am extremely glad I did, having a great deal to add. In the first place, I had a note from Mrs Croft yesterday, offering to convey any thing to you; a very kind, friendly note indeed, addressed to me, just as it ought; I shall therefore be able to make my letter as long as I like. The admiral does not seem very ill, and I sincerely hope Bath will do him all the good he wants. I shall be truly glad to have them back again. Our neighbourhood cannot spare such a pleasant family. But now for Louisa. I have something to communicate that will astonish you not a little. She and the Harvilles came on Tuesday very safely, and in the evening we went to ask her how she did, when we were rather surprised not to find Captain Benwick of the party, for he had been invited as well as the Harvilles; and what do you think was the reason? Neither more nor less than his being in love with Louisa, and not choosing to

venture to Uppercross till he had had an answer from Mr Musgrove; for it was all settled between him and her before she came away, and he had written to her father by Captain Harville. True, upon my honour. Are not you astonished? I shall be surprised at least if you ever received a hint of it, for I never did. Mrs Musgrove protests solemnly that she knew nothing of the matter. We are all very well pleased, however; for though it is not equal to her marrying Captain Wentworth, it is infinitely better than Charles Hayter; and Mr Musgrove has written his consent, and Captain Benwick is expected to-day. Mrs Harville says her husband feels a good deal on his poor sister's account; but, however, Louisa is a great favourite with both. Indeed Mrs Harville and I quite agree that we love her the better for having nursed her. Charles wonders what Captain Wentworth will say; but if you remember, I never thought him attached to Louisa; I never could see any thing of it. And this is the end , you see, of Captain Benwick's being supposed to be an admirer of yours. How Charles could take such a thing into his head was always incomprehensible to me. I hope he will be more agreeable now. Certainly not a great match for Louisa Musgrove; but a million times better than marrying among the Hayters.'

Mary need not have feared her sister's being in any degree prepared for the news. She had never in her life been more astonished. Captain Benwick and Louisa Musgrove! It was almost too wonderful for belief; and it was with the greatest effort that she could remain in the room, preserve an air of calmness, and answer the common questions of the moment. Happily for her, they were not many. Sir Walter wanted to know whether the Crofts travelled with four horses, and whether they were likely to be situated in such a part of Bath as it might suit Miss Elliot and himself to visit in; but had little curiosity beyond.

'How is Mary?' said Elizabeth; and without waiting for an answer, 'And pray what brings the Crofts to Bath?'

'They come on the Admiral's account. He is thought to be gouty.'

'Gout and decrepitude!' said Sir Walter. 'Poor old gentleman.'

'Have they any acquaintance here?' asked Elizabeth.

'I do not know; but I can hardly suppose that, at Admiral Croft's time of life, and in his profession, he should not have many acquaintance in such a place as this.'

'I suspect,' said Sir Walter coolly, 'that Admiral Croft will be best known in Bath as the renter of Kellynch-hall. Elizabeth, may we venture to present him and his wife in Laura-place?'

'Oh! no, I think not. Situated as we are with Lady Dalrymple, cousins, we ought to be very careful not to embarrass her with acquaintance she might not approve. If we were not related, it would not signify; but as cousins, she would feel scrupulous as to any proposal of ours. We had better leave the

Crofts to find their own level. There are several odd-looking men walking about here, who, I am told, are sailors. The Crofts will associate with them!'

This was Sir Walter and Elizabeth's share of interest in the letter; when Mrs Clay had paid her tribute of more decent attention, in an enquiry after Mrs Charles Musgrove, and her fine little boys, Anne was at liberty.

In her own room she tried to comprehend it. Well might Charles wonder how Captain Wentworth would feel! Perhaps he had quitted the field, had given Louisa up, had ceased to love, had found he did not love her. She could not endure the idea of treachery or levity, or any thing akin to ill-usage between him and his friend. She could not endure that such a friendship as theirs should be severed unfairly.

Captain Benwick and Louisa Musgrove! The high-spirited, joyous, talking Louisa Musgrove, and the dejected, thinking, feeling, reading Captain Benwick, seemed each of them every thing that would not suit the other. Their minds most dissimilar! Where could have been the attraction? The answer soon presented itself. It had been in situation. They had been thrown together several weeks; they had been living in the same small family party; since Henrietta's coming away, they must have been depending almost entirely on each other, and Louisa, just recovering from illness, had been in an interesting state, and Captain Benwick was not inconsolable. That was a point which Anne had not been able to avoid suspecting before; and instead of drawing the same conclusion as Mary, from the present course of events, they served only to confirm the idea of his having felt sone dawning of tenderness towards herself. She did not mean, however, to derive much more from it to gratify her vanity, than Mary might have allowed. She was persuaded that any tolerably pleasing young woman who had listened and seemed to feel for him, would have received the same compliment. He had an affectionate heart. He must love somebody.

She saw no reason against their being happy. Louisa had fine naval fervour to begin with, and they would soon grow more alike. He would gain cheerfulness, and she would learn to be an enthusiast for Scott and Lord Byron; nay, that was probably learnt already; of course they had fallen in love over poetry. The idea of Louisa Musgrove turned into a person of literary taste, and sentimental reflection, was amusing, but she had not doubt of its being so. The day at Lyme, the fall from the Cobb, might influence her health, her nerves, her courage, her character to the end of her life, as thoroughly as it appeared to have influenced her fate.

The conclusion of the whole was, that if the woman who had been sensible of Captain Wentworth's merits could be allowed to prefer another man, there was nothing in the engagement to excite lasting wonder; and if Captain Wentworth lost no friend by it, certainly nothing to be regretted.

No, it was not regret which made Anne's heart beat in spite of herself, and brought the colour into her cheeks when she thought of Captain Wentworth unshackled and free. She had some feelings which she was ashamed to investigate. They were too much like joy, senseless joy!

She longed to see the Crofts, but when the meeting took place, it was evident that no rumour of the news had yet reached them. The visit of ceremony was paid and returned, and Louisa Musgrove was mentioned, and Captain Benwick too, without even half a smile.

The Crofts had placed themselves in lodgings in Gay-street, perfectly to Sir Walter's satisfaction. He was not at all ashamed of the acquaintance, and did, in fact, think and talk a great deal more about the Admiral, than the Admiral ever thought or talked about him.

The Crofts knew quite as many people in Bath as they wished for, and considered their intercourse with the Elliots as a mere matter of form, and not in the least likely to afford them any pleasure. They brought with them their country habit of being almost always together. He was ordered to walk, to keep off the gout, and Mrs Croft seemed to go shares with him in every thing, and to walk for her life, to do him good. Anne saw them wherever she went. Lady Russell took her out in her carriage almost every morning, and she never failed to think of them, and never failed to see them. Knowing their feelings as she did, it was a most attractive picture of happiness to her. She always watched them as long as she could; delighted to fancy she understood what they might be talking of, as they walked along in happy independence, or equally delighted to see the Admiral's hearty shake of the hand when he encountered an old friend, and observe their eagerness of conversation when occasionally forming into a little knot of the navy, Mrs Croft looking as intelligent and keen as any of the officers around her.

Anne was too much engaged with Lady Russell to be often walking herself, but it so happened that one morning, about a week or ten days after the Crofts' arrival, it suited her best to leave her friend, or her friend's carriage, in the lower part of the town, and return alone to Camden-place; and in walking up Milsom-street, she had the good fortune to meet with the Admiral. He was standing by himself, at a printshop window, with his hands behind him, in earnest contemplation of some print, and she not only might have passed him unseen, but was obliged to touch as well as address him before she could catch his notice. When he did perceive and acknowledge her, however, it was done with all his usual frankness and good humour. 'Ha! is it you? Thank you, thank you. This is treating me like a friend. Here I am, you see, staring at a picture. I can never get by this shop without stopping. But what a thing here is, by way of a boat. Do look at it. Did you ever see the like? What queer fellows your fine painters must be, to think that any body would venture their lives in such a shapeless old cockleshell as that. And yet, here are two gentlemen stuck up in it mightily at their ease, and looking about them at the rocks and mountains, as if they were not to be upset the next moment, which they certainly must be. I wonder where that boat was built!' (laughing heartily) 'I would not venture over a horsepond in it. Well,' (turning away) 'now, where are you bound? Can I go any where for you, or with you? Can I be of any use?'

Obliged to touch him before she could catch his notice

'None, I thank you, unless you will give me the pleasure of your company the little way our road lies together. I am going home.'

'That I will, with all my heart, and farther too. Yes, yes, we will have a snug walk together; and I have something to tell you as we go along. There, take my arm; that's right: I do not feel comfortable if I have not a woman there. Lord! what a boat it is!' taking a last look at the picture, as they began to be in motion.

'Did you say that you had something to tell me, sir?'

'Yes, I have. Presently. But here comes a friend, Captain Brigden; I shall only say, "How d'ye do," as we pass, however. I shall not stop. "How d'ye do." Brigden stares to see anybody with me but my wife. She, poor soul, is tied by the leg. She has a blister on one of her heels, as large as a three shilling piece. If you look across the street, you will see Admiral Brand coming down and his brother. Shabby fellows, both of them! I am glad they are not on this side of the way. Sophy cannot bear them. They played me a pitiful trick once – got away some of my best men. I will tell you the whole story another time. There comes old Sir Archibald Drew and his grandson. Look, he sees us; he kisses his hand to you; he takes you for my wife. Ah! the peace has come too soon for that younker. Poor old Sir Archibald! How do you like Bath, Miss Elliot? It suits us very well. We are always meeting with some old friend or other; the streets full of them every morning; sure to have plenty of chat; and then we get away from them all, and shut ourselves into our lodgings, and draw in our chairs, and are as snug as if we were at Kellynch, ay, or as we used to be even at North Yarmouth and Deal. We do not like our lodgings here the worse, I can tell you, for putting us in mind of those we first had at North Yarmouth. The wind blows through one of the cupboards just in the same way.'

When they were got a little farther, Anne ventured to press again for what he had to communicate. She had hoped, when clear of Milsom-street, to have her curiosity gratified; but she was still obliged to wait, for the Admiral had made up his mind not to begin, till they had gained the greater space and quiet of Belmont, and as she was not really Mrs Croft, she must let him have his own way. As soon as they were fairly ascending Belmont, he began,

'Well, now you shall hear something that will surprise you. But first of all, you must tell me the name of the young lady I am going to talk about. That young lady, you know, that we have all been so concerned for. The Miss Musgrove, that all this has been happening to. Her christian name – I always forget her christian name.'

Anne had been ashamed to appear to comprehend so soon as she really did; but now she could safely suggest the name of 'Louisa.'

'Ay, ay, Miss Louisa Misgrove, that is the name. I wish young ladies had

Old Sir Archibald Drew and his grandson

not such a number of fine christian names. I should never be out, if they were all Sophys, or something of that sort. Well, this Miss Louisa, we all thought, you know, was to marry Frederick. He was courting her week after week. The only wonder was, what they could be waiting for, till the business at Lyme came; then, indeed, it was clear enough that they must wait till her brain was set to right. But even then, there was something odd in their way of going on. Instead of staying at Lyme, he went off to Plymouth, and then he went off to see Edward. When we came back from Minehead, he was gone down to Edward's, and there he has been ever since. We have seen nothing of him since November. Even Sophy could not understand it. But now, the matter has taken the strangest turn of all; for this young lady, this same Miss Musgrove, instead of being to marry Frederick, is to marry James Benwick. You know James Benwick.'

'A little. I am a little acquainted with Captain Benwick.'

'Well, she is to marry him. Nay, most likely they are married already, for I do not know what they should wait for.'

'I thought Captain Benwick a very pleasing young man,' said Anne, 'and I understand that he bears an excellent character.'

'Oh! yes, yes, there is not a word to be said against James Benwick. He is only a commander, it is true, made last summer, and these are bad times for getting on, but he has not another fault that I know of. An excellent, good-hearted fellow, I assure you, a very active, zealous officer too, which is more than you would think for, perhaps, for that soft sort of manner does not do him justice.'

'Indeed you are mistaken there, sir. I should never augur want of spirit from Captain Benwick's manners. I thought them particularly pleasing, and I will answer for it they would generally please.'

'Well, well, ladies are the best judges; but James Benwick is rather too piano for me, and though very likely it is all our partiality, Sophy and I cannot help thinking Frederick's manners better than his. There is something about Frederick more to our taste.'

Anne was caught. She had only meant to oppose the too-common idea of spirit and gentleness being incompatible with each other, not at all to represent Captain Benwick's manners as the very best that could possibly be, and, after a little hesitation, she was beginning to say, 'I was not entering into any comparison of the two friends,' but the Admiral interrupted her with,

'And the thing is certainly true. It is not a mere bit of gossip. We have it from Frederick himself. His sister had a letter from him yesterday, in which he tell us of it, and he had just had it in a letter from Harville, written upon the spot, from Uppercross. I fancy they are all at Uppercross.'

This was an opportunity which Anne could not resist; she said, therefore, 'I hope, Admiral, I hope there is nothing in the style of Captain Wentworth's letter to make you and Mrs Croft particulary uneasy. It did certainly seem, last autumn, as if there were an attachment between him and Louisa Musgrove; but I hope it may be understood to have worn out on each side equally, and without violence. I hope his letter does not breathe the spirit of an ill-used man.'

'Not at all, not at all; there is not an oath or a murmur from beginning to end.'

Anne looked down to hide her smile.

'No, no; Frederick is not a man to whine and complain; he has too much spirit for that. If the girl likes another man better, it is very fit she should have him.'

'Certainly. But what I mean is, that I hope there is nothing in Captain Wentworth's manner of writing to make you suppose he thinks himself ill-used by his friend, which might appear, you know, without its being absolutely said. I should be very sorry that such a friendship as has subsisted between him and Captain Benwick should be destroyed, or even wounded, by a circumstance of this sort.'

'Yes, yes, I understand you. But there is nothing at all of that nature in the letter. He does not give the least fling at Benwick; does not so much as say, "I wonder at it, I have a reason of my own for wondering at it." No, you would not guess, from his way of writing, that he had ever thought of this Miss (what's her name?) for himself. He very handsomely hopes they will be happy together, and there is nothing very unforgiving in that, I think.'

Anne did not receive the perfect conviction which the Admiral meant to convey, but it would have been useless to press the enquiry farther. She, therefore, satisfied herself with commonplace remarks, or quiet attention, and the Admiral had it all his own way.

'Poor Frederick!' said he at last. 'Now he must begin all over again with somebody else. I think we must get him to Bath. Sophy must write, and beg him to come to Bath. Here are pretty girls enough, I am sure. It would be of no use to go to Uppercross again, for that other Miss Musgrove, I find, is bespoke by her cousin, the young parson. Do not you think, Miss Elliot, we had better try to get him to Bath?'

CHAPTER NINETEEN

WHILE ADMIRAL CROFT WAS taking this walk with Anne, and expressing his wish of getting Captain Wentworth to Bath, Captain Wentworth was already on his way thither. Before Mrs Croft had written, he was arrived; and the very next time Anne walked out, she saw him.

Mr Elliot was attending his two cousins and Mrs Clay. They were in Milsom-street. It began to rain, not much, but enough to make shelter desirable for women, and quite enough to make it very desirable for Miss Elliot to have the advantage of being conveyed home in Lady Dalrymple's carriage, which was seen waiting at a little distance; she, Anne, and Mrs Clay, therefore, turned into Molland's, while Mr Elliot stepped to Lady Dalrymple, to request her assistance. He soon joined them again, successful, of course; Lady Dalrymple would be most happy to take them home, and would call for them in a few minutes.

Her ladyship's carriage was a barouche, and did not hold more than four with any comfort. Miss Carteret was with her mother; consequently it was not reasonable to expect accommodation for all the three Camden-place ladies. There could be no doubt as to Miss Elliot. Whoever suffered inconvenience, she must suffer none, but it occupied a little time to settle the point of civility between the other two. The rain was a mere trifle, and Anne was most sincere in preferring a walk with Mr Elliot. But the rain was also a mere trifle to Mrs Clay; she would hardly allow it even to drop at all, and her boots were so thick! much thicker than Miss Anne's; and, in short, her civility rendered her quite as anxious to be left to walk with Mr Elliot, as Anne could be, and it was discussed between them with a generosity so polite and so determined, that the others were obliged to settle it for them; Miss Elliot maintaining that Mrs Clay had a little cold already, and Mr Elliot deciding on appeal, that his cousin Anne's boots were rather the thickest.

It was fixed accordingly that Mrs Clay should be of the party in the carriage; and they had just reached this point when Anne, as she sat near the window, descried, most decidedly and distinctly, Captain Wentworth walking down the street.

Her start was perceptible only to herself; but she instantly felt that she was the greatest simpleton in the world, the most unaccountable and absurd! For a few minutes she saw nothing before her. It was all confusion. She was lost; and when she had scolded back her senses, she found the others still waiting for the carriage, and Mr Elliot (always obliging) just setting off for Union-street on a commission of Mrs Clay's.

She now felt a great inclination to go to the outer door; she wanted to see if it rained. Why was she to suspect herself of another motive? Captain Wentworth must be out of sight. She left her seat, she would go, one half of her should not be always so much wiser than the other half, or always suspecting the other of being worse than it was. She would see if it rained. She was sent back, however, in a moment by the entrance of Captain Wentworth himself, among a party of gentlemen and ladies, evidently his acquaintance, and whom he must have joined a little below Milsom-street. He was more obviously struck and confused by the sight of her, than she had ever observed before; he looked quite red. For the first time, since their renewed acquaintance, she felt that she was betraying the least sensibility of the two. She had the advantage of him, in the preparation of the last few moments. All the overpowering, blinding, bewildering, first effects of strong surprise were over with her. Still, however, she had enough to feel! It was agitation, pain, pleasure, a something between delight and misery.

He spoke to her, and then turned away. The character of his manner was embarrassment. She could not have called it either cold or friendly, or any thing so certainly as embarrassed.

After a short interval, however, he came towards her and spoke again. Mutual enquiries on common subjects passed; neither of them, probably, much the wiser for what they heard, and Anne continuing fully sensible of his being less at ease than formerly. They had, by dint of being so very much together, got to speak to each other with a considerable portion of apparent indifference and calmness; but he could not do it now. Time had changed him, or Louisa had changed him. There was consciousness of some sort or other. He looked very well, not as if he had been suffering in health or spirits, and he talked of Uppercross, of the Musgroves, nay, even of Louisa, and had even a momentary look of his own arch significance as he named her; but yet it was Captain Wentworth not comfortable, not easy, not able to feign that he was.

It did not surprise, but it grieved Anne to observe that Elizabeth would not know him. She saw that he saw Elizabeth, that Elizabeth saw him, that there was complete internal recognition on each side; she was convinced that he was ready to be acknowledged as an acquaintance, expecting it, and she had the pain of seeing her sister turn away with unalterable coldness.

Lady Dalrymple's carriage, for which Miss Elliot was growing very impatient, now drew up; the servant came in to announce it. It was beginning to rain again, and altogether there was a delay, and a bustle, and a talking, which must make all the little crowd in the shop understand that Lady Dalrymple was calling to convey Miss Elliot. At last Miss Elliot and her friend, unattended but by the servant, (for there was no cousin returned) were walking off; and Captain Wentworth, watching them, turned again to Anne, and by manner, rather than words, was offering his services to her.

'I am much obliged to you,' was her answer, 'but I am not going with them. The carriage would not accommodate so many. I walk. I prefer walking.'

'But it rains.'

'Oh! very little. Nothing that I regard.'

After a moment's pause he said, 'Though I came only yesterday, I have equipped myself properly for Bath already, you see,' (pointing to a new umbrella) 'I wish you would make use of it, if you are determined to walk; though, I think, it would be more prudent to let me get you a chair.'

She was very much obliged to him, but declined it all, repeating her conviction, that the rain would come to nothing at present, and adding, 'I am only waiting for Mr Elliot. He will be here in a moment, I am sure.'

She had hardly spoken the words, when Mr Elliot walked in. Captain Wentworth recollected him perfectly. There was no difference between him, and the man who had stood on the steps at Lyme, admiring Anne as she passed, except in the air and look and manner of the privileged relation and friend. He came in with eagerness, appeared to see and think only of her, apologised for his stay, was grieved to have kept her waiting, and anxious to get her away without further loss of time, and before the rain increased; and in another moment they walked off together, her arm under his, a gentle

In another moment they walked off

and embarrassed glance, and a 'good morning to you', being all that she had time for, as she passed away.

As soon as they were out of sight, the ladies of Captain Wentworth's party began talking of them.

'Mr Elliot does not dislike his cousin, I fancy?'

'Oh! no, that is clear enough. Once can guess what will happen there. He is always with them; half lives in the family, I believe. What a very good-looking man!'

'Yes, and Miss Atkinson, who dined with him once at the Wallises, says he is the most agreeable man she ever was in company with.'

'She is pretty, I think; Anne Elliot; very pretty, when one comes to look at her. It is not the fashion to say so, but I confess I admire her more than her sister.'

'Oh! so do I.'

'And so do I. No comparison. But the men are all wild after Miss Elliot. Anne is too delicate for them.'

Anne would have been particularly obliged to her cousin, if he would have walked by her side all the way to Camden-place, without saying a word. She had never found it so difficult to listen to him, though nothing could exceed his solicitude and care, and though his subjects were principally such as were wont to be always interesting – praise, warm, just, and discriminating, of Lady Russell, and insinuations highly rational against Mrs Clay. But just now she could think only of Captain Wentworth. She could not understand his present feelings, whether he were really suffering much from disappointment or not; and till that point were settled, she could not be quite herself.

She hoped to be wise and reasonable in time; but alas! alas! she must confess to herself that she was not wise yet.

Another circumstance very essential for her to know, was how long he meant to be in Bath; he had not mentioned it, or she could not recollect it. He might be only passing through. But it was more probable that he should be come to stay. In that case, so liable as every body was to meet every body in Bath, Lady Russell would in all likelihood see him somewhere. – Would she recollect him? How would it all be?

She had already been obliged to tell Lady Russell that Louisa Musgrove was to marry Captain Benwick. It had cost her something to encounter Lady Russell's surprise; and now, if she were by any chance to be thrown into company with Captain Wentworth, her imperfect knowledge of the matter might add another shade of prejudice against him.

The following morning Anne was out with her friend, and for the first hour, in an incessant and fearful sort of watch for him in vain; but at last, in returning down Pulteney-street, she distinguished him on the right hand pavement at such a distance as to have him in view the greater part of the street. There were many other men about him, many groups walking the same way, but there was no mistaking him. She looked instinctively at Lady Russell; but not from any mad idea of her recognising him so soon as she did herself. No, it was not to be supposed that Lady Russell would perceive him till they were nearly opposite. She looked at her however, from time to time, anxiously; and when the moment approached which must point him out, though not daring to look again (for her own countenance she knew was unfit to be seen), she was yet perfectly conscious of Lady Russell's eyes being turned exactly in the direction of him, of her being in short intently observing him. She could throughly comprehend the sort of fascination he must possess over Lady Russell's mind, the difficulty it must be for her to withdraw her eyes, the astonishment she must be feeling that eight or nine years should have passed over him, and in foreign climes and in active service too, without robbing him of one personal grace!

At last, Lady Russell drew back her head. – 'Now, how would she speak of him?'

'You will wonder,' said she 'what has been fixing my eye so long; but I was looking after some window-curtains, which Lady Alicia and Mrs Frankland were telling me of last night. They described the drawing-room window-curtains of one of the houses on this side of the way, and this part of the street, as being the handsomest and best hung of any in Bath, but could not recollect the exact number, and I have been trying to find out which it could be; but I confess I can see no curtains hereabouts that answer their description.'

Anne sighed and blushed and smiled, in pity and disdain, either at her friend or herself. – The part which provoked her most, was that in all this waste of foresight and caution, she should have lost the right moment for seeing whether he saw them.

A day or two passed without producing any thing. – The theatre or the rooms, where he was most likely to be, were not fashionable enough for the Elliots, whose evening amusements were solely in the elegant stupidity of private parties, in which they were getting more and more engaged; and Anne, wearied of such a state of stagnation, sick of knowing nothing, and fancying herself stronger because her strength was not tried, was quite impatient for the concert evening. It was a concert for the benefit of a person patronised by Lady Dalrymple. Of course they must attend. It was really expected to be a good one, and Captain Wentworth was very fond of music. If she could only have a few minutes conversation with him again, she felt all over courage if the opportunity occurred. Elizabeth had turned from him, Lady Russell overlooked him; her nerves were strengthened by these circumstances; she felt that she owed him attention.

She had once partly promised Mrs Smith to spend the evening with her; but in a short hurried call she excused herself and put it off, with the more decided promise of a longer visit on the morrow. Mrs Smith gave a most good-humoured acquiescence.

'By all means,' said she; 'only tell me all about it, when you do come. Who is your party?'

Anne named them all. Mrs Smith made no reply; but when she was leaving her, said, and with an expression half serious, half arch, 'Well, I heartily wish your concert may answer; and do not fail me to-morrow if you can come; for I begin to have a foreboding that I may not have many more visits from you.'

Anne was startled and confused, but after standing in a moment's suspense, was obliged, and not sorry to be obliged, to hurry away.

CHAPTER TWENTY

SIR WALTER, HIS TWO DAUGHTERS, and Mrs Clay, were the earliest of all their party, at the rooms in the evening; and as Lady Dalrymple must be waited for, they took their station by one of the fires in the octagon room. But hardly were they settled, when the door opened again, and Captain Wentworth walked in alone. Anne was the nearest to him, and making yet a little advance, she instantly spoke. He was preparing only to bow and pass on, but her gentle 'How do you do?' brought him out of the straight line to stand near her, and make enquiries in return, in spite of the formidable father and sister in the back ground. Their being in the back ground was a support to Anne; she knew nothing of their looks, and felt equal to every thing which she believed right to be done.

While they were speaking, a whispering between her father and Elizabeth caught her ear. She could not distinguish, but she must guess the subject; and on Captain Wentworth's making a distant bow, she comprehended that her father had judged so well as to give him that simple acknowledgment of acquaintance, and she was just in time by a side glance to see a slight curtsey from Elizabeth herself. This, though late and reluctant and ungracious, was yet better than nothing, and her spirits improved.

After talking however of the weather and Bath and the concert, their conversation began to flag, and so little was said at last, that she was expecting him to go every moment; but he did not; he seemed in no hurry to leave her; and presently with renewed spirit, with a little smile, a little glow, he said,

'I have hardly seen you since our day at Lyme. I am afraid you must have suffered from the shock, and the more from its not overpowering you at the time.'

She assured him that she had not.

'It was a frightful hour,' said he, 'a frightful day!' and he passed his hand across his eyes, as if the remembrance were still too painful; but in a moment half smiling again, added, 'The day has produced some effects however – has had some consequences which must be considered as the very reverse of frightful. – When you had the presence of mind to suggest that Benwick would be the properest person to fetch a surgeon, you could have little idea of his being eventually one of those most concerned in her recovery.'

'Certainly I could have none. But it appears – I should hope it would be a very happy match. There are on both sides good principles and good temper.'

'Yes,' said he, looking not exactly forward – 'but there I think ends the resemblance. With all my soul I wish them happy, and rejoice over every circumstance in favour of it. They have no difficulties to contend with at home, no opposition, no caprice, no delays. – The Musgroves are behaving like themselves, most honourably and kindly, only anxious with true parental hearts to promote their daughter's comfort. All this is much, very much in favour of their happiness; more than perhaps –'

He stopped. A sudden recollection seemed to occur, and to give him some taste of that emotion which was reddening Anne's cheeks and fixing her eyes on the ground. – After clearing his throat, however, he proceeded thus,

'I confess that I do think there is a disparity, too great a disparity, and in a point no less essential than mind. – I regard Louisa Musgrove as a very amiable, sweet-tempered girl, and not deficient in understanding; but Benwick is something more. He is a clever man, a reading man – and I confess that I do consider his attaching himself to her, with some surprise. Had it been the effect of gratitude, had he learnt to love her, because he believed her to be preferring him, it would have been another thing. But I have no reason to suppose it so. It seems, on the contrary, to have been a perfectly spontaneous, untaught feeling on his side, and this surprises me. A man like him, in his situation! With a heart pierced, wounded, almost broken! Fanny Harville was a very superior creature; and his attachment to her was indeed attachment. A man does not recover from such a devotion of the heart to such a woman! – He ought not – he does not.'

Either from the consciousness, however, that his friend had recovered, or from other consciousness, he went no farther; and Anne, who in spite of the agitated voice in which the latter part had been uttered, and in spite of all the various noises of the room, the almost ceaseless slam of the door, and ceaseless buzz of persons walking through, had distinguished every word, was struck, gratified, confused, and beginning to breathe very quick, and feel an hundred things in a moment. It was impossible for her to enter on such a subject; and yet, after a pause, feeling the necessity of speaking, and having not the smallest wish for a total change, she only deviated so far as to say,

'You were a good while at Lyme, I think?'

'About a fortnight. I could not leave it till Louisa's doing well was quite ascertained. I had been too deeply concerned in the mischief to be soon at peace. It had been my doing – solely mine. She would not have been obstinate if I had not been weak. The country round Lyme is very fine. I walked and rode a great deal; and the more I saw, the more I found to admire.'

'I should very much like to see Lyme again,' said Anne.

'Indeed! I should not have supposed that you could have found any thing in Lyme to inspire such a feeling. The horror and distress you were involved in – the stretch of mind, the wear of spirits! – I should have thought your last impressions of Lyme must have been strong disgust.'

'The last few hours were certainly very painful,' replied Anne: 'but when pain is over, the remembrance of it often becomes a pleasure. One does not love a place the less for having suffered in it, unless it has been all suffering, nothing but suffering – which was by no means the case at Lyme. We were only in anxiety and distress during the last two hours; and, previously, there had been a great deal of enjoyment. So much novelty and beauty! I have travelled so little, that every fresh place would be interesting to me – but there is real beauty at Lyme: and in short' (with a faint blush at some recollections) 'altogether my impressions of the place are very agreeable.'

As she ceased, the entrance door opened again, and the very party appeared for whom they were waiting. 'Lady Dalrymple, Lady Dalrymple,' was the rejoicing sound; and with all the eagerness compatible with anxious elegance, Sir Walter and his two ladies stepped forward to meet her. Lady Dalrymple and Miss Carteret, escorted by Mr Elliot and Colonel Wallis, who had happened to arrive nearly at the same instant, advanced into the room. The others joined them, and it was a group in which Anne found herself also necessarily included. She was divided from Captain Wentworth. Their interesting, almost too interesting conversation must be broken up for a time; but slight was the penance compared with the happiness which brought it on! She had learnt, in the last ten minutes, more of his feelings towards Louisa, more of all his feelings, than she dared to think of! and she gave herself up to the demands of the party, to the needful civilities of the moment, with exquisite, though agitated sensations. She was in good humour with all. She had received ideas which disposed her to be

With all the eagerness compatible with anxious elegance

courteous and kind to all, and to pity every one, as being less happy than
herself.

The delightful emotions were a little subdued, when, on stepping back
from the group, to be joined again by Captain Wentworth, she saw that he
was gone. She was just in time to see him turn into the concert room. He was
gone – he had disappeared: she felt a moment's regret. But they should
meet again. He would look for her – he would find her out long before the
evening were over – and at present, perhaps, it was as well to be asunder. She
was in need of a little interval for recollection.

Upon Lady Russell's appearance soon afterwards, the whole party was collected, and all that remained, was to marshal themselves, and proceed into the concert room; and be of all the consequence in their power, draw as many eyes, excite as many whispers, and disturb as many people as they could.

Very, very happy were both Elizabeth and Anne Elliot as they walked in. Elizabeth, arm in arm with Miss Carteret, and looking on the broad back of the dowager Viscountess Dalrymple before her, had nothing to wish for which did not seem within her reach; and Anne – but it would be an insult to the nature of Anne's felicity, to draw any comparison between it and her sister's; the origin of one all selfish vanity, of the other all generous attachment.

Anne saw nothing, thought nothing of the brilliancy of the room. Her happiness was from within. Her eyes were bright, and her cheeks glowed, – but she knew nothing about it. She was thinking only of the last half hour, and as they passed to their seats, her mind took a hasty range over it. His choice of subjects, his expressions, and still more his manner and look, had been such as she could see in only one light. His opinion of Louisa Musgrove's inferiority, an opinion which he had seemed solicitous to give, his wonder at Captain Benwick, his feelings as to a first, strong attachment, – sentences begun which he could not finish – his half averted eyes, and more than half expressive glance, – all, all declared that he had a heart returning to her at least; that anger, resentment, avoidance, were no more; and that they were succeeded, not merely by friendship and regard, but by the tenderness of the past, yes, some share of the tenderness of the past. She could not contemplate the change as implying less. – He must love her.

These were thoughts, with their attendant visions, which occupied and flurried her too much to leave her any power of observation; and she passed along the room without having a glimpse of him, without even trying to discern him. When their places were determined on, and they were all properly arranged, she looked round to see if he should happen to be in the same part of the room, but he was not, her eye could not reach him; and the concert being just opening, she must consent for a time to be happy in an humbler way.

The party was divided, and disposed of on two contiguous benches: Anne was among those on the foremost, and Mr Elliot had manoeuvred so well, with the assistance of his friend Colonel Wallis, as to have a seat by her. Miss Elliot, surrounded by her cousins, and the principal object of Colonel Wallis's gallantry, was quite contented.

Anne's mind was in a most favourable state for the entertainment of the evening; it was just occupation enough: she had feelings for the tender, spirits for the gay, attention for the scientific, and patience for the wearisome; and had never liked a concert better, at least during the first act.

Towards the close of it, in the interval succeeding an Italian song, she explained the words of the song to Mr Elliot. – They had a concert bill between them.

'This,' said she, 'is nearly the sense, or rather the meaning of the words, for certainly the sense of an Italian love-song must not be talked of, – but it is as nearly the meaning as I can give; for I do not pretend to understand the language. I am a very poor Italian scholar.'

'Yes, yes, I see you are. I see you know nothing of the matter. You have only knowledge enough of the language, to translate at sight these inverted, transposed, curtailed Italian lines, into clear, comprehensible, elegant English. You need not say anything more of your ignorance. – Here is complete proof.'

'I will not oppose such kind politeness; but I should be sorry to be examined by a real proficient.'

'I have not had the pleasure of visiting in Camden-place so long,' replied he, 'without knowing something of Miss Anne Elliot; and I do regard her as one who is too modest, for the world in general to be aware of half her accomplishments, and too highly accomplished for modesty to be natural in any other woman.'

'For shame! for shame! – this is too much flattery. I forget what we are to have next,' turning to the bill.

'Perhaps,' said Mr Elliot, speaking low, 'I have had a longer acquaintance with your character than you are aware of.'

'Indeed! – How so? You can have been acquainted with it only since I came to Bath, excepting as you might hear me previously spoken of in my own family.'

'I knew you by report long before you came to Bath. I had heard you described by those who knew you intimately. I have been acquainted with you by character many years. Your person, your disposition, accomplishments, manner – they were all present to me.'

Mr Elliot was not disappointed in the interest he hoped to raise. No one can withstand the charm of such a mystery. To have been described long ago to a recent acquaintance, by nameless people, is irresistible; and Anne was all curiosity. She wondered, and questioned him eagerly – but in vain. He delighted in being asked, but he would not tell.

'No, no – some time or other perhaps, but not now. He would mention no names now; but such, he could assure her, had been the fact. He had many years ago received such a description of Miss Anne Elliot, as had inspired him with the highest idea of her merit, and excited the warmest curiosity to know her.'

Anne could think of no one so likely to have spoken with partiality of her many years ago, as the Mr Wentworth, of Monkford, Captain

Wentworth's brother. He might have been in Mr Elliot's company, but she had not courage to ask the question.

'The name of Anne Elliot,' said he, 'has long had an interesting sound to me. Very long has it possessed a charm over my fancy; and, if I dared, I would breathe my wishes that the name might never change.'

Such she believed were his words; but scarcely had she received their sound, than her attention was caught by other sounds immediately behind her, which rendered every thing else trivial. Her father and Lady Dalrymple were speaking.

'A well-looking man,' said Sir Walter, 'a very well-looking man.'

'A very fine young man indeed!' said Lady Dalrymple. 'More air than one often sees in Bath. – Irish, I dare say.'

'No, I just know his name. A bowing acquaintance. Wentworth – Captain Wentworth of the navy. His sister married my tenant in Somersetshire, – the Croft, who rents Kellynch.'

Before Sir Walter had reached this point, Anne's eyes had caught the right direction, and distinguished Captain Wentworth, standing among a cluster of men at a little distance. As her eyes fell on him, his seemed to be withdrawn from her. It had that appearance. It seemed as if she had been one moment too late; and as long as she dared observe, he did not look again: but the performance was re-commencing, and she was forced to seem to restore her attention to the orchestra, and look straight forward.

When she could give another glance, he had moved away. He could not have come nearer to her if he would; she was so surrounded and shut in: but she would rather have caught his eye.

Mr Elliot's speech too distressed her. She had no longer any inclination to talk to him. She wished him not so near her.

The first act was over. Now she hoped for some beneficial change; and, after a period of nothing-saying amongst the party, some of them did decide on going in quest of tea. Anne was one of the few who did not choose to move. She remained in her seat, and so did Lady Russell; but she had the pleasure of getting rid of Mr Elliot; and she did not mean, whatever she might feel on Lady Russell's account, to shrink from conversation with Captain Wentworth, if he gave her the opportunity. She was persuaded by Lady Russell's countenance that she had seen him.

He did not come however. Anne sometimes fancied she discerned him at a distance, but he never came. The anxious interval wore away unproductively. The others returned, the room filled again, benches were reclaimed and re-possessed, and another hour of pleasure or of penance was to be set out, another hour of music was to give delight or the gapes, as real or affected taste for it prevailed. To Anne, it chiefly wore the prospect of an hour of agitation. She could not quit that room in peace without seeing

Captain Wentworth once more, without the interchange of one friendly look.

In re-settling themselves, there were now many changes, the result of which was favourable for her. Colonel Wallis declined sitting down again, and Mr Elliot was invited by Elizabeth and Miss Carteret, in a manner not to be refused, to sit between them; and by some other removals, and a little scheming of her own, Anne was enabled to place herself much nearer the end of the bench than she had been before, much more within reach of a passer-by. She could not do so, without comparing herself with Miss Larolles, the inimitable Miss Larolles, – but still she did it, and not with much happier effect; though by what seemed prosperity in the early abdication in her next neighbours, she found herself at the very end of the bench before the concert closed.

Such was her situation, with a vacant space at hand, when Captain Wentworth was again in sight. She saw him not far off. He saw her too; yet he looked grave, and seemed irresolute, and only by very slow degrees came at last near enough to speak to her. She felt that something must be the matter. The change was indubitable. The difference between his present air and what it had been in the octagon room was strikingly great. – Why was it? She thought of her father – of Lady Russell. Could there have been any unpleasant glances? He began by speaking of the concert, gravely; more like the Captain Wentworth of Uppercross; owned himself disappointed, had expected better singing; and, in short, must confess that he should not be sorry when it was over. Anne replied, and spoke in defence of the performance so well, and yet in allowance for his feelings, so pleasantly, that his countenance improved, and he replied again with almost a smile. They talked for a few minutes more; the improvement held; he even looked down towards the bench, as if he saw a place on it well worth occupying; when, at that moment, a touch on her shoulder obliged Anne to turn round. – It came from Mr Elliot. He begged her pardon, but she must be applied to, to explain Italian again. Miss Carteret was very anxious to have a general idea of what was next to be sung. Anne could not refuse; but never had she sacrificed to politeness with a more suffering spirit.

A few minutes, though as few as possible, were inevitably consumed; and when her own mistress again, when able to turn and look as she had done before, she found herself accosted by Captain Wentworth, in a reserved yet hurried sort of farewell. 'He must wish her good night. He was going – he should get home as fast as he could.'

'Is not this song worth staying for?' said Anne, suddenly struck by an idea which made yet more anxious to be encouraging.

'No!' he replied impressively, 'there is nothing worth my staying for;' and he was gone directly.

Jealousy of Mr Elliot! It was the only intelligible motive. Captain Wentworth jealous of her affection! Could she have believed it a week ago – three hours ago! For a moment the gratification was exquisite. But alas! there were very different thoughts to succeed. How was such jealousy to be quieted? How was the truth to reach him? How, in all the peculiar disadvantages of their respective situations, would he ever learn her real sentiments? It was misery to think of Mr Elliot's attentions. – Their evil was incalculable.